Canary in the
Coal Chute

Canary in the Coal Chute

A NOVEL
SET AROUND FACTUAL CHAPTERS OF:
THE LIZZIE BORDEN TRIAL

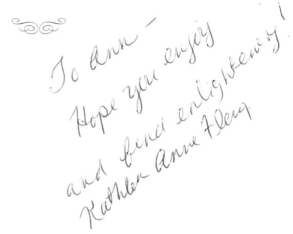

To Ann —
Hope you enjoy
and find enlightening!
Kathleen Anne Fleming

Kathleen Anne Fleming

Canary in the Coal Chute
by Kathleen Fleming

Published by BakerBrowning Press

Printed by CreateSpace, an Amazon.com company

Fleming, Kathleen Anne
Canary in the Coal Chute
Kathleen Fleming – 1st Edition

Publishers credits:
Cover by Lisa Klare, Lisa Klare Photogrphay
Author photo by Lisa Klare, Lisa Klare Photography
ISBN: 1515344185
ISBN 13: 9781515344186

Disclaimer

This is a work of fiction, and of fact. The work uses names, character(s), businesses, places, events and incidents from the author's imagination and are used in a fictitious manner. Any resemblance to actual persons, living or dead, or actual events, is purely coincidental.

Aside from the facts expressed in the "historical facts" chapters, which are drawn from primary source E.H. Porter's *The Fall River Tragedy*, and several other sources, the fictional chapters which touch upon the facts are simply the author's opinions and interpretations of said facts, as expressed through fictional characters.

In addition, due to the voluminous amount of historical and theoretical information surrounding the case, including books, blogs and articles, the author has gathered as much accurate factual material as possible. Theories and evidence continue to surface. All efforts have been made to interpret E.H. Porter as well as possible. Some writers and readers may possess differing theories and perceptions.

The author disclaims any liability to any party, for any errors or omissions, or to those who feel they have different or more definitive information. Also, the interpretation of the facts is also merely the opinion of the author.

Dedication

To:
Rachel,
Clare and Nicholas,

and Veronica

Prologue

In August of 1892, in Fall River, Massachusetts, a young woman aged 32, one Lizzie Andrew Borden, was accused of murdering her father and step-mother with a hatchet.

An exceedingly violent crime, the two murders occurred between 9:15 and 11:00 am ET. Abby Borden, struck from behind, had her skull severed and suffered a wound which reached through to her brain. She was hit a total of eighteen times, initially from the front until she fell to the floor, face down. Apparently, it was surmised, that one hit in particular from the hatchet, which entered her back all the way up the helve of the weapon, would have killed her. One of the wounds included a severe conical wound to her spinal column which was two and one-half inches long and two and one-half inches deep. Closer to 11:00 am, Andrew Borden took ten hits of the hatchet while napping on the sofa in his sitting room, which obliterated his face beyond recognition. He was struck from behind which some felt may have accounted for the control of blood splatter. His left eye was apparently loosed from its socket.

The tragedy resonated at the time, and continued to affect readers of the crimes for decades to follow. A likely motive for the atrocities may not have been indigenous to Fall River. In fact, the likely motive may have involved another crime, one committed against men, women and children as a malignant fury both then, and now.

Chapter One

W hat jarred her awake was the bracelet. Rolling onto her side, she massaged the skin under the Victorian slide bracelet she'd purchased recently at an antique store in Long Grove. A connoisseur of all things vintage, Colette Browning knew the bracelet was doubt-less 14 k gold all around. So why in the weeks since she'd been wearing it, did it seem to heat up the skin on her wrist, feeling kind of like the warmth from a bright light bulb? And it felt tighter at certain times. She was certain of that too. It would then leave a faint lavender mark, and awaken her from a sound sleep. Never enough to really hurt, but just to the point of making her sweat all over. How could one bracelet do that? The curious little cameo and art nouveau snake motif had been dictating her life. This innocuous piece of jewelry played tricks on her. Because since the first day she'd put it on, she'd been unable to undo the clasp and be free of it. It would have to be cut off with wire cutters, or perhaps a simple trip to the jewelers. She just hadn't had time, and in the interim, she didn't have the heart to disfigure such an object of beauty.

But this unrelenting clasp in the bracelet's personality would only be the beginning.

First off, the room had a different scent. Unable to place it, and knowing her tendency to be messy, she checked under the bed for leftover pizza. It might have been fresh paint? She could not be sure. The room looked somewhat fresher too and was not as ramshackle as it had seemed the day before. Was it just her mindset? Then she swallowed. No. She was certain now that the walls now were blue. And yesterday, they'd been a bright seafoam green. Even the paint was less glossy and more subdued, with a quiet matte finish.

Her wrist was really hurting. She wondered if the bracelet was resulting in some sort of allergic reaction. She rubbed the purple mark left by it, and massaged the skin on her wrist. On the bedside table was a book she'd picked up on the trial of Lizzie Borden.

At the window, she knelt down and peered out at the neighborhood. Several behemoth houses, comprised in her opinion, of cardboard, had replaced what some on the North Shore referred to as "tear downs;" those smaller, yet far better built houses from a humbler time. The "blight" of Cape Cods from the 1940s and Bungalows from the 1930s had been eliminated. Developers had steam-rolled the older homes on some rampage, like some serial killer in the form of a wrecking ball and dump truck.

Colette felt out of place in Valley Stream, in this small North Shore town of only 8,000 residents, which fell somewhere between Wilmette and Northfield. In fact, she'd been lonely since her most recent divorce. One had only to contrast her Bohemian skirts and Victorian jewelry, to the uniform of wealth on a majority of the women in town; Burberry Pashminas, khaki capris and Cole Haan shoes, displayed the full effect of the disparity. Although tall, Colette worried often about her weight as she was full-figured. She also refused to acquiesce to societal stereotypes and kept her hair long, past her shoulders, and past the age of fifty. She detested stereotypes and for that reason, regretted that she also had large green eyes. On the outside she touted the look of the blonde, buxom extrovert and yet on the inside, she felt most comfortable as the introvert, spending time alone reading and painting small watercolor canvases. Perhaps for this reason, she'd always attracted the wrong kind of men.

Colette was reminded of her solitary non-domesticated situation simply by her daily dinners of store-bought soups, and a weekly rent she paid out to her landlord Marilyn, for this small rental room. Marilyn had once been her neighbor when Colette and her ex-husband had owned the only brick bungalow left in the neighborhood. Still standing for now, it was located directly across the street from the very farmhouse where she now lived. And quite stubbornly it stood now, for nearly seventy years thus far, its beautiful wooden door adorned with stained glass from the Frank Lloyd Wright studio in Oak Park, Illinois.

Leaning over with her elbows on the window sill, for some reason, both her exes came to mind, Max and Dimitri. Admittedly she'd brought her own personal baggage of her parents' divorce, and her general distrust of men to each marriage. Weren't there stories about crimes of passion and subsequent betrayal and murder on the television every day?

But what would really drive a woman to murder? When did a wife, or daughter or sister's indignity grow just strong enough to push her over the edge? Perhaps this line of thinking was the impetus which had driven her to buy the book on the Fall River, Massachusetts tragedy around the murders of Andrew and Abby Borden.

She took a deep breath, resting her chin on her hands. Her mother Ursula came to mind. There was intensity there, like Lizzie's rage in a way. Except Ursula's depression was turned inward and the result was immeasurable sadness.

Colette thought of children in general. The Prairie door on the bungalow was a bit unusual. On the back side of the door, below where the old mail slot with a flapping metal opening was located, there was a built-in music box. When she'd first discovered the music box, she was amazed that it was built into the door. Attached to it was a type of coiled metal cord, which used to attach from the music box to the trim on the wall around the door. She recalled her father telling her that the cord, the one attached to the music box on this bungalow door, was made that way to keep track of children running in and out of the house. At the time she'd thought what a sweet way to love one's children. The music box and the cord made certain that each time the music played, a child was likely running in and out of the house. That way, the children, in their Buster Brown shoes and pinafores, would not get lost playing around the Depression era streets of the neighborhood, and would make it inside the house in time for a homemade dinner. Her father may have been mistaken, but Colette chose to believe the story.

Now seated cross-legged on the floor, she picked at the fringe of her ailing, threadbare oriental rug. Yet what about the children who were unsafe even inside their homes? Those children of abuse, she wondered? Could such a crime drive someone to murder?

Rolling to her feet, she strolled over to the far wall of the rented room. The hardwood floors creaked like arthritic joints as she did so. Her mother's PhD was hanging there, as were other diplomas. Since moving in, she'd unpacked her office stuff first. Still, eying the diplomas, she often wondered how two women so concerned with women's rights, helping families facing alcoholism, and all kinds of familial dysfunction and abuse, could have messed up so much in their own lives. She'd tried to be mindful of the old lath and plaster walls and used adhesive hooks that would remove easily. There was her mother's Ph.D. in Psychology from the Illinois Institute of Technology; "confers upon Ursula Lucinda Grant," she read to herself, and Colette's Bachelor of Arts from DePaul University, and then Colette's Masters Degree in Gender Studies. Colette had grown up idolizing every feminist from Susan B. Anthony and Carrie Chapman Catt, to Erica Jong and Gloria Steinem. She recalled finding a copy of Jong's *Fear of Flying* in a bedside table as a kid, wondering at the time about her mother's sudden fascination with airplanes. It took her several years to learn the true erotic nature of the book.

If she only knew how far she would travel on this particular day.

Stretching, she rubbed her eyes and thought about coffee. Turning toward the open window, the familiar and intoxicating breath of summer drifted to her. With that, she felt inspired by her momentary peace, and decided to concentrate on something else besides the mystery of her mother's lifelong sadness, or her own divorces.

Several birds chirped merrily right outside the window. Thinking perhaps a nest had been created nearby, she leaned over, listening to their song until she caught her breath all at once. She spotted Olivia, a toddler of only nineteen months old, teetering along in the front yard across the street. It couldn't be? She had to be mistaken?

What Colette did not know, was that this was only the beginning. How could she know there would be a connection between the prairies of the Midwest and the nineteenth century societal expectations of the East Coast? The razing of her old house at 1804 Prairie Street in Valley Stream, Illinois, and the Prairie front door itself would transport her back to 1994. Then the continuum would push her even further back, to the late nineteenth century.

Tearing it down would be the house at 1804 Prairie Street's death sentence, but not the end of its soul. For every house had a soul. Colette truly believed that. However, the destruction of this house would be just the start, the start of a foray into the lives of women in 1892; about murder, insanity, and one sinister and highly significant secret overshadowed by the tabloid mania of what would be called, the Borden tragedy. How could Colette know that the rage, inflicted so violently out East, would become important, and that it would inexorably lead back to coal black scribbling contained on the stairs of the house at 1804 Prairie? Added to that, in a very short time the contents of a forgotten and buried coal chute in the basement of 1804 Prairie would possess Colette Browning's daylight consciousness, and put a stranglehold on her nights. Everything around the coal chute as well, the physical room around it, the house overhead, they too would all be gone. Like some macabre siren out of time, the Fall River, Massachusetts double murder, believed to have been committed by one Lizzie Borden, would hack its way into her life. Somehow, that bony claw from across the United States would reach all the way to

Illinois, in the present year of 2011, and throttle her. And it would all happen because of the bracelet.

In this moment now, there was her daughter right before her eyes, as a small child. This fact in itself, made no sense to her.

Carrying a yellow plastic shovel, Olivia meandered toward the front sidewalk which originated from the door of a brown brick bungalow. It was, in actuality, the same bungalow Colette had once shared with her first husband, Max. Olivia was their daughter. That wasn't her Olivia now? In fact, Olivia hadn't been two years old in sixteen years. In fact, as of that morning, Colette thought, pinching herself to see if she was sleeping, Olivia was eighteen. Colette blinked several times, studying the toddler across the street again. Any mother would know her own daughter. That was Olivia Schmidt. That was Olivia Schmidt in the old yard of the house they'd lived in sixteen years before.

Rubbing her wrist, she adjusted the bracelet. Due to a faulty clasp, she'd been unable to get it off. Now it had left a purple line on her wrist again.

Regardless of who exactly this toddler really was, she had to stop her before she reached the street.

The pounding in her chest propelled Colette out of the small room. Tumbling down the stairs, which were surprisingly steep, she realized it had only been two weeks since she'd rented this room across the street from her old house at 1804 Prairie. She had two children. Olivia, who would be turning 19 soon, was traveling during the summer, and son George was on vacation with his dad, Dimitri. Divorced twice, Colette was grateful to Max because they'd had Olivia, and Dimitri because they'd had George. Not exactly the Brady Bunch, but modern America in a way.

Seeing this child that resembled Olivia was so strange, even though it was not the first time that something very strange had happened here in Valley Stream.

At once she was down to street level. A boxy Toyota honked at her, jarring her to a full stop. Her eyes were glued to Olivia's blonde curls and round porcelain face. She hesitated, not wanting to call out to the toddler, not wanting to startle her into movement toward the street.

Thankfully, Olivia was in her own toddler world. Right now she squatted down to yank out a dandelion which had burst forth along the cracked pavement of the front walkway.

Looking past her daughter from another time, Colette noticed the old original doorway to the bungalow. It was thick with stained glass built in on either side, with purple and forest green squares and crème-colored rectangles depicting Frank Lloyd Wright's tree of life. If she recalled correctly, there was a built-in music box on the back of the door, inside the house, with a cord extending from the box to the wall. So whenever someone opened the door, the music box string would get pulled and the sounds of a tiny harpsichord like tune would play and be heard throughout the house.

Colette stepped purposefully across the street, approaching the little girl as gently as possible. On some level, she knew this had to be a dream. After all, Olivia was eighteen now and entering college, having just completed four years at New Trier High School in nearby Winnetka. Although Olivia was indeed her daughter, Colette was uncertain how the small child would react to her voice.

As she drew closer, she could see the diaper under Olivia's flowered sun dress sagging in the back. Where was Max? Now she was annoyed. Olivia had reached the front of the walkway, flush with the sidewalk. Colette bent forward, hands pressed to her knees.

"Finding any ants, Olivia?" she said, smiling, hoping the good will showed in her voice and would soothe the toddler.

Olivia turned her round face, alabaster soft to the sun, her blue eyes awash in youth, replete with trust. She pointed with the yellow shovel to a flurry of ants which crowded the cracks in the sidewalk.

"Mama. Play now?"

It startled Colette. This dream was too lifelike. It disturbed her how much she enjoyed it, like she often enjoyed her other nighttime explorations into the subconscious imagination. Until now, she simply figured this sojourn from everyday thought was her reaction to her daughter finally turning eighteen. It was a milestone. Colette and Max had prayed and utilized modern science for five years before being blessed with little Olivia Schmidt.

"I think those are red ants, Olivia. Better stay away from them, okay?"

Colette touched her daughter's shoulder. It was soft. This confused her. And the air was so warm and sweet. In fact, Colette could smell the freshly cut lawn of her neighbor John, who was now emptying the side bag to his mower. She hadn't seen John in years, yet now he waved and smiled at her, as naturally as if it were a daily occurrence.

Colette squatted next to Olivia. "Where's daddy?" she asked her, growing somewhat alarmed.

"Daddy on boat, mama," she said, laughing shrilly, her face the usual mess of dirt and sweat and saliva, and that said, she fell back on her diaper butt.

Colette straightened up and stood over the toddler. She wiped her forehead with the back of her hand, feeling overheated suddenly. Looking at her forearms, she saw she'd begun to sweat. This dream state was heating up into a reality. Kneeling down, she kissed Olivia on her warm head, the fragrance of the little girl's baby shampoo, combined with a bit of sand from her frog-shaped sandbox in the back yard, mingled to one taste. The taste of childhood.

Opening the side gate which led to the back yard, Colette walked to the long expanse that comprised the style of the lengthy Prairie-style brick bungalow. She'd once read that the beauty of the Prairie school of architecture was bringing the outdoors in; and in essence, building the house at the level of the open prairies of which Illinois and the Midwest were so well known. The side garden along the house was plump with full summer. The fragrance filled her mind with purple and lavender delights, until, walking onward, she spotted the bent-over shape of her husband Max. He worked away on his 28-foot Star sailboat. It was parked in the back driveway which led out to the alley.

"Max," she said, walking up.

This familiar salutation amused her. This was, after all, only a dream and yet here she was, acting the part of the wife she had once been, fifteen years before.

How odd. It felt so natural. It was as if not a day had passed and no divorce had transpired, and that her teenage daughter really wasn't spending the summer with Max near Boston, for her last month before college. Max had transferred for a new job out East the year before. Right now, the two of them were perhaps sailing out of some small harbor town along the coast. Sadly, Max's health had deteriorated in recent years due to years of hard work and even harder drinking.

Suddenly revived, she turned back, and called out to her daughter.

"Olivia. Come back here now, honey!"

From atop the small craft, Max looked up, wiping his forehead with the back of his hand. When he turned, Colette was shocked at how youthful he looked; his eyebrows were thick and brown and he had a full head of blond hair. Although short in stature, Max's magnitude came alive in the glint of his pale blue eyes.

"You look great," she blurted, unable to stop herself. "But look. Why did you leave Olivia out front like that? By herself?"

"Oh God," he said, standing and jumping off the boat gingerly. "She wandered off again? I thought I had the gate closed, hon. I'm sorry. You know how fast the little Olivia Bear can be." Then he pointed to a cooler nearby. "Hand me a beer, would you?"

Colette huffed at this request, hands on her hips.

"You just got out of treatment, Max," she said. "What's come over you?"

He tilted his head and eyed her curiously. Not angrily so much, but looking confused.

"Treatment? For what?"

Colette stepped back. My God, she thought. His mind is gone. The sun felt stronger. It glared into her eyes and she fought dizziness.

Olivia suddenly threw her arms around Colette's leg, nearly knocking her over.

This dream was almost invasive it was so intense, so real.

"I'm sorry," Colette said, picking Olivia up and hugging her closely. She rocked her, taking in the sweet powder smell, and tried to ignore how quickly her pulse had sped up.

"What day is it?" she asked.

Max looked at her again, for a long moment. Straightening up, he walked to a bucket located next to the sailboat, leaned over still watching her, and moistened a large blue rag.

"You okay?" he said. Then sighing, he muttered, "it's August 3rd."

"Well, no wonder I'm thrown," Colette said, throwing her shoulders back. She set Olivia down, watching the little one ramble off to the nearby sandbox. "Why isn't Olivia at Happy Day Playhouse?"

Max hoisted himself back onto the boat and started washing down the deck, water from the hose splashing her. He laughed. "If you hadn't given up alcohol years ago, I'd think you'd been hitting the bottle this morning, honey."

Colette smiled. Then that strange feeling in her stomach returned. She tried to catch her breath. She felt queasy, enough so, that she immediately fell into a nearby Adirondack chair.

Allowing her eyes to wander across the back yard, she noticed a fully blossomed bed of impatiens situated in a far corner, flowers she would routinely plant in early summer. One year, when Olivia was about the age she appeared to be now, in this dream, Colette had gotten an angry rash from poison ivy on her arms that wouldn't subside for weeks. She'd insisted on going into the office anyway, until her boss simply asked her to go home because he couldn't "look at those painful arms another minute." That had always been Colette's work ethic in those days. Unless she was close to death, she always went in to the office.

Back then, she and Max had had dreams. And they once had plans for their future, and for Olivia's future. Why was she seeing spots? Was it the sun pulsating on her head? Directly in her eyes as it was? At the same time, her wrist felt the tightening of the slide bracelet and slightly warm again.

So many plans. And then she looked back to the house. Why wasn't the family room there? That's right, she thought. They'd put that addition on the following fall. And immediately after that, she and Max had broken up. Pressures from jobs, new baby, or just living in a house perpetually under construction – any of those reasons could have been the final straw to the marriage.

All of the pain of those days was still to come. She knew all of this now, at this very moment. It was as if she could anticipate what would happen. They'd planned to send Olivia to a public grade school a block away, the same school Max had attended as a child in the 1960's. So, the pattern had been set; the road map had been spread before them. Max came from a long line of Germans where traditions ruled.

It's not going to happen, she thought. "None of those things happened."

"What's that honey?" Max called from the boat.

Olivia was rolling in the sand now, her little pinafore dress wrapped around her upper torso. The girl had never liked dresses. In fact, she would grow into quite the tomboy in the years to come.

"By the way," Max said. "Hazel Schubert wants you to stop over and see about some chair she wants to unload. You know, Marilyn's mother. Thought you'd like it."

Colette nodded, rising up from her chair.

At the same time, Olivia had somehow raced down the back sidewalk, defiant, babbling nonsensical words and heading straight for the gate at top speed, the gate of which Colette had left open by mistake.

"Olivia! Olivia Browning Schmidt! Wait for mommy!"

Colette charged after her daughter, somewhat astounded by an odd abundance of newfound energy. Perhaps, she reasoned, she'd actually been getting enough sleep, more than enough sleep, now that she lived across the street in the old farmhouse.

Now how could that be? What was going on? She lived across the street from her young daughter and husband? This would be the truth as she understood it. Clearly, it made no sense.

I am in the throes of a bizarre dream, she thought. Certainly. The house was so long. She'd forgotten this, until she finally caught up with Olivia, who seemed engrossed in the front steps of the bungalow.

"What is it, dear?" she asked her. Colette squatted down, right next to the little girl.

Olivia wasn't listening, so intent was she upon tearing away at tangled vines that clung to the concrete base of the front stairs. Colette too, looked. Underneath the mass of greenery, spiders scrambled out, and as she helped Olivia clear away more debris, a crack was revealed, running up the perimeter of the molding.

Olivia's small hands were covered in dirt. Still, the toddler persevered to find something. Frustrated, the little girl looked up at her mom, her face a smear of dirt and sweat. The clear blue eyes possessed some confounded puzzlement, as if she knew she was supposed to be accomplishing something but that she wasn't sure what that something was.

"You're so dirty, honey," Colette commented, taking the small hands of the child into her own. "I'll get a baby wipe and clean you up."

As she stood up, she guided Olivia away from the stairs. The toddler fought back, pulling on her mother like a stubborn terrier. Normally a free-floating, easy-going youngster, Olivia started to grow panicky somehow. She babbled loudly, protesting against her mother. A young couple pushed a stroller past them and studied Colette, a bit harshly.

Colette smiled back. "Everything's fine," she said, as if to explain. "She's very determined, as you can see."

Although appreciative of the refined neighborhood she and Max had chosen, even in their humble little nest planted in the midst of the excessive wealth of the North Shore, Colette still resented glances which translated to judgments. It was as if it never occurred to any-one that something more serious than a good old-fashioned scolding could be going on here. Colette also seriously wondered if the next generation of wealthies, Olivia's peers, were actually being raised sole-ly by their Russian nannies.

Leaning over, Colette gripped the round sides of Olivia's torso, and started to lift her up. Suddenly, in a move so unlike Olivia, she squirmed and shimmied her way out of her mother's arms and lunged for the concrete wall beneath the stairs. All it had yielded so far, had been a clump of ancient ivy and a colony of spiders and ants. Why would Colette expect to discern something else? Something she'd never noticed before?

"Tic, tac toe," Olivia muttered. "Tac, toe, mama," she kept repeating.

Scooping her up, Colette held onto Olivia like a groom carrying a new bride across the threshold of their home. At the street, Colette waited a moment for a car to pass, again, another boxy-looking Toyota compact.

Lots of old cars around here, Colette thought. Just as her mind wandered to this thought, Olivia had wriggled her way out of her mother's arms and was racing back for the bungalow.

"Fine," Colette said, extending her hand to the little one. "We'll have you stay here with daddy. I guess there's no reason for me to take you to the rented room."

At this comment, Colette stood there, hand to her chin. Why again, was she living in a rented room? It seemed the move had exacerbated a deepening gnawing depression she'd had since her divorce from her second husband, Dimitri. Within moments, Olivia was kneeling down on her chubby white knees, wiping away the dirt from the cement on the side of the house. It was the same side, right by the stairs.

Colette loved her daughter's independent spirit. At the same time however, she sometimes lamented that she'd been thirty-three when she had her. Admittedly, the girl had worn her out. Suddenly, Olivia let out a squeal.

"Ball, and tic tac toe and lollipop!" Olivia blurted with some urgency.

Finally, Colette knelt down alongside Olivia and the two sat there, mother and daughter, gazing at the wall together. This was quite a dream. Olivia was eighteen and had just finished high school now. Yet, sitting cross-legged next to her daughter as a toddler, even the little one's skin was soft against Colette's bare arm. As they studied the wall, Colette was at first, apt to agree with Olivia. It was just a tic tac toe game scrawled on the concrete. Leaning forward, Colette took a second look.

It showed several lines drawn, three horizontally and two vertically through the other three lines. The odd variation was that the drawing was on an angle. And then, directly adjacent to that depiction was a carefully scrawled circle, as well as what indeed looked like a lollipop. The candy part was in the shape of a diamond.

How odd to find such a strange message? It appeared quite old but the symbols were still legible. And the message, whatever it meant, seemed to fascinate Olivia.

It was all just too deliberate to ignore. The drawings seemed to have been etched into the concrete with some permanent marker of some sort. It reminded her of a dry cleaner's pencil markings, the kind that used to decorate the collar of Max's shirts when they were first married and lived on Lake Shore Drive, so many years before when they could afford the regular dry cleaners.

"I see now, honey," she said.

She too, reached out her hand so it was juxtaposed next to Olivia's small hand. She touched the symbols. They were clearly written in permanent ink. They looked decades old. At that moment, Max swung through the gate.

"I'll take her in and give her an afternoon snack, honey," he said.

Colette smiled, but she looked at him carefully. "What's with the 'honey' stuff, Max?"

Wiping his brow, Max stopped, and leaned over. He scooped up Olivia. Wiping off her bare feet, he knit his brows together, looking puzzled.

"What do you mean, hon?"

"There it is again. We've been divorced for fifteen years, Max. But I do, of course, appreciate your efforts at getting along with me."

"What?"

Then he said nothing, and simply plodded up the front steps, hugging Olivia tightly to him. She shook her head as she stood up, and wiped her pants off.

"Oh well, no matter," she said.

He walked into the house. Colette stood there a moment, then noticed the yellow plastic shovel on the sidewalk. She leaned over and picked it up.

Waiting a moment for several more cars to go by, she thought to herself how the cash problems must be affecting the choices in automobiles of late. The economy in the year 2011 was certainly bad. Unemployment was at 10.5%. These cars, they were at least ten to twelve years old, or even older, from what she could tell.

At the front door of the old farmhouse across the street, she instinctively reached around the corner to find a spare key hanging on a hook. No high security in this town, she thought. What Colette did not know, which was actually fact, was that she had just time traveled to 1994. The present day was the year 2011. Via the bracelet, which now seemed to tighten on her wrist and demand her attention, was actually a mystical guide and messenger, and the Prairie door, the same one she'd begged Marilyn to save for her, acted as portal. Her next stop within a day's time would be the year 1892. Her time travel flight would take her out to the East Coast and beyond.

Now standing inside the aged foyer, she breathed in the slightly dusty scent. Slipping off her shoes, she headed up the straight wooden staircase which led to her room. Perhaps it had been odd that she'd rented a room across from the house she'd once shared with her first husband, Max, over sixteen years before. She'd been lonely. She knew that. Against all the better advice from her sister and best friend, Julie, she knew she was over the heartache of the breakup. She'd always liked Marilyn, the woman and one-time neighbor of Colette's, who maintained the one-hundred-year old house. In fact, Marilyn had been living in the place for over twenty-five years.

"Marilyn!" she called out to the house at large, peeking around the corner into the kitchen. For some reason, it hit her how similar this farmhouse was to the nineteenth century black and white photos she'd seen of another house in Massachusetts, where the Borden murders had taken place. The accused, one Lizzie Borden, had a rage that always struck a familiar chord in Colette's psyche.

It confused her. The woman was always right there whenever Colette came home. Shaking her head, she started up the stairs, which seemed even more creaky than they did the day before. She rubbed her arms, and noticed the lavender mark on her wrist had grown purple. She found it hard to believe they'd just paid to have the stairs redone in April.

The sun beat down as she climbed the stairs. There was a Mariano's grocery bag at the top of the stairs. They'd just opened one in 2011, she knew that. So maybe the odd dream was over for now. Back to her senses, but she felt extremely lethargic.

Entering her small, but comfortable rented room, she threw her shoulder bag onto the bed. She stared a minute after the bag, not recalling having brought it across the street with her. At this thought, she crossed to the window again and knelt down, giving the old bungalow another glance. The red gardenias in the cement pots out front, and the freshly cut lawn made her smile at the thought of Max. He'd put so much tireless work into that small yard, having weeded and rid the old lot of crabgrass. Max always liked things to look just so. As she thought this, she saw Max himself, emerging out the front door and settling down on the stoop. He positioned Olivia on his knees.

What the hell is going on, she thought? The Mariano's bag at the top of the stairs told her she'd only been dreaming and that she indeed lived in Marilyn's farmhouse in 2011. Then why did she still see Max and Olivia in the front yard of their old bungalow?

Her feet felt heavy and it took a great effort to stand. Slowly, she slipped off her shorts, pulled on sweat pants she kept tucked under her pillow and threw herself onto the twin bed pushed against a far wall.

Banging sounds came as menacing interruptions to her deep sleep. Opening her eyes, she lay there, studying the dark tinted wood of the ceiling overhead. It took her a moment to recall she'd just moved into the rented room weeks before. She'd just left her second husband. Then the dream hit her; the bright red gardenias in the pots on the stoop of 1804 Prairie, her beloved bungalow. She recalled the odd dream she'd just had about her first ex-husband, Max, and Olivia, their daughter, when she was only a year and a half old. The sunshine in the old yard at the back of the bungalow, and then the odd hieroglyphs on the stairs.

Sitting up, she rubbed the skin under bracelet which felt tight again, and then walked to the window. Stretching her arms over her head, she leaned over to absorb the soothing breeze that was one of the benefits of the North Shore. Then she caught her breath. In an instant, she remembered that the bungalow was being torn down. All she'd asked the condo builder was if Marilyn could collect the gorgeous front door for her.

Across the street, where the day before, 1804 Prairie Street had stood as an 80 year old behemoth of a bungalow, there now sat instead, a mammoth tractor, replete with cement wrecking ball. A true-link fence surrounded the property. The fence was impenetrable, and acted as the calling card of a demolition crew.

Anger flushed up her neck, rising to her face. It was indeed the year 2011 and she was back in her present day.

How could she know that her own furor over the demise of her old house would soon come face to face with another's rage, a rage broiling east of Illinois?

In her mind's eye, she recalled a documentary she'd seen about similar hieroglyphs to the ones they'd seen on the stairs of the bungalow. And the bungalow had been built in 1930, that much she recalled. Could that writing have been the work of a Depression-era vagrant? They called such writing hobo hieroglyphs. The words would indicate whether or not the resident would feed you or if it was an unsafe place for drifters.

How could Colette Browning have known that an unbridled rage, released from the psyche of one Victorian resident in Massachusetts would visit her in her sleep, and abduct her from the safety of her dreams? Or that Olivia's discovery of hieroglyphs scrawled on the stairs of the bungalow in the Midwest, would aid in unraveling a tragic frenzy, which in 1892, the year Colette would visit soon, had caused a genteel woman in the Massachusetts of that same year, to exact her tumult on her father and step-mother?

Chapter One (A)

The Historical Facts

I t was a double murder right down the street. It happened in a neighborhood just like any other in nineteenth century America. On the fourth day of August in 1892, deadly pandemonium exploded at 92 Second Street in Fall River, Massachusetts.

Lizzie Borden, "spinster" of 32 years of age, was indicted and tried for the double murders of her father, Andrew Borden and step-mother, Abby Borden. The murders were committed in the Borden house in the bright sunlight of an August morning in 1892. Lizzie eventually went on trial for murdering them. There was only one other person at home at the time of the killings – a young family maid from Ireland named Bridget Sullivan, also called Maggie.

Andrew Borden, age seventy, and Abby Borden age sixty-five, were hacked to pieces by someone wielding a hatchet. The nature of the crimes was horrific for several reasons; the severity of the murders, and the simple fact that the accused was a woman. The woman under suspicion was their daughter Lizzie, age thirty-two. Yet in 1892, such brutality was unheard of, in fact, it was later stated that a Christian woman would never do such a thing.[1]

Never do such a thing, apparently as murder her father and step-mother. Yet at the same time, all evidence pointed to Lizzie, and too many questions remained unanswered. With heavy heart, investigators descended upon the Borden house immediately following the reported murders. The house swarmed with people. Investigators and police speckled the scene like bugs. Out front on the sidewalk, shocked bystanders and neighbors stood around for the entire block, gawking, with their mouths agape.

Ironically, Andrew Borden's brother-in-law from his first wife, John Vinnicum Morse arrived and, apparently unaware of the murders, waltzed through the Borden's back yard and helped himself to a couple of pears off one of their sumptuous trees.

Another interesting account of Lizzie's behavior came from a different brother-in-law, one Hiram C. Harrington, husband of Andrew Borden's only sister, Luanna.

Mr. Harrington spoke extensively with Lizzie following the murders, and listened carefully to her describe how lovingly she'd "tucked her father in for his nap" on the sofa, just before he was murdered, even offering him an afghan blanket. As the story went, once she was satisfied that he was comfortable, she described to Mr. Harrington how she had walked to the barn and searched for lead pieces with which to make sinkers for a fishing trip she was planning.[2]

Perhaps the most unbelievable fact around the murders of Andrew and Abby Borden was the issue of timing. If Lizzie's various accounts detailing the amount of time she utilized on her trip to the barn were to be believed, then Andrew Borden was seen alive, and then was reported murdered only fifteen minutes later.

Also called into question at the outset was Lizzie's demeanor immediately following the murders. Both she and her older sister, Emma, were described as non-emotional, hearty women. It was also said that Lizzie was the more outspoken of the two, but that both sisters were deeply resentful of their step-mother Abby. Abby came into the two daughters' lives when they were young, and was disliked for trying to act as a mother to them. Lizzie's birth mother died when Lizzie was around two years old.

Out front of the house immediately following the crimes, the street was crammed with wagons, horse teams and pedestrians. Despite the full one-hundred degree heat of a bloated summer day, people waited and lingered around the Borden house to glean any word on what had happened to the upstanding Andrew Borden, the sharp financier and frugal family man of flawless lineage and decorum.

As she conversed with police, family acquaintances and friends, Lizzie went into great detail about the supposed sightings of mysterious strangers who had been milling around the house in recent weeks. She also claimed that the house had recently been burglarized but that her father did not want people to know.[3] In this way; she could perhaps throw suspicion off of herself.

During Uncle Hiram Harrington's questioning of Lizzie, he asked why she did not wonder about her step-mother right away. This conversation was perhaps soon after the discovery of Andrew's body, before anyone thought to look for Abby. Because in point of fact, once the examiners had completed autopsies and investigations, it was determined by investigators, that in all likelihood, Mrs. Abby Borden was murdered first.[4] In fact, investigators surmised that Mrs. Borden had been lying in her own blood for at least an hour and a half.

In addition to strangers lurking in the area, Lizzie claimed that the family's milk had been poisoned in the previous couple of days. Ironically, the local apothecary identified Lizzie as a young woman he'd waited on, who had denied her the purchase of poison the day before the murders. The witness verified that it was indeed Lizzie and that she had claimed she needed the poison to clean a seal-skin cape.[5]

In fact, Hiram Harrington confirmed Mr. Borden's extreme capacity for monetary thrift. Mr. Harrington seemed quite impressed with Andrew Borden's way with finances.

Soon after, when referring to Lizzie again, and their conversation right after discovery of Andrew's body, Mr. Harrington stated that she was stoic and unemotional. Interestingly, when he asked if she had gone in search of her step-mother, after discovering her father's body, she did not answer. It was then, in her next breath, that Lizzie mentioned there'd been a strange man roaming her neighborhood in recent days.[6]

It also became evident that Lizzie and her sister Emma did not get along well with Abby Borden. Lizzie wanted to entertain at the level of the upper-middle-class residents of Fall River who lived over on the hill, across town. But Mr. Borden thwarted any such ideas by not giving her enough funds to live such a life. Concurrently, he made financial allowances for his wife Abby, and even Abby's sister. This last fact became crucial in the eventual trial. It was a different time. The sisters were unmarried and likely needed healthy inheritances from their father. Women only enjoyed financial freedom if they married, and married well. Lizzie Borden, just having turned 32, was well into spinster-hood. So the resentment was based in Lizzie's sense of survival as well.

Lizzie wanted to be treated as an equal by her father or at least on the same level, especially financially, as her step-mother. Ironically, Mr. Harrington's description of Lizzie is, in itself, contradictory. In one breath he described her as having a "repellant disposition" and in the next, described her as a "brilliant conversationalist."[7] In Lizzie's mind, she apparently felt equally esteemed to others in Fall River of the same financial background, and that she was entitled to uphold her end of society via gatherings and entertainment festivities in town. Her father's refusal to enable her to compete on this social scale angered her very much.

Along with this bit of personal knowledge, there followed even more contradictory revelations about Lizzie Borden. First, there was no concrete evidence against her with regards to the murders. At the same time, Lizzie would not allow the police to examine her bedroom immediately following the crimes. It seemed for every action that worked in her defense, there came about some sort of damning evidence against her.

Judging from the orderly condition of the Borden home upon discovery of the bodies, the motive for the murders was clearly not burglary. There was nothing taken from the place. However, one of the examining officers mentioned how cool Lizzie appeared and in fact, that her demeanor was oddly calm and serene. He noted this was especially true even just after she'd discovered her father's brutally chopped apart body. The officer even clarified that when he saw carcasses in battle, such that, "thousands" had "lay mangled and dead," he'd not witnessed such extreme calm under duress even by fellow soldiers.[8]

Mr. Borden, the murdered father, had been spotted talking to a Mr. Charles Horton at 10:30 a.m. on the morning of the murders. Bridget Sullivan, the maid, admitted Mr. Borden into the house after unlocking the front door between 10:45 and 10:50 a.m., Miss Sullivan was certain of this fact.[9]   In essence, Mr. Borden was reported dead by Lizzie in less than fifteen minutes from the last time he had been seen alive.

What was established, judging from the crime scene and condition of Abby Borden's body, was that the murderer was not undeterred at the sight of blood. Also, it was determined that he or she focused clearly on the goal at hand; ending Abby Borden's life as quickly, and as completely, as possible, no matter how bloody or difficult it became.

The question was soon raised, could the assassin have been wandering the house for over an hour in between the two deaths?

Eventually, a funeral for the victims was held. In a most sinister fashion, Mr. Borden was laid out in a black cloth-covered casket, next to his wife Abby in the very sitting room where he'd been murdered. The badly damaged heads of the victims were turned with their faces down, to camouflage the severe and fatal cuts.[10]

Soon it was discovered that Mr. Borden left no will behind; despite his frugality and his concern with money, and a sizeable fortune. Consequently, the estate fell to the two daughters, Emma and Lizzie.

According to a lawyer questioned at the time, one Andrew J. Jennings, it seemed highly unlikely that some strange man could commit such brazen violent crimes for the following reasons; this was during the mid-afternoon, in a prominent house located on a busy street where such a person would not have gone unnoticed. He also would likely have been covered in blood, and even perhaps been carrying a bloody hatchet. Yet at the same time, he stated that Lizzie had on the same clothes she'd been seen wearing before the killings. He then stated that, "this, together with the improbability that any woman could do such a piece of work, makes the suspicion seem altogether irrational."[11]

At around 10:00 a.m., a Miss Addie Cheetham, who lived nearby the Borden house, sat writing a letter. She then walked to the post office, and yet on this trip, she saw no sign of a cloaked stranger, nor a deranged street person. In fact, she saw no one entering or leaving the Borden property. Perhaps this would have been insignificant if this were the only eyewitness, but there were actually two more.

First there was a Mrs. Churchill, who also lived nearby. This older woman was out and about of her house until 10:15 a.m., and then went to the market for groceries and was back home by 10:50 a.m. The first person Mrs. Churchill saw was Lizzie Borden herself around 11:30 a.m., rushing out the side door of the Borden residence. By now Mr. Borden's bludgeoned body had been "discovered" by both Lizzie and the maid, Bridget Sullivan.[12]

Mr. Buffington, a third witness in the vicinity of the Borden house had been tooling around in the back yard. Should a stranger have done the murderous deed, that same stranger would have had to jump over the Buffington fence, or another neighbor, the Kelly's fence – where there were laborers in the yard. Therefore, a third-party, someone located outside the Borden family and their employees, would have been seen leaving, or creeping about the house by someone who lived nearby.

A point to remember was that it was bright daytime, at a busy time of the morning when any number of persons would have spotted someone, even a glimpse of someone in transit, running, covered in blood, in the vicinity of the Borden house. This would have been true even if a witness did not immediately recall seeing someone, because he or she may well have recalled later on. And yet, no such person came forward. No such strange harbinger of death was recollected.

Another crucial occurrence happened one week before the murder. Apparently, a horse-drawn buggy turned down Second Street with two men in it and sat outside the Borden house. One man disembarked from the buggy and rang the Borden doorbell. Mr. Borden let him in. The man spent only ten minutes in the house, and then returned to the buggy. Another important event involved a small girl who had been sitting on the doorstep at the Chagnon's house, the neighbors directly adjacent to the Borden house. This young girl did not see any alleged "man" or "stranger" leaping over any portion of that fence which adjoined the two properties, at any time.[13]

In a sermon on the Sunday after the murders, according to E. H. Porter's *The Fall River Tragedy*, the Reverend W. Walker Jubb said:

> What must have been the person who could
> have been guilty of such a revolting crime?
> One to commit such a murder must have been
> without heart, without soul, a fiend incarnate,
> the very vilest of degraded and depraved
> humanity, or he must have been a maniac.

The crucial details related to Lizzie herself centered around the timing. Experts investigating determined that the murders happened roughly between 10:50 a.m. and 11:15 a.m. Yet even with all the numerous witnesses, not a single soul noticed anyone entering or leaving the Borden property. More importantly, no one saw Lizzie enter or leave the barn at any time. The barn, of course, had been her purported alibi for the twenty minute time period when her father was butchered to death on the sofa in the sitting room.

Even more damning to Lizzie's story was the fact that she claimed she went up to the loft of the barn in search of lead for a fishing line. However, an investigator discovered no tracks in the exceedingly dusty floorboards of the loft. In other words, there was no indication or proof that anyone had been up there in a very long time. The investigator even went so far as creating his own tracks just to see if they would leave any marks behind. Indeed they did.[14] The unlikely but fortuitous conclusion reached, which favored Lizzie, was that in all her distress over the murders, she had forgotten that she actually had not climbed up to the second story loft. That in the near one hundred degree heat, while upstairs looking for lead in the dust of the attic, that fact did not stay in her memory.

There was also much discussion about the "mysterious note" that was supposedly delivered to Abby Borden. This note apparently summoned her to the bedside of a sick friend. Someone delivered this note, which was never discovered, which had called Abby away from the house. It was because of this letter, that Lizzie claimed she did not call out to her step-mother upon the discovery of her father. She explained that she knew that her step-mother had received a note. She called instead to "Maggie" which was the name they called Bridget Sullivan, the maid. The odd, but obvious discrepancies with the note story were twofold; no "sick" friend ever came forward to corroborate Lizzie's claim, nor did a boy of independent age step up and admit he was the messenger of the note.

By the Monday morning following that Thursday, August 4th, rumors flew across the town of Fall River and back, that a member of the Borden family was suspected.

Other points were raised. It was surmised by some that the "cunning" murderer would have had to plan ahead, donning a loose wrapper, which was a Victorian apron of sorts, to wear over her clothes, as well as gloves. Key to the validity of this theory was that there was a small fire burning in the kitchen, on the stove, at the time of the tragedy. Had someone arranged for the fire to be burning ahead of time?[15]

The surprising behavior for the time period which was a society infused with propriety and decorum, was that people were scattered around the sidewalks. People made no attempts to keep a proper distance. Despite this being during a time period in American history which was genteel and the pace was slow, the investigator moved at a furious pace.

Officer Doherty was sent to the Borden house to pick up Bridget Sullivan, the maid they referred to as Maggie, to serve as the first witness at the inquest. Apparently in 1892 it was common for the upper class to refer to any and most Irish maids as "Maggie."

In answer to her whereabouts close to the time of discovery of the bodies, Bridget explained that she'd been washing dishes in the kitchen, and that Lizzie passed through the kitchen once, possibly twice. Once Bridget had completed the dishes, she resumed washing windows on the second floor. And it was soon after that when Bridget had gone upstairs to nap, that Lizzie had called out to Bridget in a panic. By the time Bridget arrived at the sitting room door, she saw Mr. Borden as nothing but a bloodied mess on the sofa. Lizzie was standing by in the doorway.[16]

Ironically there had also been talk about some sort of "mysterious" unknown letter, not the note about the sick friend, but rather one that had been sent to Abby Borden well before the murders, warning that she was going to be poisoned. Surely, it may be surmised that this mythology was perpetrated by Lizzie herself.

Inevitably, Lizzie was charged and was not allowed to leave the police station with other members of her family. Keeping in mind that Lizzie was simply a delicate woman, as many women were considered to be at the time, when the police accused her, they used the utmost care.

Lizzie immediately waived her right to hear Marshall Hilliard read the warrant for arrest out loud to her. The matron had been asked to leave the cell, where they'd placed Lizze, so it was Marshall Hilliard, Detective Seaver and Lizzie in the room.

Lizzie's demeanor, of which the community was cognizant, was described as being one in an "unemotional state."[17] So it surprised some later on, when the tears which had welled up in her eyes upon being accused, metamorphosed into sobbing and "violent vomiting." The matrons returned and tried to help her, but to no avail.

Although a nightmare for Lizzie Borden, Judge Blaisdell, District Attorney Knowlton and Marshal Hilliard, were all considered to be intelligent men, well-versed in the law. However, the arrest, upon the discovery of the body of Andrew Borden and the investigation which ensued, of a woman of such high social standing, started many in the town to questioning the capabilities of the Fall River police and their procedures.

Part of those procedures included invading a farm which belonged to the Borden family. There were farmhands suspected of having involvement in the murders. Still, there were no clues or connections found. And there were others suspected, including family member John V. Morse. However, he was indeed able to account for his whereabouts after all.[18]

A day or so into the investigation, a carpenter named Maurice Daly, the Marshal and Officer Harrington entered the Borden house and were then seen leaving the house later on. They carried out parts of the woodwork in the house, including certain doors and windows, which contained blood splatter evidence. These would be examined carefully as part of the investigation. Carriages and pedestrians were seen milling in and around the streets of Fall River well into Thursday, the final day of the inquest. Wheels of carriages were heard "rattling" over the rough pavement.

The special treatment afforded Lizzie continued into the environs of the courtroom. Mr. Jennings, Lizzie's counsel, objected to Judge Blaisdell presiding over Lizzie's trial, due primarily to the fact that the judge was also overseeing, and hearing all sorts of evidence of which Lizzie was unaware at the inquest, which was still in process.

It was still decided that Lizzie would be moved to Taunton jail, a different jail, more suitable to house her. Flowers, provided by Reverend Buck adorned the cell, while Lizzie was being held at the Fall River Station. They were clearly visible through the window. Still, they were not enough to make Lizzie's internment bearable.[19]

Emma Borden soon offered a $5,000 reward to anyone who could identify the real butcher responsible for murdering her father and step-mother. She also hired a private detective. In this way, if Emma did suspect her sister, it upheld a façade of blamelessness for the Borden family.

Ironically the matron and Sheriff, a Mr. and Mrs. Wright, who oversaw the Taunton prison, remembered Lizzie as a child from years before, when Lizzie used to play with their daughter, Isabel.

The preliminary trial began around ten days after Lizzie had made herself at home in the Taunton Jail. Fall River had no prison facility in existence that could house someone suspected of murder; much less, a Christian woman in 1892, upstanding and upper middle class, and suspected of murdering her parents with a hatchet.

Ironically, once the trial started, Lizzie was repeatedly referred to as the "unfortunate."[20] In actuality, one would have thought her dead parents would actually have been the most "unfortunate" at this stage. Nevertheless, Lizzie's attorney went on to object to the stern wording of the Complaint which had been read aloud to the courtroom on a previous date. Apparently the words were considered too "harsh" to be used in addressing a genteel woman such as Lizzie.

The judge responded simply that this wording had been devised at least one hundred fifty years before Lizzie was born. So obviously, the intent was not meant to distress the urbane woman in the present day; this woman who may also have been an axe murderer.

Interestingly, Miss Borden's pastor from her church, where she had been active as a Sunday school teacher, had a few choice words for Judge Blaisdell. Reverend Buck, upon whose arm Lizzie had been seen on numerous occasions since her arrest, was purported to have said, in reference to Judge Blaisdell's action at allowing such a document, and presiding at the inquest as "indecent, outrageous, and not to be tolerated in any civilized community."[21]

The trial was set to start the morning of August 25th. Women, considered to be below Lizzie Borden's social station crowded their way into the courtroom, wielding individual lunch boxes as if expecting fabulous entertainment. First they sat through a drunkard's arrest and court appearance, and then a battered woman exposing her brutal husband, and lastly, and most prophetically, children being admonished for disobedience to their parents.

Perhaps this accusation should have been held over for Lizzie's upcoming appearances. Surely murder by a hatchet would qualify somewhat as insubordination.

The courtroom would eventually be bursting with attorneys from neighboring cities, members of the bar association, men of medicine and science, and spanning the mahogany room, clergymen of every possible denomination gathered, awaiting the start of the proceedings.

Among some of the people called up was a Thomas Kiernan, an architect, who had drawn the plans of the Borden house. He was asked to spell out the parameters of the study where the carpet had been taken up. Kiernan was also instrumental in describing the measurements of the outside yard and the fencing. This would perhaps become important when a "stranger" would eventually be cited as a possible murder suspect, instead of Lizzie.[22]

Several doctors were called upon. Their testimonies may have been described as nothing less than gruesome. They went into details about the condition of the skulls, and the length and breadth of the holes in the heads caused by the hatchet blows.

All the while, Lizzie sat by in the courtroom, wearing again the dark blue suit she had worn when whisked off to Taunton many weeks before. And on her head she wore a black hat with a cluster of flowers at the front of it. The only sign of emotion was the occasional twitching of her lips.[23]

The Medical Examiner, Dr. Dolan, testified that when he first saw Andrew Borden, lying back on a camel-back Victorian sofa, in an uncomfortable looking reclining posture with both feet on the floor and his head resting on a pillow, (what remained of his head), he stated that Mr. Borden's lifeless face seemed to gaze out the window. He further described a Prince Albert coat resting atop the sofa cushion. In a second testimony, Dr. Dolan described Mr. Borden's head as "one of the most ghastly sights he had ever known." Although at first readying to read his notes to the room, Lizzie's lawyer forbade it. So, from memory, Dr. Dolan described ten hits to the head in all. The largest hit was four inches long, and two and a half inches wide.[24]

The most macabre description was perhaps the blood spots. There were eighty-eight in total. They were described in various clusters here and there, some having flown against the wallpaper, some others which had messed the floor.

The most heinous blood description of all was a spot on the west door jamb of the study which led into the dining room. Specifically, the doctor described it as, a "string of blood" two and a half inches long" and it was "drawn out."[25]

It was concluded, definitively, that a weapon weighing four or five pounds could have made the wounds.

Next, Dr. Dolan described finding Mrs. Abby Borden's lifeless body. Lizzie's step-mother had received eighteen whacks with a hatchet. Her face was difficult to see at first, because both of her arms were positioned up beside her ears and covered both sides. Approximately seven or eight of the hits penetrated her skull and reached into the brain. Abby also had a contusion on her nose, and two over her left eye, all resulting from, most likely, the act of falling to the floor. Rather a malevolent wound like some "pound of flesh" it was a 2.5 inch long and 2.5 inch deep slice made by the hatchet to Abby's spine. So Mrs.

Borden at some point, for whatever fury she must have inspired in her attacker, was literally stabbed in the back.

There later came to light, via letter, a strange man who had been seen walking out in the middle of nowhere along a roadside, covered in blood, on the very day of the murders. Supposedly, he was seen by a Jewish peddler around one in the afternoon on the day of the murders. The letter, dated August 17th, described the encounter in detail; and how the bloodied man had gotten in a fight with a landowner of a farm, where the man had once labored. The fight was concerning wages. Apparently, the peddler helped the man clean up, and gave him polish to cover the blood on his shoes.[26]

The Jewish peddler, one Samuel Robinsky, claimed he could not notify the police or come forward sooner because he did not have a sales license to legally work and was thus afraid. He also said that because he was a foreigner, his English was not very good and he might not have been able to explain clearly. So like Bridget, the peddler too, perhaps because of his lack of social standing in the American hierarchy of the day, was careful about everything he admitted to knowing.

Attorney Jennings for the defense attempted to contact the mystery man in Waltham, Massachusetts, where he claimed to have been from, but there was no one there named Samuel Robinsky. There was someone by that name in Boston, however. The defense attorney was satisfied that the man existed and that this fact would ultimately bode well for Lizzie's case. In any event, it would work well for Lizzie because if this man created any doubt in a jury's mind, that someone besides Lizzie may have been guilty, she would perhaps be acquitted.

Chapter Two

S he tried to roll over in bed. Something squeezed her wrist and she unconsciously rubbed the skin under the slide bracelet. Hand to her nose, it felt like she had splinters there. Someone rapped sharply on the door of her room and it jarred her, shocking her into the moment.

A heart attack? Something weighed upon her chest as well, crushing her now. Her body was immobile. She could not turn her face. Oddly, a waxy oily scent of polished wood filled up her nose and she instinctively pushed with both hands, with all her strength until something large and loud crashed to the floor. It was explosive, thick and solid.

Rolling to her side, she flipped about and threw herself out of bed, then stopped when her toe stubbed a heavy wooden door. What the hell, she thought? The door had been on top of her. She knew it. It was the front door from the bungalow across the street. They had saved it for her. THE door. Maybe Marilyn brought it up? But why was it here, leaning against her bed? It had been the front door of their bungalow - the one she'd shared so many years ago with Max and Olivia. The built-in music box on the back of the door was facing toward her.

Standing, she stumbled to the door of her room and opened it.

"Colette," her landlord began her speech. "You promised you'd have something toward the month's rent. It's the third week into the month, dear."

Colette just stared at the woman. Marilyn was the same age as Colette. Ironically, they'd been neighbors when Colette had lived in the bungalow across the street years before.

"No need to bang the door down, Marilyn," she said, running her hand through her bangs. "Say, what's going on across the street?"

"What do you mean?"

"The bungalow. Where Max and I used to live when Olivia was a baby. Why is there a fence around it?"

Suddenly she already knew.

"Are you kidding?" Marilyn said. "That's the reason you moved in here. You wanted to watch the place before they tear it down." She shook her head. "Now, about the rent…"

Colette frowned. "I don't understand. Why did you leave the front door by my bed? The door from the bungalow? It was half on top of me? I bumped into it. I even got a few splinters."

Marilyn just stared.

"What are you talking about?" she said at last.

Colette caught herself, and then went on. "The door. Over there," she said, pointing to the bed.

"You said you wanted it. I grabbed it before the wrecking crew could finish it off with the house. You wanted it, right?"

"But why did you put it next to my bed?"

"I didn't. I leaned it against the far wall over there," she said, pointing to the wall on the far side of the room.

Colette stared at the floor. She touched the slide bracelet absentmindedly. No purple mark now. Just a bracelet. Nothing was making sense.

"About the rent. You'll get some money this week, I promise," she said. Then her eyes went to something Marilyn held in her hand. It was a small yellow shovel. It was Olivia's shovel.

Marilyn noticed her staring. "Oh yeah. Is this yours? Found it in the foyer downstairs."

Collette reached out, saying nothing. She stared through Marilyn. Then her eyes focused, and an odd question tumbled out of her mouth before she could think to stop it.

"When did your mom die?"

Marilyn frowned. "You remember. Long time ago now."

Colette took a step toward the woman. "Around fifteen years ago? When my Olivia was a baby?"

"Why yes, Colette."

Marilyn stood there, her expression somber. After a moment, she turned and walked off.

Colette said after her, "I had the strangest dream last night."

No response.

"Your mother was still very much alive."

Marilyn's steps sounded from halfway down the stairs just as Colette finished her statement. Marilyn was often short on time, and on patience. Colette turned back to the room, gazing at the troubling door. It lay flat on the floor; thick and bulky and aged as it was. She was almost afraid the thing would move, or stand up and start talking to her at any second. Why did she feel like this door had broken into her room and violated her privacy?

Stepping around it now as if it were a body, she crept to the window. She glanced around the small room, and then pulled a small wooden chair, one that accompanied a roll-top desk she cherished, to the window. This was one of five pieces of furniture wedged into the small room. Simplify. That had been her life of late. She owned a music shop in town and had taken the summer off from work, leaving her business for someone else to run.

Now it was as if someone were staring at her from behind. She sensed eyes boring through her. So she turned, slowly, looking back, at the apartment door. But it was the energy from the door on the floor, the damn door from the bungalow. The front door from the house she'd shared with her ex, Max and daughter Olivia.

Perhaps it was a general malaise she'd felt since her last marriage had ended.

Were she a true Chicago North Shore wife, she'd have the time, and know exactly how to restore it and paint the thing. She was not a tennis club sprite, a frequenter of Louis Vuitton, a champion in a game of paddle at the club, nor a Botanic Garden volunteer. In other words, she was not a cookie cutter soccer mom like all the others. In fact, she liked the door in its present condition; faded, cobwebby, a little creepy and somehow able to move around all by itself.

Then there was her small music shop, which had survived a crumbling economy, and the financial wrecking balls of credit and collections. That was, until the previous year hit. All businesses suffered in Valley Stream, especially the smaller ones.

Despite the fact that she'd slumped through yet another divorce, and her daughter Olivia had simultaneously entered high school and the world of manic hormones, Colette had kept it together. Musicale, her eccentric music shop, had to cut its hours but had somehow managed to stay in business. Inside the cavernous shop, one would find Celtic fiddles hanging from the ceiling, oddly shaped flutes and recorders, hand-painted concertinas and Cajun and Appalachian CDs with remastered recordings from the 1930s.

So Colette had left her assistant, Jason, in charge for the summer. Colette's son George was spending the next few weeks fishing in Canada with his dad. Two bad marriages, two great kids.

In recent months, Colette had fallen into a depression. And although she'd acquired over twenty years of sobriety, she'd still had conscious thoughts of taking a drink. Of course, she knew twenty-some years of regular recovery meetings would be toast in one sip. Now that she no longer spent as much time at her music store, at least for these hot summer months, she'd had to resort to a position as an administrative assistant at a local food distributing company. Her days were spent dogging around after egocentric executives and servicing middle managers. Some, unfortunately, exploited her position of subservience, and took every opportunity to advise her on how to "manage her time better," "not laugh so loudly with co-workers," "clean up the filing cabinets," or make yet another mind-numbing invoice binder. Thus, her confidence level had slipped of late.

Looking out the window now of her rented room, her "little apartment that could" as she liked to call it, she sat in a small straight-backed chair she'd picked up at a garage sale. Then she spotted Louise Martin. The thirty-ish blonde strolled up the sidewalk with her prodigy child in tow. Likewise a tow-headed blonde daughter, Talia, had been cultivated in the art of the piano since she was barely able to reach the keyboard of their Steinway.

Louise Martin absolutely had to impress others. She had always seemed determined to make certain that her daughter soared above the rest of the symphonic hopefuls of the North Shore community. But of course, in the end, the expectation would be that Talia graduate from a prestigious college, find a wealthy husband and keep a functioning, dazzling North Shore home replete with Kohler fixtures in the bathroom, Plunkett leather furnishings and oil paintings of the children in her seven bedroom home. She could play her piano in between cookie exchanges, book clubs, gallons of Chablis and facials at Elizabeth Arden.

Colette was astounded at the overwhelming determination that seemed to drive Louise Martin to outrageous perfection. She was often seen running mid-day on weekdays with her miniature Poodle, while her husband, whom she'd met in law school, toiled on LaSalle Street downtown. In the same way their Victorian home burst with too many accoutrements, wall adornments and signs of her husband's immense wealth, just as such a house would in 1892. Louise, like many a modern woman, wanted to extend this perfection to her own persona. Didn't matter where she was going. And like the numerous strands of opera-length pearls the well-kept Victorian woman would lasso around her neck, Louise Martin paraded around in Cartier watches and Jimmy Choo shoes at the local post office, or even at the drop-off driveway at the grammar school. The pick-up/drop-off driveway often served well for countless other North Shore wives as a red carpet runway of sorts.

So many women had perfected the North Shore suburban uniform of pressed khakis, slim fitting top, and platinum Tiffany chains on wrist and neckline, any onlooker would be challenged to tell the women apart from one another.

Sounds of courteous verbal exchanges carried up in the quiet from the downstairs. There passed between piano teacher and mother, niceties and encouragement. Conversation like this was foreign to Colette. Her life was so out of place, so out of step with this community.

Shuffling about the room, waking up gradually now, she grabbed her clothes off the floor. After a quick shower, she emerged in a modest bathrobe. The metrical careful chords of the piano traveled up the stairs to her from the lesson still being taught downstairs. Talia was sparkling on the piano, her skills evident as her fingers traveled up and down the keyboard. It was Debussy.

Colette paused at the top of the staircase, her hand on the wooden knob. She listened. The sounds of the music floated up the stairs. Once she'd ascertained the lesson was still in progress, she slipped down the stairs and out the front door. Louise nodded superficially as Colette passed by.

Surely in her own way, Louise felt sorry for Colette, the crazy twice-divorced woman? Colette could feel eyes upon her. She crossed the street and grasped the true link fence surrounding the helpless house now held captive. Leaning into the fence, she studied the bungalow now. Impending loss hovered over her. She had thoughts of the house when it was alive, when she and Max had spent Olivia's first year and a half of her life. There had been days of delight with their child, as she'd scrambled around the hardwood floors and plucked out keys on the old upright piano.

Walking to the left side of the house, she peered inside the windows of the old place. There was the never painted wooden archway which divided front from back, the living room from the dining room. The bungalow had been built in the days when quality took precedence over quantity, now being defined as square footage by overzealous North Shore realtors. These smaller homes had featured seemingly innocuous extras such as built-in kitchen hutches, sturdy oak archways and trim and hardwood floors built to last one hundred years, and not eight.

A youthful, upwardly mobile couple ambled past, the young mother rushing along with two bellowing toddlers in tow. The sharp young husband checked the time on a bulky Rolex watch on his wrist.

Colette stood by, watching. Her mouth set. They conversed around her, as if she weren't there.

"Finally. They're tearing that eyesore down," the woman commented impatiently.

Colette leaned forward into the fence, trying to disappear into the final remnants of life coming from the house. She closed her eyes, fighting tears.

"Kinda sad," the man said. "The place was here since I was a kid. I think the Sullivan family raised 8 kids there."

"It's ugly."

Colette studied the growth of ivy on the house as their steps receded. The ribbon of windows had always struck her as a bit of the Prairie school of architecture, borne out of Oak Park and Frank Lloyd Wright. Hemingway too had been a product of Oak Park, Illinois and yet his take on the place had been quoted as a town of "broad yards, and small minds." Even Hemingway's sparkling life had ended in alcoholism and suicide. Colette thought how she'd barely survived high school there.

Looking at the bungalow now was like watching a friend facing forced retirement. Forced, permanent retirement without any pension. Townhouses were due to blight the landscape within a year's time.

She turned to see Louise scurrying out of Marilyn's farmhouse, yanking Talia along by the hand. Her voice carried across the street.

"Talia can't work this way," she said, slamming the door of her Lexus.Marilyn Schubert remained standing on the dilapidated doorstep of her farmhouse, resolute, her arms crossed over her chest as the car drove off. This was her method. She'd made the mistake of pointing out that Talia needed to put down the iphones and the games, and practice more. Marilyn was considered the best piano teacher on the North Shore and she wouldn't give in. Not even to Louise Martin.

In addition to piano, Louise Martin also forced elocution and French upon Talia as well, not to mention soccer, girl scouts, Young Rembrandts and private skating lessons. As Colette watched the Lexus recede around the corner, she mused that inevitably, the poor kid would end up an honor student at New Trier and likely attend her father's alma mater Northwestern. Her life of over-achievement and stress had been well-planned out, as were most in the area. Yet with all this work and effort, Colette wondered if the ultimate goal of every North Shore mom was to raise yet another North Shore mom? To be sure, Talia too would one day play paddle and shop at Saks while her husband toiled away downtown.

Ironically, also well known around town to everyone except Louise herself, was her husband Ryan's other life. The fact that while she spread herself between book clubs and pilates, her husband Ryan spread the legs of his lover, Brandi. Brandi was the nubile wife of the soccer coach who lived just down the street from the mammoth Victorian home which Ryan and Louise shared.

Perhaps Colette was the only one who knew that Louise Martin was, in her younger days, known simply as Louise Schnell. She'd hailed from a small rural community in Wisconsin. No doubt the descendent of humble German immigrants who'd trudged North upon hitting American shores, she'd graduated from Northwestern with great expectations from her parents. She was the first in her family to attend college. Her parents' goals for their daughter had included perhaps becoming a lawyer or an executive in some big Chicago loop corporation. As it happened, Louise had been motivated upon graduation, to simply upgrade her social status, and spit out five children. Perhaps her thought had been that there needed to be a sufficient number to discourage Ryan from divorcing her, for fear of going bankrupt from alimony and child support. Louise needed to excel at black tie affairs, shine by her husband's side, and maintain a neat garden.

With some chagrin, Colette's mind went to Louise's condescending nod from half an hour earlier. Colette believed that Louise, like ninety-eight percent of the wives in Valley Stream, felt sorry for Colette. Colette Browning had just finalized her second divorce. However, her heart rejoiced at the two blessings which had resulted; two children; a daughter and a son, one from each marriage.

Louise piqued Colette's interest. Similar perhaps, to a wriggling specimen in a biology lab. Where did that determination and focus come from? Why would any intelligent woman compete in high society Olympics? But Colette had a secret. It had to be a secret she'd figured out over the years, because no other women, at least in the suburbs of most of Chicago, recognized it. As Susan Faludi had said in *Backlash,* her extensive non-fiction study of how women contribute to their own demise, the 1950s saw a relapse into the old tradition of the woman as housewife and mother only. Colette recalled the 1970s, and Erica Jong and that there had been hope, and then another backlash where women perpetuated the myth that they could concurrently be executives, as well as housewives in the oldest sense of the word.

No one recognized the hypocrisy, the inequality of roles. And those who recognized it the least were those educated women. As Colette studied this solid house built in 1929, in America, in the decades since, after Amelia Earhart in the 1930s, and Eleanor Roosevelt in the 1940s, women had kicked off the 1950s by assigning themselves, once again, to former roles reminiscent of the nineteenth century. How far had women really come even since 1890?

She leaned in on the fence again, peering straight inside the front windows of the bungalow and all at once, she was back in that marriage with Max in 1993.

"Tell me again why you want a divorce?" he had asked her years before.

As she studied the distant outlines of the couple with the baby, that fateful conversation in the bungalow kitchen with her ex came to her again.

"Max, don't make this harder than it has to be. I don't know how to put it into words. Our concern should be Olivia right now."

His eyes darkened. "She is my main concern."

Then the inevitable fight had ensued. Colette had paced the length of the gourmet kitchen, front to back, and finally turned around. Max had followed her, berating her, unleashing years of bottled up rage.

She turned on him. "I don't want this anymore," she had said, swinging the refrigerator door open. With tears in her eyes, she indicated a shelf lined with beer. "There's every possible brand in here, from American to German for God's sake. I'm done." Hands on her hips, she studied the floor. "I can't live here pretending the constant sight of alcohol doesn't upset me. I don't drink Max. And I want to continue to be a recovering alcoholic. Not a relapsed one. Our life-styles are different. You're the North Shore party circuit and I'm try-ing to not drink and stay alive. In her mind, she acknowledged that once she'd sobered up six months into their marriage, she realized she'd married a stranger.

Max had sat at the kitchen table, perhaps just becoming aware of the Beck's beer he clutched in his hand.

"I live here too," he said. "It's not like I push it on you. I don't of-fer you beer."

"No. But going to parties until two in the morning and having to drive separate cars just so I can leave before everyone gets sloppy drunk? That's not fun, Max. Neither is waiting up on weeknights be-cause you've stopped for drinks with the guys from the trading floor."

He smirked. "It's not like you've ever had dinner waiting, is it?"

"I never pretended to be the domestic wife you seem to now want so much. "

He nodded. "Look. I tried to make it work. You know that."

His words trailed off. That very cessation of sound, the silence, was very telling. This was the point they had reached. Colette also sat in silence now, at the table. They would spend the next hour half-heartedly hammering out their separation after ten years of marriage.

Now Colette checked the street for any other pedestrians, and then pushed her way inside the true-link fence. Glancing left and right, she slipped along the length of the house, along the side all the way to the back yard. Passing the wooden deck which jutted out from a sunny bay window. She paused. In her mind's eye she saw Olivia in the sandbox years before.

It had been right there, in that very window, where Colette had sat with Olivia propped on one knee, reading to her from the book *Goodnight Moon*. Some nights she'd read it three times in a row at Olivia's insistence. Olivia would study the moon outside while Colette read, then turn back to the book and trace the words she could not yet decipher with her small index finger. The transparent blue of the child's eyes rivaled the moon itself.

Colette's gaze froze upon the dilapidated window boxes along the railing of the patio. She'd once stuffed them full with multi-colored impatiens.

Turning to the driveway at the back of the yard, she recalled how Max had tossed all her belongings she'd not been able to move with her, out onto the concrete, including a cross-stitch of a sailboat and "I love you, Max" she'd spent six months secretly making for him one year for Christmas. Granted, that was as far as her homemaking skills had reached. There was no home cooking and it had taken her a year in the house to discover a built-in ironing board behind a door in the kitchen.

Lizzie Borden was ironing handkerchiefs on the morning of the murders of both of her parents. Why did this fact she'd just read the week before, come to her now?

Unfortunately, the voices from the couple who lived next door reached her. The place had at one point been converted into a two flat and now housed several apartments. But Ted and Susan had restored the place. Numerous landmark, and older home magazines, had featured their beaming faces in feature articles detailing their labors.

Now she spotted them hauling in groceries from their Jeep Laredo. They stopped when they saw her. The man, in sleeveless t-shirt and covered in tattoos, seemed somewhat displeased to recognize Colette.

"Your old place is getting torn down first thing tomorrow," he said.

"How've you been?" she managed.

But he simply nodded as he answered his ringing cell phone.

Within seconds, Colette's goal became clear. Squeezing between the fence and the narrow space allotted between the house and the two-flat, she slid her way up along the side of the house again, back to the front. Typical of Valley Stream and its ridiculously low criminal activity, she could hear the impending sirens filling the cloudless sky.

Why didn't I grab a camera, she thought? How could she have known?

Patting her Capri pants pocket, she held her new ipod touch phone in her palm. Her son, George, had found it in his father Dimitri's bedside drawer. As usual, he had decided to give it to his mother. At age twelve, George always seemed to be looking out for her.

"This way you can call me if you need to while I'm fishing in Canada with dad," he had told her.

But more importantly, he'd showed her the camera feature.

Fumbling with the colorful touch buttons, she tinkered around until she pressed a button and something flashed. Her smile faded when she realized she'd photographed her feet and the concrete sidewalk.

"Great."

Skimming along the side of the house, she returned to the front and knelt down behind some solid horizontal rows of brown brick and mortar. Again, she saw nothing but foundation. The bricks themselves were still solid, without any crumbling. The first police car would thunder on the scene at any moment she figured, taking deep breaths. Then, she spotted the vines.

Hardly distinguishable up until now, the hieroglyphs were definitely nothing she'd noticed in her five years living in the house with Max and Olivia. More overgrown now, she noted a cluster of green ivy. It was more lush and vine grown, certainly, than it had been fifteen years before. Extending her hand, she brushed them away gently, to one side. The crescendo of police sirens was upon her. Just as she yanked the vines aside, she caught her breath. There were the scribbles, the hieroglyphs she and Olivia had seen. The first sign to reveal itself, appearing as something indistinguishable, was the slanted tic tac toe symbols from her nightmare. She caught her breath. The next symbol was some sort of house and lastly, what Olivia had repeatedly called a "lollipop."

Kicking at the cement with her toe, she spotted what looked like a shoebox. Wedged between crumbling bricks, she pulled at the box gently. It was green and rectangular. After a moment, she realized there was a hard cover book inside. The gold title on the front read "History of the Borden Murders. Illustrated." The author name on the spine was E. H. Porter. She was about to open it, when a passing car motor made her stand up suddenly with the book hidden under her arm.

Perhaps she'd not been certain about very much this summer. Everything was uncertain and she'd forced this self-imposed sabbatical away from the world, living in a rented room after her second divorce. What did she know?

What she did know was that she'd never seen these symbols while living in the house. They had lived there five years and they'd never seen the symbols.

Backing away now, she squeezed all the buttons on the iphone, waiting to hear that telltale click of the tiny camera. Squatting one last time, she focused on the symbols close-up, then backed up, then backed away further and took another picture. Standing on the sidewalk, she clicked the backdrop of the entire house, including the stenciled original Depression-era 1804 address plate of the front door. That's when the first squad car appeared. She turned and dropped the book and grabbed it, just as two cops got out of the car and slammed the doors.

Unfortunately, Detective Halloran was not among them. Only McCormick, the police officer she'd unfortunately dumped when they were in high school, emerged from the car.

She reached the back of the house and jimmied a gate open, threw it wide to the alley and ran down the road, up the sidewalk, and back to the front of the house. Officer McCormick led his new partner up to the tru-link fence. She kept on walking, right past them.

Minutes later, Colette was sipping a Starbuck's iced coffee from the little fridge in her rented room. Her eyes were on the bungalow again, just out the window. A parade of two-legged hounds snooped the yard where the house was encased in its tru-link prison, awaiting demolition.

Above the soundlessness of this pursuit by the police, it would be incumbent upon Colette to travel to Fall River, Massachusetts out of time, and become enmeshed in a personal tragedy.

Like a child, who always desperately wanted to go behind the velvet ropes in museums, and literally spread out on Abraham Lincoln's bed when she was eight years old, or sit in an ornate chair in Colonial Williamsburg, this trip would bring a ghastly museum to life.

As an unwitting witness, Colette would hold the same hatchet that drove itself through the flesh of loved ones, and the minds of a horrified community. A century-old slaughter would shed fresh blood.

Now she closed the window of the rental room and succumbed to the rhythmic hum of the silence around her. Perhaps she would realize soon, that each time this hum reached her, enough to cause a telltale ringing in her ears, and the tingling purple from the squeeze of the bracelet, her body, and soul would take flight.

"This affection between a teen-age Lizzie and her father would not be inconsistent with a past history of sexual abuse."[27]

"All the hatchet blows directed at Mr. Borden were aimed at his face. As the prosecuting attorney described it in his closing argument, the hand that held the weapon was 'not the hand of masculine strength. It was the hand of a person strong only in hate and the desire to kill.'"[28]

Chapter Two (A)

The Historical Facts

The testimony of Bridget Sullivan, the maid who was chronically referred to as "Maggie" by the members of the Borden household, was probably the most incriminating testimony against Lizzie. Bridget recounted how she, like other members of the household, had vomited outside on the morning of the murders, supposedly due to tainted milk.

The key time frame began precisely when Bridget opened the front door to the house to let in Mr. Borden following his rounds at the banks, at around 10:45 a.m. It was apparently Mr. Borden's routine to visit his business concerns during workday morning. A Mr. John Shortsleeves claimed to have seen Mr. Borden in town, at a shop on South Main Street at 10:30 or 10:40 a.m.

Keep in mind as well, that most of the doors, both inside and out, were kept locked at all times, and that different members of the household had keys to certain doors, usually their own bedrooms. For instance, when Mr. Morse, Lizzie's uncle, left the house on the morning of the murders at 8:45 a.m., he had to be let out the front door via Mr. Borden's keys.[29] Mr. Borden's keys acted as an extension of his need for control. This was, of course, the male power dynamics of the nineteenth century.

So it was odd that at around 10:45 a.m., Mr. Borden was unable to gain access with his own key to the front door. This was due to the fact that the door had been bolted. Also, at the moment he entered the house, Bridget, who had just opened the door to let him in, overheard Lizzie laugh from upstairs. At this point, the assumption persisted that Mrs. Borden had been called out of the house as a result of receiving a note to go quickly and visit a "sick friend."

Why would such a "sick friend" not simply have telephoned? But then, there would have had to have been a ringing sound heard throughout the house. Or perhaps they had no telephone? Perhaps it had just proven easier to claim a note had arrived, if it had indeed been a ruse, and then mysteriously admit no one ever saw the note again.

A sordid detail centered around the odd laughter Bridget overheard at the precise moment Mr. Borden was allowed through the front door by the maid. Lizzie had been standing at the top of the stairs and let out a boisterous laugh. As it would later have been attempted to prove, from the stance on the stairway, Lizzie could have feasibly seen the dead body of Mrs. Borden lying on the floor. It was later proven, in fact, that she would have possibly have had a clear view of Abby under the bed. Also, at this point, Mrs. Borden would have been dead almost an hour and a half.

Regardless, if one were to examine why Lizzie Borden would have laughed aloud at that moment on the stairs, loud enough to have been heard by Bridget and possibly Andrew Borden, a whole new set of scenarios would have required examination. For instance, if Lizzie indeed had been upstairs alone, what would have caused her to laugh? She obviously was not chatting or cajoling with anyone? To laugh for no apparent reason would have made it seem maniacal. Or was she just, as suspected by prosecutors, laughing at the prospect of next having the opportunities to kill her father at last. No matter how it was analyzed, it revealed instability in Lizzie Borden's makeup.

Soon after Mr. Borden arrived home, Lizzie went to the dining room to iron handkerchiefs. It was significant that Lizzie made a point of asking Bridget if she would be going out, to which she replied that she would not. Lizzie was perhaps gauging the whereabouts of everyone in the household.

Ironically, this was even after Lizzie mentioned a sale at a local merchant called Sargent's. Despite that fact, Lizzie could not convince Bridget to leave the house.

Soon after that, at around 11:10 a.m., Lizzie called out throughout the house for Bridget. The exact words she uttered were "father is dead."[30] It was also interesting that, not only did she seem certain her father was dead, but also, quite suddenly, that Mrs. Borden needed to be found. This sudden urgency to locate Mrs. Borden may have seemed odd. Hadn't Lizzie claimed Abby Borden was called out of the house to visit a sick friend? So why would she suddenly have believed that Abby had returned? Why would Lizzie have assumed her step-mother may have been murdered or attacked somewhere else in the house? Because Mr. Borden must have been murdered literally minutes after he'd arrived home.

There were two other points to consider; Bridget said there was a coal fire going in the kitchen when she went upstairs to nap; that she didn't recall what dress Lizzie was wearing and that they found a box of hatchets behind the furnace when the house was searched. Upon further questioning, Bridget said Lizzie told her she'd heard someone groan around the time her father was killed and that that was how she came in and discovered her father had been murdered.[31] Realistically, how could Lizzie have been able to hear a "groan" all the way from the barn, where she had claimed to have been while the murder would have taken place?[32]

Soon after, Mrs. Adelaide Churchill, a neighbor of the Bordens, was to testify on the third day of the trial, that Lizzie told her that from her location by the barn, and while in a state of upset, that Lizzie had been able to discern "a distressing noise," ran back to the house and found the screen door open. Lizzie then informed Mrs. Churchill that although her mother had indeed been called out to see a sick friend that "she'd somehow thought she'd heard her come in" and that she wished they would find her because she may also have been killed. Lizzie also immediately claimed that her father must have had an enemy because they all had been poisoned several nights before.

It was interesting that Lizzie would already have been forming a hypothesis, and speculating about motive when she would certainly have been very distraught or in a state of a shock. When Bridget was questioned, she recalled that she'd not seen Lizzie shed a tear at all, "not in all the day."[33] Perhaps in public, Lizzie may have shown only a quiver of her lip now and then, but in private, apparently, she did not reveal distress.

Mrs. Churchill described soon after how she had been walking from City Hall toward home, and down the street – and at the end of the block she could see Lizzie standing just inside her door.

Of course, Mrs. Churchill's description of Lizzie was that she "looked distressed." However, why would a young woman, who had seen the aftermath of her father beaten and hacked into pieces in an extremely violent manner, choose to remain in the house? Couldn't the maniacal killer still be lurking somewhere, as yet, unseen?

Once Mrs. Churchill arrived at the Borden house, she asked Lizzie where her father was. After explaining that he was in the sitting room, Lizzie claimed to have been in the barn looking for a piece of iron, until she'd "heard a distressing noise" and hurried back into the house. Then, she inadvertently explained that she feared her mother may be "killed too" for she thought she'd "heard her come in." [34] At this point, Lizzie desperately wanted someone to go looking for her mother because she thought she'd heard her come in. But how plausible was it that Lizzie would have conveniently overheard a "distressing" noise? All the way from her stance in the barn? Somehow she'd heard the noise, and then later heard her mother come in the house amidst a crowd of people milling about the property. These facts were all too odd, because it was later determined that Abby Borden had been bludgeoned at least an hour and a half before Lizzie's father. She may have seen or spoken to her step-mother, long before her father had been killed. Was it not odd, then, that Lizzie would present her fears for her step-mother's life so late in the game?

Soon after Mrs. Churchill's recollection of events, a Miss Alice Russell, another neighbor, and Lizzie's closest friend, claimed that Lizzie mentioned that she'd gone to the barn to attain "tin or iron" to "fit to the screens" in the Borden house. Whatever Lizzie was truly looking for in the house, it is odd that the information surrounding such a simple errand in the barn, would result in two different explanations as to why she chose to go there, especially in the close to 100 degree heat.

An interesting witness, and one which speaks to the unlikely idea that a "stranger" had burst into the Borden yard, and then ventured into that triple-locked house, murdering the two people with excessive rage, was one Miss Lucy Collet. Miss Collet had been asked to sit on the stoop of Dr. Chagnon's porch, which was a neighboring house to the Borden's. She arrived there at 10:50 a.m. She remained until 12:00 noon and saw absolutely no one, not in the yard, nor even a soul to pass through to another yard.

The next bit of evidence proved visibly disturbing to Lizzie Borden herself. Three different witnesses, presumably all pharmacists at Smith's Drugstore, heard and identified Lizzie as the woman who had entered the store just the day before the murders. This woman had attempted to buy ten cents worth of Prussic Acid also known as hydrogen cyanide. The Prussic acid was known to have a faint, bitter, burnt almond-like odor. Historically, it had been used to kill both rodents and humans alike.[35]

Clearly, this was damaging evidence. In efforts to confuse the jury, defense attorney Jennings called in a furrier as well as the pharmacists. The furrier had no knowledge regarding proof that Prussic acid could or would have been useful. He thus successfully baffled the jury enough to eventually acquit the young woman.

As already mentioned, another witness, Assistant Marshall John Fleet, also heard Lizzie respond to the question of "who killed her father and mother" with an angry retort from Lizzie that reiterated that Abby was not her "mother" but her "step-mother."[36] This was a key differentiation Lizzie repeatedly made; that Abby was her step-mother and not her real mother.

A sign that someone was not telling the truth would reveal a story with novel twists and outcomes. Assistant Marshall Fleet noticed that initially, Lizzie claimed that she was gone to the barn in the 100 degree summer heat, looking for sinkers for fishing rods for half an hour. She then claimed it was more like twenty minutes to half an hour. And for some reason, Lizzie became adamant about insisting that the time frame was precisely between twenty minutes and half an hour.

Soon a Professor Edward Wood was called up to take the stand. At this point, Lizzie started to appear haggard and worried. [37] Professor Wood was a known expert who examined the contents of the stomachs of Andrew and Abby Borden. One could have assumed that Lizzie's upset hinged upon what exactly the contents of the stomach would reveal? Professor Wood was the expert assigned to examine the contents of a large trunk from a Dr. Dolan. The contents of the trunk included a hatchet, two axes, a blue dress waist, a white starched skirt, lounge cover and a large envelope which contained three smaller envelopes.

One may assume that Lizzie was concerned about Professor Wood's findings. In the end, the hair and blood found on the hatchet was concluded to have been from an animal. Due to the fact that there was obviously no DNA testing in the late nineteenth century, even from modern standards, the hair could have easily been transplanted to the hatchet so as not to appear like either the skin or grey hairs of Lizzie's parents. Even Attorney Knowlton asked about the "suspicious" stains on the hatchet handle and the blade. Still, Professor Wood maintained that none of the stains were actually blood stains.

Next a Captain Harrington was called. He related that Lizzie claimed to have been in the barn for twenty minutes. Although Lizzie made certain to say that she'd not seen anyone in the yard, she did plant the seed of doubt in the minds of the jury by describing having seen a "man who had had angry words" with her father of late, apparently in the last couple of months. [38]

Somewhat damaging too was the fact that Lizzie persisted, even in a courtroom full of people, in her claim that she and her stepmother did not get along. So aside from the issue of a house or property that had been bestowed upon her step-mother's step-sister, a Mrs. George Whitehead, which caused some ire five years before, that most recently, she and her stop-mother had been getting along. However, Lizzie continued to reiterate that she referred to the woman as "sometimes Mrs. Borden" and "sometimes mother."

Soon after this explanation, Lizzie mentioned that on the day of the murders, earlier in the day, she had had on a blue dress. She went on to claim that she'd changed in the afternoon and put on a print dress. Why would she have first, changed her dress (unless there was blood on it) and secondly, have admitted to the fact in an open courtroom? These were perhaps some of these idiosyncrasies in her testimony and at times, her belligerent attitude which expanded the mythology of Lizzie Borden, and furthered her enigmatic persona.

Further on in the trial, Lizzie was quoted as saying, in two consecutive sentences; from Porter's *The Fall River Tragedy*, with regards to the crucial time period when her father returned home that, "I was in the kitchen reading when he returned. I am not sure that I was in the kitchen when my father returned." Immediately following these contradictory statements, she claimed she was "in my room long enough to sew a piece of lace on a garment."[39] Ironically, right after this, Lizzie further stated in the inquest testimony that she believed Maggie (Bridget) had let Mr. Borden in the front door and that she (Lizzie) had been upstairs at the time. This is most likely because Bridget related in her testimony how she had overheard a bizarre laugh from the top of the stairs just as she opened the front door for Andrew Borden. All this information must have appeared to have been a case of one trying to remember the "story invented" as a result of telling untruths.

One of the key points during Lizzie's inquest and questioning by the District Attorney involved the specifics not only about her father's arrival home on the day of the murders, but also Lizzie's interpretation of her mother's whereabouts earlier that morning. Lizzie explained in detail how she had seen Abby Borden dusting in the dining room, and then how the older woman conveniently mentioned to Lizzie that her intention had been to go back upstairs, now that she'd already made the bed in the guest room, to put on pillow slips.[40]

Lizzie went on to contradict herself numerous times as to her whereabouts once her father had returned home, and supposedly, about the precise time her mother went out. In the end, it was Lizzie, and Lizzie alone who claimed there was a "note from a sick friend" which asked that Abby come and see her. The District Attorney managed to wrangle the information out of Lizzie that she had actually had no fishing rods even at the farm, nor was there any fishing line. She had searched the barn for twenty minutes in a quest for lead sinkers, so specified, to go fishing in the coming weeks. Apparently without a fishing rod.

At the same time, Lizzie claimed to have picked up several pears from the ground while standing under the tree, and having eaten three of them or in some accounts, she was in the barn. Apparently, even in the one hundred degree heat, she chose to eat the pears upstairs in the loft of the barn. Eventually, she claimed that although she could see clearly out the barn window, that she saw no one. This information was contained in the original inquest. And yet earlier, at some point, she had claimed that she could not see out the window at all.

Lizzie contradicted herself as well in the original inquest notes. She said at one point, that she was descending the front stairs just when Mr. Borden was let in the front door of the house by Bridget. Prior to this statement, she'd claimed to have been in the kitchen when he came in. The point was, according to the original statements made to the police, it was revealed that she had been under the effects of morphine. The defense attorney claimed she was not lucid. Thus, her contradictory comments at the inquest were ultimately not admitted during the final trial one year later.

Ironically, once the defense attorney Jennings began his lengthy opening statements on the sixth day of the trial, and although his words were intended to demonstrate how "innocent" Lizzie was, and how loving she was of her father, he also inadvertently raised more questions about her. Ironically, this very act of revisiting all the facts of the case threw probable cause and clear motives right back in the defendant's lap.

In actuality, early on in Lizzie's testimony, she claimed that she had assisted her father in getting comfortable on the sofa in the sitting room as soon as he had laid down to nap. This was precisely where he was killed. She testified that she'd arranged an afghan blanket over him. In fact, according to Mr. Harrington, Lizzie said she was in the kitchen when he came in at 10:30 a.m. and that she helped him off with his coat, inquired about his health, asked if he wanted the blinds closed and then helped him recline on the sofa. [41]

As stated before, Mr. Jennings pointed out in his closing arguments, that the person or monster who committed these heinous murders had to have been someone whose "heart was as black with hatred as hell itself" [42] and that the personality suggested someone having "insanity or brutal hatred."[43] Also, it was pointed out that the person who ultimately wielded the hatchet was quite experienced with it. And yet, later on the judge eventually stated that the blows from the hatchet were unskilled and savage.

According to recorded accounts, there was a tiny drop of blood on Lizzie's petticoat that was never fully explained. It was determined to have not been "menstrual" blood. Even so, it had been established that Lizzie was indeed menstruating at the time of the murders.

Interestingly, Jennings went on in his closing statements to practically point the finger at Bridget Sullivan, stating that wouldn't a stranger have been more likely to viciously attack Mr. Borden? Yet ironically, he was quoted as saying, not sweet Lizzie whose "baby fingers" had been "lovingly entwined about her father's head." Because those very details, Lizzie's last moments in her father's presence, varied according to several different accounts.[44] Mr. Harrington, the brother-in-law, claimed at the outset of Porter's *The Fall River Tragedy*, that she asked her father about his health and helped him get into a reclining position on the sofa, and then inquired whether or not he would like an afghan laid over him.[45] So this bit of information was obviously reported several times, perhaps by Lizzie herself.

Jennings continued to reiterate that the Commonwealth insisted that the murderer would have been covered in blood. But perhaps the jury may have recalled too that there had been the curious questions around the burning of Lizzie's blue dress. Lizzie claimed it had paint on if from recent work done in the house. Her sister Emma concurred. Clearly, although the evidence was largely circumstantial, the errant actions of Lizzie so soon after the murders, painted a likely picture of guilt.

Several items of interest included the following; that she attempted to buy Prussic acid the day before the hatchet murders, and that she'd brazenly descended the front stairs in front of police, carrying a bucket of bloodied rags. This was apparently typical of the time. Women used slop pails to dispose of their rags during the menstrual cycle. Of course, this move down the stairs carrying the slop pail was bold on Lizzie's part, but obviously she knew the police would assume they were simply her private rags and that they'd have been too embarrassed to say anything. And third, there was the dress covered supposedly in paint that Lizzie burned over an open flame in the kitchen three days after the murders. There were, of course, more bits of evidence. But certainly, these three alone would easily have sealed the suspicion of her guilt.

The inconsistencies continued around Lizzie's story. Jennings even mentioned Bridget Sullivan and the fact that no one had looked into her whereabouts while she was supposedly washing windows? The key here however, might have been that they claimed Bridget's motive would have been her anger over her station in life, and the fact that Abby Borden ordered her to wash windows, on what, with the layers of clothing women wore, felt like a one hundred degree day. Some sources described the day as near one hundred and others claimed it was indeed one hundred degrees. The hatchet was wielded with extreme force, leaving a horrific aftermath. Truly, the motive, if emotionally based, was extremely intense. Would a maid have been perturbed to such an extreme because she'd been forced to wash the windows? Or would the ferocity have been more in alignment with the suggestion of some experts, that Lizzie was a repeated victim of incest? According to Marcia R. Carlisle, as spelled out in a 1992 issue of *American Heritage* magazine, in her article entitled "What Made Lizzie Borden Kill?" she stated that "all the hatchet blows" were "aimed at his face" and that the murders were by "the hand of a person strong only in hate and the desire to kill."[46]

Jennings continued to point out that the initial interrogation of Lizzie had been unjust and unfair. Yet he contradicted himself stating that Lizzie would not have killed her step-mother with her father in the house, and then immediately determined that she would never have gotten her father out of the house, if fully intending to kill her step-mother. Jennings appeared to cover every angle as far as Andrew Borden's being home or not, and yet at the same time, his insistence on when or why Lizzie would not have committed the murder of her step-mother made the very relevance of it seem moot. It was still difficult to understand, despite his attempted explanations, why a stranger in the house (versus an emotionally-charged and enraged family member), would choose to wait an hour and a half to kill Andrew Borden? It has been purported that Emma herself may have been the first victim of the incest, but she would perhaps have become too old right around the time their beloved mother died. This might also have explained why Emma, for many years anyway, never spoke harshly or judgmentally of her sister, even in the face of overwhelming evidence of Lizzie's guilt for the murder of their parents.[47]

There were others in the house who could have been murder victims, such as Bridget Sullivan. Why would a stranger have risked waiting around in someone's house that was not their own, unless they knew there was only Bridget to contend with? As it was, she was taking a nap. And that knowledge would have worked out well for a family member, aware of the domestic comings and goings, whose intent that day was to kill two persons in particular in the household.

At times, Jennings was going in many directions with his defense strategy. Often he would bring up precise facts that would easily have condemned Lizzie, such as her uncertainty about how long she was truly in the barn? Ironically, Jennings pointed out that upon returning to the house and finding her father as "having been killed," in her words, by someone that Lizzie did not call out for her mother. Interestingly, upon further thought, it would have been a more logical reaction to cry out right away for her mother. Because wouldn't it have been understandable for her to call out for a family member versus the maid, despite the fact that she knew her mother had supposedly been called away to see a "sick friend."[48]

In the next breath, Jennings pointed out that only an "insane" person would laugh at the top of the stairs, on the heels of having murdered her own step-mother. Also, Lizzie asked her friends, once they'd arrived at the house, to search for her mother, and that she "thought" she "had heard her come in." If so, why didn't she call out for her mother? And why did she know that someone had killed father?"[49] Granted, Andrew Borden was bleeding quite a bit. But why did she herself, determine him to already be dead?

How would Lizzie have "heard her mother come in" if she had been in the barn for as long as she claimed? [50] Either she heard her mother come in or she did not. If she'd heard her mother come in she would have instinctively searched for her first, for two reasons: to gain assistance and perhaps to be consoled by a family member. And perhaps, just to see if Abby Borden was all right. Worth examining was why Lizzie stayed inside the house while sending Bridget off to get help. For what reason? To guard the dead body of her father? Wouldn't she have feared that a sadistic murderer could have been wielding a hatchet and could possibly still have been in the house? Logically, a normal young woman of that time period, or any time period, would have been frightened to death at the prospect of remaining in the house at all, much less alone, unless she already knew who the murderer was.

Discovered later on, with reference to the laugh on the staircase, was the fact that anyone standing at the top of the stairs would have had a clear view of Abby's body, stricken down in cold blood and laid out adjacent to the guest bed. Regardless of whether or not Bridget overheard the maniacal laugh of Lizzie's, one she claimed to have heard, it would have proven that Lizzie did indeed, at the very least, see Abby's body under the bed.[51] The two women (Mrs. Churchill and Alice Russell), who were eventually sent to look for Abby Borden, simply because Lizzie thought she'd "heard her come in," claimed to have spotted Abby's body quite clearly from the landing on the staircase.[52] This was precisely where Lizzie would have been standing. So once the idea that Lizzie had been on the stairs was affirmed, that then raised the question as to how she could not have seen her stepmother's body in plain view at the top of the stairs.

It would have been easy for Lizzie to have feigned illness the day before the murders. After all, she claimed she had stayed all day and only traveled across the street that evening to see her friend Alice Russell. Yet somehow, it could not have been denied that three separate witnesses testified to having seen and heard Lizzie enter a drugstore that same night and attempt to purchase Prussic acid. Deadly, Prussic acid. The witnesses were no less than exemplary; two were pharmacists in the drugstore and the third was a medical student. Not only was Lizzie recognized by sight, one of the three also claimed to have known her by her voice.[53]

The truth was that Lizzie may easily have informed her stepmother that she'd stayed in sick all day, without the step-mother really knowing one way or the other. Yet one had to realize that the house was replete with locked doors, repressed silence and distrust. It was nowhere indicated that Abby Borden paid attention to Lizzie's whereabouts or vice versa. In point of fact, on the very day of the murders, Lizzie was supposedly not entirely certain as to who had sent the note for her step-mother to "go see a sick friend;" nor whether or not the woman had actually gone.[54]

Jennings also explored motive and claimed that in the "natural course of events," the money would have been Lizzie's.[55] His belief was that once Mr. and Mrs. Borden had died, all monies and properties would fall to the young women. However, as was proven later on, this was not at all the case. In actuality, the will of Andrew Borden had been changed quite recently, and was purported to have cut Emma and Lizzie out of a substantial inheritance. It may have had to do with the farm which was a major piece of real estate Andrew Borden had owned. However, some claimed he left no will.

Quite literally, unlike a woman's stifling existence in nineteenth century America, as compared to even thirty years later when American women finally earned the right to vote, a change in Andrew Borden's will may have left the two women literally destitute. Also, unlike a woman even ten to twenty years later, with Lizzie's lack of educational background or basic training and lack of experience in a trade, or a factory, she would have had no means of supporting herself. Added to that, the likelihood that she would marry so late in life was very slim. This would have been a bleak outlook for anyone in the late nineteenth century, especially to two young women who were proud, and cognizant of the town's gossip and criticisms of them.

Around Lizzie's thirtieth birthday, she embarked on a nineteen week Grand Tour of Europe. In a sense, without a man to take care of her, a home of her own and especially the luxury she'd experienced on this trip, such a situation would have added to her angst. Europe had proffered plumbing, fashionable clothing, running water and exquisite food. The contrast of Lizzie's Fall River home, which consisted of an austere, distrustful and mirthless life, one with no possibility of a husband, children or a life of her own and a life of financial freedom could surely have been a motive. So to many, that would have been her motive. However, the experience of Europe, and the disparity between her life in Fall River and the shame of her existence compared to a comparatively good life, may have been fueled by this extensive tour of Europe that lasted several months. All this excluded the most convincing and likely motive; retaliation for a life wrought with sexual and emotional abuse.

According to Marcia Carlisle, after Lizzie's mother died:

> Mr. Borden refused offers of help from other family members, including his sister. He chose to keep his household his private domain, establishing a kind of family isolation well documented in the case histories of incest survivors.
>
> As the result of a sense of entitlement and the absence of an appropriate sexual partner, Mr. Borden might have abused first Emma, then Lizzie. Research on serial abuse is sketchy, but it may occur in as many as fifty percent of all cases. The shift from one sibling to another often takes place as the older child begins to resist the abuse. in the Borden household the transfer might have taken lace when Emma was about fifteen and Lizzie was about four.[56]

In essence, Lizzie Borden was at her wit's end. At the trial, her attorney for the defense Jennings, next launched into an explanation about the "inherent" difference between men and women and their reasons for committing murder. He claimed that certainly a man would do such a thing when "pressed for money." He went on to argue that Lizzie would never be the kind of woman who would have committed such a heinous crime simply because she was "pressed for money."[57] Ironically, Jennings here, in my mind, inadvertently reiterated the likelihood that, in light of the macabre and extreme violence of the crimes, such as obliterating Mr. Borden's face and loosening an eye from its socket, that such a maniacal motive would indeed have been over much more than simply money. So in point of fact, this would have led to a family member, young and strong enough, to wield a hatchet wrought with rage.

Jennings further claimed that Lizzie would have "inherited in the natural course of events."[58] In actuality, it was later discovered that there had been rumors that Andrew Borden was indeed going to amend his will to accommodate his wife. In fact, there were many theories set forth that Borden planned on changing his will. Although, this was never clearly established as to whether he did or not, some records even indicated he was going to change his will within twenty-four hours of the time he was murdered.

Most importantly, it appeared that the more Jennings presented his opinion, stating that Lizzie had never attempted to buy the prussic acid, the more ridiculous his justifications became. For instance, he claimed one of the three witnesses, the pharmacist named Eli Bence, only heard her voice, and that it sounded "tremulous." And yet later on, it became apparent that she had tried to purchase the prussic acid and at the time, claimed it was to clean a seal-skin cape.[59]

Interestingly, there was also mention of a seal-skin cape or covering that had been given to Lizzie upon her departure for her grand European Tour. Perhaps it was the same cape. Ironically, a thirtieth birthday would have marked a spinster in 1890. In actuality, Lizzie enjoyed the trip overall and it exposed her to the idea of luxury. During that tour, Lizzie celebrated her thirtieth birthday.

Soon attorney for the prosecution Knowlton came back with numerous details around motive. He asked quite simply why, if it had indeed been the work of an angry or disgruntled businessman involved with Andrew Borden, would such a man hike upstairs to find Abby, kill her first, then wait an hour and a half to destroy Andrew Borden's skull? Also, Knowlton pointed out that such a person must have been a coward.

This last point may have had several explanations. If Lizzie was a victim of incest, her goal would have been to obliterate Andrew's face, wiping out his visage. This was accomplished tenfold. In fact, as noted, one of his eyeballs was out of its socket and was literally dangling. At the same time, if it had been a business venture gone awry, typically one may have surmised that not only would the perpetrator not have minded if Andrew saw him, but rather, would have wanted to see him. Thus, Attorney Knowlton's theory that the man must have been a coward, was erroneous only in its motivational stance behind the sofa, where Andrew Borden lay napping.

The next set of key points Knowlton raised involved the entire idea of an actual "stranger" having committed the crimes. Knowlton raised several basic facts; the entire Borden house was under perpetual lockdown. Unlike most Victorian homes where windows were often thrown wide for fresh air, especially in one hundred degree heat, the Borden house had all the windows closed tightly. Such a tight hold on windows, door and keys only heightened the suggestion of incest in the house. All the doors between each room were also kept locked. Regardless of the reasons, a suspicious and most likely internal burglary in the house which had taken place a year or so before was the purported reason for the lockdown. This security extended to the barn and cellar, and would have made it virtually impossible for anyone to gain access to the house. Perhaps if the culprit were a circus performer or trapeze artist, he or she may have perpetrated a method. It was more likely though, which Knowlton here exposed, that the deed was internal and was most certainly committed by someone within the confines of the family.

Such a conclusion brought observers back to the fact that Lizzie and Bridget were the only two individuals at home when Abby and Andrew Borden were murdered. Therefore, that the culprit was likely an insider was an understatement.

Chapter Three

This time the heat was stifling. It woke her up. The bracelet emitted the light simmer of warmth, like an internal sunburn. Yet it tightened again, to the point where she could see the distinct purple line on her skin. The bracelet left a light dusting of lavender particles. She ran her finger under the maddening slide bracelet and rolled toward the window.

Colette sat up in the bed struggling, reaching out instinctively to adjust the air conditioner. Instead of her foot touching upon carpeting, her toes felt hardwood floor. Upon standing, she realized she wore a voluminous white nightgown. Lifting the sides of it, she studied the intricate lacework, and then sneezed suddenly. Opening her eyes through squints, she noticed that the floor, as well as a roll-top desk in the corner, were covered in dust. She'd definitely time traveled again.

Blinking several times, she pulled herself up to the window sill, and reached for the Kleenex box she always kept on the floor next to her bed. Instead, there was a small pile of white handkerchiefs. She shook her head, confused and turned her attention back to the window. Expecting to see the Prairie bungalow about to be torn down, she readied herself for the wrecking ball and that unsightly tru-link fence that would inevitably be around the place. Although she'd taken a walk in 1994 the day before, somehow, in a strange trip via time travel, there, she'd said it; she knew today she would be back in the year 2011.

Hands on her hips, she leaned over to gaze outside. That's when her throat tightened. This was not 2011 at all.

In place of the bungalow, there stood an unusual, wooden-framed farmhouse. She opened the window to take a better look. Sweet summer came to mind. That was the phrase she would use to describe the incredible scent of the air. The sidewalks gone. The road itself was unpaved. There was a haunting silence about the street and all around the block.

The farmhouse now situated across the street was certainly not the sort she'd ever seen before. Not anywhere. It was wooden, but the two-by-four wooden siding was in vertical rows rather than horizontal. The front of the house had fussy lattice work and the trim had eaves which jutted out. Colette took a deep breath at the sight of the grandiose house. Something felt wrong. The paint was so fresh on the wooden siding and she could practically smell the scent of freshly cut lumber. Time was out of place. She was out of step with whatever was going on.

Was it true that extreme emotional distress could cause one to hallucinate? Or perhaps, time travel? She'd read about these theories. In fact so many had written about it. If that were the case, she would have traveled years before; perhaps during her first divorce or her miscarriage. Why hadn't she? Why was she time traveling now?

Her mind diverged into several directions. Colette realized that her life of late, after her second divorce, had left her wondering not only about herself, but the state of women overall? It had left her in a deep depression. She'd even had thoughts about drinking, and yes, now and then, even of suicide. This scared her because she didn't believe in either one. Not at all. On some level, she knew her very life was a gift, as much as the gorgeous color purple and the swaying of Weeping Willows. So were these time travel stints just her mind manifesting her stress? But if she'd been dreaming, how did Olivia's yellow shovel suddenly show up? Even the scents of the air, which seemed more organic in these travel periods, somehow convinced her, without a doubt, that these trips were authentic. The olfactory sense never failed her. It always gave her a sense of place. The scents in the rented room on this day dappled across her mind, and wavered between horse manure, bleachy soap, and a deeply sweet smell of grass and foliage.

Looking to the left of the house across the street, there stood, as it had for years and would continue to stand well into 2011, a tall, singularly proud American Foursquare farmhouse. From chatting with her neighbor once or twice fourteen years before, in real time, Colette had learned that the house was built in 1885. To the right of the farmhouse, on the other side of where the bungalow would be built in 1929, stood another farmhouse, similar in style which would, almost one hundred years later, be converted into apartments. Then she got it. The bungalow had not yet been built. It would stand between the two farmhouses.

Oh good God, she thought. Now where had she traveled to? No. When the Hell had she traveled to?

A breeze blew through the window suddenly, strong and fresh. It swept under the capped sleeves of the obscure lace nightgown which had dressed itself on her body somehow. Clearly, the time travel took place during her sleep. Looking around the room, there sat a Victrola and another dresser with a vast mirror, and vanity in a far corner. Stepping over, she touched a splintery large wooden wardrobe closet which had not been there the night before. She touched it. It was real.

Turning, she opened the left door and caught her breath quickly. It was her reflection in a full-length mirror that stared back at her. She had on no makeup and her hair was a dishwater blonde instead of the lighter color she'd sported her entire adult life. It was her natural hair color. Reaching inside the wardrobe, she traced her hand along the fabrics. The closet was replete with silks, cottons and lightweight wools. She pushed one aside, then another, and another. At the very end there was a high-collared lace blouse, three or four of them, in fact. She flipped back to a cluster of full-length skirts grey, blue and black, some with lace trim at the bottom. Each was comprised of the organic green and brown colors of yesteryear.

Someone pounded on the apartment door. She snapped out of her reverie.

"Colette? It's time to go. We don't have much time. Mr. Sewell won't want to be kept waiting. It's time for the visit."

"The visit?" she said, glancing out the window as she noticed a small crowd forming, moving along the sidewalk. She could see the sways of long skirts, the black tailored jackets here and there.

A woman stood there in the hallway and clutched a brown shawl around her shoulders. She looked less than amused.

"Of course," Colette blurted, pretending she knew what "the visit" was. She stepped forward, gazing at the woman's gray hair and translucent eyes. The eyes smiled at her now. Colette's shoulders relaxed.

"What should I wear?" she asked, fully cognizant that she had no idea where she was going nor who she was visiting.

"What you always do."

A rumble of voices and movement reached her from through the open window.

"What is the crowd outside all about?"

The door had closed swiftly, quietly. Colette stared after it, thoroughly bewildered. She touched the ornate crystal doorknob and turned her hand around it, admiring it. So intact and permanent, so well-built, and definitely not there earlier in the day. That doorknob was not part of the door that very morning. It was the type of doorknob renovators searched through garbage cans for. It seemed as if someone had come in and converted the room while she slept.

Whipping around, she scanned the room, marveling at the trim around the ceiling. It appeared to be newly built, with high gloss to the wood. This also made no sense. In fact she was certain this ceiling had not endured the twelve coats of paint that would eventually happen.

Colette paced back to the window and slid it open, just ever so slightly. It opened so easily that it surprised her. There was a calendar on the wall. Who had put a calendar up in her apartment? In fact, who used calendars at all? She patted the bed, and then her draping long skirt she'd put on, searching for her cell phone. Was the landlord slipping in while she was out?

The crowd had gained momentum and had moved around the corner out of her field of vision. Something in the neighborhood had brought everyone out. And the heat. She took a deep breath but the air was so thick, it was just a physical exercise.

Then she checked the calendar more closely. It depicted a young couple registering for a marriage license. The clothing characterized the Gibson girl, the ultimate woman as defined by the Arrow Shirt Company in the late nineteenth century. It was August, according to this calendar. Of course it was. She knew that. This calendar claimed it was August of 1892. Colette grabbed hold of the dresser nearby to stop from falling over.

The heat enveloped her. A mere wisp of a breeze lifted through the window. Without any alternative, she turned back to the wardrobe closet. Vast, intrusive, and taking up much of the room, she was certain it had not been there before.

The unmistakable sound of horses' hooves clopping carried through the open window. This dream of another reality was becoming three dimensional. This was no dream.

Sifting through the clothing in the wardrobe, she finally settled on a lacy blouse to match the skirt. She hardly had a choice. No Capri khakis or Polo t-shirts would be found here. She squeezed into the skirt; certain it was no bigger than a size eight.

Tripping a bit on the skirt, she shimmied down the front staircase and had reached the front door five minutes later, pausing by an oval mirror in the hallway taking just a moment to adjust a cameo she'd pinned at the neck of her blouse. Outside, the sun was ruthless as she waited on the stoop, watching children playing with giant hoops and porcelain headed dolls on the lawn next door. Soon, an adolescent young man peered at her from the back of a black carriage which had just pulled up. Across from the young man sat the grim angular face of an older man.

"Come along, Colette," the older man demanded. "It is crucial that we are on time."

As she stood up, sweat broke out around her neck and she felt drops of perspiration running down her back. She ran her fingertips just under the collar of her blouse. She mustn't topple over; she had to get it together. Stepping to the carriage, she grasped the older man's hand. It was rough and the grip was too strong. Still, he guided her up the fold-out steps into the compartment.

Once on board, Colette touched the leather seats, at once marveling at the craftsmanship as well as confirming the fact that she was indeed, not dreaming. The air was filled with the scent of the oil used on the leather of the carriage, and the sounds of squeaking wheels. It was imperative not to appear in awe at the novelty of being in an actual carriage of the late nineteenth century. It was tough though. She loved this old stuff. And then she noticed it, a distinct change in the air. And when she looked out the carriage window, it was slightly hilly and the terrain was completely unfamiliar.

Colette sat very still, with her hands folded. Prim and proper. She could manage this charade for now. Colette must play the part of the nineteenth century woman; demure, obedient and unassuming. No one could know that she was not who she was supposed to be, or at least, who they seemed to think she was.

But how did one play the proper woman of 1892? The gay nineties in America? The heat in the carriage was dizzying. The younger man's gaze took her in, his eyes full of intensity. She opened her mouth to speak, but decided to remain silent. A woman wouldn't start a conversation in the presence of men. Not in 1892.

"Mister Sewell," the driver yelled from up top. "We will make good time today." The driver's accent was strange to Colette. She couldn't place it? She read the cover of the book Mr. Sewell was reading, "What Every Gentleman Should Know about Institutional Banking." The young man next to her, who looked to be around fifteen years of age, finally spoke.

"You were missed on our last visit," he said. "Isabelle," he started, and then stopped. "She was less well, than before. Father put her in today after she broke out of our house." He hesitated. "He keeps her captive," he said, his voice low. Then after a moment, he added, "Isabelle really values her friendship with you."

Colette blinked. "And I, was here," she murmured, "exactly where are we?"

The young man nodded. "I know. Sometimes Fall River is strange and foreign to me too."

"Fall River?" she managed, her voice hushed.

Mr. Sewell went on reading. "Massachusetts," he said gruffly. "Don't you have your wits about you, young woman?"

She sensed that Mr. Sewell was not authentically reading the latest financial advice. In fact, Mr. Sewell seemed inordinately tense, even by Victorian standards. At the same time, he seemed to control everyone in the carriage.

"They're teaching her about being a young lady," the young man said, not without sarcasm. "Because they think she acts too old for her age. She's an embarrassment to our father."

"Do not discuss your sister," Mr. Sewell interrupted firmly.

The words were benign, perhaps to the naked unassuming listener. But Mr. Sewell's eyes were black. They registered a man broiling with rage; something festered, almost volcanic just beneath the surface of decorum.

As Colette watched the open fields pass by slowly to the left, her mind envisioned all the 1920s bungalows and later 1970s developments, that would be built years later. Chickens and roosters rambled about everywhere, following alongside the carriage with occasional cackles.

Half an hour passed. Colette couldn't gauge how far they'd traveled. At a carriage pace, they'd made their way to a train station which was replete with archways and overhangs. The station breathed in the grey day and appeared to register their presence as the carriage cobbled past. Someone pulled a shade down in the station, like closing one eye, as if to block out the sight of them passing. Colette surmised the horse and buggy mode of transport would persist only for another twenty years, until 1915 when the automobile would rumble alongside them.

Soon they pulled up to a hill, a massive hill which seemed to loom up out of the ground, insistent upon being noticed. It was surrounded by an iron gate. The sky was awash in charcoal and she noticed the sun's disappearance behind clouds, slipping away as if aware of some evil in its midst.

That's when she knew. The massive mahogany door from the old bungalow had transported her further than even to the nineteenth century. This was nothing like the flat prairie lands of Illinois. She'd driven through New York state years before for a wedding. It was hilly. Funny she recalled now how happy her friend had been to marry; although she'd been a graduate with honors from Cornell. She talked of nothing else than having four kids and staying home while her husband pursued success as a neurosurgeon. And so this little town exhaled East Coast as well. She was indeed now on the east coast. The door from the bungalow, as some sort of portal, had first sent her to 1994 right across the street in Illinois. And now it had transported her east to Massachusetts? Why? Was she supposed to do something?

Reviewing it in her mind, she'd awakened in the farmhouse very similar to the one across from where she, Max and Olivia had once lived. Was it the carriage? It had taken her into the next realm. The carriage had carried her into the East coast. The Sewells picked her up at a boarding house in Fall River, one very similar to Marilyn's in Illinois. But the view out the window looked so much like Illinois. Yet now she'd awakened in actuality, in Fall River. One town can certainly look like the next.

Checking her wrist, she noticed the slide bracelet had left a bright purple streak on her wrist. She touched it with her forefinger, moving it aside to see if the bracelet was indeed the cause. Sure enough, the small lozenges of purple marks coincided with each slide on the bracelet.

Colette leaned out of the carriage now, stretching her arm out the side window, the sensation of her starchy white cuff and tight sleeve feeling very foreign. She tried to get a sense of where they would be logistically, in the twenty-first century, versus the nineteenth century.

To the right was a two story carriage stop. There'd been one similar to it back in Illinois, like the one in Valley Stream; it too would become a watering hole in the twenty-first century. Of course, it would have to survive the wrecking ball.

That had been one of Colette's pet peeves. The greed of the North Shore in Chicago, where excessive square footage took precedence over architectural form and beauty. This real estate gluttony led to the rampant destruction of eighty to one-hundred-year-old homes in the Midwest. In her mind, it was nothing short of mass murder. Often Colette would gasp simply driving down a street she'd not driven down in a while, horrified at the sight of yet another Victorian farmhouse surrounded by the tru-link fence, the death knell for old homes. Another tru-link fence meant soon there would be another hole in the ground where hardwood and lath and plaster once stood. Sometimes half a porch would have been crushed in, just to test any remaining strength the old girl had in it, she figured, as if the crew needed to know just how easy it would be to demolish the façade. The shell would stand there, quivering in its skeletal frame, waiting to be wiped out from the landscape of the town and forever erased in everyone's minds. Never would it be appreciated by generations to come.

For a while, Colette would snap a picture of such houses with her iPhone, as if she could somehow lengthen the life of the structures. But they were doomed.

Eying this carriage stop now, in 1892 Fall River, the roofline was in the shape of a barn. And instead of the cheap advertisements on the side, and neon in the window flashing "cold Budweiser Beer" it had the words "Fall River Stage Coach Stop" printed in ornate gold letters across the top. On the side of the building there was a brightly painted Pears Soup advertisement.

Twenty minutes later, the carriage pulled up to a vast high-arched entranceway. Leaning out as far as she could, she scanned the creaking sign once, quickly, as they click-clacked through a set of mammoth iron gates which read, "Perfect Pines Insane Asylum." A disheveled man stood there, hunched over, and fiddled with the cumbersome padlock, moving at a maddeningly slow pace.

As the three, Edward, young William and Colette passed through the gates, they were assisted out of the carriage and forced to continue on foot. The degenerate man followed, slowly, hunched and defeated. They were led through dense trees and a winding, disorienting pathway. This was certainly on purpose, to perhaps prevent unwanted visitors.

The building itself was grey stone, and the windows eyed them coldly. Once inside they approached a small reception area.

"You're all here for Miss Sewell?" a severe-looking matron asked. She was swaddled to the neck in apron and black dress.

Mr. Edward Sewell craned his neck, turning to look stiffly, his head moving with the cold precision of a blackbird. His eyes, black with secrets, bulged as if he believed everyone listened to his thoughts. The place echoed loneliness, with the longing of souls who had been forgotten. The hallways appeared to lead nowhere, making their vast length as vacant as the expression in the nurse's eyes.

To all superficial appearances, the place served as a lofty refuge for those who could afford it. Despite a bleak exterior, the furniture was plush. Burgundy patterned chairs matched several windows swathed in heavy pinstriped draperies. The floor was marbled with black and white tiles. It reflected the images of their boots, like jagged unfriendly mirrors.

Colette knew better. The cold tiles, the black of the nurse's clothing and her severe expression told her. This was no place of luxury and healing. The angst in the eyes of the man at the gate outside had lingered with her. It spoke of cruelty and judgment. Mental illness, as always, then and now, elicited disdain from those on the outside, those family members who were "normal."

Women in 1892 America suffered from any number of neuroses from "hysteria" to "uterine issues." Essentially they were catch-all phrases meant to deal with all the general female maladies.

Before she was fully aware of it, Mr. Sewell was being directed away, disappearing down the dark corridors. As his frame receded, his gait grew more like a swagger. It was the entitled march of some patronizing commandant, overseeing an underhanded operation. His angular frame grew smaller, but no less commanding as they diminished down the hallway.

William sunk into a chair with his head bowed. He stared at the floor, dutiful, and stone-faced. Like the nurse, he seemed to have been assimilated into the place simply by its atmosphere.

Soon the nurse and Mr. Sewell disappeared as nothing but two minute shadows at the end of the spotless corridor. Pinpoints. Then gone. Colette sat up suddenly. She had to know.

"What is this place, this asylum?"

William's face was drawn, aging him beyond his apparent youth. He turned to her. His face was grey.

"He's the devil. But he's powerful."

Somehow in merely five minutes time, a twist had transformed the young man's entire countenance, to the point of appearing ill. Colette leaned over in the broad leather chairs, and touched his sleeve. He simply leaned back and closed his eyes. There was something sinister at work here.

"I am not like other young men my age. I don't believe women should be locked up."

"Who is the "devil" you're referring to? A doctor here?"

"My father." He laughed, mirthlessly. "I guess that's what you'd call him. He is supposed to be a stellar example of Fall River's finest. A nineteenth century gentleman. Makes an ample amount of money. He's a well-known financier. And he knows everyone of prominence around town. But the way he has treated Isabelle..." He stopped and shook his head. "The doctors here are suspect too."

"What do you mean about your father?"

"He does not act toward Isabelle as a father should. I really think he dislikes her, because she's too much like mother. That's what he always says."

A strange, yet familiar nausea washed over Colette. It was not just his otherworldly pallor. It was his words as well. They were full of pain, of shame. Gone was the amicable personality of the young man. This boy harbored the wisdom of an embittered survivor.

The nurse at the desk eyed her suspiciously. Colette leaned toward him. "What is it?" she said.

His eyes flashed. "It's this place." He looked away. "It's only August 4th, but I know he's insisting on getting her home by mid-day."

"August 4th?"

They sat in silence a moment. A large clock, round and crème in color with stenciled black hands, ticked away in the hush. Suddenly he turned and grabbed her by the hand. His grasp tightened until it hurt.

She freed herself. He was unreadable. Tormented, but unclear.

"Do you understand the devil's motivation?" he asked. "I mean, I'm not the good Christian who practices what he learns in church. But the men here, and everywhere. There are brothels, and young girls. They're all mistreated."

Colette hesitated. "Do you question his decision to lock up your sister here?" She knew from her own studies of history how bad these places were, and continued to be well into the 20th century. She could only imagine. "What did she do?"

"My father planned her demise, gradually. It's imprisonment. My sister's only crime has been using her brain. She's very smart. Isabelle has goals and ideas. Isabelle is not your typical young lady. She does not fit in with the others. God help her, she has opinions."

"How does that justify his locking her up?"

William smirked. "There was a musician. A trumpeter who traveled with the John Philip Sousa band. He encouraged her to, be who she was."

"Surely that isn't a crime?"

"They became too close. And she is obsessive. She struggles with her mind. It haunts her. Darren helped her. But before anyone would listen to her, or the troubles of her friend Lizzie," he stopped.

"Lizzie?"

"Right down the street. Something was not right in that house! And Isabelle knew it. Just like life is not normal in our house. The devil doesn't know that I know."

Colette thought about the crowd she'd seen that morning. It had spread along the street like a pack of ravenous wolves. The looks of disbelief and hungry curiosity on their faces came to her. That's when it hit her that the farmhouse itself allowed her to see into 1892. That's why she could see the crowd forming. She was seeing 2nd Street from her rented room. And once in the carriage, she too had been completely transported. In 1892 however, the rented room became part of Mrs. Burns' boarding house in Fall River, Massachusetts.

"She finally did it. Isabelle tried to get help for her."

"Who did what?"

William's eyes were averted as he uttered the words, "Lizzie Borden."

"Then that crowd today? The Borden murders?"

"Someone was killed." He looked at her. "How would you know anything about it? It's rumors that something has happened at the Borden house." Then he took a deep breath and looked at the ceiling as he continued, "Isabelle told me. She said she was not alone in her misery. This was how Darren cared for her. In his way, Darren's attentions to Isabelle may have saved her from the fate which has apparently overtaken Lizzie."

"What happened to Darren?"

William frowned. "I'm not certain."

His demeanor transitioned again, as if a heavy barbell weakened his shoulders. He leaned forward, his head in his hands. William had moved past the realm of innocence. Defeat lay upon him like an ozone.

"To survive in this horrible place she has to keep her mouth closed and hang tight to her skirts."

When he looked up, his eyes were red. "The few times I've been allowed to see her in this place, she's been doped up and looks as if she's been physically tested. Once, she tried to tell me more about Lizzie, about her friend's outrage and sense of total helplessness. But the devil, he keeps her down."

"Your father? How well does he know the Bordens?"

William laughed, shaking his head. "Andrew Borden and Edward Sewell are two men of the same cloth. Don't know about Mr. Borden, but in addition to their banking and real estate conversations, the devil likes his mind-altering spirits."

All at once Edward stood there, watching them, his dark form not moving. William was up and at the front door within seconds. By the time Colette had followed, the carriage, black matte with gold trim on the doors, was awaiting her outside. It seemed to know her. This made no sense, and yet when William assisted her inside the beast, and she grasped the inky black door of its flank, a shock ran through her body.

Chapter Three (A)

The Historical Facts

U pon closer study of the floor plan of the Borden house, it was readily apparent that one could not gain access to Mr. Borden's room at the back of the house, from the front of the house.

In fact, the villain would have had only one way to get from the front of the house to the back of the house, and that entailed passing through the downstairs and all its rooms on the main floor. This also involved being seen by several members of the household.

Added to that knowledge was the fact that the house was located in the heart of busy downtown Fall River, where hundreds were known to pass the residence on a daily basis.

Obviously, the murderer would have had to have known all the precise movements of each member of the household. Like any home filled with three or four family members, often one member did not always know the whereabouts of the others from day to day, and moment to moment. This was true even for routine events which may have varied with each day. As discovered later on, the events in the Borden house on August 4th, 1892, were exceedingly unpredictable.

The fact remained, that certainly anyone, especially a dubious-looking stranger, would not have gone unnoticed in downtown Fall River. Added to that, the neighbors Adelaide Churchill and her best friend across the street had all known one another for years. An unknown person would have been seen and noticed by anyone and everyone in the close-knit metropolis of Fall River.

Knowlton further pointed out that Lizzie was the only one left in the kitchen after John Vinnicum Morse, Lizzie's uncle, left, and later, Lizzie was the only one upstairs, along with Abby Borden. Bridget had, of course, been previously ordered outside by Abby Borden, to wash windows.

In the downstairs of the house, there was no one around, besides Lizzie. The only two persons inside the house were Lizzie and her step-mother, and according to the timing of witnesses, like the neighbor Mrs. Churchill, Mr. Borden scurried off on his errands at the same time that Bridget was in the blistering heat and dressed in full-length dress no doubt, washing the windows. So, if that witness was to be believed, Bridget was indeed seen by the neighbors, outside washing windows at the precise time that Abby Borden was determined to have been murdered. [60]

Again, it was duly pointed out that were Lizzie and her step-mother alone in the house, which they indeed were, Lizzie would have heard the body of Abby fall. Abby Borden, it was estimated, weighed close to 180 pounds. Most certainly, the sudden violence taken out upon her would have caused her body to fall to the floor quite heavily, and quite loudly.

Secondly, when Mr. Borden was left alone with Lizzie, and when Bridget had gone upstairs, not fifteen minutes later, Andrew Borden was bludgeoned. The prosecution pointed out that emotionally, Lizzie would have known. She may easily have recalled more precisely where she was at the time her father was killed. Bridget would later claim that she'd heard a somewhat sinister laugh from the front stairway, from the top of the stairs just as she'd allowed Mr. Borden in through the front door. And Bridget was also convinced that the laugh had been Lizzie's.

Lizzie contradicted herself at the inquest. The prosecutor here brought up that although now it was Autumn, that they should try to picture why a murderer, or Lizzie, would have wanted to have been upstairs in the doubtless 100 degree heat. Would Lizzie have spotted such a murderer around the house, or outside? A window? The last place Lizzie saw her father before he was murdered, was downstairs. Lizzie had been ironing handkerchiefs.

Next, the prosecutor pointed out that Lizzie confused her story several times. First, Lizzie claimed to have been in the kitchen, and then she stated that she was on the steps on the front stairs coming down. Lizzie had no clear explanation for why or where she was, for a full hour and fifteen minutes. In one of her explanations she'd stated that she'd been waiting for the iron to heat up in order to iron the handkerchiefs.[61]

Questions around Lizzie and her supposed reasons for going out to the barn were varied. Even if Lizzie went to the barn for twenty minutes, that did not explain how she missed seeing some culprit responsible for the murders. Again, an outside murderer would have had to hide out for an hour, waiting for Mr. Borden to get home and then emerge and pounce on him at precisely the right moment, without being seen.

Next, the prosecutor explored the fallacy of the note story. Clearly, he did not believe her story. He further pointed out that Eli Bence, the pharmacist, and two other witnesses at the drugstore, recognized Lizzie when she attempted to buy prussic acid. Although the defense attorney reiterated that the witnesses only identified her by her voice, the prosecutor instead stated that the pharmacist both "recognized her and her voice."[62]

The prosecutor also indicated that once Lizzie's hopes of buying prussic acid were thwarted, she decided to go forward with her acts of murder. The fact that the attack on her father was "from behind" in a day and age of honor, trust and high morals, was to have been considered extraordinarily callous and crude.

Next Knowlton took a direct attack on Lizzie's femininity all together. The claims that she lacked "feminine feeling" was brought out. In fact, he shared the fact that Lizzie was so unfeeling that she wouldn't even allow anyone to search her room. There was Detective Fleet trying to find the murderer of her parents and Lizzie refused to let anyone in.

In fact, Dr. Bowen was in the room with Lizzie and supported her decision, keeping the police at bay. Knowlton went on to point out that she'd had a good fifteen minutes to hide away any bloodied apron or bloodied shoes.

Near the conclusion of his speech, Knowlton left the room in silence. At last, Judge Blaisdell, with great sadness, created an interesting scenario. He presented the hypothesis which purported that a strange man, the murderer, had been the first to come upon the tragic scene in the drawing room and found the horrific remains of Andrew Borden. What if, as Knowlton pointed out, he had claimed he'd just been in the barn looking for sinkers to go fishing? Would it have been likely that this strange man would have been believed?

Judge Blaisdell, with a tear in his eye, announced that Lizzie Borden was likely guilty and would soon have gone to trial.

Due to the fact that they really had no appropriate facility to house a female prisoner, Lizzie was sent off to Taunton Jail, eight miles away from Fall River. A newspaper in Worcester, Massachusetts featured an article stating that they hoped all those persons connected with prosecuting Lizzie Borden would be struck by a wave of cholera, which scared the residents of New York.[63]

Before the jury reconvened on December 1st, Lizzie's good friend, her best friend, in fact, Alice Russell, visited with authorities in charge of the case. She revealed the fact that Lizzie had come to see her the night before the murders. During that visit, she described what had been said. She also revealed that she saw Lizzie burning a dress in the kitchen three days after the murders.[64]

The date of Lizzie's trial was set to begin on June 5, 1893. The trial was in response to three indictments passed down on December 2, 1892. These actions kept Lizzie imprisoned in the Taunton Jail from

December 3rd to May 8th. Lizzie received several visitors while being held at the jail. Most were women.

Next discussed in Porter's *Fall River Tragedy* was one Henry G. Trickey, a reporter for the Boston Globe, and Detective Edwin D. McHenry. This was also referred to as the Trickey-McHenry affair. The history of it was basically a plot devised to publish a "fake" story in the Boston Globe. Detective McHenry supposedly provided a story about the Borden case for $500. In the end, the story was proven to be false, and in fact Trickey was mysteriously killed by a train in Canada soon after it was disproved.[65]

Detective McHenry related how he'd heard of the Borden murders while traveling in New York, and that he'd hurried to Fall River. He received conflicting stories as to what had actually transpired at the house. So he began by thoroughly investigating each thread that had been presented. The first one suggested that a fictional stranger jumped the fence located in the back of the house. John Cunningham also informed Detective McHenry that the cellar door had been found to be locked immediately after the murders. McHenry went as far as counting the number of cobwebs just inside the door of the cellar, which indicated, and perhaps proved, that no one had gone in or out of the cellar entranceway recently.

Soon it was discovered that Henry Trickey completely manufactured a lover-boyfriend love story involving Lizzie. Trickey was quoted as saying, "has Lizzie Borden got a lover? Can't I allege that she has in my story tomorrow morning?"

There soon also came a check in the amount of $5,000 drawn by Andrew Jennings, attorney for the Bordens. It was in payment for the government's case. Jennings was after information about the State (Knowlton's) secrets.[66]

There was much speculation that the original defense attorney for Lizzie, Mr. Adams, had agreed to pay $1,000 to the prosecution for the evidence they had against the defense. Further, Jennings also apparently went along with the idea.

There was a supposed letter handed over to Trickey, reporter for the Boston Globe, that was written by the wife of Attorney Adams. She had been aware that Lizzie was guilty because she knew the content of Adams' conversations with Lizzie. One conversation, in which Lizzie admitted guilt to Adams, was also apparently overheard by McHenry, the private detective. The letter, which the following quote was taken from, was itself extracted from original witness testimony by the reporter Trickey. It said the following words; paraphrased –"I am ashamed to think that my husband has interested himself in the defense of this woman, when you know she is guilty. You had no business to have anything to do with her case."[67]

Witness testimony via Trickey, Boston Globe reporter, and McHenry, further spelled out the necessity for certain witnesses for the Prosecution that needed to be kept under control. Taken from original witness statements, the following conversation was said to have taken place:

Trickey asked if Bridget knew more than she claimed. McHenry replied that yes, she did. In fact, he said there were three or four witnesses that needed to be kept out of the state. There had supposedly been affidavits. In fact McHenry suggested that Bridget be sent out of the country.[68]

She was. Bridget Sullivan eventually was sent to live out of the United States and returned to her homeland of Ireland.

The beginning of the Superior Court Trial for Lizzie Borden began on June 5, 1893. The start of the trial recounted several instances when Lizzie reiterated to her interlocutors' repeated references to her "mother" that Abby was her "step-mother." This was a common reaction on Lizzie's part, any time someone made that mistake. The reason cited for this unrest was the fact that there'd been bad blood between them over a disagreement some five years before the murders, having to do with real estate.

A more in-depth account involved a trip to the dressmaker's. Apparently, while at the family cloak makers, the spring before the murders, Lizzie was quoted as saying in response to a reference to Abby as follows: "don't call her mother. She is a mean thing, and we hate her, (she and Emma). We have as little to do with her as possible." Soon after the murders, a policeman had asked Lizzie quite simply, when the last time was that she'd "seen her mother" and she replied brusquely, "she is not my mother. My mother is dead."

At the start of the trial, the issue of household illness had been introduced again. Apparently, a sickness had mysteriously struck the Borden household days before the murders. Members of the household had grown sick to the point of vomiting. This had included Bridget the maid, although there would be differing accounts around this particular fact.[69]

As before stated, it was possible that even the trip itself, the Grand Tour of Europe, had set the stage for Lizzie's growing unrest about her lifeless, and dead-end situation back in Fall River, Massachusetts. It has been speculated, that perhaps once Miss Lizzie Borden had sampled the food, couture and other European delights of the continent, even including proper plumbing, electricity and the like, that she had made up her mind not to return to the former life of drudgery and mediocre living arrangements.

What exactly was the situation at home? According to experts about Victorian America in the 1890s, women had little or no rights. Women were essentially expected to learn the mundane workings of a home, and basically master all tasks domestic; cleaning, cooking, cultural care of the children and proper etiquette and education. Women who did not master these highly demanding skills risked the horrific fate of which Lizzie was perhaps aware; the very real possibility that she would have neither home nor standing in the community.

Ironically, Lizzie's closest friend, Alice Russell, did eventually go to the authorities about the visit Lizzie made to her the night before the murders. To Alice and others, Lizzie's action was obviously a way to establish the suspicion that Mr. Borden had serious enemies in business. Lizzie emphasized that the entire family had been poisoned the day before, and in a doubtless, great performance, stressed that it indeed had to do with her father's business. She also exhibited authentic concern for her father's safety. Lizzie talked about being depressed. She went on to describe all the troubles her father had been having with tenants and business associates. Yet later, the incredible timing of this visit to her friend's house, to impress upon Alice her fears the very night before Abby and Andrews' murders, may have been too transparently convenient.

The two women ruled out the baker's bread which most members of the household had consumed. Surely, they figured more Fall River residents would have been taken ill. That narrowed any possible poisonings down to the milk.

There was the foreboding man Lizzie had seen "lurking" around the Borden house just, as she said, "the other night."[70] This dubious stranger apparently coincided with the disgruntled business associate of Andrew Borden's. Apparently both concerned, wished ill will upon the old gentleman. One had to wonder, however, how simply ill will over rent, or office space, would have driven a man to obliterate his associate's face with a hatchet. Repeatedly. Beyond the point of death. To what end? Wouldn't the longer he spent murdering Andrew have possibly led to his being caught? The wounds inflicted upon Andrew Borden screamed emotional rage and violation. These were not the wounds over business dealings. The person, who imposed such an inordinate amount of violence upon Mr. Borden, was insane with anger.

William Moody, Assistant District Attorney to Attorney Knowlton for Essex County, went on to explain the importance of understanding the layout of the shotgun style, rectangular house that was the Borden residence. The structure had apparently at one time been a double-tenement house. Thus the locks, which were in place and which added to the intricate system of closed doors and keys, as well as the burgeoning unrest and disdain, added to the angst which existed within the family. Those who resided in the house left the entire atmosphere fraught with dissension and perhaps, even evil. In other words, if the idea of incest and marital dysfunction were to be considered, the physical structure of the place only furthered this possible theory.

Also of great import, which Moody pointed out, was that the house at 92 Second Street was situated on a busy thoroughfare. In this way, the idea of someone, of anyone, spotting a foreboding or sinister-looking man would have greatly increased in likelihood. Moody went on to clarify that there were only three entrances to the house; the side door which led to the kitchen, visible from Mrs. Churchill's house, the rear cellar door (which was eventually found not only to have been locked but also to have had numerous cobwebs), and of course, the front door, which led out onto a highly traversed street, both by pedestrians and by carriages.[71]

Moody also described how from the staircase, one was able to look directly into the guest room where Abby Borden was eventually found lying on the floor, dead. Moody made this point to clarify that when Lizzie was supposedly positioned on the staircase, Bridget saw Lizzie there, just as she allowed Mr. Borden through the front door. This would have been minutes before he would be murdered. She said she'd heard a cryptic laugh coming from the stairs. What Moody presented for later reference was the fact that Abby Borden's body was visible from the stairs at that time. Due to the fact that the body would have been visible, that meant that the hideous laughter Bridget had overheard on the stairs when she let Mr. Borden in, may have been Lizzie. Lizzie might have laughed at the sight of Abby's body, because she was the murderer. Because in contrast, if she'd been an innocent bystander, she would have been more likely to have screamed at the sight and called for help.

The only accessible rooms at the top of the stairs included a wardrobe closet, the guest room (where Abby's body was found), and Lizzie's room. These three rooms were the only ones accessible. However, also important to the heart of the murders was the door which connected to Andrew Borden's room, from inside Lizzie's room. Apparently, it was always kept locked. However, in light of the incest theory as it related to Lizzie's motive for the two murders, Andrew's easy access to Lizzie's room, as well as what turned out to be a taciturn acceptance by Abby, may have fueled Lizzie and the rage which had festered for years. If indeed, abuse began when Lizzie was a young girl, when her room had been the smaller room (Emma's room at the time of the murders), a room which was only accessible through the larger room, (the one connected to Andrew Borden's by the locked door), and the abuse had continued from perhaps age three until around age eleven or twelve, then Emma would have had full knowledge of what had been going on. This may have accounted for Emma's firm support of Lizzie throughout the trial. Ironically, years after Lizzie was acquitted, the two sisters parted ways due to a serious dispute.

Chapter Four

At first sight, it looked like a long, jagged crack, wriggling its way across the ceiling. The walls had been stripped of wallpaper overnight. Colette peered at it, blinking. The room was now painted a painfully dull crème color. Alarm seized her insides. A crashing, like a pendulum hitting glass, erupted from somewhere outside, from the direction of the street.

Standing at the window, her head felt light. A sudden jolt shook the ground. To her abject dismay, half the bungalow across the street was missing, and all that remained were crumbling bricks. Most of the walls were toppled over, with only trembling slabs of house still standing, like those extant Easter Island monuments she'd read about as a child, trying to prove there was history there that could endure. The painted walls of the house looked dismal, and exposed, lath and plaster crumbling, some walls stubbornly holding on, as if determined to prove they could last as long as they were intended to.

Colette stumbled for the door, stopping to grab her trench coat off a strange desk chair. Where had that chair come from? She skipped every other stair and barely stopped just short of the curb outside. Two rounded, aerodynamic looking Toyotas sped past. This was definitely present day 2011.

In fact, she had time traveled forward to a day in 2011 yet to happen.

At that very moment, she felt the same sinking despair she'd experienced three months before when she'd left the corporate world. After twenty-eight years of ceaseless "whoring herself" in offices, as she'd often referred to it, she'd decided to pursue her lifelong passion for music and open a unique music shop. Patrons could enjoy Von Holst on one visit and rock on to Fleetwood Mac on the next. The place was eclectic? Positively rogue, and rare, and certainly not North Shore. Exiting the Starbucks in the center of town, Prada-clad wives had trouble masking their disdain when they'd pass her store.

During the last six months, Colette had slaved at a large successful corporation in town. She had tried to move up just enough to get hired and benefit from health insurance. Yet any sense of security for herself and her two kids eluded her. Mindless drivel from the manager was a typical day. Often, managers, who seemed to be frustrated women, would spell out in ambiguous corporate-ease, why and how Colette had been failing at her job. The job, one Colette deemed solely task-oriented, was in her mind, better suited for a mindless chimp.

Added to that, the house at 1804 Prairie, born in 1929, was being torn down.

Hands to her face, she started to cry. A neighbor boy of about eight yanked on his mother's sleeve and pointed to the woman who was bent over the tru-link fence, sobbing.

As Colette watched the home where she and Max had once lived being torn from its roots in the concrete base of the ground, she too felt unearthed, turned upside down, readying as she was, to face a sea full of financial storms and emotional chaos. Aside from this, was the sinking realization that she felt, no matter how hard she fought it, like either the Scarlett Woman, ala Hester the Adulteress, or Ryan's Daughter the Irish heroine who dared to love a British soldier. Why they'd shaved her head publicly in the courtyard. Would the local townsfolk of good old Valley Stream butcher her hair or have her institutionalized? Because in the end, didn't even the "French Lieutenant's

Woman," Miss Sarah Woodruff, played by Meryl Streep admit, in her socially damaged state that "yes, I am a remarkable person."

Because despite her own feelings of being ostracized, Colette too felt like she was a remarkable person. She'd not give in to this insanity over the past or her recent confusion at waking up from enigmatic dreams, she thought, as she turned back to the farmhouse. As she ascended the creaking staircase, she wondered if she'd really time traveled again. Did it really happen? Because the night before, her sleep had been exploding with nightmares about Lizzie Borden. She'd looked in a mirror in her dream, and seen instead of her own long face with green eyes, the rounded visage of Lizzie – why she'd even touched the pug nose as if to ascertain she was actually Lizzie and no longer Colette Browning.

In the hall upstairs, Marilyn the landlord was waiting for her. Even her short stature seemed to fill and blacken the meager light which filtered through the stained glass window at the back of the house. Colette thought how random that window was, situated there, at the end of such a long hallway. Little did she know a window at the back of a farmhouse would insinuate itself, quite importantly into her life, via the life of Lizzie Borden. It would be the back window of the Borden residence, and the key to how Lizzie would get away with murder.

There was something about her landlord Marilyn's expression on this day, even though she was only a year or so older than Colette, which struck Colette as bizarre. Almost too inquisitive. In her way, she was not allowing Colette to pass her on the landing.

Her own perception of time was skewed. She'd learned that in time travel, one week could equal ten months in 1892 and vice versa.

"Where were you last week?" Marilyn demanded.

Colette bowed her head and sighed. "Behind on rent, I know."

"It's not that," she said. "Forget that. You've worked a lot of years and I know you're trying."

Marilyn's observation reiterated the bleak circumstances of her abrupt exit from corporate America. Businesses had become soul suckers, everyone in fear of losing jobs, losing pensions, losing health insurance. The place had bled her dry of all sense of self, any human-ness, any creative spirit. It reminded her of her own mother's depression in the 1970s. Ursula Grant fought to maintain equilibrium in the face of her own devastating divorce.

And now, the house was being torn down.

The house at 1804 Prairie which somehow represented a stalwart life, however erroneous, planted as firmly as the embedded cement and bricks.

"So it's happening. They're tearing down the house," Colette mumbled to herself.

"They fenced off the place two weeks ago, Colette. That's why I'm asking where you've been? It's your old house. I mean, I know you knew about it, but you just went on and on about those concrete steps. What is it about the steps anyway? Never seen anyone so bent out of shape about a couple of steps? It's an old bungalow. It's a tear-down. That's what they call it in real estate."

Colette closed her eyes, infuriated, and pained by Marilyn's words. Finally, she turned the corner on the landing. Like some magical Buddha, she massaged the rounded knob of the top of the stairs, thinking about the old house, about that "tear-down" bungalow.

Marilyn leaned over and gazed out the window in Colette's humble room.

"It's gone," she said, raising her voice, oblivious to Colette's misery. "Half the front of the place is already gone. It's a tough old bird."

"It is."

Colette stepped into the small room and pushed past Marilyn. At the window, Colette leaned over and regarded the trembling remains of the old house. She thought of Olivia bouncing in the bungee swing that used to hang between the dining room and kitchen. Colette's son would be born five years later with her second husband, Dimitri. Olivia would bounce up and down and up and down, pushing off with her little alabaster feet on the hardwood floor. In her round little face was pure unaffected joy, illuminating everything around her, growing stronger and stronger with each day of exercising in that swing.

The crew was taking a break. It was too late. All that remained of the stairs was rubble. Despair filled her up, relentlessly.

Marilyn had moved back to the doorway. Light and shadow seemed capricious in this house lately. In some ethereal way, Marilyn seemed shrouded in the colors set forth from the waning sunlight through that stained glass window at the back. According to the clock and the sunlight which dappled its way across the tops of her haphazardly shelved books, the shadows signified it was well past dinnertime.

"I can't stop sleeping," Colette said, a bit embarrassed. "And I wake up like I've run a marathon. Exhausted."

"Well at least we salvaged the door to the house, right?"

She nodded.

All at once, the causal connection hit her; the fatigue, the confusion, the time travel that was becoming more and more authentic. The endless nights of long sleeping.

"Where is it?" she said.

"What?"

"The door. Where is it?" She tried to control the tremor in her voice.

"Well, you said it was in the way here in your room. I had the Johnson boys next door move it to the basement."

Her throat was dry. "The basement?"

"Don't know why you're saving the old thing," Marilyn went on. "I mean, is it valuable? Do you think the stained glass in it is Frank Lloyd Wright's design? But the door is so heavy."

"That's because it's solid," Colette said, heading toward the stairs to go down.

"But you said it gives you splinters? How? Are you sleeping on it? Why don't you just get a firm mattress?"

"I'm not exactly sleeping on it."

Minutes later, they'd descended the stairs in grim silence leading to the basement. The walls felt clammy under Colette's hand as she guided her way down. "I've been watching the workmen," she was saying as she walked into the black of the basement, "and the wrecking ball." She was smiling, broadly, in the darkness. "And they've had a hell of a time knocking down the walls."

Yet as Colette sunk into the dank abyss of the room, even her attempt at bravado sounded hollow. The house had lost. The days of her children as small; either wearing a Brownie uniform or having ice cream dribbling down their chins, or the look of shy achievement on the face of George when he'd won a small derby trophy, those days were over. Her quick breaths came on so suddenly that it left her surprised, and a bit embarrassed. Suddenly her soul felt the empty space, the lonely gaping hole left behind when one's children grow up, and go off to college; her son was no longer capturing lightning bugs and announcing how beautiful the beach was and "wasn't this a nice picnic" they were having, even though she'd simply bought cheese and crackers and Orange Fantas at the beach snack shop.

Her soul had died along with the house. Colette felt herself sink into the expectant atmosphere, standing below ground as they were. Here in this basement, she felt the heaviness of being buried alive. So why did her mind go to the coal chute? Indeed, they had demolished the house. Did anyone know about the insidious coal chute? The room with a window, and a chair that neither she nor Max were ever able to explain? They'd also never told anyone. In fact, they'd even avoided speaking of the room to one another. In the basement of 1804 Prairie Street, there had been an exceedingly old coal chute. It looked much older than the house itself. Then there was the room at the back of the coal chute that contained a small window, too small for a person to wriggle through. And a single chair was inside the room.

Colette followed Marilyn to where the door had been left propped against the wall. In a sense, she felt as if she'd entered into some illusory gloom that felt purple and mystical. Colette believed in the saying about not judging your insides by other peoples' outsides. But this space, this room, it suffocated her with its sense of omega, of ending. And the house was gone.

The door was a part of her now. As a portal, it was revealing to her a world in which, what her son once defined in one of his long-winded science fiction speeches, that the door may have been accessing a parallel universe of sorts. George often spoke of the amazing subcultures of almost surreal science. She always listened. In fact, she felt her son George was one of the wisest people she knew.

As if the door knew she was thinking about it, she thought she noticed a slightly darker outline; a shape and essence, whereby the perimeters of the door revealed itself in the blue black of the room. She sighed relief. She thought she'd lost the door forever. At one time in its life it welcomed family and friends to 1804 Prairie Street. Now, it led beyond 1804 Prairie, now that its essential body had been obliterated. The door persisted. Even the air around her suddenly felt lighter, and her mind went to the door's ability to help her take flight, while she slept. Yet something stirred in her now.

An awakening of another time seemed to manifest in her thoughts. In her mind's eye she saw herself and her father standing in front of the door, posing for a stiff reunion embrace, when he'd traveled from San Francisco to visit her. Olivia had been barely a year old.

It was all about the door.

Maybe that had been the first sense of time travel, in the door's own way. Because in that moment, time had coalesced. In her mind she envisioned her grandfather dying suddenly and her father, left behind at age eleven, struggling through the Great Depression and spending his own life trying to carry on and become a man. As the sounds of the music box slowed down, she could practically see him in a 1930s tank top swimsuit and bony knees.

So standing there now, in the numb blue of this farmhouse basement, there remained the door before her, the last remnant of the house where Olivia had romped those years before with the fireplace in the family room alive behind her, until just a year later, her parents had discussed in hushed tones, their inevitable separation.

And the door waited.

When she finally looked up, Marilyn was staring at her.

"Who were you talking to?" she said.

She snapped out of her reverie. "What? She felt heat traveling up her neck to her face. "Who was I talking to?"

Marilyn shook her head and kept talking as she walked toward the stairs again. "I have a recital here this Saturday. Of course Louise Martin is in overdrive as far as her daughter and the pieces she insists Talia play. There's the restraining order with Lorraine and Chad. They are both coming. Don't ask me how that's going to work out."

"Lorraine finally got a restraining order, huh?" Colette commented, feigning involvement, her eyes still on the door.

"No. Chad got one against Lorraine."

The two women started up the stairs. These conversations never held her interest. Still she followed suit with a final comment. "No doubt she'll wear her usual plunging neckline to a kid's concert, right?" They had reached the upstairs and both women walked to the front window. "Think I can get some of those demolition guys to help with carrying the door back up to my room?"

Marilyn turned, shaking her head.

"First you want it out, now you want it back?"

Colette wasn't listening. She rummaged in her purse, searching for a pen and paper. There still might be time.

"They're not done destroying the place yet," she said, going out the front door.

"Where you going?"

"I'll be right back."

"They're just having a lunch break. You can't go on the property, Colette. You know how the Valley Stream cops are. They live for nabbing you. They have nothing better to do than give you a ticket for trespassing or something ridiculous. You know, it's their quota they have to meet."

Ignoring Marilyn, Colette scurried across the street. She knew she might be too late already. Looking left, in the twilight she could just see that the crew sat around in a half circle, eating sandwiches and drinking coffee from Thermoses. One of them looked like he'd spotted her. Regardless, she pulled up the side of the fence to the right, bending it out of shape so she could get to the concrete stairs.

"Come on, lady!"

On her knees, she wiped away the now browned ivy which traveled in wild zigzags on the side of the stairs. A majority of the steps were gone, corroded and crumbled. It hit her suddenly that the scribbled sign language was likely gone. Still, she leaned over and wiped away dust and mud, where she thought she and Olivia had found the signs, years, and yet actually only several days, before. A stray black streak emerged. She'd found them, indeed.

Scrawling as quickly as she could, she tried to draw exact replications of the symbols. The lollipop symbol, and several others, some straight lines, some curves. None of them made any sense to her, but she knew they were important. And then, just like that, a shadow blocked any light that remained in the dusk.

"You gotta know," the man said, towering there, "that you can't be here." He had one hand on his hip, and was wiping away crumbs from his mouth. "It ain't safe. Cops won't like it either. My neck is on the line."

Her eyes traveled up the denim legs to his face, a weathered man of forty or so, now lighting a cigarette. He was frowning. His eyes were extremely blue, and even in the darkness, they were intense.

"Colette, Sweetheart," he said, in a singsong voice, recognizing her, "I could call the cops on you."

Great, she thought. It's Bob. He's one of those types. Did she have any feminine wiles left to utilize? Standing, she flipped back her bangs and smiled.

"Sorry. You know I used to live here," she managed, thrusting out her chest a bit.

"I hate to tell you, but the place is gone. Nothing left."

She nodded toward the concrete. "Except for the front stairs, right?"

Although deep in color, his eyes were cold. No movement in them, even though they hinted at light and laughter, maybe at other times. Maybe with another woman. But not now. His eyebrows were thick, and his face wrinkled in smile lines replete with long days of sun and even longer nights of drinking. And other things.

She felt her face flush red. Another worker, about age twenty, someone they seemed to call Jason, barked at them. He stood next to a smaller red bulldozer, about ten yards away from them. He was actually situated, if Colette figured correctly, precisely on the spot that used to be her and Max's back yard. He stood on the small patch where Olivia's sandbox had been. Colette's instinct was to tell him to clear out. That had been Olivia's magic space of sand. Except now the guy was on his knees, peering down at something.

"Something odd here, Bob," he said, hard to hear from just behind the machine. As they drew closer, the man's fervor increased. He was digging with his bare hands now.

"I'm serious, Bob," he went on excitedly. "You gotta come here."

Colette ran ahead, not waiting for Bob's permission. His voice boomed from behind her, demanding she get clear of the property. Within seconds, she nearly stumbled into a devastating hole in the ground. Meanwhile Jason, with burly hands choking the handle of a shovel, had hit the surface of something hard, somewhere inside the ditch.

Standing near the edge of it, Colette threw herself down, lying on her stomach to get a better look at whatever the man had hit upon with the shovel. There spread before them, what she had already known would be there; a large vacuous room.

"Lady," Bob said, "get back. Jason? What the hell is it?"

Colette ignored him, and leaned further down into the space.

"It's a damn room," Jason said. "A big one."

"What do you mean a room? Behind the coal chute? We tore down the house. There weren't any other rooms on the plat of survey?"

"It's a room," Colette said, her voice even. "I knew it was here." She went on, without looking up. "I've known about it for years."

"How?" Bob said.

Colette pushed herself up, wiping dust and mud off her skirt. "We were never able to get into the room. There was no door. Only a window. It was as if the coal chute was part of a previous house, or maybe the room was, and the coal chute hid it in a way."

Bob jumped in and wiped away dirt from the walls of the room. "Judging from the lath and plaster and the condition of these walls, I'd swear this room and the coal chute date from the late nineteenth century."

Hand to her mouth, Colette gasped. The bizarre ride out of time in the black carriage came to mind. The two men stood there, dumbfounded. Colette sat back, cross-legged, next to the discovery. Whatever rabbit's hole she'd fallen into was a direct conduit to 1892. It hit her then, that perhaps this had been the very reason for her time travel. Colette Browning was connected to the Prairie bungalow from 1929 and the hieroglyphs on the stairs precisely because it all led here, to this coal chute from 1892. The chair in the room indicated someone locked up alone. It all related to the Borden murders somehow. It had to. Why else would she have traveled via the Prairie Street block in Valley Stream, Illinois, 2011 to Fall River, Massachusetts in 1892?

Standing there listening to Bob talk, the bizarre ride out of time in the black carriage came to mind. Jason just stood there, dumbfounded. Colette sat back, cross-legged, next to the discovery.

"There's a chair in the room," she said.

"What the hell are you talking about?" Bob demanded.

"It's a chair. It's a black chair. A very nice one too, and very old."

"Look," Bob insisted, "the only access to the room is this small window. Wouldn't even let a small kid through."

As the three of them gazed down into the semi-darkness, twilight started to gloom into full night. The sun slipped behind the horizon and the room was almost impossible to see. Coal black dust seemed to flake off the walls, and there was a bit of gritty powder rising in the air. It was in her nose and eyes. Colette blinked. Her eyes teared. Indeed, it was a chair. A chair inside the large room. The room without any door. But it wasn't about architecture, she knew that. This was about something sinister, punitive, long-forgotten.

Until now.

The two men stood there, staring down at her. Bob lit a cigarette, and then coughed, deeply, the cough of a lifelong smoker.

"You really should quit," Colette said. He just looked at her, distantly, dispassionately.

"What the hell," he muttered. "How'd the chair get in there?"

Colette moved closer to the hole, hoisting herself to her feet and leaning forward. Bob grabbed her arm. His grip was rough.

"Watch it. Legally you ain't even supposed to be inside the fence around the property. Get back for the last time."

"Unless," Colette murmured, "someone was abandoned here and the room was constructed around her."

She stepped back and looked inside the hole while the men continued to examine the archaic walls. "So back then, neither my husband nor I could fit through the window. So I sent in Einstein."

"Who the hell is Einstein?" Jason put in.

"Some scientist," Bob said, laughing, and then coughing again.

"Einstein was my cat. A real curious one. So I sent him in on a feline reconnaissance. I attached a book light to his collar. So when he went in, I looked, and I saw it."

"It?"

"The chair."

"Why is there a *room* attached to a twenties coal chute?" Bob asked.

"It is kinda strange, this old coal chute, and then a room," Jason mumbled.

Colette looked up at the two men. Then she edged closer to the room. Bob eyed her severely. Still she moved even closer, like a two year old vying for the cookie jar, and just as Bob went to grab her again, she leaned into the room. "Because what shocked me," she went on, her voice farther away now, her outline shadowy, "was the very chair itself. That's what Einstein's hard work showed me."

Bob shook his head and exhaled smoke. He dumped his cigarette and ground it into the dirt with his boot.

In her mind, she knew crazy all at once. Because her knowledge of what had happened here, right here in this house, was the result of time travel. She knew for certain, there had been a house there before the bungalow. She knew, because she had seen it. Recently. She'd seen the house, traveling with William and his father, Edward, on that recent day when they'd pulled up in the black matte carriage. This expanse had not been flat farmland. It had been an oddly gothic wooden house with vertical slats. Surely, she didn't imagine it? The asylum and that vast lobby with the heavy burgundy drapes. Perhaps a similar wooden house with vertical slats had stood here too?

"No," Bob went on with a worn out sigh. "Sorry to disappoint you. I've seen the paperwork. This here was always a brick Ranch house."

"Bungalow," Colette mumbled from the coal chute.

"Fine. A bungalow. It's always been just a small brick house." With that, he jumped in the hole and pushed his way over to the window; at the end of the coal chute, face to face with the room.

Standing next to her, his voice was hushed. It sounded almost intimate as it faded in and out of the darkness. In some inexplicable way, the coal chute magnified his voice. It endowed him with the vibrato of the haunted. At last, he stepped into a sliver of light emitted by the bright work lamp set up on Jason's Dodge truck. Bob wiped his brow, his face shiny with sweat and his eyes dark. In the half-illumination, for a split second, Colette envisioned him as one of those dogged hard-working souls from the nineteenth century. He wore the weary work ethic of a coal-miner in his entire countenance; the broad, but slightly drooped shoulders, and the smoky somewhat grimy face. Added to that, the timelessness, like sepia tone, was topped off by the sharp blue of his eyes.

"Well," he said in the half-light, "the cat on reconnaissance was right."

Colette stepped toward his voice. "What do you mean? The other room? And the chair?"

"Yeah. It's definitely a chair," he said, leaning down, looking into the low, small window. "But the window is way too small. It's like someone didn't want anyone in there. Ever."

"More importantly," Colette added, "why is the chair in there in the first place?"

She crawled out onto the embankment. On her knees again, she reached her hand out to assist Bob out of the vast hole. Clouds rolled across the moon, transmuting dusk into something more dire. Bob looked on, saying nothing. Colette felt she could hear his thoughts; the confusion, the annoyance at a job that was supposed to be a simple two-day knock down.

Colette hid it well. The hurt, the heartbreak, the memory of Olivia crawling along the hardwood floors in the former house, the edifice with hearty brick arms, which Bob and friends had obliterated. It had been a structure which had stood on that parcel of land for over eighty years. Colette's chest ached.

The older house, she thought. That was the time period of the Carpenter Gothic. So someone built the bungalow over the coal chute, as if to hide something. Or someone. That means too, that the coal chute WAS from the 1870s.

In various corporations for over twenty years, Colette had aided others in promoting the slightly arrogant American dream via big business, and having the edge on the competition. Now this. This was not just an injudicious demolition of an old bungalow. This was the murder of a historic home, an icon of a simpler, unpretentious

America. The American Bungalow, with large rooms and front stoops, with concrete stairs just like the ones with the hieroglyphs. From these porches, neighbors in the Prairie State could converse together on lazy summer afternoons. Eighty years of survival was expunged in just one hour.

"So what happens now?" Colette remarked, breaking the silence.

"We finish the job," Bob said. "Not today though. We'll come back tomorrow."

Jason yelled from the truck. "I'm on another job. I can't do it."

"I'll be here," Bob said, rolling his eyes and shoving another cigarette in his mouth. "There will be other crew. Not sure what the hell I'm going to do about that."

Colette stood up. She studied Bob's face in the grey. How much could she get away with asking him? His face was world-weary from a life of battling on the streets for what he wanted. Although he was certainly only forty, he easily looked fifty.

"Don't worry about it," Bob said, waving him away. "I'll handle it."

Jason shook his head and started up the truck. He was short. The size of the Dodge Ram perhaps made him feel more powerful. Anyone would have trouble standing up to Bob, even in a Dodge Ram. Bob's presence behind her now was overpowering, and a bit aggressive. She felt like he knew she knew something.

"When?" she said, turning to him, her head bowed, trying to be covert.

"Don't know yet. I'll contact you."

Ten minutes later, as Colette closed the door to her rented room; she faced the Prairie door leaning against the far wall. She touched the crystal doorknob, holding it for an extended moment.

Chapter Four (A)

The Historical Facts

In Porter's *The Fall River Tragedy,* he described how Assistant District Attorney Moody went into great detail regarding the numerous locked doors within the Borden household. The vital aspect of the system was that the front of the house was only accessible by going up and down the front staircase, and the rear of the house only by climbing a staircase which led to a hallway, and then back into the kitchen.

The point to all this explanation, as it related to historical credence relative to the incest theory, had to do with the locks. At some point in the history of the family living in the house, it was likely that the door between Andrew and Abby Borden's bedroom and the larger room, at first occupied by Emma and later by Lizzie, was accessible by Andrew Borden, to facilitate his entering the girls' room. He may also have crept down the stairs at the back of the house, walked through the kitchen, through the dining room and sitting rooms and ascended the front staircase to enter Lizzie's room.

Added to the familial tension was the fact that the second Mrs. Borden came into their lives when Lizzie was four years old. At that time they lived in a different house, one less desirable than the one on Second Street. The notable point was that when the family moved to the odd house of locked doors on Second Street, it was seven years into the second marriage of Andrew Borden. At the time, and by all accounts, it was a crucial time in the life of a daughter who may have been a victim of incest, Lizzie was eleven and Emma was twenty-two.

As pointed out in Carlisle's "What Made Lizzie Borden Kill?" the very move itself may have been orchestrated by Andrew Borden to assuage suspicions they might have had about what was going on inside the house. If, as Carlisle pointed out in the article, there was a transfer of abuse from Emma to Lizzie, it would have coincided with the move to the other house on Second Street.[72] In fact, what if the locks on the doors, especially the door between Andrew's master bedroom and the girls' rooms, were purposely implemented by Andrew to keep Abby out beyond a doubt, and from discovering if something was going on?

Carlisle pointed to several reasons why the incest theory was likely to have been precisely, the only motive, for Lizzie to have murdered her parents. It was borne out of several theories.

In Martins/Binette's *Parallel Lives; A Social History of Lizzie A. Borden and her Fall River,* written by Fall River historians Michael Martins and Dennis Binette, there had always been talk around the town that the Borden family was "odd." At a time when mental disorders, including depression, were neither understood nor tolerated, "eccentric" behavior on the part of the Borden women, or just women of 1892 in general, may have been nothing more than depressive personalities or even post partum depression.[73]

The "uterine congestion" which Lizzie's mother suffered with before her death was a catch-all phrase used by doctors at the time to explain away a host of female complications. Mrs. Borden had given birth to and buried "Baby Alice" before having had Lizzie. Added to post-partum, the loss of a child, and then the subsequent birth of another would have been devastating. Therefore, the observations of townspeople at the time may have been harsh. Due to the subjugated role of women in the 1890s, a catch-all assumption by observers, especially townspeople in the aftermath of the murders, would have been that the family, the women in particular were always "odd." There was little tolerance for mental disorders, much less the chronic complaints of women in and around childbirth and other female is-sues. Laudanum, or tincture of opium, as it was also called, which in modern society would one day be labeled as poison, was given freely to appease such ailments, often without any prescription.

So, if the layout of the Borden house was taken into consideration, in light of the dysfunction also active there, one could easily have mapped out the tragic time line to the inevitable murders which even-tually exploded on August 4, 1892.

After all, in Victorian times, a woman would have been locked away in an asylum for lesser transgressions against the "civilized," male-dominated, Victorian society.

In her article, Carlisle went on to describe the Borden family as one "at war with itself." There were key elements present within 92 Second Street, which Carlisle described as clearly having led to the murders. Some of the key words from her article included: "ab-sence" – the absence of the wife-mother after the death of the first Mrs. Borden; the "isolation" of the family by the autocratic father right in the heart of downtown Fall River, even to the point of re-fusing outside offers of help, which at one point included his own sister; the failure of the family to bond as a unit once the new Mrs. Borden joined the family; the "structure" of the second house they had moved into, which was long, and separated by two halves and locked doors, and the "tensions" between the two sisters and the step-mother, and the failure of them to bond.[74]

Although taken separately, these facts may simply have divided a household. However, this combination of events led inexorably to the violence of the murders.

Typically, the Victorian man was the head of household. And, in the Borden house, Andrew Borden allowed for no freedom for the women in the home, nor would he allow outsiders in.

Therefore, if the move to the house on Second Street was intended to increase the chances for Emma and Lizzie to find husbands then that plan failed miserably. If indeed, Lizzie was eleven years of age when they moved to the 2nd Street house, and the abuse continued, it may well have been assumed that Lizzie's nights were filled with the horrific sounds of her father's footsteps, traipsing down the back stairs to the kitchen, across the main floor and over to the front of the house, then up the stairs located on the girls' side of the house.

In this way, Lizzie's life on Second Street would have continued to have been that of a child prisoner. During the trial, Moody and the other attorneys referred to Lizzie as "the prisoner," although they labeled her as such because she was literally in police custody. Lizzie may very well have been considered already as a prisoner in her personal life. She was a captive of abuse in her own home. Even the system of complicated locks, and difficult-to-access rooms and hallways, served a purpose in order for Andrew Borden to maintain his firm control of the family and situation. Apparently, he kept the keys to the bedrooms on the mantel over the fireplace almost, as if, in a way, to taunt those who knew of their location.[75]

It was verified by Bridget that a distinct "laugh" was heard on the stairs; a laugh or an "exclamation" by Lizzie. Mr. Borden was apparently fumbling with his keys to the front door because it was bolted. As was previously noted, Lizzie would have seen clearly the dead body of Abby Borden if she were indeed standing on the stairs, which, in fact she was.

Also interesting was the conversation Lizzie immediately engaged in with her father when he arrived home. It was as if she wanted to misdirect the conversation by reiterating to him that Mrs. Borden had gone out. After Andrew Borden went upstairs, via his back staircase, at the opposite end of where Abby was already laid out on the floor, to do whatever he was going to do, he then returned back down the stairs. Bridget was finishing up on the windows in the dining room and readying to go upstairs to take a nap. As Bridget was preparing to do so, Lizzie made a point of informing Bridget that there was a sale on fabric, of eight cents a yard, downtown, and encouraged her to take advantage of it. This maneuver could clearly have been seen as an attempt, on Lizzie's part, to get Bridget out of the house.[76]

In actuality, the flow of events which followed was, if examined more closely, a bit unusual. One may wonder, for instance why, if Lizzie did indeed "sound the alarm" by calling out to Bridget, "Maggie, come quickly, someone has killed father," why she would then have called for a doctor at all? What good would a doctor do when someone is clearly dead? [77] Again, why did Lizzie remain in the house, and why wouldn't she have called for the police instead of a doctor? Arguably, sometimes a doctor was called first in such instances.

At this point, a closer examination of the facts and the redundant recounting of the initial events around the murders, both by the defense Jennings, the Assistant District Attorney Moody, and District Attorney Knowlton, at the request for Dr. Bowen, could have been more thoroughly examined. Apparently, Lizzie and Dr. Bowen had a close relationship. It was said that at one point in the recent past, when Lizzie's parents were out of town, that Dr. Bowen was spotted riding in a carriage with Lizzie together and even more suspiciously, that they'd been seen seated side by side at church.

Dr. Bowen played a key part in the initial hours as the events unfolded following the murders. E.H. Porter made a point of describing how Dr. Bowen stayed in Lizzie's room with her while the police were examining the house. Surely, in today's society such a course of events would not have been tolerated. But in 1892, women, although not treated as equals to men, were also, ironically, allowed certain tolerance when it came to procedures and practices that may have been considered uncomfortable, or unsuitable to pursue, if such practices would insult or embarrass a woman.

Dr. Bowen would not allow the police to enter Lizzie's room. His reasoning at the time was simply that Lizzie needed to be alone. The stress had clearly been too much for her. Dr. Bowen wanted to protect the young woman. One may wonder why Dr. Bowen felt Lizzie deserved protection; in other words, knowing full well she may have been guilty of the crimes, he seemed, perhaps, to sense that there had been equally grievous crimes committed against her.

Even so, it was ironic that despite two dead bludgeoned bodies lying within the vicinity, Lizzie still needed some quality time alone, in the house. Although the police grew annoyed and impatient with his interference in the investigation, as upstanding Victorian gentlemen of the police force, they had to comply with Dr. Bowen's demands. Thus, if for no other reason, because he was honoring the wishes of a young vulnerable woman, this breakdown of protocol before, during and after the trial of Lizzie, may well have contributed to a miscarriage of justice in the end. The Victorian befuddlement around the mysterious enigmas that were women, to the men of the time, caused men in law enforcement, the judge, the all-male jury itself, and countless other men overseeing the progress of the case, to show sexist lenience toward Lizzie.

So although some may have said Lizzie Borden was acquitted because of sexism in favor of "the fairer sex," all other countless indignities Lizzie may well have endured just in the everyday life of a nineteenth century woman, up until 1892 and the murders, may have precipitated her murderous actions; not justified them, but contributed to them. Lizzie was not alone in these circumstances. Certainly many women of the gay nineties in America suffered the same inequalities, desperation, domestic hard labor and lack of opportunities as Lizzie did.

In this way, then, suffragettes, some Christian groups and women who were forward thinkers, would have rallied around Lizzie during her time of being unjustly accused. No proper woman would commit such heinous acts. Or would they? How many women may well have secretly believed her to be guilty and also may have understood her motivations? Of course this would not have indicated that they believed her behavior was acceptable. Absolutely not. But perhaps they may have empathasized with her.

No one could say if, at the very moment Lizzie sounded the alarm with the scream, "someone has killed father!"; that for that one moment, Bridget did not already know what may have happened.

In later years, Bridget Sullivan, having returned to Ireland, was reticent about discussing any knowledge or assumptions around the murders. And yet, if one considered the "gossip" prevalent in the town of Fall River, which described a great deal of tension, then Bridget, who had lived in the Borden house, would surely have felt it. To the degree that unrest existed, the distaste in the air would have been palpable.

Assistant District Attorney Moody brought up several crucial points; the facts which follow here, were contained in Porter's *The Fall River Tragedy*. Moody pointed out that once Bridget was alerted by the suspect, Lizzie's initial response was supposedly that she was "out in the back yard," and she went on to say that she "heard a groan," came in and found the door open and discovered her "father dead."[78]

These statements were perhaps false and misleading for several reasons. Bridget Sullivan posed the question to her, one which was repeated countless times by authorities, judges, police and lawyers: "where were you?" in reference to Lizzie. Because Lizzie's initial answer to the question, which played a vital role was, "I was out in the yard; I heard a groan, came in and found the door open and found my father."

There were several issues which eventually appeared amiss with regards to Lizzie's initial responses. First, one may have wondered, from a psychological perspective, why Lizzie did not, at the horrific sight of her father mangled and bloodied, start screaming immediately, reacting with anguish and terror? In light of her supposed feelings for him, if this was something she, as a respectable woman, would never have done, why would she have remained so eerily calm?

The next part of Lizzie's statement which defied logic was her having "heard a groan." This comment could not have been true because due to the immediate violent and definitive nature in which Andrew Borden was killed, she actually would not have heard a sound at all. There would not have been time for him to make a sound. Andrew Borden had just reclined on the sofa for a nap. It would have been impossible for him to "groan." The violent blows which were driven into his face would have killed him instantaneously. The numerous additional blows to his head were excessive, gratuitous and maniacal. The man would have been dead after the first several hits.

Later on, Lizzie's story changed so that rather than ever being in the yard eating pears, she later claimed she was definitely inside the barn. Now the barn was at least twenty paces from the house. Lizzie had supposedly been upstairs where there was apparently only one open window. This was likely true because during the trial it was reiterated how stiflingly hot it was in the barn.

Immediately following her return from Lizzie's instructions to fetch Dr. Bowen, Bridget asked if she should go to Mrs. Whitehead's to find Mrs. Borden. Lizzie's next statement was odd for two reasons; First, she said, "No, I am almost sure I heard her come in," meaning Abby Borden, and yet this was certainly a lie because in retrospect, according to facts, her statement would have been impossible (because Mrs. Borden was already dead), and secondly, that indicated that Lizzie was lying. Abby Borden was already dead; therefore Lizzie had to have fabricated the story of having heard her come in. She may have thought she heard someone come in, but in light of the ensuing facts which followed, one would have realized she'd made it up. This would have also been her way to get someone else to discover Abby Borden's body so that Lizzie would not have to pretend to find it herself.

The second reason her behavior was bizarre was twofold. Again, why stay in the house if a murderer may still have been lurking there and secondly, why the insistence on looking for Mrs. Borden at all? If Lizzie truly had gotten a note that Abby Borden was visiting a "sick friend," why would she have assumed her step-mother was back?

Because if she were, wouldn't Lizzie have already looked for her, herself – if, for no other reason, out of concern, or just for help?

Mrs. Churchill, another neighbor, asked Lizzie where she had been during the time Andrew was murdered. Lizzie responded with, "I was in the barn looking for a piece of iron," whereas she had told Bridget, "I was out in the back yard."[79] Also, with this explanation to Mrs. Churchill, instead of the "groan" she'd described to Bridget, that she'd supposedly heard, this time Lizzie described a "distressed noise." Also, she'd told Bridget she found the "door open." Supposedly, the family was diligent about locking and double-locking doors? Why too, would Lizzie have claimed she'd "found the door open," if indeed she'd been the last person to go out the screen door from the kitchen?[80]

Lizzie also reiterated to Mrs. Churchill that she'd "found her father dead." A logical reaction would have been to run from the house screaming. Taking it a step further, why would she have called out to Bridget at all when, quite logically for all she knew, Bridget may well have already been killed? Unless Lizzie was certain, as the murderer herself, that only Andrew and Abby were dead.

Regardless, running out of the house may have made the most sense. This would have been a natural reflex, regardless of how far away the station was logically, and even someone on the street would have been capable of assisting.

Chapter Five

Colette rolled onto her side in the small twin bed, rubbing her wrist under the bracelet. The sun beamed a dusty angle across the room. In the light, she could see the faint purple markings under the slide bracelet. It was gentle, like a powder and not like a bruise. Like lavender baby powder.

Loud arguing. Angry men and harsh voices. The tears of women. The screams of children. Words transmuted by a damaged breeze, carried up and through the window of Mrs. Burns's relatively new house, built in 1891. For whatever reason, the stained glass door or, the "Prairie Door," as she'd grown to think of it, had grown reticent. Colette hadn't time traveled. She hadn't "flown through the door", and returned to 2011. She hadn't left 1892. She was still in Fall River.

August would not go out like a lamb. It would bulldoze and burn Fall River, blistering everyone after the insanity of a double homicide; the murders of Andrew and Abby Borden. Doors were closed tightly now. Everyone locked up, just to cross the street.

Dreaming about Abby Borden, Colette sat bolt upright in bed so quickly she startled herself. But her cloudy reflection in the oval mirror, located at the side of the room really woke her up. Located next to the wardrobe, the same wardrobe where the long black skirts and starched white blouses were stored, the pale woman in the bed surprised her, caught her off guard. For some reason, the sight of even the clothes themselves seemed sinister. The mirror was alarmingly clean and new, without blemish or faded gray spots. It was indeed, still 1892.

As if in acquiescence, she swung her legs out from under the heavy sheets and double layers of blankets and planted her feet on the expectedly cool floor. When she'd gone to sleep, just the night before, her hands had been holding the gentle round folds of a crème-colored comforter, one she'd just gotten on sale at Bed, Bath and Beyond.

Now, she ran her hand across a finely crocheted and ornamental bedspread; white, like most everything in the room, with tiny eyelets and pale pink embroidery. Everything that wasn't comprised of dark wood seemed to be white.

Colette had grown up hearing the mythology around the bizarre killings on Second Street. The Borden house itself had been made into a bed and breakfast recently, in the present day. It amazed her that time travel had brought her straight to the day of the murders. It was almost as if her need for answers about the crime had ignited the mystical experience in itself.

The night before, she did not time travel. She'd awakened with a start at about three a.m. in abject terror because she dreamed of Lizzie as a malevolent force. In the nightmare, Colette had succumbed to the fantastical stories which had surrounded the deaths of Abby and Andrew Borden; in her dream she erroneously believed the ludicrous and historically inaccurate nursery rhyme which chanted "forty whacks with an axe." This too was incorrect, as it was a hatchet. But in this dream, it was as if Colette had bought all the exploitative caricatures of the truly troubled Lizzie; she was bigger than life and covered in blood. Her face was contorted with frenzy as she held the bloody hatchet over her head about to strike.

What was disheartening to Colette, was that she knew the authentic details, which created the uncontrollable rage of Lizzie Borden, had been distorted into a carnival sideshow through the years.

Colette's own crime, she felt, was that she'd not time-traveled earlier than August 1892, perhaps to Fall River, MA in July 1892? Perhaps before the murders had happened. Could she have prevented something? Instead, each visit to 1892 focused on August 4th.

She knew better. As did the science fiction books by the likes of Ray Bradbury or Jules Verne. One does not mess with time travel. And she didn't want to distort the time-space continuum, whatever the hell that was.

Standing before the mirror, she sized herself up in the granny nightgown with white ribbons and pin-tuck stitching. Not bad, she thought. Even in circa 1892 gear, she thought she looked rather fetching for nearing fifty. It suited her.

Glancing around the room, she tiptoed over to a delicate porcelain basin as big as a large salad bowl, just like the ones she'd used at backyard birthdays for her children over the years. But this was different. There was water in it. Leaning over, she cooled her face with a couple of splashes. The noise outside on the sidewalk grew louder. Hurrying now, she jumped over to the wardrobe and wiggled into one of the voluminous skirts. She found herself fumbling with the excessive number of buttons on a white blouse, until she finally faced herself in the mirror. As a last minute thought, she threw her hair up into a bun.

At the top of the stairs, she breathed in the freshness of the hallway; it smelled of freshly cut wood. A new house smell. A house built recently, indeed perhaps in 1890 or 1891, and completely comprised of mahogany and lath and plaster. Missing now was the musty lingering scent that would accompany the house over one hundred years in the future.

The stairs didn't creak as she descended them. They felt solid under her steps. The walls were decorated with variously-sized shadow boxes containing human hair wreaths, and black and white photographs of stoic family members. The wallpaper burst red with flowers and green leaves. As she entered the foyer, where a curvaceous blue vase on a small table held a spray of pink hydrangeas, she heard someone sniffling in the parlor, the room located to the right.

Entering the space, just around a corner she spotted William seated on a red velvet camel back sofa. He rose as she entered the room, his eyes devoid of emotion. The older woman, who'd directed her to the carriage, was seated by a baby grand piano, squeezing a white kerchief to her nose.

"Mrs. Burns," William said. "This is Colette Browning."

"Oh, good afternoon Miss Browning," she said, rising very slowly. "I hope you had a restful nap?"

Colette caught on. It was still August 4th.

Colette was taking it for granted that when it came to everyone else, they all seemed to already know her, despite the fact that she knew no one, save for the key players from the history books. "No, please sit," she said. "I heard all the noise on the street and came down right away."

"Well it's never happened before. The whole town is up in arms," Mrs. Burns said. "Miss Lizzie Borden has lost her mind. It is so tragic, I cannot…"

She didn't finish. She sat back in her chair, bringing the kerchief with green embroidery trim, to her nose again.

"I wanted to welcome you properly to my boarding house, Miss Browning. I am sorry I was less than cordial early this morning. I'm much more civil after my morning tea. You're Isabelle's friend from Chicago? I know William took you to see Isabelle. She's back home now and I think Edward is taking good care of her."

The woman looked from Colette to William, then back to Colette.

William clearly bristled. He cleared his throat. Her final comment spoken, Mrs. Burns rose again, and exited the room via a door which led into what appeared to be a massive library at the back of the house.

William shook his head. He frowned.

"It's insanity," he said.

Having rushed back to the room for an additional comment, Mrs. Burns added, "None of us, not a one, really knows who is guilty of the crimes against Mr. and Mrs. Borden? But the good thing is, Isabelle is out of that crazy place. That asylum."

Colette sat motionless. At last, she leaned forward and poured herself some tea from a floral pot Mrs. Burns had brought in.

"Thank you." How to pretend she recalled her? "I'm so bad with names."

"Mrs. Burns, dear. My family just came to this country a year ago. It is a violent place, this America. Isabelle, she watched my young ones. She used to. I have two boys, Ian and Henry."

Colette heard a distinct brogue in Mrs. Burns's voice. This was not watered down from a couple generations; this one was as green as St. Patrick's Day and clearly a fresh arrival to America's shores. Colette started to sit next to William, then chose a comfortable chair instead where she could look out the window. Mrs. Burns swept out of the room again, nothing but a rush of fabric and breeze.

"He hides her." William mumbled.

Colette turned. "Who?"

"My father thinks that Isabelle needs to be kept hidden away. She's locked in our cellar again. Home from the asylum and back to the basement."

"Is she insane?" Colette asked. She wondered what the definition in 1892 was of "insane." She thought about her mother Ursula, coming home from work in 1978, drawing all the curtains closed in her bedroom and lying down for the night after working all day as a psychologist. Clinical, of course. Research. That way there was less intimate contact with other humans. And across her bedroom there was a small black and white television with a hanger acting as an antenna. The curtains she'd made herself. Out of bedspreads. That way there was not even a slim chance that any daylight would slip in. That was the picture of severe Depression in 1978. Untreated Depression. As a Research Scientist, Ursula was brilliant at analyzing data, but she could not help herself.

"Father thinks so," William said. "I keep trying to help Isabelle, but he keeps putting her back in the place. You've seen it. It's an abomination that place is."

Mrs. Burns rustled back into the room. "You know she and Lizzie are friends, despite the age difference."

Colette nodded. The preponderance of male voices outside reminded her of what time period she was in. Sure enough, when she glanced out, she noted that now the women merely huddled together, sharing tears and whispers, while the men erupted in impetuous outbursts, waving their arms as they spoke.

"There's to be a recital," William went on, turning to Colette as if the other women were not in the room.

"So much drama unfolding here in town, right in Fall River," Mrs. Burn went on, regardless of whether anyone still listened.

"A recital?" Colette asked, aghast at the significance of it, in light of recent events.

"Yes," William said, looking up at her from beneath thick brows, his expression measured. "It's the only way I can break Isabelle out of her malaise. I'd like a future for her that will gain her any freedom from living with our father. It will be an outdoor event; music around a picnic of sorts. Isabelle needs guidance and direction. She's incapable of taking care of herself. It's actually a traditional fundraiser. A garden party at Perfect Pines Asylum. I'm hoping Isabelle will be well enough to sing."

A slow, cold realization hit Colette now. She sensed, for the first time, a bit of judgment, no, more than mere judgment, had taken hold of William. Or was she perhaps seeing him for the first time in this light?

Mrs. Burns was sniffling again. "How can you talk about music? With what has happened at the Bordens?"

"Well I guess you didn't hear me," William explained, evenly, eying the woman. "Such a fete will be the best curative for everyone concerned. I'm sure the patients will be very upset by the news of the murders."

Mrs. Burns prattled on, "there must be a frightening madman on the loose, there must. Someone said they saw some crazed derelict on the street with blood on his shirt." Her eyes wide, she looked very meaningfully from William, to Colette and back to William. "In our very neighborhood."

William stared at the floor. He made no eye contact, especially with Mrs. Burns. Her very presence appeared to disturb him in some way. Maybe it was how she gossiped, like so many women did.

It occurred to Colette that even her thought patterns were too contemporary for this conversation. Sometimes things were said, references were made, that she didn't wholly understand. Plus, she knew exactly what had really happened at 92 Second Street. She knew everything in fact, while all these people were in a dizzying and brutal state of shock. The situation was strange. Bizarre, in fact, even by modern standards. And Colette was right there, on Second Street, in Fall River, Massachusetts. Now only a couple of hours had passed since the double murder from America's shameful past. There was nothing she could do. At least, not for the Bordens. Their time had passed. But maybe she could find out more about Isabelle, Lizzie's young friend?

Why was it, she wondered? When she thought about it, Colette had spent her life struck by the immense rage that had driven Lizzie Borden to murder. Not the tabloid side or the sensational aspects of it. The reason. The mental state of Lizzie. Perhaps Colette had time traveled precisely because of her interest. Could that have been why?

Slowly, over the years, Colette's mother's extreme Depression struck her in the same way. Because essentially, Ursula's depression, was her aggression against herself. Colette had once heard from a newly recovering drunk who was facing cancer, that Depression was basically anger turned inward. And Ursula's past as a child growing up in Tennessee had been cloaked in mystery. However, Colette had heard enough talk to make some assumptions on her own. Lizzie's rage was turned outwards. Ursula was turned in upon herself.

It took Colette a lifetime to unlock the enigma that was her mother, and the woman's debilitating sadness and rage. Ursula had trouble hugging people, even her own children. Especially her children, in fact. It was as if she were afraid to touch them in the wrong way. Colette found some peace in this theory, through understanding that such distance was indeed Ursula's way of showing love. It was her odd way of protecting her children. Ursula had also been very critical of others, which Colette eventually recognized as her mother's own self-loathing.

Eventually then, Colette Browning had traveled via the same time-space continuum, to Fall River, Massachusetts, on the very day of one of America's most notorious unsolved crimes in history.

Colette stepped to the window and pulled back a lacy white curtain. On the sidewalk outside, several men protested at the top of their voices, pointing down the street in the direction of the Borden house. Children had come to complete stops. They clustered, sweaty and mud-stained in overly-excited circles. Soon, several of the children lay back on the grass, stretched out in their pinafores and black boots, the grass still conversely rich and green with the last fruits of summer despite the onerous displays of death merely steps away from them.

Taking a deep breath, Colette sensed the extreme moisture through the open window. It begged for new life.

Mrs. Burns rustled out of the room with a "tsk tsk" of discontent.

"Colette," William said from behind her. "I'd advise you to come to the house and see her. She may not have much longer with this life."

Colette knew he meant Isabelle. "Is it possible with your father around?"

Apparently Colette was a friend to her in this dimension.

"My father has to go to work. Just like Mr. Borden had to. Father is tremendously calculating about his financial concerns."

Turning to face him, she noticed that at only sixteen years of age, William wore the expression of an old man. His suit was dark blue and he wore a sharp white shirt, no doubt, freshly starched and stiffened by a hot, wrought iron of the day. The notion of heating up an iron on a hot stove reminded Colette of how far society had come with the advent of electricity. It also made her recall Lizzie's claim, which she would eventually make to the police, that she had been ironing handkerchiefs before the murders, immediately preceding, going out the back screen door to the barn for that infamous "twenty minutes" or "half hour," depending upon which testimony one adhered to.

"Lizzie told police that she'd been ironing right there in the dining room," Colette said, "not ten minutes before some stranger came in and murdered her parents."

William turned to look at her, his face oddly complacent. He wore a slight grin.

"I heard some women talking on the street, "she added quickly. "That's how I know."

Unable to read his expression, she watched him look through her. The words hurt him to his very core. There came sounds of dishes being washed and kitchen activity, sounds of heavy metal pans and crockery. Colette poured herself more tea. She then glanced at William. She held the teapot in her hand.

"Tea?" Then, when he didn't answer. "Have I said something wrong?"

"No," he said finally. "It's just I wonder. How do you know about Lizzie? That time, father forbade Isabelle to associate with Lizzie. That came from Andrew Borden, I think. Isabelle started having her own opinions." He frowned. He lowered his voice. "There was this man from the Sousa Band." He stammered, faltered. "It is believed that she was intimate with him. He paused and took a deep breath. "At the end of that year, that's when mother just vanished to Chicago. Father claims she deserted us." He stopped, looking thoughtful, and then as if he remembered something he said, "to get Darren away from her, he put her in the asylum. My father and Andrew Borden were not only close business associates, they were gentlemen, and friends too.

Colette turned to the window again, still holding her tea which had gone cold. Had his opinions started to sound less critical of his father, she wondered? How could he call them gentlemen?

She never drank tea. Her days in the twenty-first century demanded Starbucks and Dunkin Donuts coffee, but she figured that while with the natives of Massachusetts of 1892, she'd better wear her prim as loudly as she could. She would drink tea, wear the long skirts and not complain about the heat.

As William spoke, he gazed outside. Colette nodded now and then, but her mind was racing. She felt unsettled. Glancing at William, she sensed a shift in him somehow. She couldn't pin down what it was exactly. This was East Coast society in the late nineteenth century. On this day, she found it fraught with an inordinate amount of drama of which it was totally unaccustomed to.

She turned back to William when he stopped talking. "Edward?"

Whipping around, he smiled a bit crookedly. "What did you call me?"

"I mean William, of course." He studied her, and then said, "there is nothing genetically wrong with Isabelle," he said. "We are a good family from good stock. Old New England stock. The very highest caliber of East Coast America. Isabelle simply made a mistake, with a music man from the Sousa Band. And they can be of the lower sort, I suppose. The entire town knew about it. It was, admittedly, hard for father."

"Some things never change."

"Excuse me?"

"Musicians, a town full of gossips, an intolerant sexist father. Nothing," Colette said. "Go on, please."

"There were rumors too," he went on, his face grave, "that Isabelle was consorting with suffragettes and other women interested in the movement. I know she went to more than one meeting. I followed her."

"Why?"

He studied her, a bit too carefully, she thought.

"Out of concern, of course, for my dear sister."

"Maybe Isabelle doesn't like the way she's been treated. As a woman, that is."

William's eyes were black. "Lizzie grew into something sinister. I cannot explain it to you. Her anger, it was out of control. Extremely excessive for a young lady. It increased with the more restrictions Andrew Borden seemed to put on her. Like the locks and keys and limiting her social life to church, teaching Sunday school and meals at home. And then, of course there was Dr. Bowen."

"Yes," Colette said, hopeful to gain real insight. "What about him?"

William took no notice of her interest and was back onto Isabelle again. "She sings."

"Isabelle?"

"Like a canary. Mother taught her. She gave her voice lessons complete with ear training, and accompanying her on the piano. It's perhaps Isabelle's only sense of freedom. That's what she tells me. When Isabelle sings, the birds stop just to listen to her."

This sentiment, coming from her somewhat enigmatic brother, made her smile. Setting her tea on a small wooden table, she sat down and looked at William, her hands in her lap. Although only thirteen, her own son George could be like this young man in three years. Except there was something different about William. Aside from the obvious fact that he was nineteenth century, there was an inexplicable omniscience about him. Almost as if he knew more than he was supposed to.

"How much younger are you than Isabelle?"

"I'm older," he said, and his face changed. "Isabelle has always had the mind of a man. Father resents her for that. Always asking questions when she was growing up, and he'd say to her, 'you don't need to trouble yourself with that, you're just a woman.' Still, she kept up. Always getting in trouble trying to get into a game of stick ball in the street, and chasing the other boys around the block." He stopped, eyes averted, gazing through a large area rug with a bright red rose pattern on it. Then, when he saw her looking at him, he smiled suddenly. Perhaps he was conflicted about Isabelle. The more she knew of him, the more he resembled twenty-first century men.

"I guess your father doesn't like her ideas or her actions?"

"Would have been best to marry her off," he said.

For some reason, William's words alerted her to the fact that he was indeed, no different than his father, Edward.

"She just doesn't cooperate" he went on. "I need to take the reins of the business so I'm not certain how long I can protect her. Who knows, maybe she'll just end up like mother." His face was hard.

"What happened to her, exactly?"

"She abandoned the family."

"You sure of that?"

"It's a logical conclusion. Father had her grand Steinway piano lowered out the parlor window and chopped into firewood. No more music in the house from that day forward."

With that, William sniffed, and stalked to the window, pulling back a curtain to watch the crowd. "I worry too that Isabelle's life will result in disaster, just like mother's."

"No one knows where Madeline is?"

"People in town talk. But that's what people do."

William followed Colette to the door and the two stepped outside. The day took her aback, as she was consumed by the billowy heavy heat of the blazing mid-afternoon. The swelter was relentless, and with it came the scents of horse manure, burning rubber, grass and oil used to lubricate wheels and machines. Colette couldn't identify the sources of all the smells. They were new, to her. They were old; over 100 years old. The crowd moved about the street like a living organism, like some amoeba.

Colette ran her index finger under her high-neck collar again, a habit she was surprised all women of the day hadn't adopted. Her covert smile was due to her knowing that, unlike the other women on the block scattered out front, with their measured sobs and exclamations, that she wore only Hanes panties under her voluminous black skirt. Once she'd opened the drawer of the massive bureau in her room, she'd decided to leave the bloomers and slips and cotton underthings neatly tucked away. It was hard enough wearing 1892 on the outside, much less layering it up under her skirt.

Besides, the issues of women's freedom had grown acute since she'd been here in Fall River.

Once she and William left the front porch of the Burns' boarding house, they became part of the mass on the sidewalk. A single mouth was not moving. Some talked. Many shook their heads. Women wept quietly. One young woman apparently noticed Colette and William, as Colette spotted her eying them. Her hair was an indescribable strawberry blonde, much like Colette's would be had she not frequented the Teddie Kossof salon back home in twenty-first century Chicago. One of the young women in the group scrutinized William, eying him up and down. It seemed she waited for him to lock gazes with her. Her nose was chiseled and her eyes were quite large and intense, with black lashes fluttering under high-arched brows.

Colette started eavesdropping on the conversations.

"I think it would be best if Isabelle disappeared," William blurted.

Sweat trickling down her back, Colette's reaction was delayed, "why would you say that?"

"I've seen her packing. She's been loading up mother's steamer trunk. That was odd too. Never could figure out why mother left it behind? Isabelle has confided in me. There is apparently something she needs to get out of the Borden house, desperately. But she won't tell me what it is exactly."

Colette glanced around furtively. "Are you saying," she whispered loudly in his ear, "that Isabelle was involved in what happened to Lizzie's parents?"

"No. Oh no. There was a note. All I know is she's been asked to help Lizzie."

"Lizzie needs her help?" Colette said.

He nodded, and pulled her aside. "Something about a small travel bag. The Johnson boy brought a note to Isabelle. At first, I thought Isabelle was just talking in that incoherent way she adopts now and then. But then, I too saw the note written by Lizzie herself, delivered within the last hour."

"Interesting."

"What is?"

"What you just told me," she said, glancing around again. "And the fact that I overheard some women talking about the exact words Lizzie said to police when they asked about her mother. Lizzie corrected the cop and said, 'do not call her my mother. She is my step-mother,' and then something about the fact that her own mother died years before. Gossip travels like wildfire. You are right about that."

"Lizzie's too outspoken," William said, shaking his head. "She cannot talk to the police that way."

The two had pushed through the milling crowd and now stepped back onto the front porch of the Burns' boarding house. Edward leaned back against a white pillar near the front door, crossing his arms over his chest. Colette noted the thick black Jacket he wore over his white shirt and black tie. For someone with such forward thinking ideas about women, he certainly dressed a lot like his avaricious father.

"Aren't you hot in all those clothes?" she asked him, then stopped herself.

He looked taken aback. Colette realized she'd perhaps violated some nineteenth century moral code about women saying what they thought.

William eyed her like she was some odd creature, perhaps a tarnished woman in her own right, and a bit too provocative. His expression implied that she could be a danger unto herself.

"Could have been an unstable laborer from the Borden farm," he said. "The lack of pay just became too much for them. They wanted Andrew Borden's money."

"What do you mean?"

"Well Lizzie didn't do anything. She couldn't have. It had to have been a couple of the workers from the farm. I know my father hasn't helped any. He and Andrew Borden believed in limiting their daughter's lives. No relationships. Maybe the ladies wanted more freedom. Probably for their own good. So Lizzie and Isabelle got a couple of the workers from the farm to rise up against Andrew Borden?"

He stopped, shaking his head, then muttered under his breath, "maybe like mother, they attracted men and had them do their dirty work for them?"

Colette turned on him sharply.

"I'm just saying," he went on, "father hurt Isabelle with a strong iron hand. He doesn't understand that women react to that. Mother certainly took it into her own hands when she left us."

Having plopped into a rocker next to the door, Colette stopped the movement of the chair. Wiping away sweat from her forehead, she asked, "if your mother is really missing, why haven't you gone to the police?"

"Father is an eminent business man, an upstanding member of Fall River society. Mother wanted a different life. She wants to be missing. It's best that she left. Isabelle has even talked about going to college some day."

"What's wrong with that?"

William swatted at a fly and made a face. "She's not stable enough. Women need protection. Imagine all the men who would be after her. A woman in her condition?"

"Condition?"

"Well, she's got hysteria." His face changed. He was somber. "She uses Laudanum. To an excessive degree. Still, I don't think father needs to keep locking her away in the asylum. There are laudanum addicts in there. The place is crawling with derelicts. Like women who use their bodies with men for money."

Colette leaned forward in her chair. William seemed to have his own ideas about women too. Apparently in his world, they needed protection, not only from domineering fathers, but from young men, other women with addictions, and of course, the desires of the flesh.

"Are you talking about prostitutes?"

"There are young girls in that asylum, girls who ran away from the safety of their homes to work the streets."

Now Colette was incredulous. "Safety of their homes? How do you know why they ran away? Maybe family was the last place they found safety?"

William's mouth was tight. Although he smiled, he shook his head ever so slightly at her words. "Women don't realize they're not always safe. Especially if they pursue odd pastimes like our mother encouraged Isabelle to do. To sing and befriend traveling musicians. That's no place for a woman, surely. Father wants Isabelle to marry well. I should say, he did before. I don't think it's possible for her now. I'm attempting to keep her out of the asylum again."

Outside the crowd appeared to be moving down the block by twos and threes. Dogs roamed in and out, sniffing frightened children as they clutched their mothers' dresses, standing amidst small clusters of people. Never had there been such a crowd, all on one street at one time in the history of the town. Women had abandoned their kitchens and hearths, still carrying dish cloths in their hands and some, not thinking about their own appearances, still wore aprons. The assimilation of the group herded forward, reaching just up to the Borden house, but being held back by nervous-looking, overtired and overheated policemen.

Colette watched intently. It still astounded her to be on the very block of Second Street, just hours after the sensational murders. Of course, in a strange way to calm herself, the ridiculous nursery rhyme kept up in her head; "Lizzie Borden took an axe, gave her mother forty whacks..." Even though she knew the song was factually wrong, and morally cruel. The total hits had been about twenty-nine for both of them combined. And Lizzie may well have been a murderer, but Colette knew she was not crazy. Colette believed, more than ever, that Lizzie had been a survivor. She suspected Andrew Borden had molested his daughter. Not just once, but over a period of years.

There were hats everywhere on the women. These were little hats, those smaller hats typical of the early gay-nineties; before the oversized hats would come into vogue some ten years later. She recalled the little red flowers on Lizzie's black hat that she would wear into the courtroom one year from this time, when she would go on trial for the murder of her parents.

Ironic too were all the prejudices at work for and against, and sometimes just muddying up, the lives of women. Because although the "devil," Isabelle's father, may have been sexually abusive of her, in the same way wasn't William also trying to wrap her up in a neat little box? In his way, he wanted to protect her. Sounded oddly familiar to some women from the twenty-first century. It consisted of not encouraging her to forge ahead with the likes of suffragettes, but to remain vulnerable and curled up in a ball. She must let someone take care of her. In his way, William blamed Isabelle for her predicament. Ironically, he could not see Lizzie as ever having the necessary amount of rage, or physical strength, to have been the murderer of her parents.

Colette walked out to the edge of the sidewalk and stood alongside William again. The crowd had started to curve away from the Borden house at the end of the street and now the focus became the Victorian gothic house directly across from Mrs. Burns's boarding house. It was William and Isabelle's house, the one they shared with their father. It was that architecture rarely seen in Chicago, referred to as Carpenter Gothic. In fact, there had been the disaster in Valley Stream in 1981 whereby a demolition crew had torn down a rare Carpenter Gothic by mistake. So there had been at least one in that style she knew about.

As she thought about it now, watching these Massachusetts natives mill about, she realized that another Carpenter Gothic house had been rumored to have been in the same neighborhood and street that eventually became the 1920's bungalow she so dearly loved, the house she'd share with Max and Olivia. Eventually, the entire existence of an odd Carpenter Gothic house in the neighborhood had become an urban legend; there was actually no plat of survey or actual record of the house. The 1920s bungalow had been the same bungalow where the door had been born, the Prairie door that liked to travel. Perhaps the door possessed the soul of the Carpenter Gothic? Perhaps that was why the door had become important to her? Because it needed to eventually be her portal to the past; the past of Lizzie Borden and Isabelle Sewell. Someone had to reveal their victimization to the world.

A similar tragedy in the city of Chicago had been when a demolition crew got the address wrong, and instead of tearing down some non-descript newer house, they'd torn down a classic Carpenter gothic, simply because it had the misfortune of being situated next door to the house meant to be razed. The house had stood in Norwood Park, Illinois from 1874 – 1981.

This house, the one in which Isabelle and Edward lived, was also of the Carpenter Gothic style; with vertical wooden slats instead of horizontal, which gave it an almost gingerbread house look. In actuality, this house would make one about as equally unsafe as Hansel and Gretel.

Could it be the door was part of the bungalow that was basically buried on some sacred burial ground? Except this time it had been a Carpenter Gothic house that everyone had forgotten about? A house that did not appreciate having been carelessly destroyed?

Juxtaposed against this insane theory in her mind, Colette felt a sudden macabre thrill standing in the midst now of a somber unsolved crime, poisoned by the stain of murder. Along with this titillation, she felt some grave responsibility. Living in the bungalow at 1804 Prairie Street in Valley Stream had not been by accident.

Looking at William, she thought about the clout his father must have carried, and the power Andrew Borden wielded having owned buildings downtown, possessing numerous bank accounts and land. William walked onward, trailing the swarm which bled its way back toward the Borden house. Colette stopped walking.

All at once, something terrifying came upon the scene.

The small group of women with which she had surrounded herself, in efforts to remain camouflaged, started to point and gasp. To her right, a woman fainted. In a bit of a delirium, Colette followed their gazes. Because this time, they were not focused on the Borden house.

Across the street at the Sewell house, there stood a young and ethereal looking woman perched at the top of a steep flight of stairs, looking like some jarring Technicolor aura. Her pallor looked dusted with chalk, and she wore a double row of pearls around her neck. Streaming wildly over her shoulders, her hair fell black against her white skin in shocking contrast. Somehow, even from this distance, Colette could make out very round, and troubled eyes.

The woman was resolute and determined, but swayed a bit pre-cariously on the porch. She stood as stiffly as an obedient soldier. Colette discerned some cajoling from some of the women. They knew her. This certainly was Isabelle. Isabelle did not seem to notice, nor care about onlookers. With halting steps, she moved down the stairs brokenly, as if listening to some preternatural song which seemed to guide her. Oddly, her pallor was somewhat waxen now, perhaps from the inordinate amount of heat. She seemed to melt as she drew closer to the group. Her eyes scanned and searched for nothing in particu-lar, breezing over the shallow crowd.

Sensing her way along, her arms stretched out in front of her, it seemed as if she'd not been outside in a long time. Was she blind? Or was she unaccustomed to sunlight?

Colette searched for William. In the chaos of the street, she'd lost sight of him. Isabelle wavered on the stoop, clinging to the porch railing. Where does one's mind go when it has been trapped inside itself for so long? Having been snared in captivity, somewhere in that landmark-style house, Isabelle's mind now absorbed every bit of stimuli around her as if she didn't expect to have freedom for long.

Feeling a wretched sense of panic, Colette ran in and out of the crowd trying to get across the cobblestone street. The young women gawked. It didn't matter what time period it was, Colette thought. Women, universally, seemed to act the same way. Why was this? Perhaps these women watching were jealous and derisive of something they didn't understand? Isabelle was a woman on the fringe. Isabelle did not fall into line. Isabelle wanted more than hearth, home, husband and children. In other words, by nineteenth century standards, Isabelle was simply insane. And this fact scared them.

Perhaps to them, Isabelle could be likened to the dark and insidious Madeline of Edgar Allan Poe's "Fall of the House of Usher." In the house of Usher, Madeline had been unleashed in death. Yet she too was buried alive. In the house of Edward Sewell and repeated sexual abuse, Isabelle had been unchained at least for this brief moment, in the aftermath of the Borden murders.

Colette reached the other side of the street, right where Isabelle teetered along the final stair. Isabelle's movements zigzagged from one side of the wooden sidewalk to the other. Was she intoxicated? At one point, she turned to look at a group of women and one woman staggered backward, and screamed, as if Isabelle was dangerous. Would such a slight woman pose a threat to them?

Perhaps her ideas frightened them. Her appearance simply reiterated her outrage.

Trailing behind Isabelle now, Colette noticed the young woman's blue dress dragged behind her on the ground. It was as if during her incarceration in the house, she'd not only thinned out, but she'd shrunk in stature too. Why else would the dress be too long on her?

It looked as if she'd been wearing it a long time. The hem was grimy, and was covered in dirt and stains. Her hair, upon closer inspection, was a tangled mass at the nape of her neck. No one really seemed to notice all the signs of violation. They realized only, that Isabelle frightened them. Her disarray exemplified something very wrong in the Sewell house, with their society.

Then it occurred to Colette where Isabelle was headed. She careened her way toward the Borden house. The young woman was trying to reach Lizzie. Colette felt certain Isabelle already knew. She knew Lizzie had murdered her father and step-mother.

Within minutes, both of them were positioned out front of the Borden house, as close as they could get. People chanted about "justice for slain innocents." Isabelle stopped just outside the perimeter of the crowd. Colette felt her heart beating out of her chest. Her breaths came quickly. Squeezed inside the crowd, the suffocation of their disdain was real, sweeping and terrifying. The anger surged, hissed from the combined voices like a cruel energy in the air, furious and driven by ignorance. They had no idea what Lizzie had suffered, Colette thought. This crowd couldn't even see that perhaps in Isabelle, there was a parallel result, a result of similar abuse, standing in their midst.

Colette covered her nose. There was a strong odor of beer on the breath of the men standing nearby her.

No. Colette could not excuse the murders committed. But also she could not condone the suffering Lizzie had experienced.

Isabelle turned to face Colette. As Colette drew nearer to the fragile woman, she sucked in her breath. There were jagged cuts which ran in criss-crosses, red and angry, on Isabelle's arms. Some were still bleeding. Colette reached out to her, but something about the eyes of the other woman stopped her. Isabelle held out her hand to Colette, palm upward. The tips of her nails were blackened with dirt, and jutting out of two large pockets in the dress were shards of glass, and what looked like strips of decorative wallpaper with red florid explosions of a rose pattern. In her mind's eye, Colette imagined Isabelle had liter-ally been clawing her way out of the Sewell mansion.

An hour later, exhausted from the heat, and horrified at the sight of Isabelle in such a state, Colette collapsed on the twin bed in her small room at Mrs. Burn's boarding house. Window ajar, the Victorian heat drifted in atop scents of cotton, grass and chopped wood.

Chapter Six

The cool was surprising and welcome. When Colette rolled out of the twin bed and walked to the wardrobe, she jumped yet again at the sight of her reflection. Shaking her head, the mirror stared back at her. She was simply face to face with herself. The mirror was faded and tarnished around the edges. Underneath her feet was the greenish indoor/outdoor carpeting she so detested. And yet, in front of the mirror, a piece of 1892 had clung to her and now made her gasp. Her head was light and she felt sick to her stomach. One thing was sure. The granny nightgown was gone.

Horror filled her as she backed away slowly, mechanically, to check her reflection from a little distance. Yes. It was a crème-colored slip, and an egg-shell colored petticoat. All along the bottom tiered ruffle of the slip, it was awash in blood stains.

Stumbling away from the mirror, she leaned over in front of the window which was opened wide. The carpenter gothic house was gone. Disheartened, she saw instead, the pitted-out remains of the bungalow.

The petticoat felt stiff in places, where there were red stains. There was some sort of smell, like rust or salt. Although the heat was the same on this August day in 2011, as it had been in 1892, at least for today, relief was available. Unbuttoning an entire row of buttons at the side, as well as untying a long cottony belt which held up the petticoat, she slid it off. It laid there, in a cottony pool of days past and unanswered mysteries from the nineteenth century.

Still very early, summer morning darkness didn't provide much light. Throwing on yoga pants and a t-shirt printed with the University of Chicago and ironically the founding date of "1892" underneath the university crest, she flicked on a window air conditioner and turned the knob all the way down. Perusing the room, she felt an emptiness at no longer being able to communicate with William, or Mrs. Burns. She was worried about Lizzie.

Sleep seemed so far away, and was hardly a source of solace now that she'd taken somnambulism to a new level. This was well beyond sleep walking. Colette was eligible for some serious time travel miles on this surreal airline.

The air conditioner puffed a cooling bit of breath into the room. It mixed with the heat outside coming in through the open window. Now that would have really angered any one of her ex-husbands; a window open and the air conditioning on. So now she languished in her freedom, and enjoyed the barometric mix of the two sensations. Of course in 1892, she mused that there would have been no relief. The air would have hung there, hot, heavy and stifling. In the case of Fall River, Massachusetts, it may have contributed to murder. Didn't twenty-first century police always claim that in hot humid Chicago, crime rates soared when the heat index rose?

Bob said he would meet her first thing in the morning. She checked her watch. It was 5:30 a.m. Good old Bulova, the only thing her mother had left her when she died. That and a Victrola phono-graph. The Victrola had fascinated her as a child; and she'd open the little front doors to increase volume. In high school, it made a good place to hide marijuana from her mother.

Now it simply connected her to the past. Because she'd always felt an intrinsic, entitled connection to the past. Was that why the door had chosen her? Or was that why she decided, after years of not hav-ing gone there, to drive to Long Grove and on a sudden whim, pur-chase the antique slide bracelet? On the surface, she and Max simply bought the house at 1804 Prairie. Perhaps Colette was predestined to live in the brick bungalow. Meant to be, for those who believed in mystical kismet, Colette mused. And Colette certainly did. But now, she was back here in the year 2011. The bracelet and the door had brought her back to the present in the midst of the murders and Isabelle and Lizzie in desperate trouble. Why?

In the hallway, she passed Marilyn who sipped coffee on the landing. At the top of the stairs, the heat rose up and pulled at her, like plump breathless arms, dragging her down. Her chest was heavy as she threw open the front door and stood on the front stoop.

Glancing across the street, the beam of Bob's flashlight danced in and out of the darkness. The way he looked around furtively, screamed "guilty of something." Colette shook her head. The Valley Stream Police Department was chronically bored. Still, Bob was seriously inviting their company. They would relish the action. The very idea of dragging a simple contractor down to the station for any reason they could devise would delight them. And for what offense? Little did anyone know, a little bit of Massachusetts was buried beneath their feet.

"Bob!"

She realized she didn't need to raise her voice. The street was terminally quiet. The lawns spread out ostentatiously left and right, and were rolled out onto lots which once housed small sturdy bungalows, but now sprawled with pre-fabricated houses. These houses were loud-mouthed. They bragged about excessive square footage but sorely lacked architectural integrity. The yards persisted in a maddeningly precise order, inauthentic like the fake grass and plastic trees of a train set. Little did the local folk know they couldn't clean up the backdrop of murder in their midst. Despite death lurking, their lawns would remain impeccable.

Bob whipped around when, the beam of his flashlight cast wild streams of light everywhere, like a fishing line in and out of the depths of the hole they'd dug just the day before. Looking up, the Pine trees appeared black, as daylight hadn't quite reached fruition.

Having reached the yard of the bungalow, Colette stood there taking deep breaths. The stairs and the hieroglyphs. It was crucial she identified the author of the odd lettering.

"What's going on?" she said to him. He stood inside the vast hole in the ground.

"Keep it down," he whispered loudly, his voice carrying up from within the hole. "You want them to hear you all the way in Glencoe?"

"I'm coming down," she said, "but I have to do something first. Over by the front of the house."

As she neared the front walkway, which now led to the shelled-out remains of the house, she fought tears. Had it really been one day since she'd happened upon her past in 1994? One day since she'd smelled the sweet skin of her daughter as a toddler? Even now, the soapy bouquet of the baby shampoo seemed to linger.

Near the same bushes where she and Olivia had knelt down just days before, she again fell to her knees and pushed. The stairs consisted now of broken up chunks of concrete. She searched, her hand scraping the ground. The accommodating morning sun, just coming to life, offered a layer of light which allowed her to see. Looking down, she saw blood running along the sidewalk and was startled, until she realized it came from her big toe. Doubtless she had stubbed it on one of the stray concrete pieces when she had charged out of Marilyn's farmhouse in her bare feet.

She opened up a large Evanston Library book bag she'd brought with her, and started to fill it up with bricks and pieces of concrete. As she did so, she tried to join them together and ascertain that all the necessary markings were still there. What about the message? What if pieces of the message were missing, or faded after all this time? This primitive note from some unknown person, from God only knew what time period, begged to be comprehended by someone.

She stood up then, hand to her forehead, blocking out the sun as the air filled up with an Illinois day coming to life.

Wouldn't the message have to have been written in the Fall of 1929? She knew, from the plat of surveys she'd studied when they'd bought the house, the ones she'd gotten at the Valley Stream Historical Society, that the brick bungalow she and Max had lived in had been built in the spring of 1929. Right before the stock market crash in October of that year.

It occurred to her that the hieroglyphs might somehow be related to the time travel. The stairs had led to the Prairie door after all.

She walked to where the front of the house used to be. The Prairie door commandeered her life at the whim of the slide bracelet. She didn't like that loss of control. In fact, it scared her not knowing where, much less when; she would wake up every morning. The rented room itself seemed to vacillate between Valley Stream, Illinois on Chicago's North Shore in 2011, and Fall River, Massachusetts in 1892.

Without thinking, she sat cross-legged on what had been the front lawn. Now it was littered with pieces of concrete and brick, strewn about like the fallout from some battle. So much in her life, in and around the two divorces, had been out of control, and in fact, a bit of chaotic. Her existence, since having left her second husband Dimitri, had been one of passion turned to pain and betrayal. Dimitri had come from a wealthy family in River Forest, Illinois, from a long line of Scandinavians and Greeks. He stood six foot four with remarkably light blond hair and light brown eyes. He was a bit of the Rutger Hauer look with a splash of the Mediterrean sea. Having met him in an alcohol recovery program, it should have occurred to her that he would have other addictions. And his addictions ranged from coffee and cigars, to impetuous costly purchases like boats and timeshares, and perhaps even dalliances with other women. It didn't matter.

Supposedly, the twentieth and twenty-first centuries purported that women had more to say about their lives and their realities than had their sister ancestors of the nineteenth century. In Colette's estimation, here was the horrific truth, it was all a farce. Didn't Lizzie

Borden feel she had no control? My God, Colette thought, you're not excusing a maniacal murderess? Of course not.

She started pulling out the grass, gazing at the flattened mound of wood and remains. She thought the pile resembled a freshly buried body right after a funeral. But barring the brutal nature of the crime, didn't women – hadn't women experienced the same sort of rage even to this day? She thought of her mother again, Ursula Grant. Ursula knew in her heart she was meant for more than cooking like Betty Crocker, with pastel cakes and sumptuous roasts, while pirouetting around a kitchen in an embroidered apron and looking perfectly poised in pumps and pearls. Such adherence to societal ideals only resulted in an uber mother on the outside, and a needy young woman feeling like a suicidal Sylvia Plath on the inside.

She stopped pulling out the grass and gazed at the back of the house behind the vacuous clearing, that used to be the bungalow.

Looking around, she made her way to the mud and grass hole where Bob was searching.

"Bob."

He looked up, his face intense.

"It's me," she said. "It's just me. You look almost, frightened. What's wrong?"

The heat started to work on her. She flipped her hair back, away from her face. Sweat had broken out on her forehead.

"You know why I'm here? Why I'm helping you?"

"Not really," she said.

"Because I've heard rumors for years. Strange happenings on this block. Talk about an underground room. Thought maybe it was a fallout shelter. But this goes way before the days of Communists and the Cold War.

"Well, I'm here to help."

Bob looked up. "Damn if this isn't stupid? We shouldn't be here. I could lose my job."

"I know it's risky," she said, scooting to the side of the hole, "but you're as curious as I am."

"What the hell are you doing?"

"I'm coming in."

"You can't."

She'd already jumped in and now crawled toward the small window in the coal chute, the one she'd recalled from her five years living in the house with Max. So many times she'd snuck to the basement, on a household errand, looking for a lamp or a certain box, and ended up all the way at the back of the basement facing the odd room.

Years later now, she was down on hands and knees headed for the same room with the window. "Got a flashlight?"

As she slipped forward, decades of pebbles, and years of sedimentary layers dropped into the hole like dirt being thrown on top of a casket. Robert backed up and now stood with his arms wide. Colette sunk to her knees, then adopted a stooped crawl, and started to yank back on the one-hundred-year-old lath and plaster around the window. For an instant, she paused, wielding a large chunk of wall in her hand.

"I knew it," she called to him over her shoulder.

Robert hesitated. "What? Bring it out and let's go."

"This is definitely not US Gypsum drywall," she said. "I knew it."

"I'm impressed," he said, "why the hell does it matter?"

"The bungalow we lived in was built in 1929. It was right after the crash. They saved money. The walls were made from US Gypsum drywall. It was a new way to build. Cheaper than lath and plaster."

Standing closer to her now, Robert scrutinized her, his eyes narrowed. The sun was directly in his eyes. Monday morning was upon them. On the sidewalk behind them, commuters were scurrying past wielding laptops and briefcases.

"Hand me a crow bar or something," she said.

Standing up straight, he met the curious eyes of a woman wearing exercise skecher shoes with a skirt, blouse and strand of pearls. Two more people followed behind her, carrying the occasional *Wall Street Journal* under their arms.

He yanked over his tool bag, found a large wrench and handed it to her.

Digging the wrench into a small hole next to the solidly built window, she pried away at the space, making it larger.

"So about the Gypsum drywall," he started, "this is an older room. And the window was for a truck to pull up and put the chute in and dump the coal. I see that. The walls around the coal chute are lath and plaster. I get it. So the coal chute was built maybe even fifty or sixty years earlier than the house over it. Right?"

Colette nodded. The sun was providing more light to her task now. She took her hands and pulled away as much of the wall as she could. Parts of it crumbled in her hand as nothing but dust, disintegrated, evidence gone.

"Do you understand, Bob, that in order for this rectangular window to be here, the truck would pull up here? Obviously, it couldn't. It wouldn't have room because this coal chute is from at least the 1870s. The erection of the 1929 bungalow would have blocked its entrance. So like I thought, the coal chute was already here before the bungalow was built. So the bungalow was really built, literally, on top of it. I am sure that the house that stood here before it was a Carpenter Gothic. It was rare for the Midwest, but it was here."

Bob shook his head. "Hate to disagree, but I know there was no house here before that bungalow. My grandfather grew up here. Said it was a field here back after the turn of the century."

Colette stopped, standing slowly. She looked at him. Her eyes were bright, as she wiped away sweat, mud and clay, and so many layers of dirt which smeared her forehead.

"But you heard the stories growing up. You know, the scary ones."

"An underground shelter?"

"And there was a house here."

"How can you be so sure?"

She started to speak, then stopped herself short of blurting, "because I was here in 1892." Instead, she said, "I know."

Half an hour passed. Finally, she'd created a hole larger than the frustrating size of the rectangular window. This would enable her to get inside the room. It struck her now how odd it was that this insidious room had existed beneath the living space she'd shared with Olivia and Max. The room pulsated with a history and a terrorized life of its own, right under the place where Olivia had taken her first wobbly steps in the wood-trimmed dining room, and where she'd once reached up on tippy toes as a toddler to play the white keys on the upright player piano.

All that time, history, with a crucial story to tell, was screaming directly beneath them.

"I'm going in," she said.

Bob got to his knees. "I can't let you do that. It's not stable."

But Colette was already down below, in the room. Pulling her bag open, she rummaged a second, and then pulled out a flashlight. Reaching one aged corner after another, the light finally fell upon the chair.

It was the same chair that had confounded her during the five years she and Max had lived in the bungalow. It had baffled her how the chair could have gotten inside the coal chute, through a window space no bigger than three feet by four feet. Someone had built the bungalow directly on top and around this coal chute which had been part of a previously-built house. It was a house which, coupled with the hieroglyphs on the stairs, had secrets.

Down on hands and knees, she crawled a bit, shining the light into each corner again, her movements becoming jerky. The floor was, quite unexpectedly, hardwood and finished, as if it was utilized as a regular living space. However, the "hardwood" was actually comprised of the wider wooden planks derivative of mid-nineteenth century construction.

Then she spotted part of the floor jutting up in an odd way. She moved as quickly as possible, yanking at the wood when she reached it, and pulling it back as hard as she could.

"What the hell are you doing?" Bob yelled to her.

She started digging in the dirt under the floor, like a kid on a beach making a sand castle. Then she stopped, her mouth agape.

"Oh my God."

Bob's voice was stern. "What?"

Wriggling back and forth, she grasped something like a white or grey stick until she withdrew what was clearly a bone. Along with the bone, she dug deeper, set what she found down, and continued to dig feverishly. Seconds later, she withdrew a skull. A human skull.

"You need to come out, now," Bob said, his voice tight.

She rotated the flashlight to the chair. The light revealed a small travel trunk with a checkerboard pattern. It too appeared very aged.

"Bob," she said, in a loud whisper, "there's a skull in here. I think we've found human remains."

"You're crazy. Get out of there now!" Bob bellowed toward the room. "I can hear my crew. They're here. I just heard the truck doors slamming. They're cleaning up the site today. It's all going in the next hour or so. You gotta get out now."

The light had fallen upon the hole. Darkness no longer hid her away from intrusive eyes. She grabbed the small checkered trunk, the size of a cosmetic case, and exited the chute. Standing, she stood there, panting

"What's that?" he demanded.

She exhaled, hands to her knees. "There's a body down there. Do you hear me?"

He didn't listen but rather raced off to greet his crew. In an instant, she held the small trunk at her side. She also felt queasy. Still hiding her finds, she slipped past him and the other men, and stumbled back across the street to her rented room at Marilyn's house.

Laying the case on her small bed, she jiggled the lock. Finally she turned it upside down, back and forth. She shook it as well. After a feeble attempt with a nail file, she set it upright again on the bed. At one point, she simply stared at it. After forty minutes of trying to pry the case open, she fell back on the bed, exhausted.

Turning, she picked up the weathered book, Porter's *The Fall River Tragedy* from the bedside table where she'd left it after finding it under the stairs. She started to read. Then she sat up on her elbows, feeling lightheaded and a bit dizzy. That wave of fear that one feels as a small child when there are shadows by the bedroom closet came over her. This book, was an original account of the Borden murders. This was the same topic she'd just taken an interest in of late when she bought her own book on the trial. Why had this original book also fallen into her hands, she wondered?

When she awakened, it was morning again. A new morning out of time. Next to her, she could smell the beaten leather of the book where it lay open halfway through, precisely where she'd left off until succumbing to sleep the night before. Most alarmingly, she suddenly realized how tight the slide bracelet felt, like a watchband would feel if the notches made it too small. That's when the unfamiliar scents reached her.

She sat up, taking in a wash basin, shiny mirror, and a strong scent of wood and horses through the window. An odd sense of relief breathed its way into her psyche. It pulsated 1892.

Just to be sure, she checked the desk for her laptop and cell phone, but instead saw a No. 4 Harris Visible black manual typewriter. Her cell phone was fickle she decided. Sometimes it came with her, sometimes it didn't.

She lingered there in that momentary serenity, that is, until she sat upright and pushed back white eyelet lace sheets and saw, for the first time, what she was wearing. Somehow she knew it had been what was in the small trunk, the trunk that she now recognized in the morning dusty light, as a small trunk, the one that had been entombed in the coal chute. It must have been the way she traveled through the time portal; because as she peeled back the sheets, she saw herself dressed in what appeared to be an underslip. How had this happened? Of fine quality, it was a crème-colored silky long petticoat.

She held her breath. Even the feel of the fine silk on her skin was strange. She'd never had on anything so well-made and intricate. Zigzagging up and down its seams was lace and stitching. Along the hem there was a patterned embroidered design and even some lettering. Turning the hem upside down to look at it, it said "hand sewn, Paris, France." Looking to the small trunk, it sat wide open on the floor. Somehow in the last time travel, the petticoat had emerged from it, and decided to try itself on her body.

Chapter Six (A)

The Historical Facts

If carefully considered, Lizzie Borden's actions immediately following her "discovery" of her father's mutilated body, revealed some
knowledge on her part, that he was definitely dead, and that she knew
precisely who was guilty.

Due to the important truth revealed by Lizzie's calling out for
Bridget, rather than Mrs. Borden, there existed a veiled awareness
that Lizzie perhaps knew Mrs. Borden was already dead. Two factors
should have been considered; first, if Lizzie told the truth about her
really having heard Abby come home, then why didn't she call out for
her first?[81] This was Abby Borden's husband, after all. If her statement
that she'd heard her stepmother come in was indeed not a lie, then she
would have instinctively called out for her, and not for the maid.

During the time after discovery of her father's body, why wouldn't
Lizzie have looked for Mrs. Borden herself, rather than send Mrs.
Churchill and Bridget on some reconnaissance mission? And first
off, why was Lizzie unafraid to be alone in her house? Her first reac-
tion in fact, was to send Bridget away from the house. In light of that,
Lizzie could have looked around the house herself when several women
returned to the house. Clearly, she wanted someone else to discover
Abby's body. In this way, she perhaps believed this would make her

appear less suspicious. Ironically, due to the purported laughter on the stairs overheard by Bridget at the moment when Andrew arrived home, Lizzie undermined her own alibi. Eventually, it was discovered that Abby's body was fully visible lying on the guest room floor by anyone standing on the landing of the stairs.[82] So why would Lizzie have been overheard laughing if Abby's dead body was visible within her sights?

Also noted in Porter's *The Fall River Tragedy,* were the seemingly cavalier movements of Lizzie in the first hours following the murders. First, some witnessed her passing through the sitting room, sweeping by her father's dead body, and then traipsing upstairs without even an "inquiry" regarding Abby. Instead, she went on to her room and lay down.

Psychologically, her movements proved interesting to Assistant District Attorney Moody. He spoke about her actions in his address to the jury on day two of the trial. Moody explained how Lizzie had put on a pink wrapper.[83] A wrapper was a loose garment worn over dresses in the late 1800s, much like a casual housedress.

The various reasons Lizzie provided to explain where she'd been at the time of her father's murder were significant, if for no other reason, than that they were varied and inconsistent. So perhaps when one did not tell the truth, which was Moody's implication, there would be inconsistencies. For Lizzie, it was difficult to keep her story straight. For the record, she told Dr. Bowen she was out in the barn trying to locate a piece of iron, or tin to fix a screen. Yet she told Officer Mullaly she was in the barn as well, for whatever reason.[84]

The true inconsistencies came into play when she started describing how she'd heard noises from the barn. Obviously, once it was realized how far the barn actually was from the house, and the fact that Lizzie was upstairs in the loft, with only one window open, the chances lessened that she'd have heard a noise at all. In fact, that concept was hard to imagine. Then Lizzie further muddled it by telling Mullaly she had "heard a peculiar noise," something like a "scraping noise,"[85] and then discovered the screen door open. Interestingly, she told

Bridget she'd "heard a groan,"[86] then rushed in and found her father. And lastly, she told Mrs. Churchill she'd heard a "distressed noise."[87]

Soon to follow were the apparently contradictory statements around the first moments when she returned to the house from the barn. First, Lizzie claimed to have heard a noise. In that instance her state of mind was one of panic and great hurry. However, seconds later, in an account which was to be repeated often later on, she described coming from the barn after looking for lead sinkers. She had claimed this followed a bit of time which had lapsed, whereby she was supposedly eating pears in the loft. However, she had also stated at one point that she'd also been in the yard eating pears.[88] Either way, she came inside again through the kitchen and checked the stove to see if the fire had heated up enough to continue with her ironing. She then set her hat down on her way back upstairs to await a mid-day fire Bridget was going to light. It was at this point, that she apparently came upon her father's body on the sofa. In one account, Lizzie came in and "set down her hat."[89] This is an important detail because later on, the defense team's crucial witness, a Hyman Lubinsky who drove an ice cream carriage, would claim to have seen a woman in the yard. However, he was certain that woman was not wearing a hat.[90]

So there were discrepancies, clearly, in her alibi. Soon after the murders, an Officer Medley discovered further contradictory evidence. Upon entering the stiflingly hot barn, and ascending to the loft, he found the floor of the barn upstairs covered in a thick layer of dust. First, he ran his hand across the surface of it, to make sure to leave an imprint in the dust, where, interestingly before, there had been no sign of anyone having stepped across the floor. Added to that, he measured the number of footsteps it took to walk across the loft and then he turned back to look. Again, he could see from imprints in the dust, exactly where he had been.[91]

Following this astute observation in the barn, Dr. Bowen was caught in the kitchen burning a note on the fire. This note was purported to have been addressed to Emma, who was away on a trip. Added to witnessing Dr. Bowen's odd behavior, there were differing opinions about Lizzie and her clothing; some claimed she was at first wearing a drab dress while others later described simply a "calico"[92] dress, and still others said "navy blue."[93] Also, perhaps as a way to camouflage her dress, she was spotted exiting Emma's room soon after the homicides wearing a loose-fitting pink wrapper.[94]

On the Saturday night immediately following the Thursday murders, Lizzie was informed by the mayor that she was under suspicion for them. It had been revealed that the very next day after the murders, Lizzie was spotted by Alice Russell, burning a light blue dress with a darker navy design on it. During this time, the policemen were all outside.[95] Alice had cautioned Lizzie against the action of destroying the dress, especially when people could see her in full view. Lizzie, in turn, said simply "oh, why did you let me do it then?"[96]

Soon Moody began a lengthy discussion of the hatchets. Apparently, there were several found in the basement.

Yet, regardless of the discovered hatchets and how they might have been involved in the crimes; one in particular for example, was found covered in ashes, and one was without a handle, Moody brought up an important point; a "stranger" as the murder suspect would have been seen by any number of people in the neighborhood at midday. A stranger would neither have the time nor the inside knowledge of the layout of the house, to have known precisely where to perform a massive and speedy clean-up of the murder weapon, and themselves. Also, one had to remember that an hour and a half passed between murders. An hour and a half. Had a stranger committed them, he or she would have had to hide themselves within the confines of the house, without spreading mess or blood remains anywhere on the premises, while also going undetected. These facts, as pointed out by Moody, would have strongly indicated that the perpetrator knew the parameters of the house and the location of available sinks in which to clean up.

In support of this theory, it was discovered later on that there were cobwebs which stretched along the doorframes around the cellar door which led to the basement from outside.[97] This little side fact further indicated it had not been a stranger going in and out of the places but rather a familiar tenant of the home.

Another point Moody brought up involved motive. If indeed, as he put it, an unknown person not living in the house had committed the crimes, such as an "intruder or stranger," who was, as he described "flying from his crimes with the bloody weapon in his possession, through the streets of Fall River at noonday…"[98] he would have been spotted immediately. Clearly, his point was that someone would have to have been careless or insane to have allowed themselves be seen out on the streets right after such grisly murders.

Moody reiterated that were it a strange intruder, why then had no drawers been pulled open, no jewelry taken and lastly, why was there a large amount of money found on Andrew Borden himself? He was found to still possess his pocket watch and chain. A last point Moody made was that it was likely that the assailant not only knew the layout of the house, but that he or she also knew the habits and whereabouts of the residents of the house.[99] This was likely factual for several reasons; Abby Borden was found in an area of the house which was accessible only via the front staircase which led to the guest room and to Lizzie's room only. Added to that, the front door was securely locked by the time Andrew Borden returned home from his rounds of his businesses downtown, and entered through the front door. Once numerous locks were opened, he was allowed access by Bridget Sullivan. Ironically, Andrew Borden was apparently also carrying a discarded lock he'd found on the ground on his walk back home after checking on his businesses downtown. The man indeed was obsessed with the idea of locks and control.[100] In this way, Andrew's concern with control, specifically the comings and goings of household members, seemed symbolized by the number of locks he utilized. How ironic too, that during the course of his last stroll in downtown Fall River, he picked up yet another lock he found on the ground.

Moody went on to reiterate that Lizzie was the only person who had come into contact with Abby Borden after she had walked up the front stairs to the guest room to remake the bed and put shams on the pillows.

On day three of the trial, various persons were called up to testify. At last, Bridget Sullivan, the maid, was interrogated by Mr. Robinson. She repeated what she'd said in the lower courts, that she did not recall whether she'd locked the screen door after coming in from the yard and washing windows.[101] This was a key point because had she indeed left the door open for certain, that would have allowed for the possibility of a stranger to have entered the Borden residence. However, such a person, at mid-day in busy downtown Fall River, would have been noticed. As mentioned previously, Hyman Lubinsky, the ice cream carriage driver, was a convenient witness who claimed to have seen a woman in the yard. However, he clearly reiterated that she was not wearing a hat. Therefore, the assumption was that he saw Lizzie Borden.[102] This worked well for Lizzie's defense. It supported her assertion that she was indeed in the barn while her father was being murdered. Later however, Lizzie would claim to have set her hat down upon returning from the barn.[103]

An interesting piece of information was the mention by Bridget of the key to Lizzie's room having been kept on the mantel in the sitting room.[104] This detail may have revealed a small bit of emotional or psychological warfare being waged within the house. Upon speculation, one may have questioned why a key to the two rooms located at the front upstairs; the guest room and Lizzie's room, was kept on the mantel? Why would it have been kept there, where anyone including Andrew Borden, taking into account the incest issue, would have had access to it? This would clearly violate any privacy for Lizzie.

During Bridget's further testimony on the third day of the trial, she described how the screen door was likely unlatched while she was outside washing the windows. This was a little before eleven a.m. Bridget claimed she could see the front door entirely while she chatted outside with a friend of a neighbor, but could not see the screen door. So conceivably, anyone, including a stranger, could have entered through the screen door.[105]

An added caveat to this theory however, was the fact that Abby Borden, by this time, had already been killed over an hour before. Therefore, the point about the screen door would have been moot. In other words, why would a murderer have left the premises and gone outside, wielding a bloody hatchet in one hand where he would have been seen, and then return back to the house after a respite outside in the one hundred degree heat?

Bridget was also quite precise about what time it was when she went upstairs, which she stated was a couple minutes before eleven a.m.[106] Lizzie, at that time, may have had flats (for ironing handkerchiefs) on the stove and was, prior to that time, eating cookies and coffee. Interestingly, if Lizzie was eating cookies when Bridget last saw her, why would Lizzie then have claimed to have been consuming several pears while out in the yard; her apparent alibi for the time which transpired when her father was being murdered?

In Porter's *Fall River Tragedy*, Dr. Bowen was quoted, upon finding Abby Borden dead as well, that he was glad Lizzie had, in effect, been out of harm's way. The fact that he made this announcement to the group of people in attendance may have sounded, in its way, as if he made this proclamation as an affirmation of Lizzie having been in the barn to "get some iron," as she had told him.[107]

Bridget had been asked and eventually brought the bedsheet which was used to cover Andrew Borden's body. Dr. Bowen from the start, continued to perpetuate the assumption that a stranger had broken into the house. This may have been his way of further deflecting any attention off of Lizzie.

Dr. Bowen went on to state that he'd instructed, right after the bodies were discovered, for Lizzie to go to her room, perhaps to rest.

Up until then, right after he'd returned from telegraphing Emma at Lizzie's request, she'd been in the kitchen getting fanned and comforted by Mrs. Bowen. On Thursday, Dr. Bowen stated he'd given Lizzie bromo-caffeine for nerves, but went on to tell how from Friday up until the time of her arrest, he'd given her morphine. It was interesting that he made a point of detailing how the effects of morphine would have created hallucinations.[108] Perhaps this revealed a further allegiance to Lizzie. Because conveniently, Dr. Bowen made a point of creating doubt in everyone's minds, especially the jury's, about the validity of Lizzie's initial inquest. In other words, his implication was, that due to drug influence, she could not have been held responsible for her words or their accuracy.

Such discrepancies, and an additional admission on the part of a doctor that one would not have been in a clear state of mind while under the effects of morphine, would have gone a long way to justify Lizzie's mistakes and apparent lies or cover-ups during any testimony given by her at the time. He even used the phrase that there was "no question of the effect of morphine on the mind; by changing and allaying their views."[109] Would it not have served Dr. Bowen's purpose well, if indeed he tried to protect Lizzie from the very beginning, as if perhaps he knew, full well, she'd been a victim of incest and further, that perhaps he knew she was guilty of the murders? What if it were true that he'd purposely given her morphine, with the full intention of creating doubt, in legal terms, about her ability to speak clearly? This would have protected her. In other words, couldn't Dr. Bowen have perhaps had some savvy in the realm of legal matters, to have decided early on to provide a valid reason for her discrepancies in testimony? What better way, for a close friend and professional doctor, to shield her from the self-righteous gossip mongers of Fall River? Especially if he felt fairly certain that she was indeed, guilty of the murders?

Because for all anyone knew, Dr. Bowen may have tended to the medical needs of Lizzie as a young girl, and in fact, perhaps the Doctor may have recognized signs of abuse; something in her physical and emotional well-being that may have corresponded to the Sheriff's wife, Mrs. Wright's, observation that Lizzie was always "grave beyond her years" to describe Lizzie's personality as a child.[110] Even if one were to look at photographs of Lizzie as a young girl, she indeed, as the adage goes, appeared to "wear the weight of the world upon her shoulders." With incest as a possibility, and its accompanying shame and self-loathing, it would indeed cast a dark shadow over a young girl's world view.

Throughout the trial, and in the past century or so since the crimes, it was often noted how calm and unemotional Lizzie appeared to have been throughout the discovery of the bodies and beyond, into the indictment, imprisonment and Taunton Jail and the trial. It was illustrated how she'd often spoken calmly when indicating she'd simply found her father in the sitting room, and exactly how the discovery had come about. If this had been her demeanor only immediately following the murders and the discovery of the bodies, one may have said it was shock. However, what proved unnerving to the public, press and prosecutors, was her continued stoic resolve throughout the trial and during her transfers before, and including her incarceration at the Taunton Jail.

Both Emma and Lizzie possessed what may have been described as an "eerie calm" throughout the trial.[111] Certainly; there could have been several reasons for such remarkable reticence. Victims of incest, as mentioned and explored by several writers around the subject of the trial and case, would attest to the fact that according to psychologists, survivors of incest, as the sisters may have been, would perhaps not have had emotional reactions. Marcia Carlisle, in her article, "What Made Lizzie Borden Kill," mentioned Emma's impassivity. In essence, the sisters may have been shut down emotionally. Carlisle further indicated that Emma's equal "calm" during the trial and around the hysteria of the murders, was due to her first off, having been cognizant of the incest, and secondly, that she was convinced of Lizzie's culpability in the murders.[112]

Also on the third day of the trial, Mrs. Adelaide Churchill was called to the witness stand. She talked about Lizzie having stated that "someone has killed father."[113] Lizzie apparently also told Mrs. Churchill that she had been in the barn looking for iron. Mrs. Churchill and Bridget attained the key to Mr. and Mrs. Borden's bedroom, unlocked it, retrieved a bedsheet and brought it to Dr. Bowen to cover up Mr. Borden's body.[114]

Several important facts come to mind even in the re-enactment of the movements of everyone following the murders. First, jurors and citizens would have been reminded of the preponderance of locked doors within the house and perhaps wondered about the reasons for such a practice? And secondly, such physical evidence of hardware and security and secrecy, certainly spoke of a lack of trust; either between the family members themselves, and with the hired servant, Bridget, as well.

Chapter Seven

At the sight of Isabelle teetering on the doorstep the day before, bleeding from gashes on her arms, Colette's chaotic life of time travel and discovery of the coal chute had intersected somewhere in time, with that same young woman, if only for a fleeting second.

Isabelle's look of turmoil the day she tumbled from the dark mansion seemed to convey all the shameful truths of women in the nineteenth century. Sitting up straight now, Colette crawled out of bed. No explanation was needed. Her hand touched the small trunk from the odd doorless room with the chair, which sat on the floor resolutely, and for an inanimate object, it appeared somewhat stubborn in its way.

She stumbled over the silky embroidered petticoat on the floor, as she stepped toward the small trunk. Definitely a high quality underskirt, she knew that. Looked as if it had been packed away for a trip. Then she looked down. Spilling in a swirl at her ankles, she too was wearing a petticoat, but one very different from the Paris handmade one. Dread started to seep into her consciousness when, upon looking down, she saw a series of dark red splattered stains. All along the hemline and even up around a foot from the floor, the petticoat she had on, which was a cheaper coarse cotton piece, splashes of what appeared to be bloodstains had hardened. Aware that what she wore now was extremely old, she untied a wide cottony belt which held it in place and let it fall, where it landed on the floor with a thud, uncharacteristically stiff like cardboard. It had been waiting for her in1892.

She sat on the bed and looked at the garment on the floor. It had her. And it seemed to know it. For some reason, it hit her that the Paris embroidered petticoat had come from the trunk. The bloodied one had come from hell.

Trying to organize her thoughts, she pictured Isabelle in her mind again. So the men in the white coats had literally, carried Isabelle by both arms and dragged her back inside. Within seconds, the woman's form had disappeared into the black gothic sea of the Sewell mansion. Why did they have to manhandle her in such a way? This made no sense.

For several days following, Colette lingered there, in 1892. There was no time travel back to the present day. For some reason, this did not frighten her, being pasted in the scrapbook of time over one hundred years in the past. One aspect of time travel that seemed clear was that a week in 1892 could simply be a day or so in 2011. For this reason, she had a bit of air sickness and felt light-headed most of the time. Or it may have been the near one hundred degree heat. She couldn't be sure.

As the days passed, she adjusted a couple of skirts to fit her on a sturdy Singer Sewing Machine with black enamel and gold lettering. As she mended cuffs that she'd torn, being so unaccustomed as to how one should move in the costume du jour of 1892, she marveled at the beauty of the old machine.

A week later, Colette was once again seated in a carriage. The stink of horses reached her and the odor was unfamiliar and heady. It surprised her when someone spoke to her suddenly. It was the driver seated up front, leaning around the carriage.

"So Madam? Where to now?"

The heat in the carriage was stifling. The burning of the leather seats was magnified too, and seemed to cook her skin under her full skirt and long sleeves. Sweat trickled down the small of her back. Just as they pulled up to a cryptic grey stone building, she'd scooted to the edge of the seat and started to get out. Oddly, even in the broiling swelter, Colette swore she could see her breath, and for some inexplicable reason, she shivered. Then immediately, it was hot again as the long sinewy driveway snaked its ways up to the place. The same grey iron gate met them with a vengeance. It was locked. A heavy chain dangled from its center. The wooden sign at the side read "Perfect Pines Insane Asylum."

"You're sure this is where you want to be left? All alone, madam?"

"Yes," Colette affirmed stubbornly. As she alighted from the carriage, she sensed that the man was baffled by her insistence on being alone. He smiled a kind and concerned smile. Although she tried to exit the carriage without his assistance, he jumped to the ground quickly and held out his hand.

His eyes glistened. "This place isn't safe for a woman," he said.

She nodded. After dropping a few coins in his hand. Totally ignorant of proper currency, she marched on without turning back. "That's all I'll need from you," she said over her shoulder. "Thank you so much."

She turned back once, and grinned when she saw him still standing there, by the carriage, very hesitant to leave her there. He had his hand to his chin, and his shoulders were stooped from years of riding, and perhaps seeing a few injustices over the years.

Although certain she needed to find Isabelle, she slowed. The place was indeed foreboding. Hadn't she always worried she would end up institutionalized? Mental health facilities in the twenty-first century were certainly less terrifying than were the torturous asylums of the 1890s.

The sound of her laced-up granny boots clicked on the cobblestones. The sound was foreign to her. The layers of clothing! Every time she moved, there was resistance in the neck and sleeves or a bit of entanglement around her legs with some underskirt or petticoat. She was certainly not accustomed to wearing so much. But this time, before setting sights on the mirror, she'd managed to locate, in the myriad drawers of her small 1892 room, yet more petticoats and thick stockings that would certainly fit her. Something she'd learned early on about nineteenth century clothing for women was that most of the ladies in those days were of a smaller stature. Somehow she'd managed to find some larger sizes at the back of the drawer.

Nellie Bly came to mind. Nellie was a courageous nineteenth century reporter who had had herself committed to an asylum in the late 1800s, in efforts to expose horrendous conditions. Colette recalled now, it didn't take much for poor Nellie, determined as she was, to get herself institutionalized. In late nineteenth century America, a woman could be put away for anything from pre-menstrual syndrome, to Depression, or to simply becoming no longer attractive to her husband.

Attractive to her husband? Colette thought about this statement relative to her second husband, George's father, Dimitri. When she'd gained weight she couldn't lose after having given birth to George, her heart was bursting with love for her blond son. In any event, she barely noticed that her own additional weight had diverted Dimitri's already roving eye to pastures so far out and away, that Colette would never be able to reel him back in again. And inevitably, Colette and her son's father became yet another statistic of divorce.

An interesting point of fact was that Victorian married men were notorious for having their wives put away when they no longer had any use for them, or perhaps just because their petticoats no longer fit their overly cinched waists. How convenient "mental illness" was for nineteenth century husbands.

Colette let the heavy door thud closed behind her. Solid. Dense. It reverberated a sound as if it sealed her fate. Striding to the front desk area, she discovered a male receptionist. He was a young man, self-possessed and serious in composure. As she approached slowly, he adjusted his black tie and white collar and looked her up and down. When she drew closer, for a moment, Colette checked her long skirt to see if it was on backwards; then fingered the top buttons of her blouse. She was still trying to get the gist of how to dress like a proper nineteenth century woman, so she'd blend seamlessly with the landscape. Of course she didn't mind so much about being proper per se, but she wanted to fit in. This was crucial. Not only did she need to blend into 1892 society, but she also did not want to ruffle Isabelle whatsoever.

"I am here because my husband wants me here," she said simply.

The clerk stood up and gave her a closer look. Then his hand ran across the rolltop desk in front of him as he sifted through paperwork.

"I don't see anything for you. Surely, Mister, your husband, would have sent word ahead of time?"

Colette manufactured the most insane expression she could muster. She let her mouth drop open and pulled a kerchief from her small black wool bag, dabbing at her dry eyes and feigning a bit of hysteria.

"You have to let me in. He'll be so angry."

"What is your husband's name?"

"Thomas Henderson," she lied. "You should have a note from him."

The clerk turned back and started to look through the desk again. As he walked to the back office, Colette could make out his dark suit Jacket moving about in the back room. Reaching across the wooden desk, she set a recently penned note, one written by herself, under the ledger book in the center of the desk. He returned and looked at the desk again. Then his face changed.

"Just a moment," he said. He opened the envelope and read through it quickly. "This does seem to be from your husband, a Mr. Thomas Henderson?"

"Yes. He believes I need a rest. A long rest."

Closing her bag with apparent difficulty, struggling with the small clasp, she smiled at him wanly, needing to appear as pathetic as possible.

"Please have a seat Mrs. Henderson," he said, indicating a severe black winged-back chair across the sparsely filled lobby area.

The sound of her boots echoed on the black and white terra cotta floors. Colette sat in the corner demurely, and pretended to read a King James Bible in her lap, the handkerchief still pressed to her nose. Over the top of the white cloth, she watched the clerk carefully. He phoned a nurse, presumably somewhere in the hospital. Sure enough, within fifteen minutes, according to a mammoth grandfather hall clock, a starched, white- aproned young woman appeared, marching toward Colette.

"Please come this way, madam. Where is your trunk?"

Colette shook her head. "I have none," she said, starting to feel real fear at her decision to help this nineteenth century woman she really didn't know. She needed to know her purpose in time traveling and she would find out, whatever it took.

"You'll be rooming with Sadie Hawthorne, a young woman who has been with us for a short while. Severe Laudanum addiction. You'd be wise not to bring it up. We don't like to talk about the women who cannot control themselves. The less interaction with her, so much the better for you."

Colette listened, feeling the ire rising in her throat. The lingo used to describe women in the nineteenth century was familiar. Unfortunately, even in 2011, female addicts continued to be described with a good deal of disdain. It was due to the erroneous belief that addiction was relegated to those with immoral weaknesses, rather than to the legitimate diseases now termed addiction.

As Colette followed the nurse into the narrow and austere hallway, accompanied only by the sounds of their heels echoing off the walls, she was at least aware of some of the advances which had been made in the twenty-first century in some mental health facilities. Not without lingering flaws, but certainly somewhat better for women. Although it had only been revealed in the past twenty years or so, there existed an understanding by the general public back in 2011, of addictions, and the toll drugs and alcohol had taken upon families. At least in this regard, America had seemingly come a long way. This much she admitted.

But in the lives of women, women in American society, Colette realized as she stepped into her narrow room, so much had vacillated between women who clung to being housewives and those who wanted to forge past an entire lifetime dedicated to the garden club and domesticity. Colette recalled author Susan Faludi, and her book *Backlash*. In it, so many discrepancies in the "advancement" of women's rights were examined, and examined closely. Her convictions were of course so strong, she'd had to come out soon after with a second book in recognition and support of what male society had been through as well. Male society apparently demanded equal scrutiny.

Still, Colette seemed to stand alone, at least in her little corner of the North Shore, in her rented Hamlet in Valley Stream. She stood alone in her stark recognition that women in 2011 simply fooled themselves. In actual fact, the very word "feminist," had grown to become derided by men and women alike, despite its arduous fight during the 1970s for basic rights. An outgrowth of the suffragettes of the nineteenth century, those same women to which Colette was becoming privy to in the year 1892, rights for women had taken a deep downturn of late in the twenty-first century.

Colette studied the nurse. The former simply frowned at her. Within seconds, before Colette could speak, the nurse exited the room and slammed the door, double locking it from the outside.

She sat on a white sheeted cot she assumed to be hers. Apparently her roommate was an addict and what they deemed promiscuous? Interesting. They'd definitely get along.

Ironically, the forebears of these women, after having been on the verge of complete sexual expression in the 1970s, had been exposed to a new freedom. Despite the study of authors such as Erica Jong and books like *Fear of Flying*, these same women gave birth to daughters and granddaughters who threw all that progress overboard. Steps forged for women in the 1970s were drowning in places like Victoria's Secret and restaurants like Hooters. And these offspring mistakenly believed they too embraced the reins of sexual freedom; when in actuality they merely perpetuated the mythology of the "ideal" female form, a pencil-thin impossibility devised by men and advertising.

Somehow the 2011 woman had been relegated back to aspiring solely for a gorgeous home, hearth and garden, and at the same time, possessing a flawless profile and figure, necessitated by botox, bust lifts, rhinoplasty and collagen. The sacrifice for excelling at these duties as a woman of the twenty-first century was placing academia or business or the arts all on the back burner of their very own gourmet steel ovens. And the back burner was key; if twenty-first century American woman could fit into her negligee and be a food bon vivant in the kitchen with little or no authentic needs of her own, then she was well on her way.

Unbuttoning the sleeves of her blouse now, Colette tried to cool off. She rolled up her mutton sleeves. The fabricated beauty of the nineteenth century nearly had her fooled. Yet thoughts of sexual abuse, mental illness, and addiction were not far away, even in this world of finery, excess and elegance.

The triple locks opened. A frail woman was shoved through the door. Her eyes were wide and an amazing Technicolor shade of blue. She gave Colette an up and down sweep. The nurse said nothing, as was seemingly her way, exited and shut the door.

Colette sat on her small bed against the wall, trying not to stare. The young woman, who looked to be in her late twenties, stood with her back against the wall, her dress shabby, with a trail of mud around the hem. She allowed herself to slide down the wall, her hands held to her knees.

"I'm Colette," she said to her.

Having landed on the floor, the woman called Sadie said nothing. After a long moment, her eyes focused on Colette's. Sadie slipped a bony hand beneath the cot mattress next to her, and then withdrew something very small. It was a tiny round compact of some sort. On the outside there were purple and black flowers. She opened it, removed a small round piece of cottony cloth, all the while her eyes directly upon Colette. Then, ever so slowly, she raised the round cotton puff and touched it to her cheek. She then started powdering them, turning them blush red after a moment or so.

"Looks good," Colette commented.

The young woman's expression did not change.

"You truly think so?" she said at last. "The young gentlemen definitely enjoy the bright blush my secret makeup seems to provide. "I'm Sadie."

Colette nodded. Despite the layers of clothing she wore, the room felt somehow clammy. She held her hand up near the window where only a slight breeze sighed its way through to her. Outside it was flowers and trees, all flawless serenity, and quiet.

She turned back to the sharp edges and cold floor of the asylum and gazed at Sadie. The younger woman smiled for the first time, sweetly, appearing ironic. It was subtle. She seemed to fight the urge to laugh with all her strength.

"I was supposed to be married," she said. "Months ago. This last June. Percy would have wanted it. I'm certain of it."

"What happened?"

Sadie straightened up, her shoulders pressed against the wall. Then she scooted over to her cot. She sat with her knees pressed together, then smoothed her voluminous blue serge dress over her knees. Allowing her head to drop forward, her dark brown hair layered its way around the delicate features of her profile. She had a pointed nose and rosy lips. Looking at the woman, even with the sensibilities of someone from the twenty-first century, Colette was astounded at her refined beauty. Truly, a timeless face.

"Mr. Percy Kolber's family happened, that's what. Do I appear as an old woman to you?"

Again, Colette was struck by the similarities with nineteenth, and twenty-first century women, and the beliefs women seemed to have about themselves.

"Hardly old," was all she could think of to say. "I assume you're around nineteen?" She was being generous.

Sadie Hawthorne's eyes softened. "I have just turned twenty-six. I am an old maid. And the scandal with my former fiancé," her voice trailed off. "I will never be married. You see, he caught me at a meeting."

"A meeting?"

"A suffragette meeting. Susan B. Anthony is the new President of our organization this year."

Standing, Sadie walked to a vast high window where drab curtains were closed. She opened them, revealing an equally dirty window. Still, the view itself was prosaic.

In Colette's estimation, the outside of the asylum was designed to mislead onlookers. It displayed an institution of refinement and specialized care. A green lawn spread back to a small grotto and woods, and interspersed across the land were several Weeping Willow trees. Here, at the asylum, like Victorian society, Colette mused, it was beautiful and ornate on the outside, hushed and shamed on the inside. In fact, the physical building itself and the interior was spartan, utilitarian. It was dreary, and offered nothing to these women except neglect. Although the lobby was more lavish, she felt that was to put family members at ease. The rest of the place was like an old factory. It reminded her of how an architect once described the Victorian houses to her; Italianate and ornamental on the outside, but the rooms were closed-in by heavy drapes which divided the narrow archways from room to room. The analogy to women themselves was not by accident. Women were supposed to be repressed, and quiet. Yet despite the narrow venues of the Victorian rooms, each was replete with fine lace, paintings and furniture intended to display the wealth of the man of the house.

Sadie sat there. Her dress, clearly, was of good quality, periwinkle blue in color with trim of eggshell colored lace around the neck, cuffs and hem of her skirt. But it had taken a beating.

Colette thought about her alcohol recovery meetings and her life back in Valley Stream. She marveled at how women still worried about their appearances to such a maniacal degree. At the same time, these women demanded their fair share of pay and position in the corporate arena. Even in the arts, women still had to look the part, and charm their way into galleries and book tours.

Here was Sadie Hawthorne, circa 1892. One year before the infamous Lizzie Borden trial would take place. Sadie, in her own way, had been through the gruesome ordeal of trial and judgment by her own peers; perhaps Mr. Percy Kolber's family could not stomach a lush, and even worse, a suffragette? A cry for women's rights? Now that was too much.

"I hate that family," she blurted suddenly.

"The Kolber family you mentioned?"

"I hate being an outcast. They have countless drunkards in their clan and they judge me! Just look at what Lizzie Borden was driven to do. She'd had enough." Her eyes narrowed. They were black. "I'm familiar with the reasons for her anger. Her horror started at home."

Colette couldn't believe it. How true it all was.

"Men knocked us down and threw tomatoes at us on the street," Sadie went on. "We women active in the cause, trying simply to get the right to vote. Why they taunted us for years. Some of us are sick of waiting."

"In my opinion," Colette began, "the Borden murders appear to be extremely anger- driven. I suppose it could trickle down from having no voice in society and maybe even less respect within her home."

Sadie hovered over Colette now, a bit unsteadily. She was painfully gaunt. Soon her face came quite close to Colette's, and she peered into her eyes, for a long moment. She nodded, then applied red lipstick to her mouth, drawing a wide and crazy line of color.

"How would you know?" Sadie demanded, her eyes narrowed, "what goes on inside someone's home. Men are so careful to keep up appearances after all."

Colette swallowed slowly, and thought about her answer a second. Suddenly, the door swung open. A nurse walked in with a determined air, accompanied by a tall angular man with jet black hair. He wore a white jacket. Cool air carried in discreetly from the hallway, somehow, smelling of antiseptic. Except to Colette, it was a different scent, something that was foreign and antique. She and Sadie stayed in this open dormitory, and could enjoy some leisure areas of the asylum, and at least for now, roam the grounds freely. Other patients were much less fortunate, as Colette would discover.

Twenty minutes later, the doctor in charge of Depressives and defiants, as he liked to call them, paraded Colette and Sadie past the main entrance. Sure enough, there were new recruits planted around the benches there with the hems of their long skirts dragging the floor, their shoulders slumped and their faces long.

Soon the two women were led into a utilitarian-type room. It occurred to Colette that this asylum must be costly. Clearly, they had plans for Sadie. Maybe it wasn't so bad after all? In fact, Sadie sat herself down in an elegant winged-back chair to rest. Yet, at this prompt, the doctor whipped around and spoke, quite fervently, for the first time.

"Get up. How dare you? Get up!"

His face, which had almost looked clean and handsome in its way just a moment before, now looked contorted. His face was pale, and his black hair, slicked back with brilliantine, made him seem even more severe, and less about medicine and health, and more about power. More about control. "Absolute power corrupts absolutely," so said British historian Lord Acton. He stood there, waiting, holding open a set of double doors that had white gauzy curtains on them to cover the windows, stretched like bandages. They made it impossible to see out of the room, creating even more dissonance and disorientation.

The two women followed. Colette kept her head bowed. Still, she felt his eyes upon her.

"You know what to do," he said to her.

She nodded, almost flirtatiously. As soon as he'd walked out, and the door to their room closed, she scampered toward a loud, hissing steam radiator, a bit antiquated even for 1892.

"I know what he wants me to do, but I'd rather do what I want to do." And reaching behind the radiator, she got down on her knees and loosened a wooden panel. Soon she removed several small canvases and some brushes, along with a round palette of paints. Noting Colette's gaze, and seemingly amused by it, Sadie's eyes grew large. Her face took on the presence of some coquette. She sat on the floor, pulling her long dress down to cover her ankles. With a sweep of her diminutive hand, she touched the paints and canvases and smiled.

"He provides these for me. They don't know."

Colette stepped over to her, then squatted down to talk to Sadie more intimately. "Who provides them for you?

At this comment, her eyes took on an intensity that seemed out of place, as if she were someone else. She had a wandering look, once again, as if her mind could fly her anywhere she wanted to go.

"Why do you want to know?"

She grinned. "Percy snuck them in through an orderly he knows. Percy and I are lovers, you know." Then, unwittingly, tears were in her eyes. "That's why I'm here."

Colette understood this woman of 1892. Because Depression had its way with Colette, whenever it felt like it.

But her children felt separate from her and she was, at times like this, confounded that after two marriages, and giving birth to two souls that perpetually would feel a part of her, that she'd ended up alone. Because "alone" for someone with Depression, equated to a pit of self-loathing and misery. Depression became an abyss.

It would hit her that perhaps if she disappeared, no one would notice. It wasn't so much something out of self-pity. Logically, she just figured it might make everyone's life a little easier to be without her. As a child, she'd write her mother a note every night, after dinner, detailing everything she'd done that day and why she felt bad about whatever it was. At that time however, her mother had been lost in her own vacuum of shame. This was the eternal pit of feeling perpetually unwanted that Colette's mother unwittingly had passed on to her daughter.

Children always need their parents. She, above anyone else, knew that. So how ironic it was now, to be listening to the heartbreak of a woman from one hundred and nineteen years before her time, and totally understand her. Absolutely, without any doubt. There was indeed a thread which connected women in a timeless way. But could this continuity transcend murder?

Chapter Seven (A)

The Historical Facts

According to Mrs. Churchill's testimony, when Miss Alice Russell arrived at the Borden home the day of the murders, she inquired of her and of Bridget, "is there another?"[115] This followed immediately after the two women had gone upstairs in search of Mrs. Borden. This phrasing of her question was presented in Porter's *The Fall River Tragedy* verbatim, according to Mrs. Churchill's testimony. It was noteworthy that instead of Alice having asked, "did you find Mrs. Borden?" she asked, "is there another?" In a way, that rhetoric was a bit unusual. Because if Alice had little or no suspicions that Mrs. Borden was already murdered, mightn't she have been more likely to have asked if Abby had returned? It was a subtle difference in wording but still somewhat indicative of Alice Russell having had some sort of sinking premonition around Lizzie's guilt. In other words, Lizzie had indeed made a point of visiting Alice the night before the murders. At that time, Lizzie apparently presented concerns about Andrew Borden having business "enemies" and that she believed someone had tried to poison the family just the day before with tainted milk, or by serving bread that had been poisoned.

So on the following day, when Bridget and Mrs. Churchill came rushing down the stairs, and Miss Russell asked indeed if there "is another,"[116] it was as if she had expected there to have been another body. In a way though, it was perhaps because Alice Russell, close friend of Lizzie Borden, already had her suspicions that Lizzie had done something. Because her first reaction was not a hopeful "did you find Mrs. Borden?" but rather, "is there another?" One may have also assumed that because Alice Russell was a long-time close friend of Lizzie's, she either knew, or strongly suspected there had been sexual abuse by Mr. Borden, with Abby Borden's knowledge, which thus made Lizzie's step-mother automatically complicit.

A police reporter himself, Porter's account, which was transcribed in 1893, utilized as accurately as possible, the phraseology used by witnesses, as would have been possible to replicate.[117] Therefore, witness statements were presented quite distinctly by Porter, who acted as a stenographer of the tragedy. The witness statements were utilized throughout the trial and up through to the acquittal.

Next called as a witness, on the third day of the trial, was Miss Alice Russell herself. It was of interest at this point, to note Lizzie's body language for several reasons; first, due to their close relationship, Lizzie would have been cognizant of Alice's extensive insight into the truth around the murders, secondly, that Lizzie might have felt some insecurity around Alice's sense of scruples because, if her friend suspected her, Alice might have revealed everything she knew, in spite of the fact that it might further incriminate Lizzie.

So upon Miss Russell's arrival in court, as she approached the witness stand, Porter described what transpired as: "Lizzie straightened up in her chair and began to watch the door. When Miss Russell came in, she looked everywhere but where Lizzie was seated."[118] Miss Russell apparently did not want to look her best friend in the eye.

Such body language on the part of Lizzie, as well as the pointed action of Alice Russell to avoid eye contact with the suspect, was a keen observation on Porter's part. As Lizzie's closest friend and perhaps sole confidant, Lizzie knew Miss Russell's testimony would have been tantamount to the outcome of the trial. And the fact that Alice avoided eye contact with Lizzie would certainly have unnerved her.

In fact, the action in itself would certainly create doubt as to what Miss Russell planned to reveal. Ironically, Lizzie's desperate attempt to plant suspicion in Miss Russell's mind the night before the murders, about strangers and poison or shady irate businessmen, could have now through testimony, have sounded very rehearsed and planned by Lizzie, especially now that she was a prime suspect.

The preponderance of alternative suspects Lizzie presented was excessive on that fateful evening before the murders. Not only did Lizzie make certain to visit Alice the night before, but she also went into four morbid possibilities which might have caused harm to the Borden family; first, she mentioned seeing a "man about the place" at night, that secondly, the barn had been broken into and that she feared someone would burn the house down (which was somewhat dramatic); third, that the house had been burglarized and finally, fourth, even insinuated that Mr. Borden had put himself in harm's way by describing how he had treated his friends poorly, even including Dr. Bowen.[119]

At this juncture, this had been a timely reference to Dr. Bowen, because, as it was explored later on in the trial, Dr. Bowen remained very close to Lizzie throughout the ordeal. In fact, he had spent a good deal of time with her. A questionable amount of time, in fact, in her room immediately following the murders. It had inspired dislike and suspicion by the police officers trying to gather evidence from the house, grounds and barn. Thus it was apparent that Lizzie established Dr. Bowen as a family friend to have been trusted. Dr. Bowen likewise, later on, presented Lizzie as a fine young woman, who simply needed time to rest in her room following the murders. It was not precisely clear just how much time Dr. Bowen carved out for Lizzie during that crucial time period. Interestingly, it could have allowed for Lizzie to conceal bloody garments, or cover up evidence in any number of ways.

Two other facts expressed by Alice Russell were significant. First of all, Miss Russell mentioned that Lizzie responded to a question posed to her, about her whereabouts during the murders, as that she'd gone to the barn to retrieve a "piece of iron to fix her screen." One may have assumed Lizzie referenced the screen door, which was described by several witnesses. However, as would soon be discovered, Lizzie also provided a contradictory story which purported that she'd been in the barn looking for lead sinkers for her fishing pole.[120]

A second important observation was that Alice Russell also stated that she saw Lizzie "going to the closet door, unlock it and go in."[121] This action may have referred to either Emma's closet, or to Lizzie's closet. Either way, the significant point was that she'd unlocked a closet door, which could have implied that she'd had the opportunity to remove any bit of clothing that might have been blood-stained, put on the pink wrapper to cover up, and temporarily hidden the blood-ied garment in the locked closet until such time that she may have spirited the dress out of the house and then eventually, burned it in the kitchen without anyone, including police, ever having seen that the dress contained blood stains.

In this way, Lizzie would have been able to hide the bloodied dress, at least temporarily. However, this may well have been the same dress with which she was eventually caught, by Alice Russell, burning in the kitchen. It was simply a quick mention in Alice Russell's testimony, and not something which was elaborated upon. Apparently, Lizzie was also tearing the dress into pieces as she was burning it.[122] Officer George W. Allen arrived at the Borden house at 11:15 a.m. on August 4th and was assigned by a Mr. Sawyer to watch guard outside. Interestingly he noted that the front door to the house was locked with a night lock and bolt. Also noted by Officer Allen was that the cellar door which led outside was locked and bolted from the inside.[123]

Another observation Officer Allen made was that although a near-by lamp and books located next to Abby's body were not bloody, there was found however, a bloody handkerchief on the floor. And although it was not a frequently discussed observation, this fact may have been relevant. What was particularly noteworthy about this fact was that it was unlikely to have been dropped by Abby. At the same time, Lizzie was known to have just been downstairs ironing handkerchiefs.[124] In fact, that had been the reason she'd been tottering off in the barn during the precise time Andrew was being murdered; in order to allow the fire to heat up the iron for her to iron her handkerchiefs.

Next up to testify was Assistant City Marshall John Fleet. He voiced an important observation. He claimed he'd found the closet at the head of the stairs to have been locked.[125] This was perhaps the same closet where Lizzie had stashed the calico dress, the very dress that may have been bloody.

Fleet next stated that he'd found Lizzie in her bedroom, and that she was with Reverend Buck. The officer asked her at that time if she knew anything about her parents' murders and she said she did not. It was at this time that she mentioned she'd last seen her father, and that she'd helped him get settled on the sofa. This detail, about helping him get comfortable on the sofa as it related to exactly what transpired once her father had gotten home at 10:30 a.m., would vary in separate tellings.[126] Because on August 4th, 1892, Andrew Borden reclined on the sofa for a nap, and it would be his final nap.

In some accounts, Lizzie claimed to have helped him get settled, and in others, she claimed she merely saw him lie down on the sofa. These two accounts, especially by way of their differences, created an atmosphere of definitive doubt around the validity of Lizzie's words, as well as the precise accounts of the events. Implausibility, due to conflicting stories, would have raised suspicion. Lizzie, in her own words, created a greater aura of doubt with regards to her innocence.

In response to Fleet's questions, Lizzie made certain to in essence, clear the names of several other possible suspects. First, she indicated that John Morse, her uncle who had been staying at the house, could not have committed the murders because he'd left the house and not returned until 12:00 noon. Regarding Bridget the maid, Lizzie was perhaps protecting her because she knew the truth; because she, herself, had committed the crimes. Because if Lizzie had truly not been the murderer, such a statement would not have been necessary or advisable. Because why would Lizzie have gone out of her way to make proclamations about Bridget, when Bridget may well have been guilty? That is, unless Lizzie was certain that she was not?

City Marshall Fleet also stated that upon searching the house he found all the doors locked except for Bridget Sullivan's. Again, finding all the doors locked so soon after the bodies were discovered, only reinforced the idea that a stranger being in the house would have been unlikely. He or she would not have been able to dart in and out of the preponderance of rooms in order to hide, especially during the one and a half hour time period which passed between the two murders.

Also during the trial, Fleet identified several hatchets he claimed he'd seen in the cellar in a box. However, when Assistant District Attorney Moody presented the hatchets in court, Fleet pointed out that they were the same hatchets. However, there was a noticeable absence of red stains on one of the hatchet handles. Also, at a certain point, when Fleet unlocked Emma's bedroom door located at the other side of her own bedroom during his search, Lizzie stated that she was "getting tired of it." (Fleet and others searching the rooms).

Lizzie next made a point of stating that searching her bedroom was unnecessary because she always kept the room locked and that no one could have gotten into it, nor could anyone have "thrown anything into it." That last statement was telling, if for no other reason, than it implied that Lizzie may have stashed something in her bedroom herself.

Finally, Fleet admitted that the hatchets he'd seen in the cellar, once they were presented to him in the courtroom, were the same ones. However, the crucial caveat Fleet pointed out was that the handle of the hatchet he'd seen in the cellar, stashed on a shelf six feet high off the floor, had previously had a red stain on the handle. Interestingly, when Fleet viewed it in the courtroom, he pointed out that the hatchet now had a new break in the handle, and that the red stain was now oddly missing. Also, as was already noted, the hatchets were somehow recently smeared in white ashes. This may have further served to camouflage or diminish any stains that may have been on them.

The fifth day of the trial revealed interesting facts that may have gone unnoticed both back in 1892, and then perhaps even into the present day, and that could have been quite important. During the questioning of Officer George W. Allen, he indicated that he'd arrived at the Borden house at around 11:15 a.m., immediately following the murders.[127] Interestingly, he described the guest chamber where he saw the body of Abby Borden as having had a "small stand upon which were two books and a small oil lamp..." and he noticed a "bloody handkerchief on the guest chamber floor lying about midway between the body and the wall." There was apparently not much mention of this bloody handkerchief from other sources. The next witness called, following Assistant City Marshall John Fleet, was Captain Philip Harrington. He was called to the Borden house at around 12:00 noon.[128] Now upon his examination of the guest chamber, he did not mention having spotted any bloody handkerchief. In fact, he made no mention of any at all. He did, however, make careful observations, as he mentioned seeing "blood on her (Abby's) dress, on the pillow sham, and some on the spread."[129]

Certainly, it would have been possible between 11:14 and 12:00 noon, for Lizzie to have ventured into the guest room and picked up the handkerchief. That is, if she were aware that she'd dropped it. Of course, the bloody handkerchief may have belonged to someone else, quite possibly another woman. Certainly, the kerchief would not have flown off the victim and subsequently landed on the floor? And it should be noted that ironing handkerchiefs was the precise task Lizzie claimed to have been engaged in right after her father had arrived home. So although she claimed to have gone outside, purportedly during the precise time that Andrew Borden was being murdered, Lizzie was actually eating pears. Concurrently, she stated she was also looking for sinkers for her fishing line in the barn. However, Lizzie as killer may have actually left her calling card accidently at the scene of the first murder, by leaving that telltale bloody handkerchief. After all, she stated that she'd been allowing the iron to get hot on the fire in order to iron. So who else would have been as likely as Lizzie, to have been carrying around a handkerchief?

Chapter Eight

W hen she awakened, her hand was immersed in velvet. Colette opened her eyes to bright sunlight and the bleak surroundings of the workroom at the asylum. Sadie Hawthorne was crouched on the floor, rocking back and forth, gazing fixedly out the window. Colette sat up, and rested her arm on the hump of the camel-back sofa. It was the only soft piece of furniture in the room. Elsewhere were placed small round tables with folded handkerchiefs and irons waiting to be warmed up on the stove. In the far corner, there was a makeshift kitchen, a kind of a corner-type room even though the entire space was open, like a loft. She glanced at the oven and noticed several baked goods sitting on top of a table in the kitchenette. That's when Colette noticed Isabelle. She'd been brought back to the asylum. At last Colette recalled they'd been relegated to the "task room" to practice their domestic skills. Not surprisingly, Colette had thus fallen asleep.

Swinging her legs around, Colette straightened up. Isabelle stared her down. Her head was tilted to one side. The cuts on her arms were scabs. Draped in a blue dress, speckled with a small flower pattern, her eyes looked equally blue, although not the surreal light blue of Sadie's. Isabelle's were dark. Now those eyes were wide and somewhat unfocused. Within moments, she was up and shuffling toward Colette, the heels of her ankle boots scraping the floor.

Colette sat back quickly. Isabelle stood over her, her face gleaming in the light. What may have been a smile to some, now seemed a scowl.

"You're here for it, aren't you?"

Colette glanced at Sadie, who she still rocked, with her arms around her legs, staring at the window.

"It's hard to quit, isn't it," Isabelle said. "It's the end of your world. The Laudanum turns the abuse and the neglect, and the men, inside out so you can live. Then it turns vile and sucks the very life out of you. I first got Laudanum," she started, her eyes gazing at nothing, "one night out with a couple of musicians after a concert in the park. They said it would make me merry. But I couldn't stop. It made me feel light, and free for the first time. Then it turned on me. Life became bleak."

As she circled the sofa, she was singing softly, always looking back to Colette. "Our lives are measured out, no less than a cup of flour," she went on. "From our earliest days of becoming young women, no, as children, we women are groomed to expect as little as possible for ourselves. Our futures will likely not include any education but will certainly revolve around raising children, as many as possible. We also know that should we die during childbirth, our husbands will likely marry again for more children. We are reproductive creatures. That is all. That and domestic servants; crucial to our self-worth will be how well we keep a clean home, and decorate it, and decorate ourselves with pearls and pendants and lavalieres and cameos, all simply necessary displays of our husband's wealth."

Colette's mouth tightened.

"I myself," Isabelle went on, "have been known for my sweet voice. That's what the men in the Sousa band often told me. I am not as scientific as my friend Sadie here. I'm the canary that can sing. But people like my father don't care for my music."

Sadie still sat on the floor. All at once, she stopped rocking and said, without looking up. "I liken myself to a mystic. I feel connected to nature."

Isabelle grinned. "She's a science genius is exactly what she is."

"Percy didn't want that," Sadie went on. "I, too started on the secret solace of the laudanum. I thought I could hide it from him."

Isabelle watched Sadie the entire time, hanging upon her words as if she'd never heard the young woman share before. Clearly Isabelle knew the pain of addiction. Pacing back and forth in front of Colette, her long hem dragged the floor as she swept past. The motion was mesmerizing. Something about the room was claustrophobic now, with the rocking of Sadie against the incessant pacing of Isabelle. The room was not four even walls exactly. A corner had been wedged off at a sharp angle. Something had been hidden there and then plastered over to cover the fact.

Sadie noticed Colette looking. "That section used to be for ice baths and being shackled to the wall. They built a wall quite hastily, I might add, to hide those unmentionable activities. Just in time for the fete. Don't want the wealthy patients to see what really goes on."

Isabelle started to sing in a low throaty voice. This was not a naive voice, dressed up in delicate lace and conformity and propriety; this was a voice of passion. The sultriness may have appeared out of character to other nineteenth century women.

"They say it's the Laudanum," Isabelle burst out suddenly. "They say that's what makes me sing like this. It's as if my insides want to express themselves."

Isabelle continued to circle the sofa where Colette sat, unmoving. Isabelle's rhythms grew more intense and determined as she stepped. She studied her boots as she moved. The fear seemed to be that she'd lose her way if she looked up, if she stopped. While she walked, she counted to herself, starting with one and repeating over and over to ten.

At one point, Colette started to stand. But Isabelle careened around and came to an abrupt halt. Colette didn't move.

Finally, the walking rampage subsided, and Isabelle's eyes softened. Her lips were slightly parted as she again, studied Colette.

Returning to the front of the sofa, she sat down in the precise spot where Colette had been seated just moments before. All at once, Isabelle spread her small pale hands out on the velvet seat cushion on either side of her, her ruffled skirt falling freely. Her eyes were troubled.

Colette relented at last and sat down, ever so slowly onto the sofa again. She continued to study Isabelle. Sadie wandered over and stood over them, clutching two large paint brushes in her right hand. Her dress had splashes of green and pinks and purples down the front of it.

Colette thought about Lizzie and how years before, Colette had read an account of the murders and the trial that followed. At that time, the account stated that Lizzie had worn a smock over her long dress and boots, when she committed the crime. Some accounts in fact, claimed that Lizzie may have done the deeds entirely in the nude.

"We meet here," Isabelle said, "because they believe we're crazy. Well," she nodded toward Sadie, "her fiancé and my father actually 'know' that we are not. They know we are not insane." She eyed Colette again. "Here we are. So we'll be out of the way. Women have to be kept out of the way. The doctor," she said, laughing, "wants us to work on our domestic arts. You see, Sadie and me? We do not measure up to the standards of a proper woman."

She turned away, suddenly solemn, holding her chin up as she looked out the window. It was the same window Sadie had obsessed over for the last hour.

Colette rose, stepped around the sofa and ran her hand along the silky soft hump of its backside. Isabelle was still. Her profile looked waxen in the mid-day light. Isabelle had an eerie timelessness about her right now.

Colette sidled up to a table nearby the two women. There was a larger table cemented next to a smaller one, both acting as permanent props for this created domestic setting. On the larger table there was piled what appeared to be thirty or so tablecloths. Next to the iron was a large bottle labeled "starch." The oven was in the artificial kitchen set up twenty paces from the row of windows. There was another station beyond that which had a pile of fabrics, and next to it several cast iron behemoth sewing machines. Colette walked up and started sifting through the fabrics. On one side of the table there were pinafores, dresses and Victorian wrappers. Picking one up, moth ball holes ran a pattern across the garments. Obviously these had been made by another set of inmates in the asylum. This had been the sewing table for a very long time.

It all reminded her of a frighteningly austere home economics class. Perhaps a home economics class primer for all other home economics classes to follow in the next century. Sadie and Isabelle were face to face. Isabelle held both of Sadie's hands in hers. These two would not cooperate with the purported home economics curriculum.

"I am not saying what Miss Lizzie Borden did was right," Isabelle began, her voice low and hoarse. "But I understand her frustration. The difference between her and the rest of us is perhaps that she is indeed, mad. She must be out of her mind to have committed such grievous crimes against her parents. But you must realize, to have experienced the cruelty, the death of her very soul...I too often wish my perpetrator, that my father, was dead."

"Stop it Isabelle!" Sadie blurted, pulling her hands away.

"In this place," Isabelle went on. "we are only trying to stay off our temptations. For me, it's the laudanum. For Sadie, here," she said, nodding to the beaten woman by the window, her shoulders hunched, "she is wrapped up in the drink."

"What about Lizzie?" Colette broached, crossing her arms over her chest.

Isabelle lifted her chin and turned to look at Colette, looking at her full on, her eyes boring into hers. In a way, Isabelle's fury was almost sinister. This young woman, who had been held against her will in her father's own house, had hardened because of it. If Colette recalled correctly, Isabelle looked more severe than she did earlier in the day on the steps. Colette disputed the idea that she'd been bleeding soley from wounds to her hands and arms. Isabelle spoke at last.

"Lizzie was past the boiling point. She played the good daughter and it consumed her, body and soul. That step-mother of hers, from what I heard, was unbearable. Not that the old woman deserved to die," she hesitated, as if reconsidering, "not in that way. A young woman can only take so much, without rights, without allies. Abby Borden did not have Lizzie's interests at hand. We women cannot work or gain our own wealth through our own deeds or employment. Of course, we can teach," Isabelle smiled vaguely, a faraway look in her eyes, "or work in grungy factories. Why I heard my friend Sally was so badly injured in a factory last summer that her husband left her. He was horrified to be seen with her since she'd had her arm severed in an accident. This, of course, gave him another excuse to abandon her. What good was she if she couldn't work or take care of the house?"

Colette took a step toward Isabelle.

"Isabelle? What does your father do to you?"

"He won't break me," she said, her voice unusually calm. "Like her father broke her."

A shadow passed in the hallway, then an aura seemed to pause like a face and stare through the glass window pane, gazing into the room. All-seeing, black eyes. Mechanically, Isabelle teetered over to a nearby table and started folding handkerchiefs. After a while, she turned her head, ever so slightly to the left, toward the window, as if to see if the eyes still watched.

She started to pile the handkerchiefs, took several off the top all at once and started to refold them. During this ritual, she started to sing a song, the same melody Colette thought she'd heard somewhere before. Sadie watched her, as if watching a Shaman, her eyes gleaming.

Sadie stalked the circumference of the room, around and around again, she circled while Isabelle set the iron on the stove to warm. Colette somehow knew and understood the mechanics of the old kitchen. Ever since childhood, Colette frequented antique stores, like most kids did amusement parks. There had been a heavy dark brown iron from the late 1800s that she used as a door stop in her apartment. Still, it always surprised her how she just "knew" certain things about antiques. Because often, it was contraptions she'd never seen in her life. As if she'd been there at the time period of the invention. The key fact was the old relics always made her feel more at home in her own skin, right with the world. She turned to Isabelle.

"What were the cuts all over your arms?"

Isabelle touched one of the scabs on her arms with her fingertips.

Then she turned, again with the same slow motion movement of her head. Lifting the iron, Isabelle pressed the handkerchief under it, holding it down, watching steam rise on either side of it. Then she lifted the iron and eyed it, for an interminable second, holding it up about an inch from the palm of her other hand. She was deep in thought now. In truth, she was perhaps somewhere else entirely. The iron was suspended there, clutched in her left hand. Colette sensed Isabelle's sudden urge, perhaps to harm herself.

Suddenly, she brought the iron down and pressed it onto the fabric, letting a rush of steam shoot out in every angle.

"Father locks me in over and over. No one can hold me. Wants to keep me away from Darren, and from singing at the gazebo concerts with the Sousa band. I embarrass him."

Sadie laughed, then walked to the kitchenette and started washing dishes in the sink. "This year, I heard," she started, "University of Chicago and Pennsylvania are letting women into their universities. It's a first anywhere in the States. They have been allowed overseas for quite some time."

Colette followed the two women as they went about their tasks. A group of men had gathered and now looked through the window, watching, studying them.

"So to focus on your question," Isabelle said, "I think Lizzie used drastic means to gain her freedom. She was enslaved by her stepmother. and yet Abby didn't look out for her at all. Andrew ruled the house, like all fathers do. Lizzie knew," Isabelle went on, closing her eyes, "She knew he had money. Lots of money. More money than most people would ever need in their lives. But those properties of his, his businesses. Those were his babies. Emma and Lizzie were no more than property." She paused, biting her lip, thinking. "In the meantime, Lizzie has been growing older and older. No prospects of a husband make a woman's life limited. Oh there were rumors; of a man, a boyfriend. She had no boyfriend. Guess they're trying to pin the murders on some poor delinquent. Nosy little town."

Colette nodded, eying Sadie. Isabelle went on.

"I know her. I know Lizzie. She did it. I know she did it. I don't blame her."

Colette leaned back on the distressed dark wood of the kitchen counter, moving ever slowly, closer to Sadie. "You're not saying you think it was the right thing to do?"

"You mean the murders of Andrew and Abby? No. But maybe she saw no other way. But what about all the slow suicides by women? Laudanum, opium, brandy, whiskey...you name it. Women do it. No one talks about it. Maybe they're not lying about in opium dens, but believe me they're living their own addiction nightmares in the privacy of their homes, in the lonely nights without their husbands."

Isabelle rolled up her sleeves. "What are these cuts?" she said, extending her arms out to the other women. "I ripped the wallpaper off the walls of my room. I was tearing my way out of my existence. When he threatens me," she stopped, looking pensive, perturbed. "I lose my momentum, the life inside me dies. My father wants to send me away. He sent my mother away. And this was beyond an asylum. He sent her out of the town, to another city. He was so ashamed of her. I keep running away. I want to find her."

With that she started to hum. Colette recognized the tune.

"You like Sousa?" she asked.

Sadie looked up suddenly, with her eyes only, and a sly grin. All at once, she jumped up and skipped around Isabelle, talking at her in a sing-song voice. "Does she know Sousa? No! You need to ask her how well she knows one of the men of the traveling Sousa band! Ask her about him."

Colette smiled, a bit taken aback, but amused by Sadie's sudden lightness of spirit. The touring Sousa band again. Colette had played in a concert band herself, for years. First clarinet. The wearied conductor had had to deal with a smattering of toddling children from the audiences, notorious for dancing right up to the ropes, just around the band gazebo. There was something so American and idyllic about playing concerts in the old band shell.

Isabelle hummed the Star Spangled Banner as she skirted around the room. Then Sadie and she joined hands and were traipsing around the faux kitchen, throwing metal utensils on the floor and taking sacks of flour and throwing it at one another.

A sound came from behind them. The doctors eyed the three women. The hems of Isabelle and Sadie's dresses were caked in flour and their faces were white with the powder. Apparently Colette too, was one of the lab rats. The men were shaking their heads and taking notes in black notebooks with fountain pens.

To Fall River, Massachusetts, what Lizzie Borden had apparently done, by the vicious act of slaying her parents, was fallen herself into a similar vein as the other women. These women, and their irrepressible drive to be more than domestics and mothers...what was wrong with them?

"Go to hell!" Sadie raged at them.

Colette stepped back and it took several seconds for her heart to slow. Isabelle simply watched Sadie, not so much calmly but with a sharp empathy. Although she appeared not more than nineteen years old, Isabelle had worry lines around her eyes, and a sadness about her. It was as if she'd seen more than her share, more horrors than anyone could imagine.

Colette wandered over to the kitchen now. All the ancient apparatus, covered in flour, baffled her; a massive black kettle to warm everything seemed to be central to the room, the mutton on the table appeared too meaty and fatty to eat but there it sat on the table, along with a loaf of bread having been baked from scratch. This was home economics for diehards.

"How do you ladies feel about being watched like laboratory animals?" Colette asked them.

"They're waiting for us to crack," Sadie said. "It's more than a constant watch they force upon us. There are the beatings for not complying with their demands. They deny us food, and lock us in the special room where we are forced to write for hours, about what it means to be a valuable young woman of the 1890s. Like I said, I'm being punished for pursuing an intimate relationship with Percy. I was told women have no need for sexual feelings."

Then she took to the floor again, hugging her knees to her chin. Isabelle sidestepped around the smaller woman as she kneaded a loaf of bread. Soon she formed it into a baking dish.

The medical men moved on, and talked amongst themselves. The same doctor, who had ordered them around earlier, swaggered over to Isabelle.

"How is your baking?" he asked her.

"I'll bring some to Darren," she said. "What do you think, Dr. Warburton? After his concert."

"You won't be seeing him tonight. You know that, Isabelle," he said. "Nor ever again."

The bread was filling up in the pan. She molded it carefully with slender, alabaster hands. All the while, she smiled.

"You realize you put yourself in grave danger at your father's house. You did it all yourself. You hurt yourself. Your father just wants you to marry well. You don't want those cuts on your arms to scar."

She stopped kneading and looked up at him. "I have scars on the inside that will never go away."

The fire was lit under the oven. Taking large wool-like gloves, she pulled the black door open and placed the bread inside the oven. Sadie glared at Dr. Warburton, still rocking back and forth.

"I've been painting again," she said to him. "Wild dreams. Sexual dreams I have covered canvas after canvas with them. They're erotic. Want to see them?"

Ignoring Sadie, Dr. Warburton spoke to Isabelle. "You have to stop running away from your responsibilities. What makes you think you can always get away?"

"Harry Houdini does it. So can I."

The doctor frowned, and he jotted notes. Two younger doctors had joined him. He gave them a knowing glance.

"Who is this Houdini person?" he said, turning to them.

Sadie started laughing, too loudly. One of her bare shoulders showed white when her dress shifted. She licked her lips and eyed one of the young doctors, trying to look lascivious. The taller of the two doctor's eyes widened and he turned away.

"Houdini has been on Coney Island," Sadie offered up, quite proudly.

Then Isabelle leaned over and whispered to the doctors. "He's an escape artist. He is me."

Chapter Eight (A)

The Historical Facts

There was a mystery around the bloodied handkerchief at the site of Abby Borden's body, chiefly, that it disappeared at all. Because apparently, between 11:15 and 12:00, when Captain Harrington observed the room, the handkerchief was no longer dropped there on the floor.[130] It certainly would have been spotted by someone had it still been there. Captain Harrington had been observant enough, after all, to notice a "drop of blood" which had been trickling down Andrew Borden's face moments before.[131]

Captain Harrington gave an intriguing testimony. He had asked Lizzie what she could tell him, and all she said was, "I can tell you nothing at all."[132] She reported that Mr. Borden came home with a package from the post office, but Lizzie made no mention of the great lengths she'd apparently gone to, to cover him with an afghan blanket, and make him more comfortable, as she had told other witnesses.

Harrington went on to describe Lizzie as wearing a pink wrapper.

A wrapper was a full-length apron-type dress worn over house dresses. Why would she have put on this pink wrapper as she had been observed doing by Alice Russell, so quickly after the murders? Could she have, in fact, perhaps changed her blue calico dress, hidden it away and put on instead, a very similar, but completely different calico blue dress? Indeed, Lizzie would have had a reason for hiding the first dress if it indeed had blood stains.

Ironically, Captain Harrington arrived after Fleet had, and whereas Fleet witnessed Dr. Bowen, in a sense, guarding Lizzie in her bedroom behind a closed door, Bowen would in fact, not allow Fleet entry at all. Harrington witnessed Lizzie wearing a pink wrapper over her dress. So there was the possibility that she may have donned the wrapper specifically to confuse the issue about the dress underneath it. One would have difficulty distinguishing one blue calico dress from another if she had put on a pink wrapper. And yet, for what logical reason would she have had the wrapper on?

In Martins/Binette's *Parallel Lives*, it was pointed out that the precise details presented by Captain Harrington were somewhat excessive and surprisingly accurate. He was a surprise to those in attendance in the courtroom, as it made him sound like a tailor or perhaps even a cross-dresser. In fact it was said that no one would have been surprised if he'd, "drawn a mouchoir (handkerchief) from a dainty satchel and deftly dusted the powder from his nose."[133]

Along the same lines, a Captain Doherty arrived at the Borden house some time after 11:39 a.m.[134] He and a Deputy Sheriff Wixon went into the house together. Like Harrington, Doherty did not describe spotting any bloody handkerchief but did describe a "bunch of hair," which would later be discovered to have been a hairpiece that Abby always wore.[135]

Interestingly too, later on when Doherty described a conversation with Lizzie in the kitchen, he had asked her where she had been "when this was done," referring to the murders, and she repeated what she'd been telling everyone; that she'd been "in the barn." However, she specifically said "she heard no outcry or screams, but she did hear some noise like scraping."[136]

Before Patrick Doherty left the Borden house, he stopped by Lizzie's room, as apparently, other officers had done. He knocked on her door. Opening it, she said "one minute," then closed the door in his face. He recalled a light blue dress that Lizzie had on, saying it had a "bosom" to it.

Next, an Officer Michael Mullaly arrived at 11:37 a.m. When he saw Lizzie she claimed she was in the yard during the time of the murders, and that when she came into the house, she simply found her father dead, reclined on the sofa. Noticeably, there was no mention of having heard any groan or scraping sound.

A difference in what was witnessed focused on the handles or broken handle of a hatchet. Officer Mullaly testified that he found a hatchet handle in the cellar box. Mr. Fleet however, did not see a hatchet handle.

On the seventh day of the trial, the testimony of Lizzie Borden at the original inquest was deemed, because of the words of defense Attorney Robinson, inadmissible to be included in the trial.[137] This was a blow to the State's case against Lizzie. That original inquest testimony had contained inconsistencies which would have helped to incriminate Lizzie. Such inconsistencies may have implied that Lizzie had been lying or making up separate stories.

Soon after this development, several interesting facts were revealed by the Medical Examiner, Dr. William A. Dolan. First, in response to Dr. Dolan's questions around the note Lizzie's step-mother had received, Lizzie oddly, indicated she'd, "supposed she had thrown it in the stove."[138] This reasoning was one of convenience. It seemed odd that it would have occurred to her to destroy the note in such a timely way. The action would cause one to think one of two things; either there never was a note and/or secondly, if there was a note, there would have been no logical reason to have burned the note so quickly.

The following details described by Dr. William Dolan included the initial scene before him in the sitting room where Andrew Borden was found. Dr. Dolan stated that he'd arrived at the Borden house at 11:45 a.m. Dr. Dolan described Mr. Andrew Borden as having been positioned stretched out and reclining. The end of the sofa was flush with the dining room door jamb.[139]

A crucial observation concerned exactly what Mr. Borden's head was resting upon. According to Porter's *The Fall River Tragedy* "the head was resting on a small sofa cushion; a coat was under that and an afghan under that."[140] If the theory was accepted, whereby Lizzie, as murderer, put on her father's Prince Albert-cut coat like a surgeon, worn backwards with the back of the coat covering her, this could have explained the coat being tucked beneath his head. It was worn in such a way so that little or no blood would have been on her or on the dress. In this way, it would have been logical for his coat to have been rolled up and placed under the pillow, or sofa cushion.[141] It would have been feasible for Lizzie to have rolled the coat and shoved it under the sofa cushion.

Interestingly, Medical Examiner Dolan did mention finding an old handkerchief, which was made of silk and was also bloody, located "near her head."[142] Supposedly, later on when the authorities buried the clothes of the victims in the yard, at Uncle Morse's request, there was a "napkin" described as one of the items buried. However, it was not necessarily designated as a bloody handkerchief. So thus far, Officer Allen and Dr. Dolan, the Medical Examiner, were the only two individuals who mentioned having seen a bloodied silk handkerchief at the scene of Mrs. Abby Borden's body. Dr. Dolan described it as being "near her head," and added that he did not take the kerchief, but claimed that it was buried with the rest of the clothes in the yard.[143] However, the only item described aside from the clothes was a "napkin" which would not necessarily have indicated the handkerchief. This, despite the fact that more specifically, the item was described as a "bloody silk handkerchief," by two witnesses.

Also according to Dr. Dolan, they discovered on Andrew Borden's person, a little over eighty-one dollars, his pocket watch and a ring on his finger.[144] Certainly if the evil culprit had been a disgruntled business associate, or even a renter of one of his properties, such a person would likely have absconded with the monies or even his watch. The fact that so much money was found on him might have further proven that the motive was neither robbery nor the revenge of a business associate.

It was interesting also to note that an examination of Lizzie's clothes yielded only a pinhead-sized drop of blood on her white underskirt on the back, eight inches above the hem.

What follows is the description of all the witnesses located near or around the Borden house, at the time the murders occurred. It was important to note that Miss Lucy Collet had been left to stand watch on the porch of Dr. Chagnon's house.[145] The view from Chagnon's house and veranda, would have included the right side of the backyard of the Borden house. This was where anyone could have seen activity going on. This was also crucial to the Borden case. So not only did this first witness not see anyone else, it must be noted most importantly, that Lizzie herself, was not spotted by young Lucy Collet.

Next, according to Porter's *The Fall River Tragedy*, there was a Thomas Bolles washing a carriage in Mrs. Churchill's yard.[146] Mrs. Churchill was of course another neighbor located behind the Borden house. Therefore, anyone passing by on the sidewalk on Second Street would have been spotted, including anyone crossing the front yard, or perhaps a stranger who didn't know the Borden house, such as an unknown person who may have searched the houses for addresses. Someone wandering along the front area as they likely would have been, would also have been in full view from the Churchill's yard. This person would have been noticed. Such a person would have been wielding a fair-sized hatchet as well. Certainly this person would have been seen, and noticed.

As the list of witnesses continued, it may have been realized the increased likelihood of Lizzie's culpability in the murders. All the witnesses, collectively, claimed to have seen no one on the premises, such as a forbidding slovenly, irate stranger, nor did they see Lizzie. As had previously been pointed out, the tumble to the floor of Abby's body would most definitely have been heard by anyone in the house.

Also nearby and in attendance on this sultry hot morning in August, 1892, were three men. These men had been situated, at the time of the murders, directly behind the Borden house, ironically, precisely where one year later in the month of June 1893, a "new-looking" hatchet would be found on the roof of a John Crowe's barn.[147] The hatchet would be discovered by some young boys, on or about day ten of Lizzie Borden's trial by the jury. Crowe's house, which had been close enough to the Borden house, could have feasibly been a good hiding place for the hatchet, by whomever may have used it for the murders. Added to that, Lizzie had been noted building up her muscle strength at the local gymnasium by several witnesses. For this reason, it may have been feasible for Lizzie to have hurled the hatchet up onto the roof once the deeds were done. Perhaps too, this could have happened while police and curious onlookers were in the house, and roaming out front at the same time. Lizzie could well have been in the back, disposing of the hatchet. This may have been at the height of few witnesses. She may easily have tucked the hatchet away somewhere until the people had cleared out of the house, and then gone to the back yard in total darkness and solitude, and thrown the hatchet onto the roof next door. After all, Dr. Bowen volunteered to guard her in her bedroom right after the deeds, having succeeded in keeping the police at bay.

The three men present in the late morning included Patrick McGowan, Joseph Desrosiers and John Denny. The three men were stone cutters. The men were at work just before noon in John Crowe's stone yard, which was "adjoining" and located at the "back of the Borden premises."[148]

So, Lizzie Borden had indeed been seen toning up at the local gymnasium. Whether or not it was loose talk, or simply a casual comment by one of the local ladies, which it apparently was, the observation did indeed lend some credence to the theory that the healthy young woman may easily have had the muscle power to fling the hatchet literally out of sight, right from her stance in the back yard.

Each of the three stone cutters claimed to have been at one of these particular locations in the Crowe's yard. As stated before, the Crowe's yard adjoined the back of the Borden yard.

So the total view, in fact practically the circumference of the Borden yard, was well-watched. The scene was observed by at least five individuals who were posted, respectively, on various sides of the Borden house.

Supposedly too, there was the theory whether concocted or not, that Hyman Lubinsky, an immigrant with an ice cream truck, had also ridden past, right out front of the Borden house on his way toward Mrs. Churchill's house. Hyman testified later, in broken English that he, the only witness to say so, spotted a woman crossing from the barn to the Borden house via the screen door. This could have been a staged testimony, as some thought, simply because he seemed uncertain, and, as would come out later, he saw a woman without a hat. However, a key point became that when Lizzie testified how she'd entered the house and found her dead and bloodied father, that she had "set her hat down" on the way in.[149] There were only two women at the Borden house at the time and Hyman knew Bridget Sullivan by sight. Again, he stated that the woman he saw crossing the yard he did not recognize.

The only side of the house not under civilian surveillance was the right side of the house, which had the Kelly house next to it. So although there was no one seated outside the Kelly house, or anyone in the windows, this proved irrelevant due to the fact that there was no entrance located on the right side of the Borden residence. In other words, any feasible ways into, or out of the house, were located on the other side, the side where people could clearly witness any movements.

Although some followers of the Borden tragedy have stated over the years that there was actually little or no visibility to be had by the witnesses, some positions around the Borden property may have afforded vantage points after all. It was surmised in recent years that the fence, and a wood pile, as high as the fence, would also have prevented

Lizzie from throwing the hatchet onto the neighboring barn. And yet one possibility may have had her do it at night, after having stowed the hatchet away in a travel bag somewhere in the house for safe keeping, right after the murders. If Dr. Bowen had had one with him, he may have secreted the bloodied garments and/or the hatchet until such time that Lizzie could dispose of them.

Next called to the witness stand, according to Porter's *The Fall River Tragedy*, on the tenth day of the trial, was a Mrs. Hannah Reagan. A matron at the Central Police Station where Lizzie was first incarcerated, Mrs. Reagan claimed to have overheard a loud discussion between Emma and Lizzie. Supposedly, Lizzie was heard to have said, "you have given me away, Emma, but I don't care, I won't give in one inch," and then she measured about an inch on her forefinger.[150]

So on the tenth day of the trial, this witness account by Hannah Reagan caused quite a stir. Words such as these; "you have given me away" and "I won't give an inch," especially in conjunction with such a violent set of killings, were certainly begging for various interpretations. Some unnamed individual on the defense team convinced Hannah to recant her story. Later on, when questioned about her story about the sisters and their quarrel, she denied ever having recanted the story at all. In other words, Hannah Reagan stood by her story about overhearing the sisters' quarrel, and in fact she denied ever having recanted the story. She maintained she heard the sisters have a disagreement. Further, she claimed she never told Reverend Buck that the story was not true.

Next in the proceedings, according to Porter's *The Fall River Tragedy*, Eli Bence, a drug clerk at the pharmacy was called. The fact that, at Governor Robinson's objection, Bence's testimony was not to be allowed became a significant fact. It was yet another blow against the State and their case against Lizzie. Because what Eli Bence was hoping to share, was the fact that Lizzie had gone into the drugstore where Bence worked, the very day before the murders and attempted to buy ten cents worth of deadly hydrocyanic acid.[151]

On the eleventh day of the trial, defense attorney Andrew J. Jennings began a lengthy introduction in his opening statement. In fact, Jennings spent a good deal of time personalizing his address, stating how he had known the victims, as well as the accused for many years. In the end, Jennings's insistence on explaining on how well, and how long, he'd known Lizzie may have been to the detriment of the case. He stressed that the relationship between father and daughter was something sacrosanct.[152] There was a lack of authentic details around the relationship of this particular father and daughter. Jennings in fact, could not supply specific examples of the great relationship between the two. What, in essence, constituted a purportedly healthy, normal relationship between father and daughter? Wasn't it essentially conjecture on the part of Jennings?

Next he appealed to the jury about his "human side." He pointed out that just because someone became a lawyer, one did not "cease to be a man."[153] He went on to state how this crime was more brutal than most, and that none, regardless of how they'd "shocked the feelings and staggered the senses" had ever presented a greater "mystery" as to what had truly happened on that blisteringly hot day in August 1892.[154]

Jennings attempted to bring in the human element, both on his own behalf and when considering the murderer. His "defense" could easily have swayed the jury either way. In point of fact, the pendulum could perhaps have swung totally against his reasoning while he attempted to present a stronger case for the defense team, and for Lizzie.

Ultimately, Jennings's method of focusing in on his own humanness, inadvertently called attention to his personal interests in having agreed to be her defense attorney. He may have claimed to have been a foremost character witness for the suspect, but at the same time, as her attorney and due to the preponderance of circumstantial evidence, this may not have worked. His constant insistence about considering her innocence in the matter, due to her church affiliations, and vouching for her, and how he had known her and her father for years, may have eventually grown thin as a tool in his defense argument.

To quote the Defense's exact words which followed, "the brutal character of the wounds is only equaled by the audacity, the time and the pace chosen here...as it would seem to most men, of an insane person or a fiend."[155]

Ironically, Jennings's intention was to avert suspicion away from his wide-eyed thirty-two year old client. He presented a Christian woman, totally incapable of such horrific crimes. Yet, in the minds of the jurors and others, this may have brought to mind that indeed, the crimes were remarkably violent. Words such as "brutal, audacity and pace" are personal words and in a way, indicate a level of emotion tied to the victims. "Brutal" revealed a level of intense dislike, abhorrence, hatred. Numerous accounts of her dislike of her stepmother followed during the course of the trial. In the end, the defense reiterated that her relationship with her father was an appropriate one between a parent and young woman.

These were crimes full of rage. These murders were likely personal. The issues around the Borden house; the early death of Lizzie's mother which left the two girls at the mercy of a controlling Victorian father, the extreme secrecy of the family, the Victorian male mentality about women and girls as part of their property, the numerous locks and keys kept on the mantle, the oddly close relationship between Lizzie and her father, the ring he wore of hers which showed an intimacy of sorts, even the locations of the two girls' bedrooms and how Emma eventually switched with Lizzie and took the smaller room – all of these facts contributed to the incest theory.[156] And such a violation would be a very personal reason for murder.

If the murderer had been a stranger, he or she would have had to wait one and half hours after killing Abby Borden. To what end? Jennings felt the timing was indeed ludicrous or insane. The "pace" was slow and deliberate. Were they to consider the killer as having been a stranger or even a business associate? Because by what logical reasoning would the perpetrator have chosen the middle of the day, on a workday, in a busy downtown area?

As Jennings said, if the murderer was indeed brimming with cunning and malice of forethought, why would he have performed such a premeditated act at such an inopportune time of day?

The ferocity of the crimes indicated that emotions ran very deep, perhaps too deeply for the good people of Fall River 1892 to comprehend. This was a society which referred to the woman's menstrual cycle as having "fleas" according to Martins/Binette's *Parallel Lives*. In fact, the entire discussion around the pinpoint of blood which had been found on her petticoat was disguised in the proper lingua franca of the day.[157] Even the "blood expert" they called to the stand during the trial, never definitively responded to the defense's questions in the affirmative as to the origin of the blood spot. This was so, despite the fact that Jennings led the expert witness back to his hypothesis of menstrual blood several times.

In the end, according to Martins/Binette's *Parallel Lives*, the argument around the spot of blood was often dismissed as menstrual blood.[158] Nothing else, in all the decades since, has been considered. In the end, the argument was simply abandoned due perhaps to the exceeding embarrassment of the female thirty-two –year-old defendant, an unmarried "spinster."

Even looking back with contemporary hindsight, the timing and the magnitude of the crimes did not reflect the movements of a disgruntled businessman. The murderer did not just happen by the Borden house at midday and become so emotionally distraught that he brutally attacked Andrew Borden, much less, Borden's wife, Abby. Certainly, had the perpetrator been calculating, he could have accosted Andrew Borden downtown much more easily, rather than in his home. Also, if that supposed stranger, who was to provide reasonable doubt to the jury, had truly been intent upon murdering Andrew Borden for dubious business dealings, he would have had no reason to murder Abby Borden. Logically, if this perpetrator had been out to target Andrew, he certainly would have wanted Andrew to perhaps have been aware that he had gone after his wife. It was likely that such a person would have wanted his deadly act to have been realized by Andrew, rather than simply attacking Andrew out right, without any satisfaction for his act of vengeance. So for what purpose would a stranger or business associate have had for murdering Abby Borden? A stranger would not have had one, per se. Murdering Abby Borden was most likely, personal.

Chapter Nine

"Why don't you let me speak to that problem?" Dr. Warburton said, swaggering over to the two women.

"You're not part of the conversation," Sadie commented simply. "Only reason I'm here is because of some gracious benefactors who said I needed help. Namely, my former fiancé's family. People can't survive these times, much less a woman on her own. Everything for the poorer classes costs more somehow. How does that make sense?"

The doctor crossed his arms over his chest. The white of his coat was blinding from repeated bleach treatments. Colette envisioned the stains; sanguine? What exactly would a doctor get on his coat dealing with patients? Blood? Vomit? She could only imagine. The profession was challenging. Colette didn't sympathize with him right now. What she heard coming from Sadie's mouth were the words from textbooks, an avalanche of books she'd read over the years about the struggles of women before the twentieth century, and for decades after for that matter.

Taking a seat in the makeshift kitchen, she sat down at a long wooden table. Along the wall in a wooden pantry there were numerous pots, a heavy kettle on the stove and a supply of wood nearby. On the table there brooded an oversized and daunting cookbook with the title "Home and Hearth, Everything the Woman of the House Must Know." She flipped the book open, reading some of the laborious ingredients; lard, mutton, treacle, candied pineapple, currants, and allspice. Then she read something in the instructions about putting "forcemeat into the craws of pigeons" and she slammed the book shut. As she watched Sadie methodically pacing and Isabelle trying to look busy by a dining room table she was supposed to set properly with china, clear, and set again, she decided to mess with the Victorian ingredients just for grins. Grabbing a large tin of flour, she started dumping whatever was at hand into a large bowl.

Reaching across the highly polished table, she started playing around with the ingredients to make bread. While Warburton and the other henchmen studied Isabelle and Sadie, Colette purposely dumped all the ingredients together into a baking dish; flour, water and a brick of lard or butter, she couldn't tell, and didn't care. The art of cooking was never a passion for her. In actual fact, making toast was a challenge.

Rummaging from one heavy wooden cabinet to the next, she opened one, withdrew several cans and started dumping kidney beans in, and topped it all off with several hearty handfuls of pepper. She sneezed as she leaned over and shoved it all in the oven.

Seated at the table again, she thought about all she knew about the Lizzie Borden case. Among other purported theories there was the suspected "boyfriend," which she knew was likely a myth. He was supposed to have been from a wealthy family. If she recalled correctly, the boyfriend idea had been the story made up to sell papers by a slightly corrupt reporter. Then there was Lizzie's "half-brother" – a young man also with the last name Borden, who lived on the outskirts of town and was known to talk to his "pet" hatchet, even years after the murders.

Rising, she spent several minutes figuring out that the wood was not for the oven, but rather the coal was to be used. After starting the fire in the ancient apparatus, which to her was a work of art in itself, she leaned back against the counter, arms folded over her chest. Another theory came to mind which held that Bridget Sullivan and Lizzie had been lovers and that Abby Borden walked in on them in bed together. Shaking her head, Colette grimaced to herself, realizing that too had not been the case.

Pacing the kitchen, she paused. Having seen Lizzie being led to a carriage a day or so before, she had gotten a firsthand look at the acquitted "murderess." Still, could she make a judgment based upon that fleeting glance? All she saw were the wisps of curls around the young woman's face, shielded under a red hat, and of course she wore a high-necked blouse even in the one hundred degree heat. A far-reaching mythology seemed to have caught fire around Lizzie.

Another speculation stated that older sister Emma had done the killings, and that Lizzie was protecting her. Then there was talk about a supposed vagrant, and even a traveling salesman, who had been seen wandering the area of the Borden house, covered in blood, who had eventually boarded a train.

Finally, she sat back on the camel-back sofa. She laughed to herself, and when Dr. Warburton gave her a sharp glance, she took a deep breath to stop her snickering. Certainly it was inappropriate here in the asylum practice kitchen. Still, she grinned again, picturing a door-to-door corset salesman happening by on the day of the murders, knocking on the door while someone held a hatchet high over her head just inside the confines of the house, right there on the right hand side in the sitting room. What an unlucky sales call that would have been.

"Do you want to end up like Miss Lizzie Borden?"

A man's voice cut through Colette's reverie. The younger of the two doctors held Sadie squarely by the shoulders and was shaking her. All at once, he drew back his hand and slapped her hard across the face. Sadie stood there, defiantly, looking at him while she lifted her pale hand to her cheek.

Colette stepped up and yanked the doctor back by his coat sleeve.

"What are you doing?" she demanded.

And with that, the other doctor clutched Colette by the upper arm, and dug his fingers into her flesh.

"Harder work and more humility. That's what you women need," he said, his voice a fierce monotone. "Get back to your chores."

The men walked out then, not waiting for a response. At the sound of the door slamming, Colette heard double, then triple locks being turned. Wasn't that what she'd read psychiatric doctors in the late nineteenth century told mental patients? Work harder.

Psychiatrists in the late nineteenth century, likely also told women who were victims of incest, that they needed to focus, and stay on task while confined to asylums. So for the sexual crimes of their fathers, or uncles, or brothers, the victims were repeatedly victimized.

Sadie sat on the floor again, her white skirt and ruffled petticoat pulled up around her. Her stare was vacant, her mouth set.

Colette sat in a dark wooden chair and watched the oven, mentally trying to will it to bake something. So, as the toddler Lizzie grew, Colette thought, from the age of two, until the age of thirty-two, when the murders were committed, perhaps Lizzie had lost faith in her step-mother as being any sort of protector from her father's abuse. It was unlikely that there had been much intimacy between the parents, perhaps having been more a marriage of convenience. It may have been Andrew's doing, to marry for practicality and, as was common in the nineteenth century, as an attempt to provide a mother for his two young daughters as a result of a mother's untimely death.

Colette watched smoke pour out from the old oven. Leaning over, she pulled the charcoal-edged bread out of the oven, thinking to herself, how could it have been, as another theory posited, that it was simply a businessman? In fact, over the years, some who'd studied the murders, had discussed the possibility of Lizzie having been in a fugue state, whereby she may have dissociated during the committing of the crimes.

Colette glanced at Sadie rocking herself with her legs pulled to her chest. Sadie cried softly, like a moan, her arms wrapped around her knees.

Sadie stood up slowly and positioned herself mere inches away from Colette's face. Colette returned the gaze without averting her eyes.

"What's going on Sadie?"

"Just watching you. You're a very interesting woman, Miss Colette."

Colette nodded and tried to smile. For as much as she felt like an outcast back in Valley Stream in 2011, she had to laugh at how this asylum, and Sadie and Isabelle seemed to understand her totally.

"Do the doctors here always treat you that way?"

"What way?"

"Order you around."

Sadie tilted her head, watching Colette intently. Her face was opaque.

"Why do the doctors act the way they do?"

"Because I'm a woman. Because I did not measure up to my fiancé's family's standards. I know Miss Lizzie Borden," she murmured. "I know her from our church group. She teaches Sunday school, you know. So do I." She paused. "So, did I."

"I'd heard that, somewhere."

Colette decided not to relate how she knew that fact, among others, despite her being new in town.

"Percy's family wanted me to spend more time with Lizzie," Sadie went on. "More time with the church activities. I was more interested in the meetings for women."

"The suffrage meetings?"

Sadie nodded.

"Isabelle got me going to them. Of course our Suffrage President now is Cady Stanton. But Isabelle started a local chapter of a group she called the Minds of Women. You know, we talked politics, and wanting a voice as women, and the right to vote like men and pursue vocations.

She stopped and studied Colette. "So I ended up here," she added.

Soon the sounds of the locks turning brought them away from their kitchen chores, and the women wandered to the door. Isabelle wiped down a stove one last time and dumped a dripping mop into a bucket of water which was pungent with cleanser.

Sadie stood directly behind Colette, her head bowed. When they reached the door, she stopped and clutched the sleeve of Colette's nightgown. "He made me believe him," she said. "He made me believe in his goodness. In the goodness of all men. You see, that had been taken away from me."

Exiting the kitchen, Colette started the trek down the darkened hallway following a stiffly moving asylum aid. Sounds of a skirmish behind her and Sadie had shoved a side door open and had scampered out onto the vast green of the back lawn. The patients waited until Colette overheard Sadie's frenzied laughter, which immediately morphed into sobs. Within minutes, Sadie was in line again.

"And my biggest crime?" she blurted.

Colette turned to her.

"I don't know how to cook." She smiled. "Or perhaps I do, but I won't do it."

Colette grinned at this.

As Colette and Sadie trudged behind the asylum attendant, Colette thought about the Bordens. The hallway had a damp, abandoned scent about it. The place emanated at once neglect and regimentation. Lizzie and her sister Emma were basically kept as prisoners at the mercy of social mores and at the hands of their father. Emma, ten years older than Lizzie, was considered a spinster, as was Lizzie. Considering the loss of his wife when Lizzie was only two years old, Andrew Borden may have unfortunately, and wrongly, turned to one or both of his daughters as a replacement for intimacy.

Finally, they climbed to the attic. The attendant waited only a moment then left them in dispiriting darkness.

Minutes later, the two women sat in Sadie's room. Colette imagined someone might catch her out of her room, but she didn't care.

Let them come after her for deranged behavior or for being out of her room. Of course Sadie had been relegated to the attic for her antics; the coldest and smallest room of them all.

Looking to a damp space next to the door, there were prayers scrawled on the walls in an uneven hand, and a Bible on Sadie's bedside table. She stared at the floor. In jagged strokes, there were written the words, "Yea, though I walk through the shadow of the valley of death, I will fear no evil..."

"Looks like you've been trying to find your faith," Colette commented. "Sorry we're no longer roommates."

"They wash them off. But they can't hide the scratches, or some of the blood stains along the floorboards. I try the Bible passages now and then," she said, grinning. "I prefer these, though." She leaned forward and pulled prints and paintings out from under the bed. They were erotic in nature – extremely so. Many nudes, and men and women caressing. The breasts and flesh of the women looked extremely lifelike, done in oil pastels. The men too, were realistically drawn, by someone clearly familiar with the male body.

"These are incredible," Colette murmured, nodding as she sifted through them slowly.

"I did them."

"Really?"

"You know something else?" she bit her lip. "I know Miss Lizzie had her fleas this past week. Do not ask me how I know. Trust me, I know. But she doesn't suffer from the woman's mania related to the fleas. I know that much too." Sadie sat back, hands in her lap. She looked very pleased with herself.

There went any Pre-Menstrual Syndrome theory some scholar may have devised in recent decades, Colette mused. Hadn't there been a court case in England where a woman was acquitted of murder due to having had her menstrual cycle?

"If you must know," Sadie went on. "As I said, I am in the same church group as she. Things are not as private as they always seem."

Colette settled into a spindly chair with threadbare needlepoint cushion.

"What do you think happened?" she asked.

"To the Bordens, you mean?"

"Yes."

"Well," Sadie began, gazing at the far wall, they were executed by someone who knew them. That's my opinion. By someone very angry."

Colette seemed to assimilate that anger now. She knew what would drive someone to such acts. In her mind's eye, she saw her mother lying in bed, the black and white television droning, her pale green eyes gazing through it. Colette would stand in the doorway of her mother Ursula's bedroom, watching her, absorbing her quiet rage, her mother's depression turned against herself. It was a silent and seething aggression. Colette recalled growing up, desperately wanting to be close to her mother, and the enigma around her mother's acute sadness. Whispers of sexual abuse perpetrated against Ursula as a child during the Great Depression comprised the wallpaper of Colette's childhood. The anger Ursula had carried inside of her mimicked Lizzie's years of repression, likely abuse and eventual deadly acts of retribution. In Colette's way of thinking however, Ursula's death from cancer at age fifty-one, felt to her, like suicide.

"Did Lizzie ever talk about her parents to you?"

"Did she ever *talk* about her parents?" Sadie studied Colette, her eyes narrowed. "Sadly no. Not to me, anyway. If she had, it might have saved her, and they'd still be alive. People just don't talk about their intimate lives."

"Sadie?"

Sadie folded her hands in her lap, as if to signify her acquiescence.

"Lizzie is going to stand trial, you know," Colette commented.

"You think an accusation will lead to court? For a woman like her?" She rose very slowly, her eyes wide, and paced. Her white petticoat swept the hardwood floor. "Don't you see," she said, "it's happening everywhere. Edward Sewell's goal was to do away with the Isabelle's mother, Madeline. He might have driven her to suicide. Now Isabelle. She wants so much more for her life. Isabelle is an escape artist – Isabelle needs freedom; to sing, to dance, to love."

At once Sadie's stare was blank as she fingered the lace of her nightcoat she'd put on over her perfunctory asylum gown. They made all the women wear them. Taupe in color, their purpose was to reinforce the utilitarian ordered life. Her hand blanched white as she touched lace which sprouted from her cuffs. Gazing at nothing in the candlelight, she braided her long brown hair. There was a fire about her, an air aloft, a spark one often didn't see in the old black and white still photographs from the nineteenth century. A requirement for posing for photographs demanded a serious expression. The pose itself often necessitated the subjects remain perfectly still for minutes on end, in order to complete the shot. No, here with Sadie, there was a tumultuous omniscience about her eyes. Her long gazes into nothing, like trances, implied years of imposed reticence.

Colette stepped to the window and looked out. She'd always had an extraordinary, almost metaphysical connection to antiques. Even as a child, she'd insist that her father pull over to the side of the road, on the old two-lane highways traveling between Illinois and Wisconsin, and beg him to take her into yet another Dutch-Colonial Style barn that often sported some huge "ANTIQUES" sign painted across it. Then she would stand there, in the midst of the dank concrete floor and hay, the smell of dust and the passage of years like perfume to her, holding a one–hundred-year-old object in her hand; a small toolbox, a photograph, a piece of costume jewelry, a doll. There had been an intangible connection, even then.

She turned to check on Sadie's reverie. Her young friend still swam in her thoughts. Looking back to the resplendent stars, they looked serene spilled as they were across the black heavens like talcum. Colette wondered; could this obsession with the past she had, have been what precipitated, and somehow orchestrated the time/ space continuum, preternatural travel between now and the past? What would a scientist call it?

She looked back at Sadie again. Colette suspected the young woman had a depressive disorder, or something else easily treatable. Perhaps just a hormonal imbalance. Certainly, it could be any of those things in the nineteenth century? Apparently, whatever it was, it had been enough to get someone locked up, perhaps locked up for years, and the key thrown away.

Suddenly, Sadie stood up and started twirling about the room, her lacy jacket dragging on the cement floor. She pranced to the window, leaned over, pressing her face to the wavy glass. She peered through the bars. When she turned around, she was biting the fingertip of her forefinger. The sway of her nightgown bent the flame of the candle in several directions, the refractions of light coming and going with each bit of breeze. There was even a scent about her, something fervent, like a combination of lavender and perspiration.

The aromas of the room filled her up, the wood scent candle burning, the waxy floors and the aged walls and ceiling. Even the cobwebs in the corners held sway over her. That's when she saw the blood. A thin line trickled down Sadie's finger, the side of her forefinger where she had been nervously gnawing.

"Sadie. You have to sit down," Colette said, standing up very slowly.

She heard movement in the hallways. A scuffling of shoes on the hardwood floor, and a series of screeches filled up the place. Sadie continued to chew and had, in fact, moved on to the next finger. Colette went to her and tried to pull the younger woman's hand away from her mouth. Sadie flinched. Her eyes were dark and she let out a snarl.

The screaming came closer now. Colette had checked out the floor when they brought her in. There were no more than four rooms in this wing. Its pitch was a high, but familiar and melodious voice.

"They've brought her back," Sadie said, her voice cracking, and then breaking into hysterical sobs. "She keeps breaking out." She held her hand to her face. It trembled. All at once, she broke into maniacal laughter.

"It's Isabelle," Colette whispered.

Chapter Nine (A)

The Historical Facts

Soon after his exploration of the intensity of the murders, defense Attorney Jennings moved in another direction. He thought it crucial that everyone in the jury should be clear regarding the motives for murder. It appeared that his intention was to show, that should the defense have proven there was indeed a motive to have killed Abby, had it been jealousy or distrust, that an equal amount of hatred could not have propelled her into having killed her father.[159] In Jennings's words, "that the defendant lived quietly with her father," and that the relations between them were those that exist ordinarily between parent and child, that such a serene relationship could not have resulted in her committing such a "wicked, wicked act."[160]

If Jennings's idea was to ascertain, and prove, that only one perpetrator committed the murders, then the defense strategy may have backfired on him. Because clearly, who else in all of Fall River, Massachusetts would have had so much dislike for Abby Borden that it turned to murderous rage? If someone had a grievance against her, and her alone, why did they go after Andrew Borden as well?

Quite simply too, the vice versa was true. If a business associate had possessed such anger at Andrew Borden, what would have possessed him to exact so much violence, upon Abby? Surely there would have been no reason for anyone to hold such a grudge against both persons?

No one, except for Lizzie Borden. If one person committed both crimes, then Jennings only furthered suspicions against Lizzie. Lizzie was indeed the one person in Fall River who would have detested both persons to such a "wicked, wicked" degree.

Some may have suspected William Borden, the half-brother and illegitimate son, who came up as a suspect for a brief time. In this instance that would have partially explained some of the wrath against Andrew Borden. At the very worst however, perhaps he was a negligent stingy absentee father to William. Still, nothing could have explained why William would attack Abby Borden. What reason would an illegitimate son have had to abhor the step-mother? She was faring no better living in the house with Andrew Borden, under the dark auspices, and disdain emanating from the two sisters.

Nevertheless, Attorney for the Defense Andrew Jennings, continued on with his speech on this, the eleventh day of the trial. The prosecution's case, he reiterated, was based entirely upon circumstantial evidence. He even pointed out that there was not "a spot of blood." Of course we recall that in actuality, there was a simple spot of blood, and it was on her skirt.[161] He continued to point out that with such circumstantial evidence, any semblance of guilt would have been based entirely upon inference. He asked whether or not the state had absolute proof? Proof that no one else could have committed the crime? At no time did any of the witnesses, or any of the key people situated around the house, such as Lucy Collet on the Chagnon's porch, the man across the street by the Churchill's, nor any of the men near John Crowe's barn, confirm that they saw anyone suspicious.[162]

Jennings went on to say there was no direct evidence which would prove, beyond a reasonable doubt, that Lizzie was definitively guilty.

Ironically he described how Lizzie "lived quietly with her father,"[163] and that they possessed the relations that ordinarily exist between "parent and daughter."[164] That this may have been a loaded statement, as well as simply a falsehood, would not have been considered. Unless Jennings had lived with the Bordens, what proof did he have that they had ordinary family relations?

Interestingly, his likening the series of events around the murders to that of a chain, in some ways, defeated the purpose of his defense. Because if one followed this chain of events theory, which was rooted in the case against Lizzie as being a sequence of circumstantial occurrences, it conversely may have aided the prosecution's case against her.

Jennings re-established the Christian background of Lizzie, and elaborated upon her highly moral, and typical Victorian upbringing. But were they, the jury, and Jennings, and perhaps even the proper folks of Fall River, to have explored her life with their reading bifocals, to see the fine print that was the undercurrent of the Borden house, a real story, buried beneath the apparent story, may have emerged.

Ironically, as cited in an article about the Women's Temperance Christian Union by Denise Noe, the WCTU initially began by staunchly defending Lizzie's innocence around the double parricide.[165] In fact, the women's group held their meetings before the trial in a space they rented located in one of Andrew Borden's buildings. Lizzie too, was an active member of the WCTU, which was headquartered in Evanston, Illinois.[166]

Ironically however, the group abandoned her after the trial and no longer supported her. Lizzie later evicted them out of their space in her father's buildings.[167]

The emotional climate of Lizzie's life leading into August of 1892 was one which, according to witnesses and people close to the Borden sisters, revealed a deeper pain restricted to within the walls of the overly-locked and double-bolted home of Andrew Borden. So in essence, those exuberant defense speeches delivered by Attorney

Jennings, where he implored the jury that they must prove guilt beyond a reasonable doubt may have only furthered the confusion as far as Lizzie's innocence. Instead, he created a sense of dichotomy, revealing a domestic scene that was less a prime Victorian genteel existence and more so a homestead fraught with painfully mixed messages and inexplicable nuances between a parent and children, between stepmother and daughters.

To name a few, the numerous door locks stood out glaringly. In this very divided house, due supposedly to a burglary of Abby's jewelry a year or so before, all the doors were fitted with locks. Oddly, as was pointed out in Porter's *Fall River Tragedy*, the key to Mr. Borden's room was kept on the mantle in the sitting room, the very room where he was murdered.[168] Perhaps this was indication of a game of control on the part of Andrew Borden.

The WCTU existed as a fickle relationship between the temperance organization and Lizzie. Typically the WCTU may have been witness to numerous atrocities which befell countless women and children at the hands of drunken fathers, including husbands and even those drunks who utilized the pre-adolescent prostitutes of the streets. Because indeed, according to Martin/Binette's *Parallel Lives*, there were active brothels in the town of Fall River.[169] Victorian prostitution, which oftentimes included children, was a rampant problem. There was always the chance that some members may have had suspicions about what went on in the Borden house. Perhaps too, this explained why Lizzie had been so active in the WCTU.

There were many concepts around the idea of "before" and "after" which needed to be studied. In large, expansive strokes, one may review the "circumstantial evidence" Jennings had likened to a chain. Because, in the years leading up to the murders, Lizzie had been involved in church activities. This much was true. Also well known, Lizzie had a solid relationship with Dr. Bowen. The good doctor, of course, lived just across the street. At some point, the relationship had been observed and studied by townsfolk, just as townsfolk were wont to do.

If one traced Dr. Bowen's whereabouts the day of the murders, his movements revealed concerns about someone at the heart of his decisions. Specifically, it may have been Lizzie herself. Several logistical movements and occurrences proved significant with regards to Dr. Bowen. First of all, at the discovery of the bodies by Lizzie, she sent Bridget in search of none other than Dr. Bowen.[170]

Dr. Bowen could have used his clout as a physician to keep the police at bay, while he perhaps helped Lizzie in any number of ways. One hypothesis may have included secretly helping Lizzie by stashing evidence such as bloodied clothes, secreted away inside his doctor bag in such a way that he would indeed be free to come and go from the Borden house without any interference from the police. Also, wouldn't it be more likely that someone familiar with the house, someone who would know how, and where, to be rid of such evidence, would have more feasibly gotten rid of such items? Something, such as bloody clothes or a bloody hatchet, could easily have been tossed out a back second story window amidst all the comings and goings. The back yard, such as the well, may have served as a way to hide away items such as the clothes, like the blue dress for instance. Eventually, the dress was destroyed on the stove over a kitchen fire.[171]

On some level the obvious nature of this logic must have occurred to the men seated on the jury. Likely too, that the morally-charged, late-Victorian-men of the jury, were pumped up by the gruesome nature of the murders. In a very real sense, they persisted in a state of denial that a woman, a chaste Christian woman created by the male-dominated society without moral blemish, would do such a thing. Perhaps this viewpoint was on a subconscious level and yet, to that point, they acquitted Lizzie Borden.

Although the defense had the testimony of Hyman Lubinsky, the immigrant carriage driver, his own statement actually cancelled the positive impact on Lizzie's behalf. Lubinsky stated that the woman he saw was definitely not wearing a hat.[172] In actuality, Lizzie mentioned in her testimony that she took off her hat upon re-entering the house from the barn.[173] Therefore, the barn story only created more questions.

Regarding again Defense Attorney Jennings, he reiterated how many individuals trampled through the barn after the murders. Despite this fact, this still would not explain the lack of footprints around the toolbox, located on the second floor of the barn where Lizzie was apparently looking for fishing sinkers.

These points were further examples of when Jennings's arguments were not only irrelevant, but worked against the defense's case. His logic was somewhat circular. It was as if the case was being churned around in his mind with no end and no beginning. It was, in essence, a senseless argument. Officer Medley did not see any footprints in the areas of the barn where Lizzie claimed to have been rummaging around either. The toolbox was located on the second floor of the barn. So whether or not the crime scene had been contaminated by other investigators and policeman later on would not have been relevant. The impact of there having been "lack of footprints" after the time that Lizzie claimed to have been up there was indeed, relevant. In that sense therefore, Jennings' argument was moot.

The next point of his argument was also immaterial, if one considered the reasoning of the action taken by Lizzie. The action had to do with Lizzie burning the dress, which she had claimed had paint on it. This was witnessed by Alice Russell as well as Emma. The question remained however, as to whether or not Lizzie's calico dress was indeed the one which had been ruined by paint stains. The fact that it was ruined only several weeks after it was made was not exactly the issue. Lizzie's choice of timing was atrociously poor. What sense did it make for Lizzie to have burned the dress right there on the stove? This was at the same time that numerous policemen were about, as well as other witnesses. Why did she take such action within days of the murders? Surely, she must have realized how suspicious this action would appear?

Soon Jennings called one witness after another for the defense. Several witnesses mentioned hearing about a stabbing or attack as the reason they'd come to be at the Borden house. Again, it was interesting that one reporter, John J. Manning, described how they actually tried the cellar door and found it was locked. Now these were witnesses for the defense and yet again, having found the door locked, it seemed to affirm the fact that no one, including a *stranger* had gone in or out via the cellar door.[174]

Soon after this, another witness for the defense was called; a Mrs. Sadie R. Holmes. Lizzie had known the defense witness through their mutual affiliation with the Central Congregational Church. Mrs. Holmes stated that she'd arrived at the Borden house around 1:00 pm on the day of the murders.[175] Unfortunately for anyone wishing to have gathered certifiable evidence, numerous people showed up and continued to traipse throughout the house.

This perhaps worked well for the defense team, especially in relation to Lizzie having spent any time in the barn. What was significant about this witness, Mrs. Sadie Holmes, was that she was summoned by Lizzie in particular, to join the suspect in her bedroom.[176] It was not revealed what was spoken about. It was key that Mrs. Holmes mentioned, in her exact words; "I think Dr. Bowen came up a few minutes after, and before Officer Fleet came."[177] Here she was referring to the time she arrived at the house. Lizzie had requested her to come up to her room. At this juncture, Sadie Holmes indicated that not only did they not allow Officer Fleet in the bedroom, but added that in fact, they "locked the door because there were so many men about that we didn't want them to come in the room."[178]

Emma Borden was called and went to great lengths to describe the "old dress," also known as the blue cord dress, which was purported to have had paint stains on it. Emma described it as "very dirty, badly faded"[179] and that she'd not worn it for "some time."[180] Emma went on to say that the dress was big on Lizzie, and that it was "very long."[181] She described it as, "an inch and half longer than her pink wrapper."[182] She also insisted that she could not have had any other dress over this big, oversized dress with the paint on it because the blue cord dress was too big to allow for another dress to be worn over it.[183]

Another comment made by Emma was key with regards to the suspicious blue cord dress. Emma referred to the dress, asking Lizzie why she hadn't "destroyed that old dress yet;" and "why don't you do so?"[184] Emma went on to describe how the dress was old and faded. She reiterated too, that it was far too long to have been worn with the pink wrapper over it.

What was important to note was that Emma made great efforts to reinforce to Jennings and the jury that the dress was exceedingly old and worn out, and that she'd not seen Lizzie wear it in a long time. If there had been blood on the dress that had been burned, the pink wrapper would not have fit over it, if indeed Lizzie had put on the wrapper to hide blood stains.

However, one may have surmised quite easily, that Lizzie could have taken the dress off and stashed it. Emma's words worked against her in a way; because if the pink wrapper indeed did not fit over the blue cord dress, and she was seen wearing the pink wrapper, that meant perhaps that she'd stashed the bloodied dress away. Dr. Bowen's doctor bag would have sufficed or even a small travel bag. Hypothetically then she may have thrown on a very similar blue dress, then worked the pink wrapper over it. This may have thrown off suspicion from anyone who had actually seen her earlier in the day. Such witnesses may have included Bridget Sullivan, Uncle Morse and any neighbor. Having put on the pink wrapper may simply have been her way to detract attention, and cloud any specific memories of the oversized blue cord dress that she had actually been wearing. The pink wrapper may have served the purpose of clouding the recall of witnesses just enough, to the degree necessary to create doubt in the jury's minds as to why the dress had been burned.

Who better, after all, than her own sister to reiterate that she'd seen the dress hanging in the upstairs hall closet with all the other dresses?[185]

Emma immediately went on to deny that there had ever been an argument at the Taunton Jail, whereby Lizzie had said something to Emma about having "given Lizzie away."[186] If the conversation had indeed taken place, which it very well may have, Lizzie may have been referring to Alice Russell having pointed out the poor timing of burning a dress, especially since the police had questioned her and Emma extensively about what dress Lizzie had been wearing.

Interestingly, the next witness Defense Attorney Jennings called was Mrs. Sadie Raymond, the dressmaker. This fact was revealed in Porter's *The Fall River Tragedy*.[187] Porter, a journalist, presented all these details in a very factual way. Why would Jennings have called upon the seamstress?

Chapter Ten

"It was too much," Isabelle repeated, over and over. "They sent me back to him. He uses me, against my will. It is better to be here, violated by strangers." There followed sounds of doors slamming and locks turning when her words started again, Colette sensed Isabelle now leaned flush against the wall which divided the two rooms.

Colette could hear her clearly. Isabelle's voice was mournful and tragic. She was determined to be heard. It seemed Isabelle preferred the asylum to her father's house. She continued to escape the mansion and meander her way back to Perfect Pines. Luckily for her, they were only a few miles apart.

Sadie's room grew hotter, or seemed smaller all at once. There were no fans and they kept all the windows closed and locked.

"I had to get rid of it," Isabelle said in a forced whisper. "I threw myself down the stairs."

"Let us help you."

"Leave me alone! It was HIS baby."

Colette felt a sickness inside. The Victorian woman's abortion. God willing it had not been the acidic burning of pennyroyal, another tragic method often used by nineteenth century women out of desperation. Isabelle had aborted her baby. She'd been impregnated by her father.

"Go ahead!" she said. "Lock me up."

Isabelle's voice trailed off. Sounds of muffled sobs reached them. Sadie had grown manic in her pacing and now her fingertips were bleeding. Sweat rolled down her cheeks. In the space of Sadie's small room, Isabelle's words had painful resonance.

Colette stood up. She walked to the wash basin, grabbed a small towel from the table. Walking back to Sadie, she leaned over, gently wiping the younger woman's hands clean.

"They said I was evil for wanting the love of my fiancé," Sadie said. "Because I gave myself to him."

As she sat there on the bed, her nightgown slipped off one of her shoulders. Although unruly and wild, her dark hair framed her face like a three-dimensional daguerreotype.

"The temptations of life can really take over," Colette said.

Sadie's face was a bit more lucid now. They had lit a small candle because "lights out" was just past eight pm. A shadow of someone walking past their door swept along the bottom, inches above the floor. Colette put her hands over the flame to hide it from whoever passed by.

"I'm out of Laudanum," Sadie murmured.

"I struggle with nightmares of relapse," Colette began. Her thoughts wanted a voice. She recalled in recent years, the scourge and pit of loneliness that would come over her. Despite years of sobriety, driving along the silent snowy streets of Valley Stream, somehow the snow, and the dark would converge and transport her back to the loveless years of high school, and then into the latter part of college, when alcohol turned her world inside out and made simply functioning barely tolerable.

These excursions in Colette's mind, into the dark depths of futility, often proved unwise for her. Highly dangerous. Dark thoughts often led alcoholics back to drinking. Colette continued to mentally extricate herself from plummeting into the occasional bleak memories which would take over with an insidious silence.

Sadie watched her, fixedly.

"I am an alcoholic," Colette admitted. "A recovering alcoholic. Thoughts of drinking alcohol come to me in my sleep, like harbingers of disaster. Sometimes I wake up with a start, terrified I've actually had a drink. In the dreams, I've left my children at the edge of a cliff while I am off in some bar dancing on a table-top, drunk, unaware of where I am. Sometimes I end up in bed with a strange man. Or I dream about seeing lovers from my past, or seeing my mother alive again. All these emotions are like daggers. I dream that I wake up from a night of debauchery. And then I truly believe I have relapsed after over twenty years without a drink."

Sadie rubbed her forehead temples briefly and closed her eyes. She touched the lacy bodice of her dress with one pale hand. Her eyes filled with tears. When she spoke, she was barely audible. A few strands of her dark hair framed her delicate jawline. "I too drink to forget my needs. My needs, as a living, breathing woman. Which are evil, I guess, because they're passionate and intimate. We women are not supposed to have such needs, or to ever desire the company of men. Laudanum helps me push away those feelings of worthlessness."

Colette nodded. Too many times, twenty-five years before, after an all-night drunk, she had rolled off the bed in the morning to find herself wearing the same clothes from the previous night except they were now on backwards or inside out. Her last recollection of that night may have been drinking a beer bong amidst the cheers of a party. Colette would have had no recollection of how she'd gotten home afterward, or with whom. Often she'd not even know what had happened to whatever man she'd been with. She even recalled trudging outside to her mother's driveway on a sweltering summer morning, hazy with regret and degradation, to check the Chevy Chevette for blood stains on the front bumper. That would be her only means of knowing if she accidently had killed someone with the car. Added to her alcoholism, was her fight with obsessive-compulsive disorder. This menacing mental disorder made her hazy morning after checks for her belongimgs, her underwear and the gas mileage on the car, that much more devastating. She was rarely without consequences for her drunken transgressions.

"My fiancé Percy always gave me laudanum. He said it would open my eyes to new vistas. He said I would see life more clearly. It only made me not recognize myself. And then there was his curse. Percy liked his whiskey. I told him it would be his ruin, which only made him angrier. He has been in several brawls and has gotten into trouble with the law. In fact he killed a man accidentally, while drunk. Of course his family has money. They got him freed. It confounds me why he drinks. Then I started too. And soon it became impossible to stop. Once I have one drink, I always want another, until the nights often don't end well. But his family, they have so many connections. He has never paid for any of his crimes. I, on the other hand, have paid handsomely for being a woman with a taste for alcohol. For being passionate and for having needs that have thus far, have been reserved only for men. For one man. But I know I am not crazy. I'm ardent in sharing love with the one man I love. And for that I'm ostracized." She bowed her head. "He no longer defends me. Once I became sexually satisfying to him he said I was no more than a prostitute. Still, it is not as bad as Isabelle's plight."

"Where does Isabelle's father keep her? In the basement?"

She nodded. "Mostly. Or he puts her to work. Excessive housework like washing the walls. Dusting every book in his study one at a time. Serving drinks to his men cronies like a maid."

"The only way I relate," Colette began, "is to the anger. My dad took off when I was eleven."

Sadie looked quizzical. "Your father left your mother to tend to domestic chores and handle the servants and children alone?"

Colette smiled. "In a way," she said, nodding.

The door handle dropped open suddenly as the knob turned. Colette sat back instinctively and put up her hand up to shield Sadie.

"It's just her," Sadie whispered.

Instantly, Isabelle slipped into the room. Her eyes were bright in the semi-darkness. The front of her taupe asylum nightgown was wet with sweat. The candle flickered. Her outline was like some charcoal drawing.

"How did you do that?" Colette asked.

Isabelle laughed. Sadie sat up straight. "Did you bring any tonic?"

"I did. But Sadie," she said, eying her severely, "it has to stop."

"It helps me. It takes away the rough edges. It's all I have." Her voice was angry. "How the hell else do I forget Dr. Warburton's cozy visits?"

Isabelle's eyes were wild.

"It's not just Warburton." Sadie said. "You don't know what the emptiness feels like inside. Isabelle, if you can believe this? Percy's family has found my fiancé an acceptable woman. Dr. Warburton told me. Takes only two signatures to get a woman locked up in this place. We all know that. But did you know it takes eight signatures to get out of here? I will never see him again. They have found him a fine woman. A woman from well-heeled society. Her father is a steel baron."

Isabelle's face was unmoved. She swept into the room. Her nightgown just cleared the door as it creaked closed behind her. She fumbled expertly with the lock, pushed with her hand at an angle, and opened the window. Then she touched the bars, running her hand up and down the metal. She leaned over and looked out. Turning back to Colette and Sadie, Isabelle reached into the deep recesses of her layers of skirts she'd pulled on under her nightgown, and withdrew a small silver flask. She handed it to Sadie.

"I don't feel good about this," Isabelle murmured.

Grabbing it without a word, Sadie slurped it down.

"Slowly," Isabelle cautioned.

Colette watched Sadie. Laudanum, the Victorian-age Korbel with a kick. It was clearly the choice of liquor for covert alcoholics in the late 1800s.

"You know what the good doctor says," Isabelle chided. "The power of the mind will set you free." She laughed, then gritted her teeth. "Don't we just need to pray harder? We must strive diligently to be cured of our sexual impulses. Only Dr. Warburton can choose our desires for us."

Sadie's eyes watered. She wiped her mouth with the back of her hand.

"I loved Percy. And he loved me."

Isabelle looked at her. "Doctor Warburton has drilled it into our heads. We're outcasts. Nothing but the dregs of society."

Colette took a deep breath. "Why are you saying all this?" she asked, even though she knew.

Isabelle's eyes were placid. "We don't go along with what is prescribed. Sadie here, for instance. She's too much of everything; too much nerve, too much personality, too much determination. The men cannot keep her down, so they lock her up. Like they lock me up. But I won't be a prisoner."

Isabelle bit her lip, but her eyes were impassive. "My father kept my mother down. Kept her in the cellar too. Same cellar, cold and strange, where he throws me every time I am forced to return to that house. There's a room in particular…"

"The one with the dark patterned wallpaper?" Colette said, recalling the first time she'd seen Isabelle standing on the front stairs of the old house.

"My father said she boarded a train and abandoned all of us." She paused, "but I don't believe it."

Sadie's eyes were downcast momentarily. Then she moved over to Isabelle and forcibly grabbed at her underskirts. She searched the pockets feverishly until she withdrew another bottle of Laudanum.

"Doctor Warburton tells you Sadie," Isabelle said evenly. "That you suffer from neurasthenia. That you have nervous exhaustion. I see this Laudanum has a hold over you. It changes you and you crave it. You're an addict."

A tear burst from the corner of Sadie's eyes. Still, she threw her head back and drank. Isabelle simply stood by, saying nothing. Sadie's rage escalated. She stomped to the window.

"It's your drinking, Sadie," Isabelle said after her. "You have to stop. It only weakens you. How can you fight the doctors if you're not thinking clearly?"

"It's all torment," Sadie went on. "Don't we want to see the world look rosier? Blurred just a bit around the edges? How else can I endure this place? Dr. Warburton? When he examined me the other day, he made me lie perfectly still. I felt a darkness in my soul. I feel wrong with the world. It can't be right. He touches me until it hurts."

Sadie lowered herself to her knees, bringing her hands to her face as she rolled onto the floor in the fetal position. Isabelle sat back on the small cot in the room, her eyes cast toward the door.

"Our dear Lizzie Borden. She didn't stand for it, did she?" Isabelle murmured, barely audible.

Colette had by now lowered herself to the floor, and sat down cross-legged next to Sadie.

Sadie's sobs intensified until she struggled to catch her breath. "No," she managed, "she certainly didn't.

"You were tossed from all good society," Isabelle said. "Just because you responded to your man's needs. Instead of sending him to the town "maisons closes" ala Madame Goodall. There is no shortage of brothels in this town. So you responded to him. Most of our good women, as you know, merely endure sexual relations with their husbands to procreate, to have children. You made the mistake of admitting to having your own sexual desires."

Sadie nodded, her eyes drooping with the further effects of drunkenness.

Colette touched Sadie's arm, rubbing her shoulder which was bony to the touch.

Sadie sat up all at once and hurled the glass bottle of Laudanum across the room. It shattered against the wall. "I don't care anymore!"

Isabelle jumped up from the cot and started pacing. "I just need to find out what really happened to my mother. It's the only way," she reflected, "that I can get to the other side of this agony."

Sadie stared at the floor. Perhaps in her mind, she felt tormented by this hideous place and was besieged by foregone hopes of a future making love with Percy, a well-established man. There were maybe visions of rolling grass picnic spreads, a brightly colored quilt, and eventually a cozy apartment for two.

These two women had clearly spent much time together, both in the asylum, and also in church activities outside its walls. The evidence was there for Colette, in the faces of these women. Written in their frustrations.

Standing up, Colette gazed out the window. A woman swaddled in a nightgown too big for her, her hair swept up in a knotted bun, was being dragged along by two male stewards of the asylum. Colette thought about the men she'd seen on the streets in Fall River, as they'd walk along the wooden sidewalks, with their heads held high, and their black lapels neatly starched, likely the result of the ironing skills of their wives. At night, the pubs spilled over with drunken revelry and the men meandered home to their wives and young daughters. Others perhaps took to the dark alleyways over to the well-known brothel in town.

One truth Colette realized was much of the wanton drunkards and resulting physical and sexual abuse against wives and children had become the original raison d'être from which the Women's Christian Temperance Union had erupted.

Sadie, as she hunched there by the window, appeared uncertain about her place. Colette imagined that Sadie had been misled by Percy. The double standard of his desire for her, was juxtaposed with his certain disdain of her if she did give in to him and become his lover.

Colette sat in a yoga pose on the floor and breathed in and out. The same double standard would persist into the twenty-first century for women. The Madonna-whore complex; whereby men expected concurrent purity combined with a voracious sexual appetite from their women. It set an unrealistic precedent for the female population. Didn't most twenty-first century narcissistic men insist their wives appear as prize ponies in the public eye, and then demean them in subtle ways at home? Further, they would provide gentle reminders about keeping the house a little tidier, or talk them out of getting part-time employment? The man would, he insisted, take care of them so there was no need to get work outside the house. Certainly, many women embraced this life. Didn't human nature dictate that on some level, the husband was to always have financial control over his wife? Total autonomy. Again the control was revealed in elusive ways such as, "you're going to leave those dirty dishes until morning?"

When she looked up, Colette saw that Isabelle and Sadie were watching her, looking puzzled by the odd stretches she was performing on the concrete floor. That's when Colette realized she was positioned in upward-facing dog.

She lowered herself and smiled ruefully at the women. Moments later, Sadie returned to hugging her thin legs to her chest, and Isabelle was running her hand across the bars of the window.

Colette's mind started racing again. She lay flat on the floor, her arms stretched over her head, breathing in and out. Her thoughts went back to Valley Stream, even from one week before. Before this week and her lengthy trip to 1892. In the twenty-first century, she mused, these were the same women these men had met at prestigious universities, many of them having just as much, if not more education than the men. Somehow they'd been relegated to roles as housekeepers and nannies. The wealthier of this set often managed to get nannies for their children and spend their afternoons playing paddle or tennis at the club. Still, what they failed to recognize was that the balance of power never shifted. To maintain the control, the husband paid the country club fees. Certainly, numerous women cherished this arrangement by simply pushing the reality of their "station" in relation to their husbands, far back into the recesses of their minds. Or, like Sadie, they took to alcohol, or pills, shopping to excess, or even affairs. Any way they could check out. However, this only undermined their own empowerment and put the control back in the manicured hands of their husbands.

So here was Sadie, who now lay on the floor somewhat passed out, having been misled in the worst, most fiendish way. She was a woman well beyond her decade in erotic maturity, like some nineteenth century Anais Nin. Colette imagined them now; Sadie and Isabelle, perhaps at the height of their lives, perhaps even one year earlier, neatly displayed in wicker chairs, their dresses spread around their ankles as they enjoyed band concerts in the park.

Isabelle now studied her hands, lying supine on Colette's cot.

Perhaps it started slowly, Colette thought, watching her, the time spent together for Isabelle and her musician lover, holding hands, enjoying Sousa marches at the local gazebo. Hadn't Isabelle mentioned that he'd been a musician, like Sadie's lover? Colette was reminded of the female character in Somerset Maugham's *The Razor's Edge*. The character, Sophie, was tempted by another woman to drink alcohol again. This woman, a childhood friend, was aware that Sophie had struggled to give up alcohol. This sophisticated, wealthy female character, knowing that Sophie was seated alone in her luxurious parlor and in a vulnerable state, had her butler wheel in a cart full of liquor. The wealthier woman had been jealous of Sophie over their mutual love of the same man. She wanted to destroy Sophie. She succeeded.

Colette had studied Somerset Maugham and his themes while in graduate school and as it so often does, shame and liquor worked their dark charms on alcoholics, and on the character of Sophie in the novel. She drank. Her life spiraled downward after that. Like Sadie and Isabelle, Sophie had been a sexually alluring woman, one who gave in to her sexual needs and desires. And like so many women who gave up, following the tragic deaths of her baby son and husband in an automobile crash, she'd become a prostitute in the dark bars of 1920s Paris.

Now Isabelle and Sadie were both snoring. Colette smiled, regretting she'd not somehow time-traveled with Breathe Right Nasal Strips for the two of them.

Her mind went to the portrayals of women in 2011.

Certainly, advertising was more racy, and the magazines and the internet sites, hurled sex at anyone and everyone without any limits. The actual feelings however, around women, remained unchanged. Feelings held, by the way, by both men and women.

Glancing at Isabelle as she slept, she noticed Isabelle's hands made repeated fists. Colette dwelled in two worlds, and felt dispirited for women in both.

Isabelle lay on the cot rigidly, and appeared shut down. She had a numb, odd stillness about her.

Colette pondered the advent of the prairie door. Why had it found her? She'd asked the demolition crew and her landlord to save it for her. Why? Then her mind crept to thoughts of the skeletal remains she and Bob had unearthed in the coal chute.

Someone was staring at her now. Isabelle was awake again.

"What do you think happened to your mother?" Colette asked her.

"I know what really happened to her," she whispered.

"What do you think?"

"I know that the asylums changed her. I know that she was no longer my mother when she was finally released. She may have abandoned us on paper, but I don't believe it."

"Your father?"

Isabelle turned to her, her eyes narrowed. "He took her life. I just have to find proof."

This captured Colette's curiosity, especially in light of the skeleton she and Bob had found. "Proof of what?"

"Proof that Madeleine was not the wretched mental defect he made her out to be," Isabelle said, shaking her head. "He followed her. I know he did. He followed her all the way to Chicago. "

In the next twenty minutes or so, Isabelle described what must have been her mother's actual journey of fear and being alone, traveling the trains as a young woman during a time when such women would have been suspicious and likely questioned. Yet somehow she managed to make it all the way to the North Shore of Chicago. That's the part in the story where Colette stopped her.

"The North Shore? Wilmette? Evanston? Do you know where exactly?"

Isabelle tilted her head, delicate fingers to her temples. "It was a smaller town. Somewhere near Winnetka, yes. Valley Lodge? Something with a Valley?"

Colette took a deep breath. "Valley Stream?"

Isabelle's face softened and blanched at the same time, as if the act of remembering forced once lost feelings to the forefront.

An hour later, Isabelle decided to stay in Colette and Sadie's room as well that night. And they paid for it the next morning, when the door was thrown open by Doctor Warburton and two male assistants stormed into the room.

Warburton grabbed Isabelle by the arm and yanked her up from the cot where she'd been sleeping. Colette sat up quickly from her place on the hardwood floor where she chose to sleep in order to stay cool. Isabelle glared at Dr. Warburton, with her chin up. Dr. Warburton slapped her hard across the face. Still, she looked away while her cheeks glowed red. With a fiendish glare, he held her with a firm grip on her arm. He shoved her out the door and grabbed her hair with his hand.

Colette followed closely behind, in the grip of one of the assistants who had pulled her up off the floor. She felt weak as they'd denied the women food for a day or so. Still, Colette managed to eavesdrop on the doctor as he rattled off instructions to Isabelle as if she were a child.

"At the garden party on Saturday, it is expected that you will show your father and all our generous benefactors that your treatments are working. Do you understand? In spite of a mother who left a blight on your family name, your father is giving you another chance to become a proper young woman."

Isabelle stared at the floor. She moved lethargically, dragging her long legs. Despite being heavily medicated on the morphine they'd forced upon her, she continued to resist the doctors. Yet it crossed Colette's mind now, as she followed closely behind with Sadie in tow, that Isabelle continued to confound her captors. Her father pressed her violently to conform. Numerous trips to the basement, without food or water for days on end, had become a regular regime in the Edward Sewell household yet not even the asylum could break her.

Isabelle's mother did not run away. She'd met with an untimely end because of her unwillingness to acquiesce to society. In her mind, Colette agreed with Isabelle on that point.

Was this factual, or was Isabelle delusional? Colette wondered this, thinking so much about it, that her head pounded. She realized too, she had not had her usual skim latte in several mornings. Mutton and lukewarm milk led her to pass on breakfasts on recent mornings. Although a widespread chain of stores, she doubted that Starbucks had expanded to time travel in 1892. This thought made her smile.

Isabelle turned and looked back over her shoulder. She had a strange indefinable grin on her face. For an instantaneous moment, Colette thought that although Isabelle dragged along, her eyes were ablaze.

They ascended a side staircase cast in white and black marble, then trudged up two, three then four flights. They entered an attic room filled wall to wall, with leather trunks and suitcases. Across the far wall, fluttering like ethereal wings, and extending the entire length of the vast attic space was an endless closet, where white lacy blouses and festive dresses, all linen and corset and satin stripes, lifted out of it.

The windows in the attic were thrown wide and wafts of hot air came in from outside. Lined up on the floor of the room, like little mock feet, were delicate pairs of embroidered shoes with pearl adornments and high-ankle boots.

Colette lingered behind Sadie and the small group of women Dr. Warburton had summoned up. She peered out the window which gave out directly onto Second Street. There were ten or so workers from the asylum setting up chairs and tents. The day was already hot once again.

Turning in the attic, her eye caught in her peripheral vision an unusual set of luggage. It was a large trunk, and several small bags resembling in shape contemporary travel bags. The initials on one travel bag said L.A.B. Edging her way over, she peered at it as closely as she could. It was a Louis Vuitton bag. It was the checkerboard Damier pattern. Colette had a working knowledge of the brand, admitting to her own consumerism; this was the Damier pattern first introduced by Vuitton in 1888.

It occurred to her, why would Lizzie, a woman who had been denied anything of luxury by her father Andrew, have owned a Vuitton travel bag? Unless someone else bought if for her? Like Isabelle? They were friends, after all. Andrew Borden knew nothing about this bag. No fancy furnishings or a proper carriage, but Lizzie Borden had a personalized piece of luxury luggage.

Gazing at the floor, Colette found herself spinning around in reverie. When she looked up, she was stunned to see Isabelle watching her intently. This wasn't simply a look, but rather a knowing camaraderie, likely a co-conspirator.

All the while, Dr. Warburton sifted through racks of clothing and additional piles of ribbons and dresses on the floor. Sadie seemed excited about it all. She had yanked down several skirts and wore one on her head, twirling with it as if it were a veil. In her way she derided the gravity of the upcoming fete, and purposely mocked the event.

Dr. Warburton had set out a vast sterling silver punch bowl with large ladle. There was something trough-like about it.

"Come my lovelies," he said, gesturing with exaggerated grace. "Enjoy this special punch I've concocted for my favorite girls."

In Colette's mind, he treated them like farm animals. Dr. Warburton's intention was to display the women, like reinvented damaged debutantes, all magically elevated to proper standards for the wealthy lobster-eating patrons; the crème de la crème of East Coast education and society. This event would be especially important to Edward Sewell, one father of many that comprised other fallen families, ridiculed by society for the mental illness within their midst, within their homes, supposedly within their daughter's or wife's minds. Certainly, these many fathers and disappointed husbands believed they just had to accept the lot of women, because they found them to be inferior.

Colette felt eyes boring through her. Isabelle still studied her. Then it began, the laughter, Isabelle's laughter. Suddenly it was too much, and it was too loud. Dr. Warburton withdrew a bottle of pills from his pocket and directed a mousy-looking assistant, suppliant and obedient, who had rushed over to him, to accost Isabelle with a large glass of water, the pills extended in his hand.

Still eyeing Dr. Warburton, Colette wondered about him. Where did he get his credentials, this man who judged women so harshly? What was his connection to Edward Sewell, and perhaps even Andrew Borden? Was this a typical good old boys club?

Turning back to the luggage, she felt an odd shift. Was it a breeze? Had someone opened a window? Eyes on the trunk again, she focused in on the L.A.B. initials. Her heart skipped a beat. She felt a pulsating in her chest. The too familiar nonsense in her brain, everything scattered and bending and fits of sickness started to come up in her throat.

He had done something. This depraved doctor, this patron of the perverse, had put something in the punch bowl, the same bowl where Colette and all the other women had been drinking. The disheartening dizzy sadness of drunkenness was overtaking her. Perhaps in days past it meant escape but to a seasoned lover of a sober and peaceful life, this felt sinister, unsafe and unsettling.

So now she couldn't be certain, staring at the Vuitton bag. It seemed to be seeping, or turning colors. Now there were lacy strands of gold, and running seams all over the length of the bag. It all looked so much like veins, like slim strings of blood riveting around the sides and front of the bag. Like the two inch sagging strand of Andrew Borden's blood she'd read about in books, which had described the immediate aftermath of the scene in the sitting room. This was indeed the bag labeled "L.A.B." Perhaps Isabelle had hidden it here for Lizzie? To avoid Andrew's wrath?

Her face burned and she knew she must be reddening. It swept up to her ears. The room was a furnace. The beams of the attic started to move, and her eyes swept along the wide plank floorboards in a dizzying queasy spin.

Making sure all the women were occupied, sifting through lace and satins, she crept closer to the L.A.B. travel bag, tripped on her long skirt, and then fell to her knees. She ran her hand along the top of the bag. It felt oddly warm. Leaning back from behind the curtains which separated the area of the luggage from the room, she checked again on the proximity of the rest of the party.

That's when the hallucinations exploded. In her mind's eye, she saw the murder scene; the sitting room where Andrew Borden had been discovered. The crime photographers moving in closely to the two-inch long drapery of blood over the door jamb behind the sofa where Mr. Borden lay, a majority of his face gone, the eye out of its socket. She imagined violins shrieking in her ears and put her hands over them to stop the noise. Turning around, she saw that Sadie was rocking on the floor, grasping a taffeta dress to her chest and sobbing.

Isabelle had thrown herself inside the closet of dresses. The hollows of her eyes were visible, as was her stony gaze. Both of the women, Colette realized, had been drugged with something extremely potent, in addition to alcohol. All three of them had.

Her hand traveled down the front of the L.A.B. bag. Even in her delirium, she smiled to herself at the craftsmanship of the luggage. She realized too, even in her fog, that the bag was securely locked.

Taking a deep breath, she turned to look ever so casually, over her shoulder. Now Sadie had wrapped herself head to toe in one of the dresses. Dr. Warburton watched her, smiling faintly. She appeared quite trapped by the dress, unable to find her way out. Dr. Warburton's eyes widened as Sadie grew more alarmed, struggling to free herself.

"Getting lost in the trappings of women, are we?" he said with a twisted smile.

"I can't breathe," she gasped, pushing one pale hand through the collar of the dress.

Afraid to release her hand from the L.A.B. bag, still feeling the wetness of the painted blood strings along the case, Colette fought the effects of the strong bromide and teetered ever so slowly to her feet. Isabelle had somehow stood up straight and was blocking a stream of sunlight that managed its way through the high windows, cutting it completely in half, blocking out vision and making it dark and full of shadows. It took everything in Colette's power to raise her chin, to tilt her head upward and regard Isabelle standing over her. The smile on Isabelle's face actually alarmed Colette with its menace.

"What do you think you'll find, my dear Colette? A hatchet?"

Colette sucked in her breath all at once, and it caught in her throat, making it impossible for her to speak. Her hand still resting on the trunk, it felt dry all at once and she turned to look, to gaze upon something that made little sense. The L.A.B. travel bag now, with its checkerboard squares of the original 1888 Vuitton pattern, looked untouched and clean. The lacy veins and blood and blur of colors had all vanished.

A bit frantically, she rubbed the surface, her fingertips searching for the signs of life, the pulsating veins of red paint or traces of lace, or whatever it was the unknown bromide sedative or opiate had revealed to her.

Had it been hallucinations? Didn't Charles Darwin have such imaginings in the early nineteenth century while taking Laudanum? What she'd observed was some horror like something out of "The Telltale Heart" or "The Fall of the House of Usher." But then, hadn't Edgar Allan Poe also taken Laudanum? Why he'd supposedly been spoon-fed Laudanum as a baby.

After over twenty years of sobriety, her true nightmare was now feeling the instability and nausea of being under the influence of a drug. For this reason, she hated Dr. Warburton. She was imprisoned in her own body, in the same way as all these women had felt for years.

Suddenly Colette fell backwards. Isabelle uttered something very strange. Colette's skirts fell above her head, and draped around her shoulders. Sitting up, she grabbed her booted feet and tried to steady herself. She wanted to throw up. Tears started in her eyes, bursting onto her cheeks, warm and strange and salty. Relapse had always been her dreaded fear in over two decades of sobriety, but now, added to that, was real terror.

She glanced at the L.A.B. bag, breathing in quick sobs now, unable to see through her tears. She reached out her hand and touched it, again finding only a smooth surface; and it left no trace of anything on her palms, even when she stared at both of them, and held them up in front of her face. Was she losing her mind?

"Miss Colette," Sadie said, standing directly over her. She knew several beings stood over her but she feared looking up.

Colette sat very still. Her body stiffened. Perhaps they wouldn't notice her, and she could slip away amongst the clothes, and hide away. This couldn't be happening. Was this a relapse? And with that she'd just remembered Sadie caught in the straight -jackets made of satin and lace. She started to rise, but a firm hand held her down.

"You think you can just continue to make fools of us?"

The voice was warbled now, unclear and menacing. "Why I do believe you think yourself a Houdini? You're just a woman. You need to remember your place. You have duties. Don't you want to make a husband happy one day?"

It was Sadie speaking to her now.

Chapter Ten (A)

The Historical Facts

The next witness turned out to be Sadie Raymond, the seamstress who mentioned that she'd worked on a dress for Emma and Lizzie. This same seamstress made the oversized blue corduroy dress, a relatively new dress, which Lizzie would ruin with paint only two weeks later. This was in the Spring, in May of 1892. In a sense, this admittance on the part of the seamstress reinforced the fact that the dress with paint on it, the dress with a lengthy train, was actually only four months old when Lizzie burned it.

Emma went into great detail about how the "old" dress could never have been "made over." She mentioned that the "material and collar" would have been impossible to repair.

Interestingly, Alice Russell, Lizzie's closest friend, also witnessed Lizzie burning the dress, and overheard Emma respond to Lizzie's idea to burn the dress, with the statements "I would" or "why don't you?"

The purpose of having had Sadie Raymond discuss making the dress may have been specifically to reinforce a certain idea. Lizzie claimed because she'd gotten paint on it, that the dress was irreparable. The jury had been swayed toward the idea that Lizzie, a sober Christian woman, had merely burned a dress which she could no longer use. In actuality, a more likely theory was that it was the act of a guilty murderess. Why else burn a dress that was only four months old, unless it was indeed, evidence? Her own sister, knowing full well how recently the dress had been made, made a point of repeatedly referring to the dress as that "old faded" thing beyond repair.

Emma went on to directly refute the idea involving a quarrel which had occurred between her and Lizzie at the Taunton Jail. However, she did admit that her sister had said to Alice Russell, "why didn't you tell him about it?" and "why did you let me do it?" The first statement was in reference to Alice feeling as if she'd lied to Mr. Hanscom when she'd claimed that all the dresses in the Borden house were still there and that none had gone missing since the day of the murders. The second statement, made by Lizzie, was directed at Emma, in a sense blaming her sister for allowing her, Lizzie, to have burned the dress.

In actuality, no matter how one examined it, whether or not Lizzie was guilty or innocent, it was senseless to have burned the dress, paint or no paint, at that point in time. It led one to the logical conclusion that only a guilty person would have chosen that time to burn the dress. That, and the likelihood that it was necessary, simply because there was indeed, blood on it.

One may have wondered too, where the dress had been up until this point. On the day of the murders, for instance, could Lizzie not have stashed it somewhere? Perhaps during the time that she and Dr. Bowen were inside her locked bedroom, not allowing police to enter? Would it not have been simple, for instance, for the good doctor, Lizzie's loyal friend, confidante and witnessed companion, to have slipped it in his doctor's bag, and then smoothly left the house?

Because indeed, according to Porter's *The Fall River Tragedy* and other sources, Dr. Bowen was spotted that very day, appearing extremely agitated as he raced about the town of Fall River.[188] One may have only speculated, of course, but his state of upset appeared to have been due to an anxiety he carried around with him. Recent events seemed to weigh upon him more than anyone else.

Regardless of this, in a sense, Mrs. Sadie Raymond, the dressmaker, may have easily set the defense team back. Mrs. Raymond essentially made it clear that the "old and faded" dress, as Emma described, was, at the time of the murders, only four months old. It would perhaps have been more believable and less suspicious, if Emma had just described it as a recently made dress that had been ruined by paint.

The final witness for the defense called on the eleventh day of the trial, was Hyman Lubinsky. The defense viewed Mr. Lubinsky, the driver of the horse-drawn ice cream truck, as a strong and viable witness. This was because, as before mentioned, he testified to having seen a woman walk from the barn to the Borden house, approximately about the time Andrew Borden was bludgeoned, and he added the important detail that he did not know the identity of the woman.[189]

Hyman Lubinsky may have mentioned this, having perhaps been coached by the defense team, to clarify that he indeed knew Bridget Sullivan, the maid, by sight, because she had purchased ice cream from his wagon before. Lubinsky therefore stated that he did not know the woman he saw walking from the barn to the house. This worked well for Jennings and his team because the woman walking from the barn to the back door of the Borden house at the precise time of Andrew Borden's murder, could then easily have been speculated by the jury, to have been Lizzie Borden herself.

Burning the dress was an odd action for anyone, much less a murder suspect. It would have been recognized as disposing of evidence. Also, it was interesting that her own sister, knowing full well how recently the dress had been made, made a point of repeatedly referring to the dress as that "old, faded" thing beyond repair.[190]

Upon closer scrutiny of Hyman's statement, he stated that "she had on a dark-colored dress and nothing on her dress."[191] This narrative may have been interpreted to have revealed that at first, she did not have the pink wrapper over the dark dress. Supposedly she was witnessed having worn it later in the day of the murders. This was at the time when police and bystanders were about. Secondly, this may have caused one to wonder why she'd donned the pink wrapper at all? The answer may have included one or two reasons; first, to cloud the memory of anyone who had seen her in a different dress earlier in the day, due to the pink wrapper, or secondly, to perhaps quickly cover any blood stains on the dress she'd had on, at least temporarily. It may also have been that she'd specifically chosen to wear the dress with paint on it knowing she would be perhaps getting blood on herself. She may have been aware of the fact on Thursday, August 4th, 1892, right when she awakened in the morning. What better dress to wear than one that had already been supposedly ruined with paint stains?

On the twelfth day of the trial, Ex-Governor George D. Robinson was called to speak on Lizzie's behalf. Amidst a great deal of lofty and florid language, Robinson began by patronizing the work of local Fall River police and the Judge Blaisdell decision. He stated that of course, they were only human beneath those blue uniforms and brass buttons.[192]

Initially, and quite ironically, Robinson's reiteration of the facts around the case, had it been a more modern place and time, would have only furthered to condemn her. Because if the following points he raised were brought up in a courtroom of today, it may likely have been interpreted differently, and not in Lizzie's favor.

Robinson's sentimental words were being heard and dissected by a male-dominated crowd, a jury which lived in a time when women were assumed to have been the weaker a sex, a creature of lesser physical strength, and definitely, a human which certainly lacked cunning, or violent malice of forethought. This insubstantial position may have worked in Lizzie's favor. A woman of 1892, especially a Christian woman, and spinster dedicated to her father in every way, would never have been capable of the volatile and masculine amount of rage and resentment, or clearly the measure of greed that only a man would comprehend.

So in a sense, even his "defense," in the name of Lizzie's fine reputation, was remiss and misinformed. At the time, what would today be considered legally negligent, patronizing and illogical, was considered acceptable behavior in light of the evidence, whether circumstantial or otherwise.

For instance, Ex-Governor Robinson stated that these vicious acts were carried out in the "broad light of an August day…in a quiet home, upon a street of a populous city, with houses within a stone's throw."[193]

So with regards to this statement, who indeed would have chosen such a time and place to carry out these deadly acts? This perpetrator chose a hatchet, a bulky inconvenient and difficult to conceal weapon, with which to murder? He or she also committed the acts in the middle of the day, in a quiet household, on an equally busy thoroughfare. It was a workday, with neighboring houses close enough to hear if there had been any struggle. The murderer had to have been aware of all these factors.

Indeed, the choice of murder weapon was unusual. If the perpetrator had been a man, perhaps an illegitimate son, Lizzie's imaginary lover, or even a disgruntled business partner or tenant, the weapon choice would likely have been different. A hatchet would be more obvious and cumbersome than even a large butcher knife. This was likely for the following reasons; although all four of the previously mentioned suspects had been considered, wouldn't each have chosen instead perhaps death by strangulation (out of rage or passion), or the slice of a knife or smaller dagger (pre-meditated), with the awareness of a busy street and close proximity of neighboring houses? Also, a different location would likely have been chosen. One point which may have been relevant was that to have been an illegitimate son, or a boyfriend of Lizzie's, or even an angry business associate at the time in 1892, the individuals would all have been men. And yet if the first supposition was true, i.e. an argument ensued, or that Andrew Borden was simply accosted by a stranger or business associate, there would not have been a weapon per se, unless it was premeditated. In fact, wouldn't it have been most likely that a man would have strangled him?

Regardless, any outside perpetrator would have had to carry a weapon, for instance the hatchet, with them through a busy downtown area. Added to that, the extreme heat would have made wearing layers of clothing to hide a weapon, appear out of place. Even if it had been the boyfriend theory, Lizzie would certainly have had to instruct him on where to locate the hatchet. And the hatchet would have had to have been easily accessible as well.

The Borden house was a maze of staircases, which only led to certain parts of the house. Also, there was a vast collection of locked doors, both inside and out, where keys were kept on the mantel or hidden away. There would have been no way for Lizzie to let the boyfriend know precisely when Abby was upstairs as well. Someone also would have had to admit this person into the house. Andrew Borden did not leave the house until nine or so. And certainly, there was no predicting when, or if, Uncle Morse would vacate the premises? Also of note was the fact that the uncle had shown up for a visit unannounced, which would have put a wrinkle in any plan conceived by Lizzie working with an accomplice to commit the crime.

Robinson then dove into details about how a "terrible instrument" must have been used, and that the "perpetrator knew how to handle the instrument."[194]

Perhaps Robinson assumed the revelation of these facts would steer the jury toward picturing a man of great strength, or someone possessing great physical agility. Of course too, Robinson made a point of revealing that the murderer knew specifically how to handle the weapon.

Ironically, and perhaps unknown to the jury, Lizzie Borden had been witnessed building up her body strength as recently as six months before the murders. In point of fact, she had been spotted at a local gymnasium.[195] Unlike the twenty-first century, 1892 was not a time period when modest women were known to be working out at local gyms.

Next Robinson went into great detail, around the numerous blows the perpetrator exacted upon the victims. Following this grisly series of facts, he described the murderer as one whose "heart is blackened with depravity, whose whole life is a 'tissue of crime...' 'a maniac or fiend,' a 'lunatic' or 'devil.'"[196] Most notably, Robinson described the perpetrator as "not a man in his senses" nor someone with their "heart right."[197] The attempt here of course, was to present a devil.

For instance, given all the facts of the case, had the accused been a man, would all the same considerations been given for him? Would the jury have taken into consideration, that the male suspect, was active in his church? Or would they believe the convoluted tale about him being up in the barn looking for sinkers for fishing, or eating pears in the yard? Not very likely. And although the defense team continually reiterated how it was all simply circumstantial evidence, it was likely that the very same evidence which glossed over Lizzie's apparent guilt, would have easily convicted a man. So the double standards worked for and against Lizzie. The depravity of the crimes may have felt masculine. Thus a man would have been convicted. But the blatant discounting of obvious clues which pointed to Lizzie; like bloody rags in a slop pail, keeping police out of her room on the day of the murders, or destroying evidence were dismissed because she was female.

Further on in his prolonged speech, Robinson stated that "you must conclude," when addressing the jury, "that such acts as those are morally and physically impossible for this young woman defendant."[198]

In addition, he went on to specify that to "foully murder her stepmother"[199] and then go "straightway and slay her own father is a wreck of human morals,"[200] and it was a "contradiction of her physical capacity and her character."[201] And yet, neither he nor the jury had been privy to her recent workout regiment at the gym.

Soon after these statements, Robinson further described that the good district attorney was just doing his job for the Commonwealth of Massachusetts, and yet then, he started in, attacking the police force of Fall River. He stated that "policemen are human, made out of men, and nothing else, and the blue coat and the brass buttons only cover the kind of a man that is inside."[202]

So in the first instance, when Robinson completely discounted Lizzie's ability to have been able to "finally" murder her step-mother, and then prance downstairs and knock off her father with several swings of the hatchet, he stated at last, that it was "morally and physically impossible" for her to do so, as a woman.[203]

In the courtroom of 1893, this was the case. In the years to come after the murders, it would come to light that such a scenario involving a woman was quite possible. Because the tragedy of August 4, 1892 was not an act of some muscle-bound maniacal man. Robinson could not have known what was truly inside Lizzie Borden.

As an aside, later photographs of Lizzie Borden, when she was well into her fifties, showed a relaxed, serene woman seated on the back porch of Maplecroft, the house she purchased with family money after the murders, petting her small dog. The evidence all pointed to Lizzie as the murderer. The circumstantial evidence was very strong. In a way however, had her motive simply been money, she could have lived anywhere in the world. Yet Lizzie chose to remain in Fall River, despite gossip.

To recap, some of the evidence included the following: the handle of a hatchet which had disappeared; bloody rags being carried in a bucket by Lizzie, and observed by a policeman. She then carried these same rags down the stairs to stash somewhere in the basement. And there was the untimely burning of the blue corduroy dress.[204] The fact that Lizzie had been witnessed working out at a gym in the weeks prior to the murders; the fact that Lizzie donned a pink wrapper to cover her clothes for whatever reason, especially when she did so over the dress she was wearing on the day of the murders.[205] Also, the amount of time, which was one and a half hours, that had elapsed between the two murders, would have necessitated that a stranger hide and remain out of sight. Conversely, someone who lived there could just have gone about their business. It was midday on a Thursday in downtown Fall

River which would have made hiding a hatchet under clothes difficult and odd for a stranger, because it was nearly 100 degrees that day. Also, no one substantiated anyone in or about the house, despite a plethora of witnesses including: little Lucy at the Chagnon house next door and three or four men working behind the house.[206]

Furthermore, there was the fact that Lizzie suggested Bridget run out of the house just prior to the murders, to go to some fabric sale happening downtown. Lizzie reiterated several times that there was a sale happening, and repeatedly tried to get Bridget out of the house before Andrew Borden had had arrived home.[207]

Simply the combustion of all the above-mentioned factors may have contributed to the time bomb waiting to go off in the mind of the young woman.

Chapter Eleven

C olette must have dozed off again. A young woman's words seeped through into her consciousness, but sounded far away. Instinctively, she touched her bracelet, still with her eyes closed. It felt very tight and warm. Opening her eyes, she saw it was Sadie speaking to her, her eyes wide. A descending sunlight beamed into the room. Last Colette recalled, they'd just chosen dresses for the fete. Yet now they were in Colette's room. Isabelle was not there.

"Her eyes are translucent. I used to stare at them in Bible study," Sadie went on, seemingly out of nowhere. "Then Lizzie would look up at me and I swear I couldn't tell if she was looking at me or at my very soul. It was as if she knew we shared a terrible secret. As young women, we both felt tainted. Everyone believed she was above reproach, but I tell you, there was something sinister in that calm demeanor. And yet, Isabelle always seemed to understand her."

Sadie stared at the floor until her words trailed off. "In fact, it worries me just how much Isabelle trusted her. She's a little dangerous, our Lizzie is."

Colette blinked, her eyes focusing on trim around the tops of the walls, all around the room, with very faded flowers, and the dingy white plaster.

"What's the date today?" she said. "Did I faint? What happened?"

Sadie grinned. "I'm glad we were roommates," she said. "I like you."

"Must have been the heat," Sadie said, nodding. "I'm afraid they're likely giving Isabelle an ice bath and some time in the restraint chair. Punishment for acting up at her father's place. Dr. Warburton said we have to pick out dresses in the attic tomorrow for some garden party fete on Saturday. It's just with the murders this morning, and then Isabelle being abruptly thrown back in here. You should have seen her hands, all cut up and bloody."

None of this was making sense to Colette. Hadn't she just gotten herself admitted to this place the day before? The bracelet had brought her back to Thursday. Then perhaps she'd gotten herself admitted on Wednesday?

"What is the date today?"

"Still," Sadie said, as if not hearing Colette, "I can't believe what happened today. August 4th is a day Fall River will never forget."

"It's August 4th again?" Colette asked, her voice low.

Sadie looked at her. "What?"

"We have to sneak into the house," Colette announced.

"What house?"

"The Borden house. Right away. What time is it?"

"You are crazy. I don't know, it's around 4:00 pm?"

Colette took a deep breath. A small rickety fan worked itself into exhaustion on a small table by an open window.

Sadie settled into a small chair and stared fixedly out the window. The heat was merciless, but clouds had passed over the sun creating a transient feeling of twilight outside. The air was moist and hot. There was a somber stillness outside and no sign of a breeze. Finally, Sadie turned to face Colette. There were dark circles under her eyes. Her skin was pale; she shimmered in a melancholy way like a ghost. She may have been an apparition invented by Wilkie Collins himself.

"I thought I was the crazy one," Sadie said. "What do you mean, sneak into the Borden house? For what unholy reason?"

"I need to see Lizzie, and gauge her demeanor," Colette went on. "I feel like that's the only way I will know for sure if she's guilty of the murders."

"How are we going to get out? Door's locked."

Colette walked to her cot and reached under the mattress.

"Isabelle left me this skeleton key she managed to lift from Warburton's office last time she was in here. Let's see if it works. I think Dr. Dolan will still be there, at the Borden's" Colette murmured, staring at nothing.

"But the people. And the crowd, why I don't even think they have an electric fan anywhere in that house. It will smell bad and be so hot. Not like this fan," she said, leaning her face toward the rounded tin-colored device, letting her hair fly. "In fact, I am surprised the hospital bothers to provide a fan for us."

Colette nodded. "I'm sure the hospital is sprucing things up because of the fete coming up." Her days felt so confused now. She jumped when the lamp above them, with shady white shade crackled and went out suddenly.

Colette stood up. "We'll find our way."

"It's a ten minute carriage ride," Sadie objected.

"Then we'll run there. I saw some white coats in the foyer closet when I was admitted yesterday. And hats. We will say we are with Dr. Dolan, who I think will be performing the stomach autopsies."

"But they'll miss us at dinner call," Sadie insisted. "And what the hell are you talking about? How could you know what's going on there?" Then she noticed something. "What're doing with that bag?"

Colette clutched the Vuitton L.A.B. travel bag. "This has to go back to the Borden house. I'm going to leave it by the front door or something." Sadie looked uncertain. "Look, we'll hurry back," Colette went on. "I just have a feeling we have to get over there. Maybe there's something I'm supposed to overhear, I don't know. The bodies will be laid out for sure. It's only 3:45 pm. Let's go."

Colette slipped the key in and the magic clicks followed. "Now we pray it's not triple-locked."

Then it opened.

"Our good fortune," Sadie whispered. "Warburton always forgets to triple lock."

As the two listened at the door to hear if anyone was nearby, sounds of moaning and periodic screams carried on the air, bellowing down the hallways to them. The staff always ate their dinner early, before the patients. Backs to the wall, Colette and Sadie slipped out, skimming the walls, and skipped every other stair leading to the main entrance. One nurse attended the front desk. They waited a moment but she was determined to stay put. Finally a male assistant walked up to her and leaned on the desk, starting a cordial conversation.

Once they'd scooted across the lobby, Colette grabbed two coats and white hats from the front closet. Outside at last, the clothing felt tight and hot. The persecutors of the establishment of the asylum had by now gathered in the darkly paneled basement room of the place, with their sinister heads bowed, and were no doubt, exchanging disappointments and criticisms of the female patient population. The massive front door was open, and Colette closed the door as gently as possible, allowing for one click only.

They shuffled along at high speed, down the sidewalk and alleyways. The hospital, located a couple miles from the Borden house, was grandiose on the outside. For 1892, it was state of the art in fact, and bordered on a lush green forest that spread out for several acres. It was tough going tripping on the long skirt, due to her breathing being restricted by the well-fitted Jacket squeezed over her blouse. The two had buttoned up the white coats, and had pulled the hats down over their eyes.

Sadie pranced several paces ahead of Colette, turning around every few seconds with a quick nervous jerk of her delicate head, resembling a nervous tic. Her dark hair appeared as reddish tendrils in the light, which stuck out from her hat.

Here and there, people were gathered on vast and wide front porches, discussions and worries being exchanged about the abominable mystery on Second Street that day.

Sadie had a wild, out of control look. Freedom had ignited the life in her again.

Caps pulled down over their eyes, they soon passed Isabelle's father's house on the right, the cement staircase still daunting, with red stains showing here and there. Across the street was Mrs. Burns's boarding house.

Twenty paces ahead on the right hand side, loomed the Borden house. The aged black and white photographs Colette had studied in books jumped to life before her eyes. The place was cold and impervious to the houses on either side, cryptic and secretive about the horrors it held inside. The trees were green and leafy and a slight, barely breathing draft exhaled, and moved the two women along.

Colette stopped to catch her breath. Her chest was heaving. She noticed the buttons strained over her bosom. She was reminded of the tight blouse and skirt she wore under the jacket. Her mind raced, trying to think of who they could impersonate in order to gain entrance to the Borden house.

Sadie still drifted along, and was now half a block ahead. Ten or so townsfolk still milled about the area and for a second, Colette lost sight of Sadie altogether. When she started to walk more quickly, her legs felt stiff. This heaviness had come upon her. It was common sense. Her body revolted, her breaths were shallow and rapid, like how a captured sparrow would feel in her hands. She felt so hot now, and it seemed her throat had suddenly dried up. There was no one directly out front of the Borden house except several policemen on the street and sidewalk.

Somehow Colette felt alone and unprotected here on Second Street, standing there with the Borden house; an icon of desperation, betrayal and evil.

Drawing closer to the place, Colette spotted Sadie darting like some unleashed nymph in and around the front steps. Sure enough, one of the policemen turned, and then approached her quickly. Sadie said something, smiling. The policeman listened, nodding.

Next, Sadie ascended the stairs and peered into one of the side windows, as if trying to see inside the house. The windows were higher than Colette had imagined. In fact, as she drew up directly next to it, the entire edifice stood at a dizzying height, the shutters narrowing their cold gaze and the windows closed in. The house was hiding something. It intrigued her because in her mind's eye, she could envision the old black and white photographs of the place.

Sadie's laughter rang out. She sounded a bit delirious, and uneven, so much so Colette searched for the officer again, to see if Sadie had drawn too much attention to herself. Her arms alerted Colette of something and she kept motioning for her to come over to her. Colette kept shaking her head, trying to allay Sadie's excitement. There was so much upset and shame and horror in the faces of the few people remaining in the area. For that reason only, her knowledge of what may have driven the murders rang true.

Colette paused. The air was thick with hell-laden heat. She had trouble breathing.

"Sadie, come here. Someone might see you."

But the young woman's smile was so wide, her teeth beamed in the afternoon descending daylight, like some garish night light.

"Can you feel it?" Sadie asked, oddly delighted.

"What?"

"The dead calm," she said. "Everyone is afraid. There are people around but for once no one knows what to say. And no one comes near the house."

"What did you tell the policeman?"

"That Dr. Dolan asked for us. We are assistants from the women's ward, here to talk with Lizzie."

Colette nodded. "Pretty good," she said. As far as she could guess, she hoped they would not show up in the history books.

Colette stood alongside her, close enough in fact, to smell the combination of perspiration and baby powder. If not for this acute sensation, Colette would again find it impossible to believe she was really there, really standing in front of this house of the reaper, the most notorious in American history. These murders trumped most tales of familial taboo. An unprecedented solution with the help of a hatchet. Standing there, Colette felt the weighty presence of ninety-five degree heat, on this August late afternoon in the nineteenth century. Somewhere in the time continuum, she had indeed landed inside the black heart of 1892.

The uneven glass of the windows lent something mournful to the story of the façade. Delicate lace curtains showed through like specters, eyelet lace that, in the context of the death within, seemed a meager peace offering of feminine domesticity. Now the curvature of the eyelets relented to something much more sinister. The vision conjured up for Colette white bandages and gauze and dried blood. In the dizzy disorientation, Sadie occurred for her as some blithe spirit.

"I think," Colette whispered, "the fear people have is all about the insanity."

Sadie straightened up. She'd taken on human form once more. "What do you mean?"

Colette put her forefinger to her lips and gave Sadie a quick look. "I think that it was pure, adrenalin-driven mania that helped a woman wield a hatchet with such amazing force. That's why this case is so baffling."

Sadie tilted her head. "What do you mean by, 'this case?'"

Colette bit her lip quickly. Her eyes looked down, pretending to study the high button boots on her feet, and the full skirt. Oddly, she was getting used to them.

"People where I come from…who will take an interest in the case that is. Let's just go in."

Sadie clutched Colette by the forearm, her white fingers tightening. "What about this 'insanity' you're talking about?"

Colette turned to look at her. Sadie's eyes were washday blue and full of trust.

"We'll talk about it later," Colette said in a hushed voice.

"Tell me what you think," Sadie insisted.

"I think people are afraid of coming face to face with someone suffering from mental demons. Especially someone they know. The human mind is capable of dark thoughts. People fear what they don't understand, or cannot see."

Colette looked up at the house, and Sadie followed her gaze. "It's the crimes of deception, from those closest to us that do the most damage."

Colette leaned over to Sadie and whispered, "what broke down in this family, do you think?"

"I've heard rumors is all I'll say," Sadie said.

Sadie had a knowing look on her face. The two women stood by a moment. The only sounds were the wind and the thrush of leaves overhead. The house brooded. The hush was sinister. All life within was extinguished.

Colette wasn't sure if she should tell Sadie that they would indeed have to pass the two corpses of Abby and Andrew Borden. Dr. Dolan could perhaps still be working on them. Because no one trapped in the confines of 1892 would be aware of that fact, not yet.

Colette took Sadie by the arm as she pondered all the extensive locks and keys necessary to get around inside the house. She smiled, recalling seeing a play in Lincoln Park once that had been a spoof on the Lizzie Borden murders. Perhaps it was sheer terror at the moment that forced her mind to imagine herself back there, sitting in the audience enjoying the musical farce. Essentially, it reminded Colette how far-reaching the murders had been, crossing time and space, even morphing from extreme tragedy in reality, to ludicrous parody on the twenty-first century stage over one hundred years later.

That musical stayed with her. In fact, Colette had made a conscious choice to not take herself so seriously. She wouldn't do that anymore. She would not fashion bedroom curtains out of bedspreads, just to make sure that no light got in, as her mother had done later in life.

Colette had given up the maudlin practice of self-pity.

"I think I know the rumors you're talking about. I think her mind, simply fractured," Colette said, answering Sadie at last." That was it. Lizzie snapped."

Sadie looked quizzical, her dark eyebrows slightly raised. "How have you got a theory already? The murders just happened today?" She tilted her head and gave Colette a long look. "You're from Chicago, right? Did Isabelle ask you to come here?"

Hand to her chin, Colette didn't answer. How to explain that the furor of Lizzie Borden had always haunted her? That in its way, it was familiar to her? Or how to reveal that an antique slide bracelet from Long Grove, Illinois and a Prairie door from a torn-down bungalow, had dictated this scenario?

Colette raised her chin and started for the house. "Let's find the side door. The door leading from the barn. The door that goes to the kitchen."

Sadie narrowed her eyes. "And that's another thing? How do you know the layout of the house so well? Have you visited with Lizzie or Emma before? I thought you were new to Fall River?"

Colette let the question dissipate in the air, lost in suffocation as the heat of the afternoon embraced them. Minds and spirits were at odds now. She could feel it in the swarming heat. As they crept up to the side door, Colette mentally rehearsed what the scene would be once they were inside this house of death. Could she stomach looking into the slop pot, for instance? The basin where Lizzie had thrown those dirtied "menstrual rags" the police had been too "polite" to ask about the day after the murders? Because by modern observers, they could likely have been the stained result of a murderous afternoon and clean-up.

Colette jiggled the door knob of the infamous screen door. The old doorknob, a knob which restoration enthusiasts would kill for in the twenty-first century, looked somewhat brassy and shiny, even in shadow. Her hand squeezed the knob gently. Her mind had the dizzying recollection of all the trial notes she'd read over the years, and all the discussions and point counterpoint with Lizzie in the courtroom as to which doors were locked and which were not. There had been a discrepancy over the back door, the screen door – which Bridget Sullivan claimed she did not lock. This, of course, enabled Lizzie to say she'd slipped back in through the kitchen after eating pears and hanging out in over one hundred degree heat in the barn out back. All this, while a purported, someone else, was murdering her parents in the house.

"It's open, is it?" Sadie said.

Colette turned and nodded, without speaking.

The two women stepped into a short hallway which led into the kitchen. Utilitarian and tidy. Would be hard to guess all the calamitous events which had just occurred in the place. Hands clasped in front of her, Colette scanned the stove area for the slop pot she'd read about. Colette thought it ironic that the police had simply looked away. They were likely embarrassed when Lizzie had descended the stairs the day of the murders, carrying the slop pot filled with bloodied rags, right past the police to the kitchen. The naiveté and the polite behavior may have cost the police, and eventually the attorneys, crucial evidence.

She saw a black teapot on the stove. On a nearby counter, there was a paste board and rolling pin. In one corner was a small wringer, used to wring out laundry. Colette also identified an old coffee canister and a tin knife basket.

Sadie had grown quiet. She reached out to touch a black scale that had a package of flour on one side of it.

"Be careful," Colette said. "don't touch anything."

Colette turned away and crept further into the mixed shadow of the kitchen. There was a large metallic round pot on the floor next to the stove. She took a deep breath, trying to ready herself for a gruesome sight. Lifting the lid, the pot had been washed clean. Ashes flew past from a fire under the stove, and she could smell coal, a bit like burning wood, which no doubt created the heat coming from the oven. As she stepped toward the sitting room, the very room where Andrew Borden was butchered, the floor creaked in the kitchen. It was a plain wooden floor. The scent was reminiscent of lumber and dust. It was pleasant and palpable and she could practically taste the fabric and curtains. It reminded her of a nineteenth century house located in Itasca, the small town where she'd grown up, just West of Chicago. One particular house there, in addition to the wonderful smell of old wood and incense, used to sell antiques. In fact, she realized now, that house smelled precisely as this one did. At least, at first. Then the scents changed as they exited the kitchen.

Already within her sights, she glanced at the top of the doorjamb. It was there that she saw strands of something red dangling from the top of the frame. She knew much of the woodwork either already was, or would be removed by investigators. Her chest heaved and she held her breath, afraid the vibrating of her heart would be heard from the upstairs. Because she'd indeed heard pacing footsteps coming from the second floor. Her heart beat within her like a Wagner symphony cranked up to full volume.

Once inside the sitting room door, Colette hesitated. A floral wallpaper pattern frothed faintly in the shadows of the room. Under her feet she felt the thin, floral oriental rug press down slightly. Sadie bumped into her because she was looking behind her while she walked blindly into the sitting room. Her white hat was low on her forehead and her blue eyes bugged out now. Colette then recalled that there was another entrance to the room coming in off the main hallway, by the front door. Colette sensed another person was nearby. Enough early evening sunlight remained, enough to reveal blackened stains on the camel back sofa where Andrew Borden must have been found. Sadie gasped, and Colette clutched her companion's white coat, shaking her head no. She pointed ahead to the door leading to the next room.

That's when she realized they didn't have much time. The initial stomach autopsies may have just been completed. Surely, the dining room had to be close? The two women crept to the next door. The first light was sun coming through a window in the dining room. Colette suspected the two dead bodies would be there, perhaps laid out on the table. That's all she needed was a shrill scream from her asylum buddy. She stopped. Sadie bumped into her.

"Sadie," she whispered. "I have to warn you about something."

The two women teetered on the threshold of the door which led into the dining room. Sadie blinked and caught her breath audibly. They stood there, feet planted, unable to move. It occurred to Colette that Sadie had no idea of the seriousness of where they stood. Did everyone just break and enter in the nineteenth century?

"What is it?" Sadie asked, too loudly.

"Just don't make a sound. There are bodies in here. So whatever you do, don't scream."

Colette stepped fully into the dining room. Two dark forms rose from the depths. The bodies of two people lay stretched out on wooden planks which made them look like a table, perhaps a card table. The one on the left had a grayish skirt and high ankle boots sticking out and over the edge of the table. Their forms were bleak, formidable and eerily inanimate. The room had an odd odor. All the curtains were drawn and the shutters closed.

Colette felt very hot. Her face burned and the room flashed white. Perhaps it was the slanting sun, trying to break through the slats or the immediate mortality in their midst. Colette held her breath, afraid to inhale the ruination. For the first time ever, as she had always yearned to do as a child, she stood inside the imaginary red ropes that used to keep visitors from entering the actual rooms in museums and old houses, much like her memories of Colonial Williamsburg. But this was far more sinister than a three-cornered hat. And now, not only did she stand within the boundaries of tragedy; they were wrung out with evil, and intimately juxtaposed with a sordid reality, in which a Victorian home had gone terribly awry.

To approach the table, Colette focused first on the structure itself, and wondered how it could support the bodies. Then Sadie gasped and Colette turned sharply. Sadie had covered her mouth and squeezed her eyes closed, and she backed out of the room, haltingly, as if being pressed back with invisible hands on her chest. Indeed, the offenses against the Bordens exhaled throughout the room. In the grey twilight, the sight of their ordinary shoes sticking out on the table was grisly.

Unfathomable how these two bodies, slabbed out on this makeshift table, would orchestrate decades of conjecture, horror and obsession for generations of historians and the curious, alike.

"It's them, isn't it?" Sadie managed to ask, barely audible.

Colette nodded. Sun slipped behind clouds and now, only darkness responded. As she turned around, the curtains looked black. She could make out in the half light, Abby Borden's long skirt which reached the top of her boots. It had only been that day and already things smelled quite badly. Pungent, nauseating. Both women covered their noses with their hands. She'd not thought of dealing with this aspect of the murders and her exploration of the facts. Of course Colette would have no idea what the odor of two dead bodies, left out on a table in the ninety degree heat of an 1892 early summer night, would smell like. Now she knew.

In the charcoal hour of this hot afternoon, Colette could make out painted trim along the ceiling, and yet another faint wallpaper pattern that seemed to move, the stenciled designs crawling and commingling.

Sounds of stairs creaking made both the women stiffen and back away from the bodies. Colette tugged on Sadie's sleeve, ever so gently and pulled her back. Eyes still shut, the two women pressed their backs stiffly against the wall opposite the table where the two bodies lay. While the sun was hiding out, and with only a sliver of light visible, Colette could make out only an occasional shadow.

And that's when she heard someone step to the landing of the other door which entered the dining room from the kitchen. There was someone else in the room, breathing heavily. Quickly, Colette had pulled Sadie with her and the two women squeezed in behind the door to the dining room which they had just entered minutes before.

Colette prayed and stood stock still. Her chest spasmed. Sadie was agitated and wriggled up behind Colette, squeezing her hand until it hurt.

All at once there were three people in the room. Five, including the dead.

The third person wore a long grey dress. A type of long light-weight Jacket was tied over it which dragged on the floor. This was neither a frail, nor diminutive person in the darkness. This woman, to be sure, was formidable.

"Who's here?" the woman in the grey dress demanded.

Lizzie's eyes, Colette felt in her heart, were transparent, and glistening. A sensation of moisture, despair, tears.

Then this being neared the dining room table and stood there for what seemed like an interminable minute.

Lizzie turned sideways, slowly, deliberately, her soft profile becoming visible by the periodic spasms of afternoon light from outside, dappling through the leaves on the trees, very dim, but enough to recognize the delicate features, and the curly tendrils of hair that sprung away from the face.

Colette had seen this profile in photographs for years. The eyes, these supposed hardened windows to Lizzie Borden's soul, glimmered in their way, more visible because of their almost diaphanous nature. The wisps of flyaway hair around her face made her appear cherubic. A murderous cherub.

Colette stole a sideways peek at Sadie. The younger woman had her eyes closed very tightly, both her hands covering her mouth. She had to avoid screaming.

No one moved for a forever minute. Colette questioned her sanity. Why did they come here? In fact, the very words in her mind now sounded ludicrous. "We are going to the Borden house." Still, Colette recalled something about a space-time continuum, and being careful not to change the future by barging into the past. She'd not intended to meet up with Lizzie Borden herself. The prairie door had enticed her with its magic of showing her Olivia at age three. But how did it all lead here? To this bleak place?

And then, there came the sounds of swishing fabric.

Colette also realized that if her history knowledge was accurate, Emma would be arriving soon after having gotten word about the murders.

And then something odd happened.

Lizzie had moved closer to the table where the bodies lay. Then, extending one arm, she touched the protruding skirt of Abby Borden, and traced the length of the long hem. Then she lifted up one of the booted feet in her hand. Moving to the end of the table, she stood with one hand holding Abby's foot and her other hand on her father's booted foot, so that she grasped each corpse at the same time.

Even in the chiaroscuro of the room, Colette could have sworn a smile crossed Lizzie's face. Just the mere change in the contours of her rounded cheeks and small chin...and the translucent eyes which now shimmered; all this conspired to reveal the young woman's somber intentions. Then Colette heard the chilling words uttered.

"Have a restless sleep in hell," Lizzie muttered.

Then she laughed, and her contralto voice cut the silence in half. In the grey half-light, Colette recalled the testimony she'd read from transcripts of the trial, when Bridget Sullivan had described hearing that maniacal laugh from the stairway. Colette's academic and personal interest in the case over the years often directed her to read articles about the arrest and trial. She recalled now that a laugh, perchance a very similar laugh, had erupted just at the moment that Bridget had let Mr. Borden in through the front door of the house on 2nd Street on the day of the murders. Bridget's claim was hardly far-fetched. Had the maid truly heard Lizzie's laughter from up the stairway, it would have been after Abby Borden had been hacked to death. Hacked so hard, in fact, that Abby's braided hairpiece had become separated from her head and was found near the body.

Wouldn't it indeed have perhaps been the laugh of a young woman who'd gotten her way in the matter? Someone who felt vindicated? Would it not strike Lizzie as somewhat funny, to have freed herself from the shame of hiding the family secrets? By doing away with Abby, she would have been destroying the accomplice. The silent accomplice who perhaps had stood by for years, taciturn, living with full knowledge of what her husband, Andrew Borden, was doing to his daughter. This violation would have left lasting wounds, searing bolts of inner malice, residual self-hatred in Lizzie herself. Who could trust when someone so close to her has trespassed upon her soul? Victorian reticence and repression, in this case, may have combusted into a maniacal rampage.

Colette's mind continued to race. The three women stood by in the stillness, the only movement in the ominous lull, a sprinkling of dust in the sun streams.

Wouldn't it follow that such a sinister laugh may easily have come from a murderess, especially one fresh from the kill? There'd not only been locked doors in the house, but locked-up souls as well, pent up with rage, bedrooms of betrayal, layered with blankets, and familial trust severed with a fine slice.

In Colette's mind, even now as she held her breath and watched Lizzie, she could sense the tangled energy that was the cerebral afterglow of someone scorned, and now someone who'd found retribution.

Mere moments elapsed, when at last the third party's breathing slowed, accompanied by receding footsteps back into the kitchen. Moments later, Colette heard a liquid being poured in the next room, and then those footsteps left the kitchen, paused for a moment in the sitting room, then ascended up the front stairs which led back up to Lizzie's room. Of course from having studied the map diagrams of the house itself, Colette knew Lizzie would pass right on by the guest bedroom where Abby had been found with the back of her head bashed in.

The footsteps paused on the upper landing of the stairs, as if considering. Did Lizzie stare into the vacuous cavern of the guestroom? Yes, she could see Abby's body the day of the murders. Right from the landing, and right there under the bed. Maybe that laugh on the stairs was because Lizzie had recalled the heated embarrassment of having run out of money on her Grand Tour of Europe. On that trip, Lizzie had been accompanied by distant Borden cousins, but they were wealthy cousins too. Cousins who, unlike Lizzie, did not run out of money on the trip. Cousins who did not have to buy reprints of paintings, but rather purchased original watercolors, fine lace and designer clothing. The cousins did not have to wire home for more money. Lizzie had to wire her father. He denied her. Her father had turned her down. She'd had to wait like a desperate dog for her sister Emma to amass enough funds to finally bring her sister home. Isabelle must have bought Lizzie's L.A.B. travel bag on her own travels in Europe, and presented it as a gift.

Sadie clutched Colette's arm. Colette, in turn, pulled Sadie back through the dank-smelling kitchen, through the hallway, struggling for breath, and shoved the screened back door open, letting it close with a bang. It reverberated in the solemnity of suppertime on Second Street.

Turning back for a quick look, the two women could see from the street one lone female form lightly filling the outline of the upstairs bedroom window in the Borden house.

As that female figure lifted aside a lacy curtain with one pale hand, perhaps she saw two angels fleeing from the house, and one of them, unaccustomed to her clothing, stumbling on the cobblestones.

Chapter Eleven (A)

The Historical Facts

So the grand tour of Europe which Lizzie experienced, had a great impact on her psyche. Observers who condemned her, assumed the murders were acts wrought with greed. The truth was more likely, the concurrence of the luxuries she'd experienced in Europe. In addition, the fact that Lizzie may likely have been a victim of incest, the trip simply solidified for her that she'd lost her soul, and yet gained nothing for her misery.

Perhaps she felt, due to her silence about the abuse, that she at least deserved an acceptable façade of being an upstanding young woman from a good family. Denying her money for a return home, Andrew Borden humiliated her once again. Instead of the trip fortifying her, this economic crisis instead transformed her subsisting on secrecy, into a seething storm bent on retaliation.[208]

Eventually, due to further examination of the evidence, the numerous hits taken out upon each parent with the hatchet were decidedly excessive. Although Robinson wanted to create the idea of some maniac or fiend, one who emerged from the house and wandered outside mindlessly, after having massacred two strangers, this concept was less likely.[239] Because the murderer of Abby and Andrew Borden was specific, and he or she wielded the hatchet with an exceedingly focused rage.

What about the pinhead-sized drop of blood on the underskirt? [240] The defense called in experts to proclaim it as menstrual blood. Had a woman been involved in that assessment, she may well have found that theory to be suspect as well, for several reasons. An "accident" caused from menses would be unlikely to leave a spot that small and would more likely have left a smudge-like stain. The "drop" of blood found on the petticoat could easily have been more likely a splatter of blood, the kind perpetrated by spraying blood and not blood that would leak through underclothes to the petticoat.

All of these circumstantial facts should have carried more weight than any human witness testimony, for that time period. Perhaps some felt that even witness testimony may have been less reliable at that time to some schools of thought, than a preponderance of circumstantial evidence. Interestingly, a closer look at what testimony did exist, such as that of Bridget Sullivan, Hyman Lubinsky and Hannah Reagan at the Taunton Jail, would reveal that each testimony was refuted by someone. For instance, the witness to the supposed argument between Lizzie and Emma, Hannah Reagan, which allegedly took place at the jail where Lizzie was being held, included overhearing Lizzie exclaim "you have gave me away." The statement about the argument was given to a reporter, and then supposedly recanted, yet then she denied ever recanting at all. [209]

For instance, Hyman Lubinsky's testimony in aid of the defense, conflicted with recorded testimony of Lizzie regarding her having worn a hat or not. [210] Why even Bridget Sullivan's distinct recollection of having heard someone laughing in a sinister way on the stairs, despite proof that Lizzie was the only person in the house, was in the end, refuted and muddled by defense counsel. [211]

Robinson soon launched into a speech about the profound, and precise duties of policemen in 1892. He found it crucial to mention that police typically had many experiences with what he called "bad people" [212] and yet this mention was supposed to somehow help to vindicate Lizzie. His theory was that for that exact reason, policemen may have been guilty of "magnifying this, minimizing that,"[213] and in efforts to finger a perpetrator and to appease the public, their goal may have been to get anyone locked up for the crimes as quickly as possible.

Next Robinson, in today's definition, started to inform the men of their duty as members of the jury. He reminded them that they had "wives and daughters and sisters" and told them "you have mothers, you recognize the bond that unites and the flash that plays throughout the households."[214]

Robinson next cautioned the jury about making a tragically incorrect decision, by returning a verdict of guilty. Why? Because they may have then found themselves unable to go back to their homes and hearths. How could they? Having convicted an innocent woman? At one emotional point in his impassioned speech, Robinson likened the power the jury had over this innocent woman, as morally suspect, and no different than if they were to "take a knife and cut this woman's throat."[215]

Robinson also went on to describe how the District Attorney had opened the case with misleading evidence, around Lizzie's attempts to purchase Prussic Acid the afternoon of August 3rd. Robinson's reasoning was that, due to the fact that it was a false accusation, that there was then no reason for it to have been presented as evidence to the jury. Robinson claimed that the reason the evidence was not presented, was because there was supposedly no concrete, tangible proof.[216] Apparently, even the eye-witness accounts, which were presented by several pharmacists, one having been Eli Bence, were not strong enough for the prosecution. This, despite the fact that two of the witnesses were absolutely certain it was Lizzie who had requested the prussic acid.[217] Robinson asked if he could get to the truth by presenting what really occurred in the days leading up to, and including the day of, the murders themselves.

The chronology of the events began with Andrew Borden having been known to have left the house at 9:30 am on the morning of August

4th.[218]   Robinson proceeded to surmise, as the evidence showed, that Abby Borden was killed at around 9:45 am.[219]   Again, Robinson believed by reiterating the facts, it would further exonerate her. And yet, what he did not realize was, that by focusing on these facts, he made it more clearly evident that whomever committed the first murder, that of Abby, had to have been somewhere in the house.[220]   So by simply proclaiming these facts, it inadvertently increased the likelihood in certain minds, that the perpetrator was not a stranger. A stranger would neither have been close enough to the house, nor privy to the private comings and goings of the members of the household, as would someone indigenous to the house.

Robinson described Andrew returning home on August 4th around 10:45 a.m. after business downtown. He mentioned that Andrew had picked up what he called an old block. Others claimed it was a used or broken lock Mr. Borden had found on the ground.[221]   Regardless, he arrived home around 10:45 a.m.,[222] went up to his room briefly and then returned to the sitting room where he was either assisted or was not, depending upon whose testimony was trusted. According to Lizzie, she helped make her father more comfortable, after which, he was promptly murdered.[223]

All Robinson was able to conjure up as a possible killer, was some stranger out of deviltry, without a motive. He followed this up with stating that it was not of the slightest importance whether such a killer had a motive or not.[224]

Ironically, this proved a very weak defense, and a transparent argument as well. He continued by stating that they had to "bind her up to the crimes,"[225] which must have meant, find direct correlation or direct evidence that put her there. In actuality, there was practically no direct evidence that put her there, by her own admission, not to mention a bonafide motive, if all the facts were to have been clearly disseminated.[226]

The acts of sexual abuse within any family, typically, may starve the soul and devastate the lives of its victims. This was true in the

American society of 1892, just as it would be in the twenty-first century. The difference in 1892, was that a woman or man who may have fallen victim to such abuse as children, would not have had outlets that would come decades later in society. In other words, it was a repressed society, whereby a woman such as Lizzie Borden would not have had the freedom to let her hair down, appear drunken in good society nor step outside any of the numerous restrictions and expectations of Fall River, Massachusetts. Nor would she have had anyone to turn to, either professionally or personally, to discuss her life as an abuse victim.

Robinson went on to state that there was no blood on her person. He downplayed the role of the pin-sized bloodstain even stating that she had her "monthly illness,"[227] and went on to surmise that she may have turned her skirt around, in order to have made this theory make sense.

Then as Robinson tried to dance around the entire scenario of the burned up paper, discovered as having been tossed into a fire contained on the stove in the kitchen by Dr. Bowen, at some point it was surmised that Emma's name was visible on the note.[228] This may have indicated that Lizzie had written to her and wanted her to come home immediately. It may have been for support, but may also have simply been more attempts to clean up the mess, and that she desperately needed her sister to help her in the aftermath.

For whatever reason, Dr. Bowen had a need to burn the paper in the fire, and do it quickly. The fact that he went to such great lengths to destroy it; when there were witnesses and observers so close at hand, indicated that the nature of the note must have been incriminating.[229] In point of fact, that note may well have been a confession of guilt to a trusted sister, from Lizzie.

In typical pontification, Robinson babbled on about Harrington claiming that Dr. Bowen was some sort of accomplice to Lizzie. He mentioned that the claim had been that Dr. Bowen somehow wrapped the missing wooden handle of the hatchet weapon, inside the said note. Officer Philip Harrington, as witness, was also assured that the note was simply of a personal nature, and related to Dr. Bowen.[230]

Robinson then went on to create as much confusion about the handle as possible. In the same way that witnesses were confused about the hatchet, Robinson said, "Fleet (Officer) did not see it; Mullaly (Officer) did see it."[231] He further pointed out how Fleet did not remove the hatchet from the box in the basement, while Mullaly actually claimed to have seen Fleet remove it."[232]

Robinson then went into detail about how the murderer must have stood astride the body, a large body at that, because Abby Borden weighed around two hundred pounds. Robinson said it in such a way, as to imply that Lizzie could not have done it. He inferred that she would have been incapable of having stood over Abby's body in such a way. Robinson believed that by explaining, in crucial detail, how one would have had to stand over Abby Borden as he or she literally, "chopped her head to pieces,"[233] that he eliminated Lizzie from suspicion. He had thought that these gruesome details, and logistics around Abby's somewhat large body, would sway opinion away from Lizzie's guilt.

Robinson pointed out that the jury had visited the Borden house, and had been asked to travel up and down the staircase to see if, for certain, one could see a body beneath the guest room bed from the top of the stairs. The answer was yes. So he proved that Lizzie would have been able to as well.

Perhaps an innocent Lizzie may not have thought to look in that direction but still probably would have seen the body, and have alerted everyone. Conversely, a guilty Lizzie would have already known it was there, and despite having seen it in full view from the top of the stairs, would have said nothing. As the District Attorney believed, she ignored it because she was indeed, the murderer.

This was a point that the prosecution wanted to reiterate. If Lizzie had been innocently tooling about upstairs in her room, then it was likely that she would have seen Abby's body under the bed.

Also, for Robinson to have gone on to claim that surely, among the jury themselves, there was "not one of you"[234] that would have squinted under that bed on that particular tread of the stairs, was to make a huge and possibly erroneous assumption. After all, Robinson would not have known what was in their minds, or even viable in their peripheral vision, just as they could not make that assumption about Lizzie, had she most definitely been innocent, and not the murderer.

Ironically, Robinson next presented a counter scenario which may have read more like an adolescent's homework, reasoning around the facts including the upstairs door. In Porter's *The Fall River Tragedy*, he began to explain that there was evidence that it (the door to the guest-room where Abby lay) was open later, but no evidence that it was open before Mr. Borden came in.[235]

By trying to create doubt as to whether or not the door to the guest room was open or closed, Robinson actually created more doubt around Lizzie's innocence. The doubt was precisely around Robinson's confidence as it related to his argument. Had Lizzie paused on the stairs on that fateful day? On her way downstairs when Andrew Borden arrived and rang the front doorbell? What Robinson accomplished by bringing up this fact, that the door may have been closed, was intended to cast doubt upon the validity of his theory that "Lizzie would not pause on the stairs to look under the bed."[236] He did not accomplish this.

Next, he rolled into a long speech about the shutters in the guest-room. The discussion involved the idea that any modern housewife in 1892, who'd been concerned with the chance that her carpets would fade, would have indeed closed the shutters. For that simple reason, Robinson claimed that it was almost certain that the shutters would most assuredly have been closed in the Borden house in the guest-room. He also said that when the doctors were called to the room, it was exceedingly dark, and even difficult for them to see anything.[237] So it followed, according to Robinson, that it would have been next to impossible for Lizzie to have seen Abby Borden's dead body on the floor, visible, as it lay sprawled underneath the bed. Why was this point reiterated by Robinson? He was attempting to press the point that no one, much less Lizzie standing so many feet away on the stair, could have seen Abby's body.

However, if regarded logically, one may have questioned his presenting an entirely new argument about darkness in the room. His own personal lack of credence in his prior argument that Lizzie would not have paused to look under the bed from her stance on the stairs, was now also questionable. Why had he presented a new argument?

In other words, in his determination to expunge any idea that Lizzie had spotted Abby's dead body, he discredited his first argument. Because he had expounded upon the fact that Lizzie would not have paused to take a look. This insistent argument was now moot. He contradicted himself. Because why would the statement "daughter going about her house chores," who would not "pause on the stairs," have been relevant? The truth was, he simply layered upon the jury excessive reasons how and why Lizzie could not have been guilty. The shutter argument could have stood alone. It was a bit of overkill on his part.

Chapter Twelve

S aturday morning awakened in Fall River, Massachusetts. The events of the previous days had left the town bare, hollow and numb. Colette and Sadie witnessed the repercussions of the tragedy, and its architect two days before, as she said goodbye to her victims. Today was brighter. Fifteen or so young women milled about in the blinding hot sunshine of the Perfect Pines Insane Asylum's vast lawn. The fete had arrived. The garden party to display the farm animals, as Colette saw it. It amazed her as she absorbed all the colors of long skirts, the shimmer of white blouses and pearls, and the tresses wound up in buns, that women had to endure so much fabric. Here it was almost a one-hundred-degree day on the East coast and each skirt was voluminous enough to make a parachute. Still, there was something romantic, and lovely, about the days of feminine attention to details like lace and medium starch.

This morning, Colette's concerns centered upon Sadie. Sadie had spent the night before shackled to a wall in the basement of the asylum. In addition to being missed at dinner Thursday night, another patient had overheard her mention the suffrage movement. Sadie had not been the same since their mission of discovery into the bowels of the Borden house. It had surprised Colette that Sadie had actually agreed to tag along. As she looked at Sadie now, and how her dark hair fell in delicate tendrils around her alabaster face, with her hair pulled up as it was into a proper bun, and a strand of pearls around her neck, it astounded her that this same woman had just a day or so before, been gasping for air, backed up against the wall of Lizzie's dining room. Who would have believed they'd witnessed the accused spending time with the dead bodies?

Although the fete had been planned for Saturday, August 6th, Dr. Warburton moved it up a day to take the town's minds off the murders. Sadie had been an accomplice in curiosity about what had truly happened at 92 Second Street. In her way, with her hair slipping out of her hat and tickling her shoulders, she looked carefree wearing just her skirt and the white long coat. Sadie had always been a rebel, spitting in the face of Victorian expectations.

The details of the case rolled through Colette's mind. She watched Sadie as she wandered about, not talking to anyone. Now and then she would race up to someone, start talking at a manic pace until the couple or family member of a patient would turn away from her, slightly confused by her.

For the first time, Colette wondered what possible good she was doing in this place. She pondered why the Prairie door, and the bracelet had chosen her?.

What good was she doing being present in 1892 in Fall River, Massachusetts? She faced the woods alongside the party that ran the length of the green lawn. It hit her suddenly that she'd already outlived her mother Ursula. It wasn't fair. Why did she have to die at age 51? So young. For what? Sometimes an inexplicable shame was indeed passed on to the next generation, even if that next generation was fortunate enough to not withstand a similar form of abuse. There would be other signs of the indignities of the parent; low self-esteem, and profound guilt. A simple hug from one's mother? Colette had spent much of her childhood trying to get physical affection from Ursula. Colette would try to be perfect, prompt, good in school, talented; anything and everything just to bring her mother out of her lethargic despondency. Unfortunately, she recalled now, Colette had found out as an adult, that Ursula had been prescribed valium in the

1970s to treat her extreme depression. Perfect, Colette thought. Let's get her addicted AND bring her down. Colette knew that modern psychiatry in the way of prescribing medications had come very far, and that many were thriving on non-addictive medications for depression and obsessive-compulsive disorder and a host of other mental disorders. She just felt that sometimes medications were still prescribed too readily.

Colette turned away now, biting her finger, trying to hold back a rush of tears. Mustn't look too crazy for the wealthy patrons, she thought, shaking her head. Yet she knew that Dr. Warburton was coming into the young women's rooms, many of them already victims from their own homes, and was further violating them. Having sex with them. Touching and prodding them like they were cattle.

She started to walk into the woods, until a firm hand yanked her back. A gangly unusually tall male asylum assistant shoved her back into the middle of the party. As she tripped back to a circle of dazed fellow patients, it hit her. Secrets make you sick, she thought. Secrets make you sick, that was it.

Those words she'd learned in years of recovery. Maybe she was here in 1892, not only to figure out who the hell the skeletons in the coal chute were back in Illinois, or the connection to the hieroglyphs and the bungalow, or maybe it was something less obvious. But Lizzie Borden had spent not only her lifetime as a pariah, an outcast, and a suspected murderer, she'd also left behind a dubious legacy in the annals of history as the maniacal "axe murderer" of her parents.

Maybe Colette's visit was simply to give Lizzie a voice, instead of a reputation.

Colette stood there, witnessing how the male doctors and male administrators charmed the wealthy patrons and families of the imprisoned patients of this institution. She realized too, even in the light of how far women had come through the decades, there still existed a bias in society toward addiction and mental illness.

Dr. Warburton pointed to her and spoke with a young couple perhaps hoping to commit a parent, or a sister. As he indicated Colette, he sputtered something about "even the older women find a place among their peers."

Colette frowned. Yanking down on her sleeves, she lifted the bodice off her chest a moment, trying to cool off. Another aid was watching Sadie with hungry, lascivious eyes. Across the patch of grass, all the way near the back of the sanitarium, a young girl was being pushed along. She'd been forcibly dressed in a pink frock. Her face was pained as another asylum assistant held her by her small, white-gloved hand. As they drew closer, Colette saw that the girl's face was red with tears.

Steering clear of the punch bowl, Colette picked up a sumptuous peach from a bowl and took a seat on a white wooden chair.

A group of male patients were being herded across the back of the picnic area toward a massive barn used for their special "crafts." Dr. Warburton made sure to keep the men separate from the women's ward. This was not out of kindness or propriety, but rather because Dr. Warburton wanted the women all to himself.

Colette looked around furtively, then got up and moved to the rear of the asylum as swiftly as possible. Walking along the far wall, away from the party, she skimmed a row of raised basement windows. Then she slowed. Thin, emaciated creatures were lined up along a cement wall. There were puddles on the floor around where they sat. Several women sat in the midst of the filth. Sadie had insisted she'd been shackled, "somewhere in the asylum, cold and cement," was all she'd said. Colette had no idea how accurate Sadie had been. She had, but now seeing this suffering, it was clear.

Two male assistants were heading her way. Darting over behind the crafts barn where the men were being housed, she ran the length of the place all the way around, and back to the fete. She straightened her skirt as she swept back into the soiree, resuming nibbling the peach as elegantly as possible.

Chewing the refreshing fruit, her mind went to 2011 again. In spite of strides made in politics and corporations, many "modern" women had become educated in universities, and then proceeded to simply marry well and stay home and raise the kids. Education bought women good husbands, who could earn a great living, and take care of their likely four or five, offspring. Didn't women, put women right back where they started in 1890? So in light of incarceration, starvation and chaining themselves to railings, for what reason then, did suffragettes go to such extremes for women, if women in the future were simply going to disregard any progress? Not only had progress been disregarded, it was impeded and even reversed in decades such as the 1950s and the 1990s.

Colette always understood it was about much more than simply gaining the right to vote with the ratification of the 19th amendment in 1920s America. For instance why was it, that as of 2011, women would still did not make equal pay to their male counterparts in the workplace?

Colette could control her grievances against suppliant submissiveness in women, at least now, in this moment. Like-minded, she felt the violent angst of these women confined to kitchens or locked in asylums back in 1892. Colette also stood in the presence of Lizzie Borden, in the same room with her, the woman whose very name conjured up a hatchet-wielding monster. Colette had assimilated the feelings in that room, in the charged atmosphere and hateful calm of that dining room. She and Sadie stood in Lizzie's world, in the dark presence of those dead bodies. In her mind, as Colette had watched Lizzie standing there in the dark, with her hands resting on the feet of those persons responsible for her life of neglect and sexual abuse, a type of connection was transmitted to Colette. For the first time even, since having learned of the crimes, as a young girl, Colette saw Lizzie, instead as a wounded survivor, someone who fought back against the ruthless expectations and standards set for the woman in the Victorian era. A murderer, yes. She'd chosen the wrong way out. But perhaps Lizzie felt she had no other recourse?

It was a savage crime. Despite the final acquittal, it endured for most scholars of the murders, as an unsolved crime.

Why now, as Colette watched the women she'd come to know in the asylum, dear Sadie and her zest for sexual freedom and Isabelle, the escape artist who harbored the shameful secret within her own family, did Colette feel a sense of sympathy for Lizzie? Kinship between women, perhaps? Sadie spoke of making love with Percy, her Sousa musician as beauty under the trees and stars. Apparently they'd taken to outdoor lovemaking usually following a concert when her Percy felt amorous. One night, according to one of the first stories Sadie told her, they'd not even made it past the band gazebo. In their zeal, they'd rolled off the stage and landed in a flowerbed of impatiens and begonias.

As she looked around the stage of green grass and groomed women, she realized Isabelle was gone again.

Sadie burst upon her. "I'm frightened," she said.

Colette turned. Sadie stood close to her, wringing her white hands together.

"Sadie? What is it?"

"What if she saw us?"

"Who?"

Sadie glanced around furtively, her eyes seeming to struggle to focus on Colette. "Lizzie. What if she saw us? We're next. She will come after us too."

Colette pulled Sadie aside and whispered. They stood behind an elaborately decorated sandwich and cake table.

"There will be no more murders. Not by her hand. Proof positive."

Sadie held her breath, still wringing her hands. "Proof of what?"

The air sifted in a pungent smell of horse manure, something Colette was certainly unaccustomed to. The swirling air only stirred around the angry heat, like some one hundred degree cauldron. In this eastern town, the heat epitomized the breaking point Lizzie too must have reached to bring her to this tragic point in her life, to her murderous decision.

"Because you know why Lizzie did it."

A well-dressed dandy of an older man, in black morning coat and neatly-tied cravat, eyed Sadie quite deliberately. The air was humid and hot and yet people strolled about, in and out of the sumptuous buffet tables. Tiny multi-colored cakes were displayed on one table. Several women with crème glove-covered hands reached for one pastry or another. There was a stark contrast between the rail-thin likes of Sadie and the other patients, and the full, well-fed shapely and healthy figures of wealthy Fall River.

Sadie tilted her chin upward, and closed her eyes in the bright sunshine. "I think I understand." Her face somehow still appeared pale even outside. "Isabelle and I have known all along."

The two women strolled alongside the outskirts of the event, not wanting anyone to overhear them. More men in cleverly creased suits, long black Jackets, high white collars and black cravats assumed the excited conversation of Colette and Sadie must have been due to their presence. Surely these women showed interest in these carefully coiffed dandies. Their smug smiles seemed to say, "we know you women would do anything to get out of this place. And we can accomplish that for you."

Sadie had admitted something about her friendship with Lizzie and that Lizzie had confided in her. "Nothing too specific. And then, Isabelle couldn't speak about it at all," she said. "She keeps running away. Because her family is evil too. And that includes her brother, William I might add."

"I get what you're saying about William," Colette agreed. "He's a charmer and an actor."

"Isabelle's mother and that dreaded basement. She couldn't talk about it. No one knows for sure. There's rumors too about some coal chute."

"What coal chute? In their house?"

Sadie pulled a couple of grapes out of her dress pocket. They'd left a purple stain in the white linen of the dress. "No. Isabelle overheard her father tell a business associate while having brandy in his posh study, that the 'canary won't be chirping any more' and they laughed. There was mention of a house in Chicago."

Colette nodded, her mind racing. She thought about the vacuous hole on Prairie Street, and that grey morning when she and Bob had discovered the human skeleton. "They say," she said, "that the saying 'Canary in the Coal Mine' means harbinger of death. So when a canary stopped singing in a coal mine, that meant there was methane or carbon monoxide. That was how coal miners knew not to go in."

Sadie tilted her chin upward, and closed her eyes in the bright sunshine. "I don't understand why it's this way for women." Her face still appeared pale, even in the outside air and with the sun warming her. "Although life would be easier if more women shared our views, Isabelle and me. We're unseemly representatives of our gender, apparently. But look where our passions got us?" She held up her arm and indicated the party-goers and then the asylum. "A lifetime stay at the Pines! Vacancies created daily!"

Sadie stared at her blankly a moment, then started laughing uncontrollably, running away from Colette at full speed.

Colette didn't move. Sadie's mood swings always surprised her. Within minutes, a hospital attendant had both arms around Sadie, and was guiding her back to the soiree. Dr. Warburton pulled her aside and spoke very deliberately to her, his eyes boring into hers. Sadie's expression went from whimsical to despair within seconds. She tried to sweep past him, her eyes on a plate of cucumber sandwiches. Dr. Warburton followed, with a bit of a swagger, and caught her hand, stopping her. There were several other men with him.

One of them gestured toward her. A prosperous couple stood by. The woman with a ridiculous feather protruding from a silly hat had her body swathed head to toe in lace and tulle fabric, with pearls falling about her in waves. Colette moved closely enough to hear.

"For this unfortunate young woman," he went on, indicating Sadie, "she had destroyed all chances for a normal life as a respectable woman."

One of the clinicians leaned over and whispered harshly in Sadie's ear, "the better food is not for patients," he said.

"What has she done, exactly?" the well-dressed woman asked directly, adjusting pearl decorated pince-nez on her nose.

One of the men looked at his pocket watch, then shoved it back in his pocket, the watch fob still dangling. It was as if Sadie was not standing there in their midst, as if they viewed her like some mouse running on a wheel in a cage.

"She humiliated a family, an important family. Her fiancé's family. Percy had a short stint in the Sousa Traveling Band. That's how she met him. She was aggressive in a way that women are not supposed to be. Never fear, your daughters and wives will be safe here. They will likely become, in fact, more compliant. Why Miss Sadie here is adjusting quite nicely. We've almost controlled her unchaste impulses."

The man nodded, taking a sip of red wine in a thick crystal glass.

Sadie watched the men, while fixing her gaze on the ground. She pressed her forefinger to her lips. She seemed to hear them, but did not process their conversation. It was about her, no doubt. It was at that moment that Colette realized they had drugged her. Certainly it was further punishment for her missing at dinner the night before. She did not give up Colette's name either.

All at once, Isabelle stormed onto the property, a splash of color against the green grass, a gaudy contrast with the delicate white lacy sleeves and hats of the more affluent, billowing around her. It was as if she'd never left. Clearly, she'd returned voluntarily. She was on a mission.

Colette covered her mouth with her hand. Wait until Warburton sees what she's wearing, she thought. Isabelle sported red velvet, tucked and tight in all the vital places. Colette approached her. Isabelle's sleeves were rolled up, and she had on black gloves which reached up to her elbows, a row of small buttons on each one. Around her neck she'd thrown a set of opera length pearls. The dress itself was short enough to reveal the tops of her boots, especially when she fell back into a white wicker chair. She hiked her heavy skirt up to her knees. One fussy man in a black and white suit merely shook his head and directed his comrades away from her. Before God and the world, Isabelle torched up a cigarette with a long wooden match. It was perhaps at that moment that the doctors spotted her, and Colette raced over to her.

Leaning over, Colette whispered in Isabelle's ear. But the look in Isabelle's eyes was defiant. She pulled away from Colette, as if she didn't know her. Then conversely, she extended one gloved hand, opening up her palm very slowly, indicating the chair beside her.

Colette sat down quickly, looking around a bit. Had anyone noticed the patient in red?

"I need to ask you," Colette began, "about the day I saw you. About yesterday morning."

"Day of the murders," Isabelle murmured with an odd smile.

Colette nodded hesitantly, "yes," she said. "Remember when everyone was milling around the block on Second Street? Yesterday around 11:30 or 12:00? You just came out of your father's house, down the front stairs? Remember? Your hands were bloody. You seemed to be holding onto ripped wallpaper. It was coming out of your pockets too? You were badly injured. Half the people in town must have seen you."

Isabelle nodded, taking a long drag on her cigarette. Her eyes were distant, the pupils dilated. Was she too medicated like the other patients? Or was she on something else?

Noting Colette's expression, Isabelle nodded. "Yes," she said, "they gave me something." She exhaled cigarette smoke forcefully. "It angers me. They know I battle with the laudanum. Even though it's all that gets me through life any more."

As she spoke, her lip trembled on the cigarette. Then she took a deep breath and tipped her chin up.

Colette pressed further. "I wanted to know," she said, "where you'd been kept that day? What had happened to you in your father's house?"

Suddenly Isabelle laughed derisively. She threw the cigarette on the grass. "I angered father that day. Yes, I did. He brought me home from the asylum and then I escaped his house. You realize they wouldn't even let me see you when you came with them in the morning that one day. They like to act like they're doing the right action. Lizzie had finally done something about her situation. Lizzie murdered the bastard. She'd had enough."

Colette was quiet.

"As you know, my mother used to sing," Isabelle commented. "She sang with an operetta group that traveled with the Sousa band. Father hated them. But that wasn't all she was open about. Mother made a mistake. She told some of the neighbors, people you see here today, what father was really doing to me. But he convinced them of her insanity. That's why she's gone. She also told some of the musicians. She knew Sadie and I had met Percy and Darren, two brass players from the band. Dear old father did not know about that. Not yet."

Colette nodded. "Your brother alluded to something going on with your father?"

"I embarrass him. Mother did too. Running around with strange musicians and actors. He called her the 'canary,'" Isabelle went on, smiling quickly, and then it faded. "She knew my mood swings were related to the drink, to the Laudanum. She tried to help me. I can't help my mood changes. At the same time though, no one believes me. They don't believe me when I tell them I knew things about Lizzie too."

A sudden shade passed as clouds covered the sun. Isabelle's eyes looked black. She took a deep breath, and tossed the hem of her dress down to her feet. "There is now a canary in the coal chute," she said.

An odd sensation came over Colette. Even the sounds around her, even a concert band they'd hired for the fete seemed to fade.

"That's what I heard HIM say." Isabelle forced a whisper.

"Who?"

"Father." Then her face changed, brightened. But too quickly, as if it were a spasm.

After a moment, Colette asked her, "did you notice anything in the attic? When we were looking at dresses?"

"That's not where I got mine," Isabelle said, laughing a bit hysterically. "I borrowed my ensemble du jour," she said, with emphasis, "from our local Madame. If only more men would just go there instead of ruining our lives."

At this statement, Isabelle leaned back and yanked her hair out of the bun. She put her hands behind her head, and rested in this way, with her face up to the sun and her eyes closed. Her dark eyebrows were curved in perfect arches against her slightly freckled face, which stood out now in the sheer sunshine. How fitting, Colette thought, that they likened her to a young free-spirited girl.

The breeze was so inviting, so gentle and sincere, and in its way, innocent. Summertime. She smiled to herself. In the days of youth, it always triggered a need for closeness, captured kisses beneath the trees or behind the bleachers.

"Father often goes on long voyages for his business. He was even on the same ship with Lizzie when she traveled abroad on her Grand Tour two years ago. I think it was two years ago?" She looked to the sky again. "We also know, for sure, that Lizzie came back from that trip a changed woman. A very changed woman. A new type of, not sure what? Anger? Yes. A new type of anger drove her. God bless her. I go to Europe often. My Lord if she wasn't so pleased when I brought her a French travel bag with her initials. L.A.B. It was from the House of Vuitton. Little checkerboard pattern. They made us two small bags special, just for me. I have one with my initials too."

Nodding, Colette listened and nibbled on grapes. She was extremely thirsty in the heat, but she knew she had to avoid any punch they'd concocted.

She turned to Isabelle.

"How exactly was she changed?"

"Lizzie was my friend. We taught Sunday school together. I had the younger kids. She would go on about the delicious food in France, and the amenities of available running water, better plumbing and electricity. You see, some folks in town claim that the Bordens have no electricity or running water. Don't know how much of that is true." She stopped, her expression distant, her small hands tracing the garish ribbons on her red dress. "Oh, and she loved the people in Italy. So expressive as a people. I guess she saw firsthand, what money can buy. Her father was indeed stingy. But that's not the main reason she killed them."

She grew quiet a moment. Colette sighed, folding and refolding a white cloth napkin on the table.

"Let's go for a walk, Isabelle."

"Glad to."

Within minutes, the two women had strolled out of the sunshine and stood in the shade at the side of the massive sanitarium. Colette could see that Isabelle's emotions were charged, to the point of hysteria. She seemed a bit too excited for 1:00 p.m. in the afternoon? Oh God, they'd probably given her more pills.

There came a rushing scent of flowers, and the organic smell of the earth welcomed them into a small clearing in the woods. How to fathom that Colette breathed in 1892? Perhaps she always assumed over one hundred years in the past would smell like an antique store? The same dusty scent of books and old leather and aged linen and cotton. She took a deep breath of it all; half expecting her neighbor's black Lexus to scream past but hearing instead the clomping of horses' hooves as a middle-aged couple bumped past in a carriage.

Oddly, all at once, Colette was overwhelmed with a need to sleep. My God, she thought. I've been drugged too. Prairie grass spread before her, encircled by trees, and hidden within them. Isabelle had wandered back and crashed into the party of patrons and parents and doctors. Just on the outskirts of the trees, there was a row of elegant massive Victorian houses. It made Colette wonder about the location of Maplecroft. For all she knew, Lizzie's future home could be one of those places?

Colette fell to the ground. Her body felt like a sand bag and she had no muscle strength. Resting on her elbows, she tried to push up. Then she felt the tightness of the bracelet again, and some light lavender dust appeared on her wrist. It told her that something was going to change. She knew it. Oh God, she wondered. Where would she be going now? Further back than the bodies in the dining room?

The bracelet had never felt this tight before.

Colette's next sensation was a yearning, a tug coming from some deep place inside of her, a profound place of slumber. She struggled to remain conscious, but the battle could have been likened to trying to stay up during an unfamiliar opera in an uncomfortable auditorium seat.

Then she sat up straight, rubbing her eyes. No need to worry about smearing makeup. No such adornments allowed in 1892. She knew she'd been sleeping for a while, but now she was seated on a sidewalk, on a busy thoroughfare. It was stiflingly hot. The sun was high in the sky, an eastern sky. She was certain it was morning. A humble horse and buggy food cart of some sort clomped by at a deathly slow march. Distinctly, she heard a newspaper boy say "hello Hyman!" to the driver. It was an ice cream buggy. She must have dozed. Even if only for thirty seconds, the bracelet was tight. This was a serious time travel. To where had she gone now?

My God, she knew him. She knew precisely who Hyman was. It was the morning of August 4th, 1892. This was the fact she'd read about, when Hyman Lubinsky, the young Russian immigrant and the man once suspected of helping Lizzie as her male agent in the murders of her parents, was riding by, right at the precise moment of which he had testified to having done so. For when she looked at her watch, it was 10:45 am. She was across the street from the Borden house. It waited there, the framed farmhouse with equally spaced windows, two and a half stories high. A picket fence traveled along the front of the small patch of yard, within an arm's throw of the sidewalk. Something about the house now seemed to scream and she imagined the place was moving, swaying from left to right. The front door was on the right hand side, deeply recessed inside massive wood framing which surrounded it. The house brooded, its wood siding and shutters dingy, angry and anti-social. By God, and there stood Andrew Borden, struggling with the front door of his house on Second Street. In his hand was the bulky lock he'd picked up on the street.

This was the moment. Colette was positive. This man would be murdered in the next fifteen minutes. A man in a black Prince Albert coat and his wife slowed their promenade up the sidewalk, checking to see if Colette was quite alright. That's when the bloodied flash came to her mind, a similar Prince Albert coat would soon be meticulously rolled up and placed under Mr. Borden's head on the sofa in the sitting room across the street. Right across the street from where she now sat.

She struggled to her knees, wiping stones and splinters off her hands. Feeling a bit clumsy in her long grey skirt, she soon balanced herself and stood upright again. A young couple paused and she nodded, and waved them away. When she looked up again, she spotted Bridget Sullivan opening the door for Mr. Borden and right on cue, the two of them disappeared inside the house.

Sweat broke out on Colette's face. At that moment, William Sewell rushed up, seemingly out of nowhere. He waved to a swarthy young man driving the horse and buggy ice cream truck.

"Hyman! How are you today?" he said.

But the driver stared straight ahead, intent upon his mission of progressing down the street. He moved very slowly, the horse plodding along.

"Colette," he started, turning back to her.

Colette's heart raced. She studied the Borden house, afraid to blink.

"My mother," William said, "has gone missing again. Father was tracking her through Pinkertons. But she's left again, somewhere in Chicago. Father is furious."

It was the first time since she'd come to know him, that William's voice sounded truly angry. Something was seriously wrong. She had to watch the house across the street knowing the precise timing of all the witnesses around the crime, and knowing Hyman had just driven past the Borden house, which meant the murder of Andrew Borden was imminent. Colette purposely stepped back to take in the side yard and see if there was any sign of Lizzie walking as yet, the path between the barn and the house. Of course, she saw no one.

"Truth is," William went on, "father is right about her. Listen to me, Colette. He just came back by train from some town called Valley Stream, Illinois. That's where the Pinkertons think they have spotted her again. He's convinced she's a fallen woman who has taken to prostitution. Woman like that? He said she has no desire to see Isabelle or myself ever again."

Colette stared at him, totally at a loss.

The concurrent timing of what Colette knew would be happening in mere minutes across the street, and William's apparent concern over his mother, brought several factors into play. The first unfortunate fact was, to William and Edward, Madeline was an inconvenient miscreant wife, not meriting any police efforts. She would likely linger as nothing but idle gossip in Fall River.

At the same time, something remarkable had been occurring in relation to the bracelet, and the Prairie door. Colette noticed that the time frame between time travels had begun to grow smaller in span. And although she knew the when and where was impossible to predict with the time traveling, she somehow felt a responsibility to try to stop what was about to happen.

And lastly, consulting her left wrist, it took her a moment to recall she had left her watch on the bedside table. It was a Bulova which looked out of time in the late nineteenth century. It hit her how odd it was, but some items, no matter from what time periods, like the watch, or any number of inanimate objects that seemed to travel with her, did not alter when she time-traveled. That bloodied petticoat for instance, had followed her through time to her rented room. It was as if the two worlds were melding, the closer she moved toward the truth; the truth about the identity of the skeletons and the psychological reality behind the Borden murders.

Wiping her hands on her skirt, she realized she still wore the dress she'd gotten from Mrs. Burns from the boarding house. Which meant she had not yet been committed to the asylum and had not yet met Sadie. She'd been given another chance and had been sent back to the time just before Andrew Borden's murder.

Perhaps someone would believe her if she barged into the Borden house now. A wave of oppressive heat made her feel nauseated. The weight of her dress, and the petticoat, and the long-sleeves of her blouse seemed to melt into the flesh on her arms. What a restrictive, uptight time this was, she thought, tugging on her cuffs for some relief.

"What time is it?" she asked him quickly.

"Excuse me?"

"The time, William!" She stopped, and started mumbling 'calm down, calm down,' to herself. "What is the time?" Don't be rude to the nice nineteenth century man.

Reaching into his vest pocket, he pulled out a large gold watch on a chain, a fob dangling on the end of it.

"It's precisely three minutes until eleven," he said. "Why?"

Lifting her skirt, she started across the street, running in front of a Model T Ford and two horse and buggies. A driver yelled to her as he pulled up on the reins of his horse.

"Foolish woman!"

Colette continued on, blindly, and stumbled up the front stairs, tripping once on her dress. She fell into the doorknob with both hands and tried to open the door. It was locked. Someone relocked it after Bridget had let Mr. Borden inside.

Down the front stairs in a half-step, she raced to the left side of the house which led to the barn. Panicked, she leapt up the four shallow stairs to the screen door, and started jiggling the doorknob, trying to get in. Back in the yard, she stood halfway between the house and the barn. Then, as if in slow motion, she turned to her left and glanced over her shoulder, trying to focus, despite the sting of perspiration in her eyes, on Second Street itself. Hyman Lubinsky was completely turned toward her in his ice cream carriage, and gazing directly at her. He gave her a simple wave.

A realization hit her like a blow to the head. It was her, Colette, who was the mysterious "woman" Hyman claimed he'd seen walking from the house to the barn. In his testimony, replete with broken English, Hyman claimed that he had spotted an unknown woman. Because he knew, and was familiar with Bridget Sullivan, Hyman was certain it had not been her. And Colette was definitely not wearing a hat.

This simple witness is what ultimately got Lizzie Borden acquitted. Added to that all the incriminating testimony of Lizzie herself, and the other witnesses that the court would not allow to be revealed in court to the jury, the wealthy Miss Borden literally got away with murder. At least, this was Colette's understanding of all the evidence she had read over the years, coupled with her bizarre, and quite recent skill at breaking into spontaneous time travel. She had her proof.

Still, whether or not the unwed woman labeled a "spinster" in society's dictionary was truly a homicidal monster, Colette had still not fully made up her mind. Having just landed in 1892, there were many issues, as they related to women, that she was still discovering and unraveling for herself.

None of this mattered now. She had to get inside the Borden house. But what would the ramifications be of her re-routing of history? It was maddening to be without a wrist watch. How would she gain access to the place? She walked to the back yard. There were windows. She tried them and found each to be locked. Hadn't Bridget just been out washing the windows? At least she would get an answer to this over-a-century-old maddening riddle that would eventually cause decades of speculation.

Scanning the yard, taking note of scattered crabgrass and dirt patches here and there, Colette spotted a red step-stool, stationed under a pear tree. THE pear tree. It was Lizzie's padded alibi. Hard to imagine now, how the young woman stooped down in the heat to grab some pears and balance them as she climbed up the stairs in the barn, donned in heavy cotton and lace, only to sit down again to eat them. Why wouldn't she eat them out in the open? Or maybe under the shade of the tree, instead of in the closed-up sauna that was the upstairs in the barn on this day?

As she looked now, there were no pears on the ground. She recalled Lizzie's testimony of munching at least three of them while waiting in the barn, supposedly looking for sinkers for a fishing line. That had been her story of where she was during the twenty minutes that an evil derelict was inside the house, slaughtering her dear old dad.

Time raced. Colette calibrated in her mind all the events that she knew were, according to the history books, happening at this very moment. The heat was thick. A trickle of sweat rolled down her back, right down her spine, just under the layers of high-collar blouse, fitted Jacket and long skirt. It was as if she were trying to move through molasses. A strong scent of grass and barn and manure filled her up. She felt dizzy. The sunlight was too bright in its way, blinding her view, refracting off the windows of the Borden house until she put up her hand to shield her eyes.

Kicking up her skirt, she wobbled over to the step stool, located at the right side of the house. Yes, she decided. From her research, she recalled the sitting room would be on the right. Even her macabre tour of the place with Sadie the afternoon before, still left her a bit confused about the layout, simply because of her panicked state.

Who would believe what two escapees from the local asylum claimed they saw in the house, the day before? Especially since in the space continuum, dinnertime last night was literally going to happen later today? This was her second time visiting August 4th, 1892. The time travel had snatched her out, right after the murders watching Lizzie in the dining room, and brought her here, precisely to the moment of enraged chaos about to ensue. It felt to her like even the time travel was emotion-driven, disordered, as if it was unsure precisely where it wanted to deposit Colette.

All the years of speculation raced through her mind as she stepped onto the lowest step of the small ladder. The stool had red patent leather cushions, and her black boot stood out starkly against the bright color. Once high enough to the window, she gazed inside.

That's when Lizzie delivered the final blow. Colette started hyperventilating and at the same time struggled to hold her breath. The silhouette of a woman wearing a dark blue floor-length dress, staggered a moment, both her hands grasping a weapon of some sort over her head. Lizzie was positioned slightly behind her father's head. As Colette's vision cleared, and the bright sun wore off, she could just discern something like a smock on the woman, except it was dark, darker than the dress. Lizzie had on a long black jacket, a man's Prince Albert-style coat. She had it on backwards, like some sadistic doctor in surgery. Then all at once, Lizzie turned slowly, robotically, and stared at the window through which Colette watched.

Lizzie's face was impassive, and her eyes were fixed. With a swift movement, she laid the hatchet on the side of the sofa, where there were already the bloody remains of her father. She rolled up the coat she had put on. She then lifted Andrew Borden's head by his hair, and placed the coat under his battered skull. Within seconds, she'd grabbed the hatchet, which was covered in bright red stains and exited the sitting room through the door which led into the kitchen.

Colette knelt down on the stool as swiftly as she could, then clambered her way to the back door. Finding it locked, she spotted a single white door at the rear of the house. She pulled with full force upon the iron handle but to no avail. Of course this door was new, perhaps installed around 1890. It wouldn't budge. She traced the wood with her hand. It was splintery and hot from the sun. Then she saw a hole in the door, a natural wood blemish. Pressing flat against its surface, she peered into the hole and blinked, trying to see if she could see anything.

Through her small vantage point, she could discern a petticoat swaying left and right, and the long blue dress where it just reached the toes of the black ankle-buttoned boots. Water gushed onto the floor. Lizzie's boots were getting soaked. There came sounds of metal scraping on what must have been the cement of the large basement sink. Then Colette saw Lizzie dabbing at the dress with a large towel.

"Come clean, come clean," she heard Lizzie muttering. More banging erupted until all at once the young woman disappeared out of sight. It would seem she had moved to a side table somewhere. Colette tried to imagine where? Perhaps to use a vice and grip? Was she removing the handle to the hatchet? Several possible hatchets would be examined in court. Soon the boots swept past her field of vision. Something wooden fell to the floor. Then she could just make out the back of Lizzie's skirt as she scurried toward the corner of the basement where the stairs led back up into the kitchen.

Colette moved away from the door and skimmed her way along the back of the wood-framed farmhouse. The last thing she wanted, was to be witnessed creeping around the Borden residence on August 4th, 1892. In fact, she would be hard-pressed to explain her presence to anyone. Her feet were sweltering in the ridiculous boots she'd been given to wear.

She glanced around the yard. It was completely empty. She saw no one pass by, no gangly stranger hurdling a lot fence by the pear tree, or slipping through the back yard into the neighbor yard of Adelaide Churchill. In her mind's eye, she pictured all the witnesses described at the trial that would follow, and the supposed sightings of bloodied strangers, and enemies of Andrew Borden, or tenants angry at him over business dealings.

There was no one. Except Lizzie.

Continuing to hug the back wall of the house, the wooden frame feeling hot against her clothing, she ducked under each window of 92 Second Street, then dropped to the ground in some type of marine crawl in her nineteenth century garb, until she reached someone else's yard, whereupon she stood up. She felt wet under her arms. Still, she grazed along, pretending to take a leisurely stroll in her Mutton-sleeved straitjacket.

On the wooden sidewalk moments later, she fell into the bustle of pedestrians and the horse and buggies. Within twenty minutes, she was back at the boarding house. If she recalled the space time perpetuity correctly, she'd not yet been sent to the asylum. She would sleep, perchance to time travel again, and land back at the garden soiree at the Perfect Pines Insane Asylum.

As she lay in bed, she thought about that place, the asylum. It was imperative to get back into the attic of the place, where she'd seen the L.A.B. bag. It had been transported there by someone. If not Hyman Lubinsky, then someone. Perhaps it had been Lizzie herself, attempting to get it out of sight and hidden until the police had finished combing the Borden house.

Dr. Bowen, on that dismal day, had actually persuaded the police to allow Lizzie to cry in peace in her room, immediately following the discovery of the bodies. There would have been ample time then, to have stashed the bloodied dress somewhere, get it off the property, and then transfer it to the L.A.B. bag.

The disappearance of a nineteenth century woman, who was once a proper wife and mother, might not go unnoticed. A wife and mother who made the fatal mistake of embracing women's causes, or the suffrage movement and snappy Vaudeville tunes? Why she actually spouted forward-thinking ideas? She would not be missed, beyond idle gossip. And in light of the fantasm which had erupted on Second Street at the Borden house, who would care if Madeline Sewell, aged 36, slipped silently into the dark and repressed Victorian night?

Chapter Twelve (A)

The Historical Facts

A midst this argument, Robinson refuted Officer Fleet's words regarding Lizzie's testimony, where she stated that she had indeed seen Mrs. Borden at 9:00 a.m., making the guest room bed. The fact that he did this, only brought more attention to the fact that Lizzie was verifiably upstairs at 9:00 a.m. at the same time as Abby.[238]

The fact that Lizzie stated that she'd seen Abby Borden upstairs put her, logistically, right next to the victim, very close to the time of her death. The fact that Robinson reiterated the fact that Bridget claimed she'd talked to Lizzie and heard about the note, did not work well for the defense. Reason being, Lizzie testified to having seen Abby, so legally the assumption was that it was true.

However, Bridget claimed that Abby Borden was in the midst of dusting the sitting room when she was suddenly called away by a mysterious note, a note that was subsequently never discovered.[239] The issue of the note became very much central to the case in the end. Robinson reiterated the fact, that Bridget claimed she saw Abby Borden run off after having announced that she had a note. However, a key possibility to be noted was the fact that Mrs. Borden may clearly have said she was running off, and indeed have received a note about someone being sick, but obviously Bridget did not know that Abby Borden actually had raced upstairs to finish up in the guest room. The justification for this having been a factual sequence of events was because there was, in the end, the dead body of Abby Borden in the guest room. And the coroner's assessment found that she'd been murdered around 9:00 or 9:30 a.m.[240] Apparently, he was able to calculate this fact simply by the state of coagulation of the blood, the temperature of the body, the degree to which rigor mortis had set in, the state of the stomach and the state of the intestines.[241]

Robinson also went on to explain away the non-existence of the purported note, to have been due to the fact that Abby must have burned it right away.[242] Thinking it through logically however, one would wonder why someone called away in such a "hurry," would pause to destroy a note, a note that was neither incriminating nor confidential? Why would Abby have destroyed the note at all? Robinson also claimed that Miss Russell was the one who suggested the note had been burned, not Lizzie, which somehow further exonerated Lizzie in his mind.[243]

In the end, all the circular logic around the note was moot. The fact remained that Lizzie had told Bridget that Abby Borden had received a note from a sick friend, specifically in order to not cause anyone to wonder where she (Abby) was. The entire creation of the note story was to keep the upstairs in the free and clear, in order to murder Abby and then leave the body there, without Bridget ever going upstairs.

Robinson went on to imply that a delicate woman should not have had to put up with all the policemen milling about her house, while she was there. She claimed she was lonely without her sister, and disliked being plied with questions. He affirmed that Marshall Hilliard did the right thing by getting the men out of the place, especially with the terrible "pall" hanging over the house.[244]

Next Robinson delved into the issues around the screen door. Apparently, Bridget claimed to have locked the screen door before going upstairs to rest.[245] Yet, Lizzie's counter-claim was that it was open and in fact, that she'd been outside.

He went on to say that it would be a woman's right indeed, to take her leisure by the pear tree, and then perhaps spend time in the barn. Possibly what he meant by that was due to all the house chores and work women did around the house, that she certainly deserved a rest. It was interesting too, that Robinson was insistent upon asking Miss Russell, Lizzie's closest friend, what exactly she replied to the question of "what did you go to the barn for, Lizzie?"[246] Her answer, and what she specifically replied was, "I went to get a piece of tin or iron to fix my screen."[247]

This response eventually became significant. Throughout the trial Lizzie had been insistent that she'd been in the barn looking for sinkers for her fishing pole.

Robinson was clearly perturbed at the fact that Officer Fleet harped upon Lizzie, regarding the timing of her trip to the barn. He obviously felt the point was repeatedly posed to Lizzie, ad nauseum. Apparently, in his mind, it was an irrelevant point much akin to splitting hairs.[248]

Fleet continued to grill Lizzie as to whether or not it was twenty minutes or half an hour that she went out to the barn. This differential in timing seemed crucial to Fleet, which further angered Robinson. The point was that Andrew Borden arrived home at approximately 10:45 a.m. and according to the physicians who were considered experts at the time.[249] Andrew was murdered between 10:55 and 11:15 a.m.[250] Because even his admission made Lizzie's claims about being completely out of the house, and completely unaware of what was happening to her father inside the house, less believable. Because indeed, if Lizzie indicated that she'd heard a "groan" or a "scraping sound," she told varying stories to different people later on. This added to the falseness of her statements when considering the following: the extreme bludgeoning which caused the immediate death of Mr. Borden would not have allowed for any words to have been spoken, in anguish or in pain, or even as a cry for help. Mr. Borden's face was obliterated at the outset, by someone with a very personal and intimate resentment against him.[251]

Next Robinson went into the minutiae around whether or not Lizzie had actually stood under the pear tree or even in the barn, then she would not have been able to hear anyone going in or out the door. He implied too, that no one would have been seen. This assumption, even if one studied the photos of the house, yard and barn, was a tough theory to fathom. Certainly, an intruder or stranger to the neighborhood would have been seen by someone? If Robinson were to be believed, then perhaps someone indeed witnessed an unknown woman. Perhaps one could have recalled that Hyman Lubinsky happened past the Borden house during the time that "a woman" was spotted leaving the barn, then walking into the house via the screen door. And then there was the young woman seated on the Chagnon's porch, as well as the men positioned behind the house by the wood pile. Not one of these nearby witnesses saw anyone, except for Hyman Lubinsky who claimed he spotted a woman he did not recognize in the yard.[252] In addition, he was certain it was not Bridget Sullivan, whom he knew from having sold her ice cream in the past.

All this insistence upon the fact that Lizzie could not have seen the screen door from the pear tree, or the barn, also would have established that none of these witnesses saw Lizzie either. So if they did not actually see Lizzie, was she really in the yard?

Someone clearly should have spotted her under the pear tree, or coming and going from the barn.

The second transparent argument involved a claim by Lizzie herself that she overheard from the barn "a moan" and/or, the "scraping sound" she testified had brought her hurrying back into the house.[253]

How would it have been possible to not have heard the screen door, as Robinson claimed? Yet somehow, Lizzie could have heard a simple "groan" or "scraping sound?"

Added to that, of course, the aforementioned fact that if the groan was supposed to have come from Andrew Borden, this argument would not have endured under scrutiny.[254] Andrew Borden was supposedly asleep. In reality, he would have been already deceased before he could have experienced pain or uttered a cry.

The entire argument that Lizzie innocently claimed she thought she'd "heard Mrs. Borden come in"[255] and then said, "Bridget, why don't you go check for her?"[256] as a legitimate defense for her innocence, was not full-proof for two reasons; how would she have heard Mrs. Borden come in if she (Lizzie) was in the barn? Secondly, with all the police and people and noise and dead bodies, if Mrs. Borden had really come in, as Lizzie had claimed to have overheard, wouldn't she certainly have gone straight to the sitting room? If not just to see what all the fuss was about? It might follow then, that Lizzie could not have actually heard her come in at all.

What woman of the house in 1892 would not immediately rush to the center of the excitement? Robinson went on to claim that it certainly may have been possible for Lizzie to have overheard a door slam when her step-mother entered the house, and yet how silly was this theory in reality, when one recalled that experts determined that Andrew Borden was only in the house a total of fifteen to twenty minutes before? So how likely would it have been that one would have heard a door close? If someone had entered the house within a twenty to twenty-five minute time frame, if such a person indeed existed, wouldn't they have seen the murderer?[257]

Next Robinson went into some detail as to when exactly Lizzie had laughed or not. At this point, his argument began to dissect the fine points, directly derived from the facts around that same laugh which had been emitted from the staircase.

No one would have known exactly what Lizzie laughed about. It would have been ridiculous to think that from her stance at the top of the stairs, that she could have overheard Bridget utter "O, pshaw" from the front door.[258]

The experts for the defense reiterated that Lizzie probably stood just inside the doorframe of her bedroom. Robinson purported this to be true to further convince jurors that she would not have been able to see the prostrate dead body of her step-mother on the floor, situated under the bed. In actuality, it was likely that Abby's body would have been visible from the stairs located outside the guest room.[259] However, Robinson's other point was that the guest room door was actually closed, and therefore Lizzie certainly would not have been able to see the body of Abby Borden.

The trouble with this argument was that if Lizzie was indeed just inside the doorway of her room, it would have been difficult to have heard a hushed "pshaw" uttered by Bridget. Bridget was all the way down the stairs by the front door. Bridget claimed Lizzie was halfway down the stairs when she had erupted into her unusual burst of sadistic laughter.

If that was the case, it would have been difficult for Lizzie to have been two places at once; for instance both standing inside the doorframe, and standing halfway down the stairs.

For whatever reason, Robinson detailed, at great lengths, how normal it would have been for sisters to refer to their mother as "stepmother." However, he went on to say how "many a man"[260] recalled his true mother, the one who "lived to see him grow up, and kind as anybody else may be, there never goes out of his heart the feeling for that dead one that is gone."[261]

The problem with this argument was that it should have brought to mind, as previously stated, the fact that Abby Borden came into Lizzie's life when she was only around three or four years old. So conversely, what Robinson had hoped to accomplish, which the jury failed to see, was that Lizzie was in essence, raised from the time she was very small by her step-mother.

Robinson went on, in an analogy to Lizzie and her temperament that it would not be the "dog that barks"[262] that would bite you. He meant that because Lizzie was so outspoken about it having been her "step-mother" and not her mother, that she would not have been the one to murder her. Ironically however, it was well-known that Lizzie was quite closed-mouthed around her feelings about her father.

In point of fact, Lizzie was exceedingly silent about her father. And yet it was important to note that he was murdered to an equally vicious degree, to that of Abby Borden.

Robinson talked about Lizzie's ring. He mentioned that Andrew Borden did not dress like a wealthy man, and definitely did not go in for jewelry or any accoutrements.[263] Yet he wore that ring, the ring which Lizzie had given him and also claimed it was when she was a "little girl." In truth, the ring was a class ring she'd worn in high school. So to have given him such an intimate and meaningful piece of jewelry, at the defining age of becoming a young woman, was if nothing else, curious.[264] Although Robinson waxed euphorically of "that ring" which was the "bond" of union between father and daughter, the implication could have been misconstrued as a highly inappropriate, and as some declared in later years, incestuous relationship between the two.[265]

August 1892

Chapter Thirteen

T here was no other way. Back in Mrs. Burns's boarding house again, Colette stared at the mirror. It was so clear, it even shimmered. It was likely right off the furniture delivery wagon.

She studied it a moment, recalling how it had silvered with age. Well, in the year 2011, it had. Finally, she lay back on the lofty bed and prayed for sleep. What seemed like minutes passed, and someone was shaking her. Eyes wide, she blinked several times, and then saw Sadie and Isabelle towering over her. Since she seemed to have no control over when, and to what time period, she would time travel, this time she had relied solely upon going to sleep for transport. It appeared to have worked. The slide bracelet too, had left lavender dust on her wrist.

"You'll be in great trouble if you don't come with us. Dr. Warburton is looking everywhere for you. He wants to show off his pet patients." Isabelle gazed at her silently, while Sadie rambled on about patrons and important family and being on best behavior and how it was all ridiculous anyway.

It felt as if she were awakening from a deep sleep, a heavily drugged sleep. She hated the feeling. It reminded her of waking up with a hangover from drinking. This was really harsh. It lay heavily in her head like a hallucinogen, or like some heavy liquor she wished she'd never drunk. Although Sadie and Isabelle hovered directly over her, she had trouble focusing on them.

Even worse was her lethargic lack of recall. She had been outside the Borden house, and it had been on THE day. It had been on August 4th, 1892, the very day of the murders. The time traveling was reminiscent of the drunken evenings of yesterday, and not being in control of where she'd end up. The next day consisted of murky and menacing memories of the previous time travel wherever the bracelet had sent her. It appeared that the Prairie door acted as the portal between 1892 and 2011, while the bracelet had been transmitting her backward and forwards within the year of 1892. If sobriety had brought her anything, it was a ready acceptance to take life on life's terms. Because she knew she had not taken the dreaded first drink. It was simply time travel.

"We have to get back up to the attic in the asylum," Colette said quickly. "Where we got the clothes for the reception with Dr. Warburton."

"We can't do that now," Sadie said. "He's a dog prowling after us. "

"He wants all of us," Isabelle added softly, her eyes faraway. Then her gaze fell to the Prairie door in the corner of the room. She stepped over to it, and traced the stained glass with her hand. "This is kind of an odd door," she said.

"I made it," Colette put in quickly. "I like to work with colored glass."

Isabelle nodded, apparently satisfied with the explanation. Sadie however, looked skeptical. Rushing to the large wooden wardrobe closet, Colette threw on a dress. Sadie helped her with the rows of buttons, and then Colette grabbed her pair of black granny boots. She was actually starting to like them. Turning back, she picked up a small silky drawstring purse from the dresser. "Let's go."

Sadie whispered to Colette as they moved down the narrow corridor. "Why did you come back here to the boarding house? Mrs. Burns let you in? Does she know you were in Pines Asylum?"

"She didn't," Colette said cryptically. Once down the stairs, the cruel heat enveloped them outside. Colette raced ahead.

Isabelle was unconcerned about keeping up, her movements graceful and languid, as if always in her own world. A world she created. For all of Isabelle's torpid movements, Sadie contrasted with her frenzied pace. Sadie trotted beside Colette, talking at her non-stop pace. Colette could feel Isabelle's ardent gaze boring through her from behind.

Soon they blended back into the asylum festivities. The fete was still bustling. The lavish reception rolled along, with sweeps of petticoats mixing with men in dark suits dabbing at their faces with monogrammed kerchiefs. A stringed quartet played up on a small stage. It was again one day after the Borden murders. August 5th. Humidity soaked the clothing, and the sun beat upon the white gazebo where the quartet played, fighting off angry flies.

In her mind, Colette recalled that Lizzie would be burning the blue dress in the kitchen stove at any time now. 1892 was prone to long silences. So it was jarring when Isabelle starting speaking very quickly, very softly.

"No one believes us," she said, rhythmically, as if praying a novena. "William and I. My mother, Madeline Sewell. The Pinkertons have even lost her according to father."

"I know," Colette said, touching her arm.

Colette walked beside her, moving in and around doctors, elite families and the much maligned patients. Purposefully, Colette walked through everyone, and circled the periphery of the event, while doctors motioned dramatically with their hands, mapping out their shrewd plans for the mentally ill members of the eloquent families gathered. These were the same families that simply wanted their wives and daughters to get "well." More specifically, they wanted the women to behave like other Fall River, properly raised daughters. The female patients here were either too outspoken; suffragettes intent upon getting women the right to vote or perhaps other sirens who'd mistakenly gotten involved with men.

Like Sadie for example. What had Isabelle been thinking? Brazen enough to pursue a career, much like her mother had? On one of many break-outs from her father's suffocating home on 2nd Street, she'd taken the train to a theater in a neighboring town to audition for an operatic part. She and her mother, Madeline had been twin songbirds who frequented other local theaters and joined whole-heartedly in the concert festivities whenever the Sousa band came to town. This may have been all right for a concert or two, but Edward Sewell would have no part of his wife becoming one of those vaudeville theater types. Talk around Fall River was that they threw themselves into music. So, despite Madeline's impeccable lineage from an old Boston family, she had completely gone "off the rails" according to Edward Sewell. Those same actors, like Nance O'Neil, Colette mused with a smile, would be who Lizzie Borden herself would one day soon be spending all her time with at Maplecroft. Maplecroft would be the lavish house on the wealthy side of Fall River, the house which Lizzie and Emma would purchase after the trial and Lizzie's acquittal.

As Colette raced along with Sadie, Isabelle followed closely behind, fighting angry tears as she mumbled lost words about her mother.

At the same time, Colette thought of her own mother. Her mind had gone to seeing Ursula, with a skeletal frame near the end of her life, struggling against cancer. Seated at the dining room table, her weight toppedd out at around eighty pounds on her five foot four frame. Propped up on pillows, she'd typed away on an old typewriter, determined to complete her Ph.D. dissertation, before she died. Ursula had the tenacity of a terrier. She completed her degree.

Sadie touched Colette's shoulder, as if to comfort her for something she didn't understand.

Isabelle's face, serene and oval, looked introspective. But the cool blue eyes were dotted with enlarged black pupils. Colette feared she'd started on the laudanum again.

"Isabelle. What about the meetings at the hospital? Sadie told me you've been leading groups to help other women with their addictions to laudanum and morphine? I don't know that we can save your mother, but you are leaving such a legacy by helping other women stay off the drugs and alcohol."

Isabelle nodded.

"And you helped Lizzie too."

Isabelle closed her eyes and sighed. When she opened them, they looked glassy. Like looking into fog. She wiped away tears with the back of her hand. Torment creased her strong brow, reminiscent of the face she'd unveiled the day she stumbled out of her father's house.

Colette had made up her mind. The Lizzie Borden case had haunted her all her life, simply because of the extreme anger of Lizzie as murderer. Because Ursula Grant had an equal amount of fury, and she'd unfortunately turned it all against herself. And now, traveling through time, in and out of the universe, this true story defied all sense of logic. But it had happened for a reason.

"I saw the travel bag," Colette said at last. "I saw the L.A.B. initials on the bag too. You helped Lizzie, didn't you? You and Emma. The way I figure it, Dr. Bowen helped Lizzie hide the bloodied dress for a little while in her room, while he kept the police at bay, all during that day of the murders. Once Emma came home, she was riding in the same horse and buggy that would take the bag from Lizzie. Lizzie had hidden the dress and the bloody hatchet in the bag, perhaps after transferring it from Dr Bowen's doctor bag. Soon thereafter, she asked Emma to stash it in the carriage and advised the driver where to deliver it. Right to the Perfect Pines Insane Asylum where Lizzie knew you would be locked up again. Edward Sewell made a regular practice of committing his daughter routinely.

"It can't be," Isabelle said, her tone unsteady.

Sadie stepped between them. "I knew that carriage driver. Joseph Simpson. He was sweet on me once, before I met my fiancé," she stopped. "My former fiancé. I introduced him to Lizzie and Emma so he did them a favor ridding the Borden house of the L.A.B. travel bag. It had Lizzie's initials on it. It had the bloody dress in it, too."

Sadie wrapped her arms around the other two women.

"It wasn't Hyman Lubinsky," Colette went on. "It wasn't the Russian immigrant driving the ice cream truck. Because," she hesitated, "he saw me. I am the mysterious woman that was walking from the barn to the house. The woman Hyman saw but knew it was not Lizzie. It was me. Not Lizzie. I was in the Borden yard at the time of the murder of Andrew Borden. I will not tell anyone. Not the authorities. Not anyone. I need to allow the acquittal to happen. The future depends upon it."

With that, she walked again. The sun glared in her eyes too brightly. They approached the back steps to the asylum. Colette tried the doors, jiggling the knobs, yet knowing it was fruitless. They always kept the place locked tightly. Approaching a basement window, she took a rock from the walkway and shattered it with one toss. Someone screamed, a pathetic weak wail. Below, inside another window, Colette spotted the ragged row of patients, seated on the concrete floor.

Sadie gasped at the sight. She remembered being locked up there numerous times. When Colette turned to look at her, Isabelle shrunk back, with her arms crossed over her chest. This was scary for her, Colette thought. She also knew that Isabelle had drunk a bit of laudanum that day. An exhausted look of interminable crisis showed on her face. Colette had seen that face on many of the patients that first morning when she'd visited the asylum with Edward and William. A support group of sorts, these women formed a bond with intimate talk, perhaps for the first time ever. Colette discovered them in the woods. Isabelle started the group. Sadie had stood up and proclaimed her addiction to alcohol, loudly, firmly. Isabelle admitted she was addicted to both laudanum and opiates. No one knew that Isabelle had formed clandestine meetings at the asylum. They met in the woods, or in the small supply closet in the basement, behind where the more, supposedly maniacal patients were shackled. The thought of Isabelle leading such meetings reminded Colette of her first meeting in recovery at a city hospital in Chicago. It was as if she was there once again, over twenty years before. She'd held hands with strangers, they'd prayed together. Everyone was so happy and yet at first she'd felt bitter and angry. Then that changed.

Suddenly it hit her. Isabelle had that same fierce devotion to Lizzie Borden. Could Lizzie have been addicted to some substance too? Certainly around the time of the murders, Dr. Bowen had pumped her full of morphine.

She turned to Isabelle. "I have to know what you've hidden upstairs."

Isabelle's eyes darkened, as if ashen clouds passed through them. Colette backed away and was soon flush against the broken window. Isabelle continued to gaze at her.

"You need to forget what you think you know," Isabelle said at last. Forget about the attic and what you thought you saw here at the asylum.

There were only a handful of other patients around the day in question. It was the day Colette remarked about the L.A.B. travel bag, and all the women were in that room, falling about the attic and the dresses and shoes. But though the dusty sunlight moved in and out from behind clouds, and filtered in through the attic windows, Colette knew for certain she'd seen a bag with the initials L.A.B. on the side.

Isabelle's expression was grim. Had Isabelle seen Colette? Had she seen Colette when she'd knelt down in awe before the travel bag, spotting the L.A.B. initials stenciled on its side? All along Colette had assumed, on that fateful day, that everyone had ignored her, and that absolutely no one had heard her, nor seen her fall to her knees in front of the travel bag. She'd pushed it back behind heavy curtains which separated the attic into two large rooms. That had been her secret hope that her action had gone unseen.

At the window finally, Colette kicked at the shards of glass still hanging on in the window frame. Outside, the sun balanced just above the expanse of lawn, almost as if the place were literally on a precipice. Down in the yard, patients, patrons and doctors still milled about somberly. In the reflection of the glass, she saw her. Isabelle's silhouette drew closer. Sadie talked to her, frantically as if trying to talk her out of something.

"Isabelle. She just wants to look. No one will know."

With that, Colette kicked in the window with a swift movement and scrambled to her knees. In seconds, she'd shimmied through it and jumped into the basement. She stood in the Domesticity room.

Making her way across the vast room, she touched her way past familiar furniture of the replicated home kitchen, and the practice parlor and fake study, all the way to the door which the doctors kept diligently locked. This was the stage set where the female patients had been locked up and forced to learn.

Through the door, pulling it with all her might, she made her way to the stairway which led up four flights to the attic. Windows were opened at each turn of the stairs, with landings and small ledges situated in each stairwell outside the windows. Of course, the ever-present bars remained secured and in place.

Sadie had by now caught up with Colette. The two women lifted their skirts and raced up the stairs, taking an occasional rest at each turn. As if uncertain about the other's mental state, Sadie continually turned back, her breaths coming more quickly. She clutched Colette's arm now and then. At times they'd stop, hearing only the string quartet in the yard, and Sadie's short anxious breaths. Then there would be no sounds until the shuffling of Isabelle's feet and the sweeping of her skirt as she rounded each flight of stairs. She was in pursuit. If not in her own dreamy state, her movements would have been more swift. Still, there was something subtly menacing about Isabelle's sudden tenacity.

Streaming in the windows was the last gasp of sun. Twilight had tuned in. The air exhaled dust and faded books.

She knelt in front of the bag, and lifted up the fine lace that had been draped across its brown and beige checkerboard pattern top. It was Lizzie's travel bag...

"You just don't understand," came a soft voice from behind Sadie and Colette suddenly.

Colette didn't listen. She fiddled with the dangling brass lock, and tapped forcibly on either side of the bag. Its shape was similar to a contemporary travel bag, or doctor bag. Isabelle, for whatever reason, fought back tears as she spoke up suddenly. "Lizzie was very disturbed. I was the only one who really believed she would act on her anger. No one would listen to me."

Colette sat back and wiped the back of her neck with her hand. She was resigned to what she would now hear. To quiet her, she touched Sadie's arm and shook her head.

Sadie too, sat back. Colette smoothed her blue skirt and raised her chin, facing Isabelle.

"Did Lizzie have a problem with laudanum?"

Isabelle fidgeted with colored pieces of paper in her hands. It reminded Colette of the first time she'd seen Isabelle, when she'd emerged, ravaged, from her father's house. Who knew at that time, that she'd just escaped from hell? What was in her hands now? Wallpaper from the asylum? The pieces fluttered out of her pockets. Isabelle had been peeling the paper here in the hospital. Perhaps the same uncomfortable horror had come up for her in this place, just as it had in her father's house. Feeling suffocated and locked away in the way her father had imprisoned her.

"Dr. Bowen just cares about Lizzie," Isabelle went on. "That's all. That's how it all started. He'd given her Laudanum. It was medicinal. He knew her as a girl. I think he knew what was happening in their house. And now, since the murders, he knows for sure. Word around town is that he stayed with her in her room. Wouldn't even let the police in the room while she cried. That's what he told the police, anyway."

Isabelle lowered her chin. She studied the floor all at once. A tear appeared on her flushed cheek. "You wouldn't understand," she began. "The anger surfaces out of nowhere. Sometimes it hits all at once. Lizzie was haunted by her demons. Demons put upon her by her father. She told me. Although I'm much younger, we've been friends for several years.

Colette knelt down on her hands and knees and crawled about the attic while Isabelle talked on. She seemed in great need of unburdening herself. This was the room. This was where she recalled seeing the travel bag on the day they'd been forced into selecting appropriate dresses for the reception. The women would be put on display. The patients were to be the walking and talking success stories of Dr. Warburton and his cronies.

Sadie curled up in her usual position of submission on the floor, like a toddler, hugging her legs in front of her and rocking back and forth. She'd loosened her blouse a bit and now her long burgundy skirt was hiked up around her knees. The position exposed her thick white cotton tights. Somewhere, she had managed to rummage up some lipstick and rouge, accoutrements Colette hadn't realized existed in 1892.

There were larger trunks and luggage in the area now. They'd been added. Isabelle prattled on in a voice both robotic and dreamlike, from her stance behind Colette.

"I confided in Lizzie about my father," she said. "About his rigid rules. The cruelty. Edward Sewell should not have had a daughter at all. I shared this with Lizzie, and with a few other women in our church group. That my father beat my mother, Madeline. God forbid, she dared to share her progressive ideas. She's brilliant, you know."

Colette pulled the bag toward her again. Having her hands on it she felt a surge of excited adrenalin. Isabelle helped her lift it over to a clear area of the floor. A layer of dust erupted from nearby heavy drapery which lined the windows, which Isabelle had thrown wide. When Colette tried to lift the two latches on either side, as she suspected, it was locked. She fell back onto the floor and crossed her legs in front of her.

Isabelle nudged her, withdrawing a small gold key. She indicated the bag. "Lizzie and I both have keys."

It was as she knew it would be. She sighed. Still, she couldn't accept it.

Turning the bag around, Colette felt along the seams on the back side with her fingertips. She recognized this was a well-built bag. It looked new to her, which was interesting. She'd seen such original bags before at estate sales, with the old doctor clasp, with the circa 1888 pattern, but they'd been worn and dusty.

She rested her hands on the bag that had belonged to Lizzie Borden. Taking the small key, miniature in size, she unlocked the tiny padlock on the side of the bag. Now as she gazed at it, she noticed there were several European travel stickers, but they were situated on the back of it, out of plain view. There were two from France and one or two from Italy and the United Kingdom. The colors were bright, in fact, the stickers looked relatively new.

The top would not open. Fidgeting with the bag some more, Colette ran her fingers along the sides of it. Soon she found two small latches that she'd not noticed before. Lifting up on each, one at a time, she still couldn't open it. Then she realized there was usually a trick to such things. She pulled up on both latches simultaneously, and the bag popped open.

Isabelle gasped. Colette too, caught her breath. Inside the bag there lay a small pile of music, sheet music. Next to that was a small glass bottle. She hesitated, thinking about forensics, and put on a white glove Isabelle handed her from the dress closet. Then, she removed the bottle from the trunk and examined the label. Laudanum. Prescription written out to "Madeline Sewell. Directions; Consume when necessary for nervous anxiety and trauma."

So now. Here was a connection between Madeline Sewell and Lizzie Borden. The trunk was longer than it was wide. In fact, it was much bigger than Colette recalled from the first time she'd seen it. Carefully, Colette lifted the music out. The composer was John Philip Sousa and it was mostly march music for the trumpet.

"He's my sweetheart," Isabelle said. "Darren."

Colette nodded, then continued to search.   Lying across the center of it was a long velvet bag with a drawstring. When Colette lifted the bag out from the trunk, she saw deep blackish stains in the lining of the bigger bag which held it.   Colette caught her breath when she saw a bloody wooden handle, about a foot in length, and the blue fabric of what appeared to be a dress, also with blood on it.

"What the hell are you ladies doing up here?"

Dr. Warburton stood in the doorway menacingly, his hands on his hips. Colette turned to face him, and shoved the bag swiftly with her foot. A stiff-looking starched white jacket accentuated his unyielding presence, as did the black pants and shoes. There were elbow patches on his sleeves. Under the jacket, he wore a fitted plaid vest with a watch doubtlessly inserted in the pocket, as a thick gold chain draped from it with a golden fob at the end.

"Isabelle," he barked. "Your father and brother are here. They must speak with you. You other ladies," he said, waving his hand wildly, "get back to the party immediately."

Sadie unrolled from her position on the floor, stood up and strolled over to him, her skin was creamy, and her movements were lithe and fluid. Even wearing an eyelet white, high-collared blouse and a burgundy fitted Jacket and skirt, she managed to emit a sensual air to everyone around her. Due to her tiny frame, her dress kept falling off her shoulders earlier in the day. Dr. Warburton had made her change into the skirt and blouse and advised her to stay away from the men at the party. She sidled up to Warburton, and rubbed her shoulder against his finely bleached and pressed cotton sleeve. He shoved her away and she broke into hysterical laughter.

Colette assumed it was Sadie's intention to divert attention away from her and Isabelle. She'd come to know the woman well. Sadie exemplified the mind and spirit of a contemporary woman, and definitely not one of the nineteenth century. Sadie utilized all her God-given prowess as a woman. So while Sadie seduced Dr. Warburton, Colette slipped the bottle of Laudanum into her skirt pocket. Rummaging around in there, it amazed her how large and roomy the pockets were. Clothing was made well made in 1892, Colette thought. Plus, these women never carried the back-breaking totes women favored in the twenty-first century.

Dr. Warburton eyed Colette. It was as if he was trying to make her uncomfortable with his stare, and somehow, violate her sense of well-being, simply by the way he looked at her. Isabelle stepped between them, as if aware of his intimidation tactics.

"The gentlemen are downstairs, Isabelle," he said. "Go down there and see Nurse Hudson. She will show you where to go."

Colette followed Isabelle. Dr. Warburton grabbed her by the arm as she passed by.

"You stay here. You and Sadie need to explain why you're up here. And without a matron."

Isabelle turned on him violently. "She WILL come with me. Father trusts her. Don't you know that's the only reason he put her in here? To keep an eye on me?"

"That's absurd. I happen to know she gained access here under a false name. I also know that she is actually Colette Browning from Chicago. Don't underestimate the power of your father Edward's ability to gain information."

Little did Isabelle know how close to the truth she was? Ever since the morning visit from Edward and William, Colette had put herself in the asylum to specifically unravel what was happening to Isabelle. She had to know why the time travel phantasm had chosen her to be a ready friend to Isabelle.

Dr. Warburton scowled, stepping over. He shoved the two women toward the door, with his hands digging into their shoulders.

Once downstairs, Colette raced to follow. Although a physically fit fifty-something, she still felt herself to be at a disadvantage. Isabelle moved smoothly, like fresh ink from a fountain pen. Her entire being was lofty airiness; at one moment earthbound, and at others, she seemed to float in some ethereal realm. It was as if she wrote her own life story, separating herself from reality.

At last, she and Isabelle reached the ground floor. There they were. Colette stood there, a bit dizzy, feeling a bit of time travel euphoria. On that first trip with William in the carriage, she had watched Edward Sewell pour over the financial pages in that black carriage, amazed at the sound of the weighted down clomping of the horses hooves hitting cobblestones. Thinking back now, she could see young William's face again, just as she had on that first time travel. She'd thought him quite a handsome young man, with his black, slicked-back hair and tidy suit jacket. It appeared that William had hoped that Colette's visit would help Isabelle.

Because neither William, nor his father, Edward Sewell, could figure out why Isabelle had asked specifically to see the enigmatic new woman in town. A woman whose clothes didn't quite match. One Miss Colette Browning, who had taken a room at Mrs. Burns's boarding house. Of course, the town figured if she went by "Miss Browning" that she was an extremely old spinster. The twice-divorced Colette decided to let them think so.

Several times Edward had glanced covertly over the top of his paper that morning to take her in, then looked away when she caught his stare. Certainly Mr. Edward Sewell, renowned financier and contemporary of Andrew Borden, wondered where Colette had come from? And why? All they knew was that she'd lived in the Midwest for a time. Somewhere north of Chicago. If they only knew how long she'd really lived there. He was, of course suspicious, that due to Miss Browning's age, she actually was a friend of his maligned wife, Madeline. And this, above all else, raised his interests beyond mere suspicion to outright dislike. According to Isabelle, he would not stand for more of that female double talk, all that bogus interest in the education of women, and the right to vote on political parties. These same women had actually frequented the restaurants and pubs officially reserved for men only.

That evening would yield no further discoveries. Dr. Warburton made sure to isolate Sadie, Isabelle and Colette from each other. Seated on her rail-thin cot in her room, the heat was merciless and persistent. Colette gazed at the bars on her window, bewildered, her brain feeling depleted, debilitated.

Much later that evening, while Dr. Warburton led a dry administration meeting in the mahogany-lined executive special situations room, Colette dragged Sadie back to the attic. Increasingly frenzied and looking a bit malnourished, Sadie followed behind Colette up the narrow wooden staircase.

"We shouldn't be going up here," Sadie uttered as they reached the final turn leading to the attic.

"Hush," Colette insisted, as she took the younger woman by the hand. They were overheated. Colette could feel her undergarments, which included tights and bloomers, and a petticoat, suctioned against her legs. As she inhaled deeply, the scent of dust and hardwood floor, and aged papers came to her. Everything was spinning and white before her eyes, as she felt herself growing more dizzy.

The hospital was a maze. Its intent appeared to be to misdirect and frustrate patients. Numerous hallways led nowhere, or down dead-end staircases. First you came to a heavy wooden door, which, like the Borden's house, had numerous locks on it. Once successfully past this first door, you found yourself stuck in total darkness. There were no sconces or lamps in the short hallway. Then one faced yet another door, albeit a thinner door, but still locked with several bolts.

"This won't work. Let's get out of the building. They have windows open in the basement and in the attic where some patients are chained."

Sadie nodded. She knew that, of course. She'd been chained there herself.

The two women trotted out to the back of the building. Sadie turned in circles, her arms extended like a child imitating an airplane. Somehow, Colette had counted which window from the edge of the building led into the attic. While Sadie waited, Colette charmed a neighbor gardener to let her borrow a ladder to "do extra chores" around the asylum. While the lofty administration decoded the futures of Sadie, Colette and all the other wretches like them, Sadie and Colette gained access to the attic from the outside. She'd thus convinced the neighbor she was simply a town volunteer. Colette had learned a few things about the art of escape from Isabelle. They could climb up to the top floor. No bars on the attic window, Colette mused, perhaps because they'd never suspect the patients of having any ingenuity, or perhaps they welcome the occasional voluntary leap from the fourth floor to inevitable death below.

Once through the window, having gently nudged Sadie through first, Colette followed and planted her booted feet on the grainy dust of the attic floor. Finding a nearby candle, she lit it with long matches placed on a table next to the candlestick. The wooden floor consisted of thick planks, a rugged less appealing wood used to save money. It reminded her of the planks in the kitchen of the Glessner House, or the Widow Clarke house back in Chicago, where she'd enjoyed the readings of Edgar Alan Poe by the same actor for nearly thirty years. Colette had reveled in that feeling of visiting another time. The actor played Poe literally until he had grown around the middle enough to bust his vest buttons. Standing poised on the front porch, this same "Poe" would await guests while Halloween closed in, for his nighttime readings, with luminaria lighting the pathway, and a crisp Lake Michigan breeze lifting his white cravat.

Finally her eyes settled upon the bag. Colette felt awash in relief. Perhaps Dr. Warburton had not realized the bag had Lizzie's initials on it, or that they'd been trying to discover its contents. In fact, she thought now, tip toeing over to the far side of the attic, why would he ever suspect that Isabelle would have smuggled in one of Lizzie's bags with her own?

"Here is the way it happened," came a soft but clear voice from behind her. Colette whipped around. Isabelle's eyes were intense, the pupils dilated. "In actual fact," she went on. "On the day of the murders, Lizzie dropped that very bag out the back window. She told me that it resembled a doctor bag, so she hoped if anyone saw her with it, they'd assume it was Dr. Bowen's. Right out the back window of the Borden house. On the second floor. She dropped the bag as close to the well as possible, the well in the Borden back yard. That way perhaps it would be blocked from view. So totally away from the eyes of the police. Can you believe it? The nerve of our Lizzie? Then she had Simpson, one of Sadie's former boyfriends, he was the carriage driver, remember? He whisked it away to the asylum for Lizzie. Has Lizzie's initials but he was told it was for one Isabelle Sewell. All she told him was Isabelle was a wealthy patient at Perfect Pines. Of course, he knew the name and how important the Sewell family was in Fall River. No questions asked. Of course, he did not know what was in the bag. God no."

She smiled sweetly. Isabelle had been the one, fortuitous patient of Dr. Warburton's, who provided ample money, as well as much needed notoriety for the asylum. The crucial standing of Edward Sewell in the business community kept Perfect Pines in full operation. The men in the town, including the late Mr. Borden, and William Sewell and Dr. Warburton, wanted it that way. The asylum was in essence, a place for their discarded women, young and old.

On her knees at once, Colette pulled out a small letter opener she'd managed to smuggle in from Mrs. Burns's boarding house the night before. If Dr. Warburton only knew of all the reconnaissance missions outside the asylum they'd taken.

She turned to Sadie. The younger woman was seated on the floor, hugging her legs to her chest. Now and then, Sadie seemed to slip into the safety of her own delusions. Colette felt powerless at those times to help her young friend. It protected her against her reality, and that she was locked away. In essence, there was nothing wrong with Sadie. She was simply a healthy woman with desires. She'd found love with a Sousa musician. Unfortunately for her, it was the wrong time period.

Sadie crawled over, allowing her white skirt to slide along on the dirty floor. Perching herself next to Colette, she sat up kneeling. She let her head drop to one side, looking in wonderment at Colette, and then at the closed bag.

As Colette ran her hands along the sides of the trunk, she again admired the treated canvas that comprised it.

Holding down the latches, she managed to open it once more. She peered inside. Sadie sat cheek to cheek with Colette. As before, there was the bottle of laudanum, and the sheet music. This time Colette reached in and touched the hatchet handle, and pulled out the blue calico dress. Both were blood-stained.

"These things will have to come back with me," she said quietly.

"To where?" Sadie said, her voice hushed.

"To the Valley Stream of 2011," Colette whispered to herself. "I just don't know what to do with this knowledge yet."

Chapter Thirteen (A)

The Historical Facts

D uring the Borden trial, in point of fact, every counter-argument that Robinson attempted to present, in a sense further buried his case. At one point, he stated, "you may tell me, if you want, that the relation between that parent and child was such, that alienation was complete, and wrong was the purpose of her heart, but you will not ask me to believe it."[266]

Within Porter's *Fall River Tragedy,* Robinson began to defend the elderly Andrew Borden's reasoning for keeping all the doors locked in the house. He referred to Andrew Borden as simply "old-fashioned," and that the old man wanted only to protect the house due to it having been burglarized in the last year.[267] In this instance Robinson evaded the obvious point; that the only reason for locks within the house, assuming the doors to the outside were already carefully locked, would have been to protect one family member from being robbed by another family member, or worse, being violated in some way, but not at all by the threat of an outsider. But those same locks would elevate privacy if one did not want to be caught during a possible violation.

If one of the jury members would have had more insight, perhaps even if a single woman had been allowed on the jury, the more relevant and perhaps likely conjecture might have been recognized. The idea may have occurred to such a juror, that someone, perhaps Andrew Borden himself, maintained control over all of these locked rooms with his set of keys. She may also have seen that some of these keys were kept tauntingly on the mantel in the very room where he was later murdered.[268] Was this practice of keys on the mantel, and their use in opening private doorways, all so arranged to meet his own devious demands?

Quite possibly, Andrew Borden required acquiescence, as well as privacy in his home. Because the locks were not confined to his own bedroom. The locks and the complex system of surety and compliance appeared to have been master-minded by Andrew himself.

In a sense, Lizzie paid a high price just for prestige and a roof over her head, only to have her father smite her, in full view of the Fall River community, both in Massachusetts, and on her Grand Tour of Europe whereby he refused to send her more money to get home.

At that time, right when Lizzie celebrated her thirtieth birthday in high style, on her first Grand Tour of Europe, she ran out of traveling money and was likened to a public scandal on par with a major high profile political candidate in full view of the world.

The analogy has been made over the years, between the closed-in, suffocatingly full rooms of the Victorian homes to the women as well, who were considered closed-up, impeded creatures, weighed down in the same way as the heavy velvet draperies of the rooms. Heavy long dresses, and wrappers dragged the floor, and women were spun in lace and pearls. This was the Victorian uniform for American women.

Lizzie brought home reprints, pictures from abroad, of castles and fortresses and put them up in her bedroom.[269] One may imagine her, as she sat upon a lovely, white eyelet lace bedspread, tucked away in her well-decorated room, alone. Certainly she felt herself growing older, seated on the bed, studying those prints of countries abroad. Perhaps she gazed upon them longingly day after day, night after lonely night. Perhaps too, she'd pondered what her life could have been. What her life should have been.

However, if one probed more deeply, one realized it was not simply a desire for finer things that would drive the young woman to murder. Twenty-nine hatchet blows were struck in total. Two murders? They were executions, purposefully committed by Lizzie Borden herself, playing judge and jury.

Chapter Fourteen

A s Colette awakened, a familiar voice was talking.
"Someone was in a real big hurry to get rid of it," Colette's landlord Marilyn was saying. "Hard to believe this bungalow got torn down? It was one of the oldest houses on this side of town? It's like we had no warning?"

Colette nodded. Having moved to the North Shore from Oak Park, Illinois, she'd indeed been horrified by the mindless razing of old homes and buildings that seemed to have become epidemic in the area, purely for monetary gain.

Sighing, Colette shook her head. She'd pulled a blue Victorian patterned chair to the window of her rental room. Leaning forward, she rested her elbows on the window sill; covered in cement dust from the basement foundation they were going to begin pouring was everywhere. Then she touched the armrests of the chair, astonished to recognize it as one of the chairs from her room at Mrs. Burns's boarding house.

"There's nothing left of the old place," the landlord went on.

Marilyn stood behind her.

Colette turned sharply. "What's that?"

"The old house. Almost all gone. But you managed to bring home some knick knacks from over there? Where are you finding them?"

Colette gazed at the fence. It now had only an empty hole in front of it. The words of her landlord didn't penetrate for a minute or so. Then she turned around.

""What knick knacks?"

Now the landlord looked confused. "Look around! Your room is filling up with them. Kinda gross though," she said, pointing. "It's like a hairpiece and that bottle of acid looks dangerous."

Colette's mouth dropped open. She reached for the items on the desk where Marilyn had left them. It was Abby's hairpiece and a bottle of Prussic Acid. Lizzie had actually purchased some, somewhere.

Colette shook her head and fidgeted around in her surprisingly deep pockets. Marilyn stared at her with a bit of distrust.

"Nice outfit. That look might catch on some day."

That said, Marilyn turned and descended the stairs. Finally, Colette looked down at her clothes. She felt a pair of bluejeans on her legs. But what she hadn't realized was that she also wore a crème colored petticoat over her pants. It was in those deep pockets she'd been digging. What the heck, she thought? Walking back to her room, she stood before the now tarnished and aged floor-length mirror. Sure enough, she had on her t-shirt she'd gone to sleep in, her jeans and a nineteenth century slip over her pants.

Her worlds were colliding.

Her landlord had had a small kitchenette put in the rental room years before. So now Colette opened a small fridge, withdrew a yogurt and frowned at the small sink brimming with dirty dishes. Leaning against the counter, she smiled to herself as she ate a triple berry Dannon yogurt.

She recalled her first husband Max, asking her soon to be second husband, Dimitri, right there, in front of her, "do you cook?"

And when Dimitri answered in the affirmative, Max had retorted, "good, because you'll have to."

What was the moral of the story? Was it, that if you wanted to stay married, you must know how to cook? She laughed.

Knick knacks, she thought? She noticed a man's gold pocket watch, several lace handkerchiefs, a fob or two. Where had she gotten them?

As she shook her head, wracking her brain, there came the crash of broken glass. Something knocked against a kitchen sink. She withdrew from the left pocket of the petticoat a small brown bottle where she'd stashed it. Her mouth dropped. The label read, among other ingredients and warnings, scripted in Victorian script, "prussic acid." She took a deep breath. Another knick knack? My God, she thought. Lizzie Borden claimed she never tried to purchase prussic acid at the local drugstore? What was this? She'd really been there.

Someone called her name. Slipping it back into her pocket, she raced into the hallway.

"Colette," it was Marilyn. "I'm leaving a note here for you in the mailbox. Just an envelope with your name on it."

"Thanks. I'll be down."

"Haven't your friends heard of email?"

Grabbing her bag, she swept past the radiator situated by the front door, where her landlord had left the note. A blue envelope. Blue Sharpie scrawled words read "Colette Browning" and was underlined with three definitive lines.

Minutes later, she sat on the crumbling concrete steps of the old farmhouse, pausing a moment to gaze at the remains of 1804 Prairie. The brick walls were halved, broken at the joints, like shattered appendages.

In addition to an affinity and respect for the style of the American Bungalow, a solid house, and in particular now the door so spiritually strong, it had become more than that, more than wood and splinters and stained glass; it was the entryway to her soul. Now she felt that she and the door had come face to face for a reason. It was as if it had to physically be close to her chest, to get her attention the only way it knew how, to tell her she needed to enter another time, another year. That it was time. Time to time travel.

But why all the way across the United States? What was the connection between Fall River, Massachusetts and the Lizzie Borden trial, and her? What about the North Shore of Chicago? What did the doomed bungalow here in Valley Stream, Illinois, which ended up being torn down, have to do with a notorious and controversial murder trial?

She gazed across the street. Commuters walked past her. Those crazy hieroglyphs on the stairs, she thought. How could she hope to decipher the puzzle at this moment? She knew why. To identify the body in the coal chute, and especially to give a voice to these who were forcibly silenced.

She ripped into the envelope now, noticing that her name seemed to have been scrawled in a hurry. The word "confidential" had been hastily added in red marker. The words on the note itself made her throat tighten. *Colette. You were right about the coal chute. There was indeed something buried there, as you know. Two somethings in fact. Meet me at the gazebo by the river tonight at 11:00 pm. Tell no one. Bob.*

After two attempts at a nap, she finally ate a late dinner around 9:30 pm. She paced the four walls of the rental room, then she slipped out of Marilyn's house by 10:45 pm. The gazebo and the river were within walking distance of the farmhouse and the remains of the 1804 Prairie Street house.

Wearing only a t-shirt and jeans, she rushed along the sidewalk, and soon ran the lengths of the back yards of all the houses. It was remarkable. How dreadfully humid it was. This was the apex of summer in Illinois. It could have been Fall River, Massachusetts in August 1892. They too suffered through an abominable heat. So many things were the same, she thought.

She jogged now. Checking her watch, she saw it was ten fifty-five pm. Night swelled with the summer silence, broken only by the various clicks and rolling chatter of the evening cicadas. Somehow the louder the bugs, the hotter it felt. Too dark to even see her watch. But she was within sight of the gazebo. She sped up, tripping as she went.

Once up the stairs, she searched the octagon-shaped structure. Bob had a travel bag at his feet. She took two strides, then stopped.

His eyes, even in the opaque dark, looked troubled. He smoked a cigarette and the sound of ash being torched made a small crackle sound. The day they'd found the coal chute, he had told her he quit. Some upset perhaps had started him up again. She remained silent and waited.

Taking a final drag on his smoke, Bob flicked it onto the dirt path encircling the gazebo. In her mind's eye, she remembered playing numerous concert band concerts with the Valley Stream community Band over the years, right on this very stage. Funny how her mind worked. The clarinet made her think of Sousa, which made her think of William and Edward Sewell, and the pitiable circumstances Isabelle and Sadie now faced somewhere in the continuum of Fall River in 1892. Right now, 1892 was there too, existing concurrently with this time period.

I will be in Fall River again, she thought, in the future but it will exist in the past, but the past will be my future? And to think a wooden door with the stained glass as a portal from an old bungalow will get me there.

"The police have partially identified the bones," he said immediately.

She caught her breath. "The coal chute? Then I wasn't crazy."

"Cops think the bodies had not been discovered until now because they'd been buried behind a supporting wall. When we knocked down the wall, it opened up the passage which was an extension of the original coal chute. You were right. There was a lot of shit in there. You wouldn't believe what was down there."

"There were two bodies weren't there?"

"There were some bones that made authorities think they were the remains of two women. I called the cops. Anonymously. That same day I stopped further work being done by the crew. They have no idea what we've found. I didn't want to get you messed up with it. I wasn't supposed to let you on the site anyway."

The travel bag practically screamed from its spot on the ground.

"What's that?"

He shook his head. "Not sure it will mean anything to you, but I found a couple of things buried with the bones."

She thought, a bit shamefully, of the small checkered box she'd taken without telling him.

"Really?" she said.

He looked at her hard; his dark blue eyes had overly focused on her somehow. "Why don't you come over for a while tonight?" he said, barely audible.

"Can't do it. Come on, Bob. I've just finished my divorce. You know that. We can't get involved."

"Right," he nodded, without smiling. "I get it."

He lit a cigarette and handed off the travel bag to her.

"I have a friend at the coroner's office if you want to get some sort of information on the bones. They might be able to shed some light on them. All I know is they're female." He took a drag and looked at her, wrinkles around his mouth creasing. "And by the way," he hesitated.

"What?" she said, looking at him, taking the bag.

"This is going to sound crazy. But at first when I looked it was only some women's clothing. Real old, like 1800s stuff. A small mirror and an overnight bag. But then I found a bottle of Laudanum for someone named Isabelle Seaward or something like that."

Colette nodded and smiled. More worlds colliding, she thought. "Now I kind of get it. My purpose in all this."

"What's that?"

"Nothing. Thanks Bob, for telling me." These knick knacks were a bit more serious than golden fobs.

Bob dropped his cigarette, stubbed it out with his foot, turned without another word, and walked off into the black night. She sat there, her hand resting on the travel bag in her lap for several minutes. It was hot. The only sounds felt heavy with the weight of bugs. The air was sodden with them. Relief washed over her.

She trudged home to within a block of Marilyn's farmhouse. That's when she made up her mind. She had to go back. No one had to tell her. She knew the bones belonged to Madeline and Isabelle Sewell. No one back in 1892, ever wondered to look for them. It was an extremely cold case. How would they identify these bones in 2011? There'd been no interest in 1892. There'd been too much else going on.

Once upstairs, she brooded. The room was dark. By now the rising air made the heat oppressive and thick. She flicked on the air conditioning. The door, broad and colorful with its stained glass in the small windows, now leaned against the far wall and seemed to regard her casually. Right where she'd left it. So why was she afraid to turn on an overhead light? Instead, she clicked on a small book light and shined it on the travel bag. It was indeed old. It was pre-turn of the twentieth century. It had a gold lock. It also had in gold lettering, the initials I.A.S. on the outside. It was the other bag from the attic. The initials this time were for Isabelle Anne Sewell. Isabelle must have taken it with her when she tried to escape to Chicago.

Sure enough, she'd hidden additional items in the bag. There was some undergarments, a bar of Pear soap, some lotion. There was even some music for trumpet. Turning around and around a brown glass bottle, she found a label. "Laudanum" prescribed by Dr. Bowen and written to Isabelle Sewell. The directions read "drink often for anxiety and to aid in sleep." In her mind, this served as definitive proof about the remains.

Colette's heart was sick.

The room now grew darker. The desk lamp flickered and went out entirely. The room had an odd scent in the blackness, something like hay in a barn. She stepped carefully to the desk and tapped the lamp. The bulb lit up again.

Colette had heard of such wrinkles in time before, whereby it would all fit together, and that she would be in the past. However, Colette had a vivid fear of impacting the future.

This would be her first time she'd taken direct action with the time travel herself. Talk about an alternative life style. She was consciously choosing time travel, which had been imposed upon her thus far. Because now that she'd actually visited 1892 in Fall River, Massachusetts, she felt a bit of an obligation to the entire case.

Standing, she turned the Prairie door around. Then she sat cross-legged on the floor next to it. Again, she reached for the string to the music box which had a small copper bell on the end of it, and pulled. It was resistant at first, and seemed to choke back, as if unaccustomed to being told what to do.

That's when the music started.

The hymn "bless this house" tinkled out its tune. Almost spontaneously, Colette could not keep her eyes open. She lay on her side on the floor, her beloved slide bracelet shimmering in the lamp light, its various stones; red, green and blue, flickered like fire. The pearl and cameo slides soothed her. Concurrently, the bracelet tightened, ever so slightly and the scent of lavender filled the room. Slowly, she reached out and lifted the bracelet where there was now a dusting of purple particles. She pushed the door shut to her room with her foot. Within seconds, it felt as if a soft creamy blanket had been laid over her.

When she awakened, she was again in her bed. Of course, the familiar weight and scent of Burns's Oil Soap filled her up. Thoroughly practiced at this game in her mind, she grasped the heavy door which leaned against the bed, firmly on either side and set it out of the way. She and the door were apparently getting this portal thing down. As expected, it was much shinier now. The wood was smooth and it glistened into a deep rich auburn color, like a lustrous head of hair. The stained glass was bright, comprised of purples and blues and reds.

Reaching under her nightgown, she realized that the fanny pack she'd put on had made the journey back. Having Marilyn point out the two "knick knacks" on her dresser, which had traveled with her from 1892, she'd left the prussic acid behind. No one in 1892 need know about Lizzie having actually purchased some somewhere. It may not have been with Eli Bence, the pharmacist who testified to seeing her, but she bought it somewhere. Abby Borden's braid however, she'd tucked in the fanny pack she'd attached to her petticoat. Perhaps because this item had slipped so far out of time, it was able to make the journey back and forth. Who knew the rules of possession and time travel anyway? All she knew was the prussic acid would not have traveled well.

Inside of ten minutes, she was dressed and outside. The braid was secured in a small reticule. She tried to recall which way to go for the police headquarters. Although she knew the police had, for some reason, buried much of the evidence behind the Borden house immediately following the murders, she was unsure how to return the braid exactly to the place where it had been stored. Because, after all, how could she be certain the braid had also been buried with the other clothes belonging to Abby and Andrew Borden? It was not clear to her why Morse had the clothes buried in the Borden's backyard after the murders.

Regardless of how the braid had made its way to 2011, Colette was convinced it was a sign, or a talisman that implored her to actively pursue what had become of Isabelle's mother, Madeline. She had Isabelle's bag, so proof was on her side. It occurred to her now, as she walked briskly along the wooden sidewalk on Second Street where she guessed the police station was, that these women could have gone missing without notice. During the late thirties and into the forties wartime, women got out and worked as part of a greater effort. Today's twenty-first century woman, she mused, was exhausted and simultaneously judged harshly by both men, and other women. For what reason? Usually for not being domestic enough.

The navy skirt she wore was voluminous and swished with each step. A crème petticoat brushed the sidewalk and gathered dirt as she raced along. The boots felt tight around her ankles. Funny how the blouse reminded her of a Brooks Brothers blouse from the 1980s she'd bought for her first job in 1982 on LaSalle Street. All she could possibly be grateful for in 1892, in conjunction with the oppressive heat, was the favored updo of the time period. At least her long blonde hair was off her neck.

The police station was in sight now. Somehow, she managed to slip into place and leave the braid on the desk in the front of the station. Of course a young deputy passed her, appearing from a side room. Colette had to manufacture an explanation quickly.

"Hello. I am," she hesitated, "somewhat new to town."

"Of course you are," he said, smiling. His face was ruddy and his dark hair was cleanly cropped. He had a nervous twitch in one of his fair blue eyes. "Yes ma'am, indeed."

He looked a bit harried.

She cleared her throat. "I'm living at Mrs. Burns's boarding house. I'm embarrassed to say that my," she hesitated again, "my dog. My dog must have gotten into the Borden's yard. He must have dragged this braid into the boarding house. I believe, if I'm not mistaken, this is evidence from the recent tragic murders of those nice Borden people. So sad. I live right down the street. Mrs. Burns's is on Second Street as well."

As she spoke, Colette realized she was frantically straightening her skirt with her hands; the flimsy reticule purse nearly fell off her wrist. She was not used to carrying such a small silken bag. The deputy's dubious expression worried her. He tilted his head and studied Colette, sizing her up from her blonde bangs, which she realized must appear a mess, to her suit coat and down to her boots. What was he thinking? Had she revealed something out of turn? Did the public not know about burying the items in the Borden yard?

Finally, he spoke up.

"Since when does Mrs. Burns allow dogs at her place?" he said at last.

Colette exhaled and started for the door. "Don't know," she said. "I do know the braid has got to be an important piece of evidence. Make sure the Sheriff sees it."

With that, she rushed out of the station and tripped back out to the blazing sidewalk, comprised of gravel and mud. She felt the sun quickly bore into her, consuming her and trapping all the heat under the clinging fabric of her long sleeves and long skirt.   As she passed women dressed like her on the wooden sidewalk, it felt good to be hiding in plain sight.

Chapter Fourteen (A)

The Historical Facts

L izzie Borden never killed again. Through violence, she had silenced forever her tormentors. Perhaps that was why a photo of her, taken at age fifty, showed her cradling quite lovingly her little dog on her lap. She was seated on a wicker chair on the back porch of Maplecroft, the house she bought with her sister following the trial.[270] She appeared to be a woman at peace. A murderer, but at peace.

This typified Lizzie as a woman and as a victim. This was not a maniacal serial killer or a random psychopath. Lizzie Borden acted out of desperation in a time when women had no rights; and no social workers or therapists to help. They may have existed, but to seek out a professional therapist would have brought shame upon the family. This did not make her actions morally or legally acceptable. This perhaps merely explained somewhat why it transpired. This was a reflection of an American tragedy. Tragic in 1892. Still a tragedy today.

Once Lizzie had exacted her punishment upon her perpetrators, one a direct sexual abuser and one who turned a blind eye, she was at peace. And this was true despite the fact that she lived as a pariah in a town she refused to leave.[271]

So this was neither justice nor socially acceptable, nor especially spiritually-driven. This was not copacetic by anyone's standards in 1892. This would include today's society as well. Unfortunately for Lizzie Borden, it was simply the manifestation of a victim lashing out against her abusers. This was the tragedy. It was simply anarchy.

There existed a difference of opinion when it came to which dress Lizzie had on the morning of the murders, versus a different dress she'd had on in the afternoon. Mrs. Churchill believed that Lizzie had on a much lighter dress in the morning. But then, Robinson presented the idea that numerous witnesses may have mistaken the dress Bridget Sullivan had on, for the one Lizzie wore.[272]

Apparently Bridget had on a lighter dress, and therefore perhaps, despite Mrs. Churchill and other credible witnesses who claimed they'd seen quite distinctly, a lighter-colored dress were now, according to ex-Governor Robinson's logic, mistaken.[273] They clearly must have confused the two women in their recall. In essence, whoever recalled Lizzie in light blue, simply confused the suspected murderer with a woman shorter of stature, like the Irish maid. In those days, one was considered remiss to not have differentiated between a young woman of some social "caliber and standing" and a lowly Irish maid, a young woman who was alternatively referred to as Maggie or Bridget, depending upon who noticed her.[274]

How could witnesses have mentally switched dresses on two different women? Especially when Lizzie's clothing would have been more carefully scrutinized than that of a young immigrant of lower status. Because who indeed, would notice Bridget Sullivan on that particular morning? She was merely a maid washing windows in the one hundred degree heat of Fall River. Like so many Victorian towns in America, Fall River was very much a class society.[275] Often the help would have been hardly noticed nor acknowledged.

So Robinson's claim soon thereafter, that there was no blood stains apparent on the dark blue dress, a fact he reiterated repeatedly, would have been a moot point. In reality, it simply was not the dress the perpetrator had on when she swung the hatchet. In fact in the end, they found absolutely no blood stains whatsoever on the dress. However, as previously stated, the petticoat did indeed have a drop of blood.[276]

Robinson went on to point out how there was not a spot of blood on her "hands, her face or hair." He further stated that Lizzie had been in full view of everyone, lounging on the sofa in the apparent dress she'd had on all day.[277] In other words, Robinson made it seem like the idea that she might have taken off the dress, the same dress she might have committed the murders in, could not have been feasible. In actuality, Lizzie may easily have slipped out of the dress she'd had on, which may well have been covered with blood stains, and hidden it inside her closet of dresses either in the hallway or in her bedroom. No one else was upstairs at the time, after 9:30 a.m. that morning. This was precisely when Abby Borden had been slain.[278]

In point of fact, it was quite possible too, that Dr. Bowen assisted Lizzie in some way. One theory may well have included his participation helping to assure that the police were barred from the bedroom, with the remonstrance to intruders, that Lizzie was "distraught" and needed time alone.[279]

The fact would have remained, it would have required no more than five minutes to roll up the dress and stash it. With the help of Dr. Bowen, the dress may have been slipped into a bag, perhaps a doctor bag? Later, they would have transferred it from the closet to his bag while the police were waiting outside her bedroom door. After that, the good doctor may have slipped out and taken the evidence, at least temporarily, to his house for concealment. Although this is entirely conjecture, in this way, the bloodied evidence would have gotten past police and safely out of the Borden residence.

One of the backdrop stories which emerged during this crucial time following the murders was that Dr. Bowen, on August 2nd, 1892, appeared to have been exceedingly distraught. Certainly, the event of the day had been harrowing, shocking, and in many ways laid bare the personal aspects of the Borden family to the entire town of Fall River, and to those closest to Andrew and Lizzie.[280] The newspaper kept close accounts. One theory that persisted was that Dr. Bowen had something to hide.

So in accordance with this theory, that the doctor indeed hid something, and kept the police out of Lizzie's room during a crucial time frame, Dr. Bowen essentially assisted Lizzie in hiding her culpability in the crime.

Robinson claimed that contained in that upstairs closet were "eighteen or twenty dresses."[281] He further attested that no government witnesses claimed, to have not seen, any dress with blood stains upon it. Added to that, there were at least eight dresses among them that were various shades of blue.[282]

How easy it would have been for Dr. Bowen, a friend to Lizzie all her thirty odd years of life, and likely sympathetic, to help hide the very dress in question in his doctor's bag? In this way they could have slipped by police unnoticed, with the bloodied dress rolled up and hidden inside.

Robinson also questioned why Lizzie would have waited until Sunday to burn the dress? And why right there in the kitchen in full view of everyone? [283] In actuality, such speculation about an accomplice, or perhaps several accomplices would have explained the determined effort to finally burn the dress and why it wasn't until Sunday. It would make sense then, that someone else may have had it in his or her possession, and then perhaps he decided having it was too risky. Someone like Dr. Bowen.

When Lizzie's dearest friend, Alice Russell, explained to Lizzie that Lizzie had done the worst thing possible by burning the dress, wouldn't that have clearly already occurred to Lizzie? Thus, the action itself was an act of desperation.

Ironically, when Alice Russell finally went to police and told them about the burning of the dress, which had heretofore been an unknown act, Lizzie was indicted.[284]

Chapter Fifteen

"My God," a woman's voice muttered from overhead. "What the hell are you doing on the floor?"

Colette could feel the hard surface under her back. And yet oddly, her vision was blocked. She could barely discern a bit of sunlight coming through a window above her. It was the door. She could feel the heavy music box digging into the flesh of her thigh. It was leaning against her bed, as always. In travel mode. But this time Colette had awakened half on the door and half on the floor.

"No way," she blurted. "How did I get back here already?"

"What d'ya say?" her landlord asked, grabbing the door with her hands, trying to help amidst stringent groans.

"I said, I always lean the door on the bed when I go out," Colette said, realizing how unlikely the explanation sounded.

"Well you should move the thing out of here," Marilyn went on. "Don't know why you had to have it anyway? What're you doing sleeping on the floor?"

Colette stood up, and touched her hand to the small of her back. "Don't know why I did that either."

Marilyn, somewhat intrusively, sat on Colette's small bed. She smoothed out the colored quilt with her hand, and regarded Colette sheepishly.

Finding herself too exhausted to ask that Marilyn get off her bed, she also took into consideration the six months in arrears of rent she owed.

"You were one of only three owners, you know," Marilyn commented.

"Of what?"

"That old bungalow you loved so much. Can't believe it's gone. I've lived in this farmhouse since 1951. Why that old bungalow was part of my world growing up. Would get up in the morning, walk outside with my Red Flyer Wagon and run up and down the street. That's when the crazy lady lived there. She had to be a hundred years old." She looked at her hand, studied a small gemstone ring on her finger, then went on. "And then there was that mysterious man everyone talked about. He built the house and then the Johnsons bought it from his family, and then sold it to you. He was the same man who refurbished the old gazebo downtown, supposedly. As the story goes, he was at one time a well-known musician, back in the day."

"What man?"

"He built the place. Spared no expense in 1929. Was insistent that he built on that exact plot of land. He claimed it had some familial history for him. But no one ever found out why. The Crash came just as they were finishing it. He lost everything and then he died a couple years later."

"All that happened before we lived there," Colette said, "fascinating. It's almost as if he was looking for something."

Marilyn nodded. "Rumors were that the man who built it, the one who lost everything, was a little crazy, sorry to say."

The conversation then ended. Marilyn often did that. She'd walk out in the middle of speaking, as if remembering a kitchen gadget that needed repair, her mind elsewhere.

That got Colette thinking. Sitting cross-legged in front of the low window as always, she leaned on her elbows, her mind pondering the women she'd met in 1892. Some said she was in some sort of dissociative state? What did they call it? A fugue state? Some experts speculated in the years after the murders that may have been the case. Colette knew better.

Colette studied the metal tru-link fence across the street where the bungalow used to be. The fugue state theory decreased in likelihood in her mind. Certainly, it had been used in other murderous crimes as a reason? Defined as a state whereby a person has some sort of seizure, or does something of which later, they are completely unaware. It involved often a type of temporary amnesia. What puzzled Colette now was, if this was as a result of trauma at the hands of her father, why, after years and years of abuse, Lizzie suddenly snapped at age thirty-two? Had the repressed memories just come to life? What triggered it? It couldn't have been simply over a potential loss of property, if Mr. Borden did indeed draw up a new will? The violence of the crimes was too extreme. What about the lag time between the two killings? How could Lizzie, had she been in a dissociative fugue state, have stood at the top of the stairs after the horrifically violent killing of Abby Borden, and been overheard to laugh? Bridget, the maid, indeed claimed to have heard a laugh.

Colette walked over to the Prairie door where it lay, looking heavy and stalwart on the floor. She lifted it slowly and leaned it up against the wall again. Pouring herself a cup of coffee from a single serving pot, she let her thoughts go a bit further. On the day of the Borden murders, hadn't Lizzie, in fact, returned to the downstairs and continued to iron handkerchiefs? She resumed some sort of domestic task, that much Colette recalled.

Half an hour later, wearing black leggings and a black jumper, Colette drove the four blocks to the Valley Stream Historical Society for an appointment with one of the curators. The Victorian house lay in wait, shutters wide, walkway outstretched and lined with vivid multi-colored impatiens. Despite the fanfare, Colette was certain they'd not had visitors in a while. Remnants of cobwebs swept her cheek as she walked across the threshold.

"I'm not sure what I can tell you," the woman said, speaking slowly, barely moving away from the door. She was easily over eighty years old. Her hair, stark white, looked somehow elegant in a tight bun. "Our older records are in the barn. Did you already try the Internet?"

Colette was surprised to see that the woman, who wore a high-collared blouse, layers of pearls and a floor-length skirt would mention the internet. Clearly she lived the part of lady of the manor. Colette fought the urge to grin. It was touching when the older set tried to keep up with the information age computers.

"The Internet? No. I like the tactile experience of suffering papercuts and the smell of old things," Colette said, then stopped, hoping the woman didn't take that the wrong way. "Old documents and plat of surveys, you know?" The truth was she knew the information was not common knowledge, and in fact likely wanted to remain buried, secreted away in dusty drawers.

`"So you want to know about that old bungalow they've torn down, is that it?"

Colette eased her way into the foyer a little more, and nodded. Just as she started to sit on a burgundy velvet camel-back sofa in the vast hallway, the woman stopped her with a firm grip on her upper arm.

"You mustn't sit on the furniture, dear. Come out onto the sun porch. I'll pour you a Coca Cola. Do you take anything in it?"

Colette straightened up, nearly falling over, and followed the woman to the kitchen. "A lime would be nice."

The woman turned to her. "No rum or anything?"

What was it about cocktails and the North Shore? "No, really. No booze for me. Not a good idea." Then she recalled the woman's question. "I'm here because I would like to see a plat of survey, with any information about the house that had been built on the site before the bungalow? It was really an interesting bit of architecture. It had a vertical wooden frame exterior with fancy latticework. Haven't really seen anything like it. Especially not in the Midwest. You know, we had that great Chicago fire and all."

The woman stopped. When her eyes met Colette's, they glistened with scrutiny. "There was no house there before. I am certain of it. I was born in 1926, and that bungalow went up before I went into kindergarten."

"You're certain?" Colette struggled with her failing memory. Her mind worked. When she woke up in Massachusetts, she always found herself in Mrs. Burns's boarding house. That much she knew. But ironically a particular photograph she'd found in the closet of the room had shown, quite clearly, a depiction of Prairie Street in Illinois. Eventually it would be the site of the bungalow. But that Carpenter Gothic style house with vertical siding, it was there in the picture, across the street from the Victorian Farmhouse that was clearly Marilyn's house and her rented room, and a great American Foursquare her old neighbors had renovated on the left side of it. So what happened to the Carpenter Gothic? Why were there no records of the house in the year 2011?

"Of course I'm sure," the woman repeated.

There was a definite change in her tone. What had happened here?

They'd reached the back porch. The day had grown insufferably hot. The sounds of cicadas merged with some unholy chorus of what she guessed to be crickets. Why were bugs always louder in August?

"I apologize for not asking before," she said to the older woman. "What is your name?"

"Penelope Grainger. Mrs. Penelope Grainger."

"Penelope, I have a photograph of this precise Prairie Street in Valley Stream, Illinois, taken in 1892. I know for certain that it is the street, where I lived. I've had the photo authenticated. And there's been no fancy computer mumbo jumbo. It's legitimate."

"I wouldn't know about that. Are you saying our records are wrong? Or that someone tampered with them? Where did you find such a photograph?"

That's where Colette felt her credibility fading like ice cream left out in the sun. How would she explain this?

"On a trip out East, a while ago. Quite a while ago, actually. I found the photo at an old pawn shop."

Eyes narrowed, Penelope studied Colette a moment. "Don't know why a picture from Illinois would be out East? Anyway, there was nothing there before. It was vacant land."

In her mind, Colette recalled the remains in the coal chute. Somehow, William had followed Madeline to Illinois. Right to Valley Stream. She was sure of it. But William seemed inclined toward his father's way of thinking of late. She'd had a different interpretation when they'd first met. Or perhaps William was the younger and more polished narcissist of the two. Perhaps his kindness was part of his repertoire.

The Prairie door, the hieroglyphs on the stairs, the reunion with Olivia in 1994--all were meant to be. And Colette's transportation had been the Prairie door, and via the bracelet, she'd been shot back to the year 1892, Massachusetts.

Perhaps it was the manner in which Penelope delivered her gruff assessment of the land in question. Because all at once, Colette was having one of her sixth sense experiences. She intuited something now.

"Is there something else you want to tell me?" she asked, hesitantly.

Penelope lifted her crystal, what was probably at one time in the 1950's, high-ball glass, and took a generous swig. Behind her, various trees in the yard swayed, as if waving to her all of a sudden. Even in the heat, there traveled a slight breeze which willowed through the leaves. It was tranquil, subtle, and now frightening. Despite the purpose of Colette's visit, and her present unrest, she felt very at home in this setting, as if she belonged here in the midst of the nineteenth century. Ironically, she was teased as a little girl for wearing maxi dresses to school every day. Yet that odd and antiquated way of dressing felt normal to her. She'd always felt more comfortable in the past. Many misconstrued her vague tendency to daydream as simply misled youth. There was nothing vacuous about Colette's mind. She'd been born with memories of the nineteenth century.

One veiny arthritic hand grasped the rum and coke. Colette noticed now that Penelope studied nothing in particular in front of her. Wisps of her white hair lifted in the breeze. Finally, she said simply, "I didn't believe the stories."

Colette leaned forward. "What stories?"

Then she sat back, decidedly. One had to be cool, to approach a woman of such age and refinement. With delicacy.

"Scared the hell out of me," Penelope blurted.

Or perhaps, not so much.

"It was 1934. Just a couple years after the Crash. It hit everybody hard, let me tell you. That's when papa's drinking got really bad. He was a nice man, but a very sad man. His name was Darren. Looked a lot older than he probably was. He was a musician and not from the Midwest. That's all I know. He lost everything. He'd built the bungalow for someone. Not for us. For someone else. No one knew."

"So that spot of land on the 1800 block of Prairie was important to him?"

"Yes. He used to talk about something buried in the ground. A room? Or a coal chute from an older house. But we didn't find a room? Not until ten years after he died when mama and her new husband expanded the house." She paused. "And the front door? Why he made it by hand, a beautiful door. Gorgeous, with stained glass. The wood it was made of was not from here. I believe it was Red Pine. I looked it up as a teenager. It was native to New England, I think. He had it all brought here by rail."

"From where?"

"Let me think. Massachusetts. That's all I knew. Red Birch. That's the wood it was."

Colette swallowed, and then blinked several times.

"He'd put in a special door with a music box. Sounds fantastic, I know. I was the only child. That music box was intended to keep track of me."

"Did he lose the house?"

"Worse than that," she whispered, her fair skin growing pink. "He lost his mind. Talked about the hatchet murders. That more people died than anyone knew out in Fall River." Colette felt the hair on her arms stand up.

"Fall River? He said that?"

"Yes."

Colette was silent. It was a ponderous silence, the kind one imparts during a moment of absorbing deep tragedy. This had been her lifelong experience of mental illness. She pictured this man, Darren Haben, in search of the room on Prairie Street. Finished the house, then lost his mind. Lost his money in the Crash, and his senses eventually, over some obsession with a strange room and finding Isabelle.

"Was there ever anyone else there with him?"

"What do you mean?"

For the first time, Penelope actually appeared frightened. Authentically frightened.

"Was anyone else living with him?"

"In our house? Besides mother and me?"

Penelope sipped her drink, avoiding Colette's gaze. Then she stood up and headed back to the kitchen. "There was," she said over her shoulder. But only in his mind. Father claimed he could hear her singing. I'd say, 'who daddy? What're talking about?' And he'd go quiet again."

Colette waited. Spinning the soda glass around and around on the table. She watched as Penelope moved stiffly about the porch.

"She was his ghost. Mama told me he'd had heartbreak as a young man out on the East coast. Mama was much younger than he was. Like I said, I was born in 1926. He'd have been in his fifties. I was only seven or eight years old when he died of pneumonia."

"Did he have any friends?"

Penelope made a "tsk" sound with her tongue. "There was a tramp you know, a hobo. A street person. His name was Percy. Was a musician friend of his from the old days. People always noticed him creeping around the old bungalow or sitting on the stairs with my father. One day mother screamed at them both because they'd written crazy drawings all over the front sidewalk."

Colette caught her breath. "Drawings?"

"What I would call symbols, had I been older. Like another language. Mother made them wash them off. The liquor did crazy things to my father's mind."

Twenty minutes later, Colette thanked Penelope. Colette's mind was full as she descended the creaky stairs of the Valley Stream Historical Society. The shadows from Penelope's childhood lingered. To a great degree, Colette at last found a connection between this life in Illinois and life in Fall River, Massachusetts.

The hieroglyphs came to her mind as she backed up her dilapidated Volvo out of the small driveway. The scribbling from her time travel to 1994 and Olivia's incredible discovery? It all had something to do with Fall River? Why else would Colette have repeatedly been summoned back to 1892 in Massachusetts? It was likely Darren and Percy drew the messages on the stairs. But no one paid any attention to the symbols because they were assumed to be the drawings of an unstable aging father and his hobo friend. What about the door of the bungalow? It was apparently made from Red Birch, sent by train directly from Massachusetts.

The symbols had to be deciphered by someone. Someone who would know. Someone perhaps, like her old friend from graduate school? Steven Harmon at DePaul. He was brilliant. He would know. She needed to call and see what he could tell her.

She pulled up into the driveway of Marilyn's farm house. In the rearview mirror, there burst forth too much space, a new patch of sun blindingly bright as it beamed through the now vacuous hole left where the bungalow used to stand. Nothing there now. Nothing but the fence and signs of no trespassing. Soon the concrete truck would become a part of the landscape, and a large basement would be the start of an either massively over-sized house or a row of unimaginative townhomes. The stairs were gone too.

Seated on the quilted comforter again, she gazed around the rented room. A dutiful obsessive-compulsive, she got up again and unplugged the small coffee pot in the corner, then checked the small stove. Everything off. All systems go, she thought.

It occurred to her now how handy the iPhone would be in 1892. But how would it work? No cellular tower? Or account? Were such details impervious to the time-travel? All she'd have to do would be to snap a few pictures of what she discovered back in Mrs. Burns's house, like the long black and white photograph of Prairie Street in Illinois, and whatever else she could find at Edward Sewell's house. Anything that could perhaps explain why neither Madeline, nor her body, had ever been found. Isabelle had told Colette and Colette believed her. Something sinister had happened to her mother. She was convinced the second body was Madeline.

As Colette lay back on the bed now, pulling the door next to her bedside, she pictured Marilyn's face if she'd happened to walk into her room and see her, reclining with the heavy Prairie door from a torn-down house, leaning against her bed again. The delicious stories would spread about the twice divorced, nut-job who'd rented a room across from where she'd lived in her first marriage. Certainly, it would go something like this; she'd taken to sleeping with the front door of the old bungalow. As if to recapture old times. It was sad really.

Amazingly, although she felt keyed up with caffeine intake, once the door lay next to her, sleep descended like something drug-induced and she experienced that same wildly fleeting free-fall into timelessness. So perfectly in concert with the door, she started to grow warmer as the sleep state deepened. She hardly felt the bracelet warming up and a slight tightening around her wrist.

Eyes opened, she looked at the high ceiling. In fact, after a minute, she tuned in to open beams and the cobwebs of the attic room where she lay, the attic she recognized as that of the Perfect Pines Insane Asylum.

Sadie leaned over her, with her high-collared blouse unbuttoned down to her chest. Her dark hair fell about her pale face. In fact it brushed Colette's cheek until she came fully awake.

Isabelle stood behind Sadie, her arms crossed over her chest, her expression grim. She stared at nothing with great intensity.

"I thought Dr. Warburton took Isabelle?" Colette asked, sitting up slowly. Immediately, she felt the weight of her layers of clothing.

"He was called into an emergency," Sadie said. "Woman on two tried to jump. I'm afraid she simply crippled herself. Now she's really stuck here, poor wretch."

Sadie smiled, an eerie yet inviting smile that took up most of her cheekbones. Somehow it was sensuous. Colette could see how the men in the world of 1892, including Sadie's ex-fiancé, would go as far as scandal just to be with her. Was Sadie Hawthorne, like Colette, a woman out of time? Was that possible? The lovely Irish woman sat cross-legged next to Colette now. Suddenly Sadie leaned in closely and whispered.

"Isabelle is worse. She hasn't spoken a word. Dr. Warburton did something to her, then let her father Edward take her home for a couple nights. So of course, she ran away again. They found her wandering the train station. Since her mother Madeline has left, he's taken a greater interest in Isabelle as if she is a replacement." Sadie looked back over her shoulder to see if Isabelle was nearby, then she went on. "He's a monster. Like so many men, he'll not go to a lady of the evening because he'd risk getting a disease. One of the myths they tell around the church and gymnasiums is that if you've had intimate relations with a virgin, it will cure a sex disease. Men believe it, isn't that absurd? "

Sadie paused, as if out of breath. She fingered a gold cross around her neck.

"Truth is," she went on, "Edward was having his way with Isabelle even before her mother left. He ridiculed her just because of what Madeline believed."

Sadie's face was urgent, her eyes pained. "He gave her a ring to wear after her mother disappeared. Too damn close for a father, I tell you. I believe that's why she keeps trying to catch a train. She desperately wants to get to Chicago."

Colette nodded. "Just like Lizzie gave her father a ring. How strange...."

The two sat in silence. Colette pulled her knees to her chest and watched Sadie now. Isabelle's silhouette lingered behind them. Her reticence alarmed Colette in a way. Maybe it was because she didn't appear alive. Like statuary, her face glowed alabaster. It was emotionless as well. Lifeless. Colette could tell even from across the room that something had died in Isabelle. Her dark hair, with alarming grey and white hairs now, had grown limp and the delicate features of her profile seemed to acquiesce to their surroundings, as if she'd become unwillingly malleable. This lovely countenance could not escape nineteenth century tyranny.

"Is there another young man in Isabelle's life?" she asked Sadie. "Besides Darren?"

Sadie at first looked at Colette disbelievingly, her brows changing her expression, and then she threw her head back with a laugh. "As if Edward would allow her any male attention besides his own? Yes, Darren loves her. He also knows he's too old for her and has to wait."

She's an attractive young woman."

Sadie leveled her face again, looking eye to eye with Colette.

"What in blazes do you mean?"

"Women are courted, aren't they?"

The blithe spirit had flown from Sadie. Her face was solemn. In the following seconds, her mouth twisted, like some caricature. When she spoke, her voice sounded older, the pitch sounded an octave lower than before.

"Isabelle Sewell is thirteen years old."

The air seemed to catch the information and hold it there, suspended. Colette was jarred from her senses. The past couple days of time travel flew like mania in her mind. Sadie looked at Isabelle and saw her for the first time. Soft reddish curls curved around her face, the slender frame still developing. She had the still developing body of a young girl. The roundness of her face increased the magic of her innocence.

The room around her faded as it occurred to her now this was not a young woman in the physical sense. In one sense, she had the mind of a bitter woman. Ironically, she saw the same washed, distilled blue in her eyes with which Lizzie Borden saw the world. It was a silent fury in the eyes, an educated and constrained compliance. No womanly prowess, but rather the prematurely wizened eyes of an abused child.

Colette straightened up. Sadie knelt next to her, with a knowing grin. She realized Colette's mistake.

The sounds of footsteps on the attic stairs did not register in anyone's mind.

That was it, she thought. Lizzie Borden and Isabelle Sewell were sadly, cut from the same frayed fabric. Such a great amount of rage, having been restricted, would likely accompany such violations. Such injurious wounds had been manifested in their makeups, which led to diverse retaliation. For some, it led to murder.

Isabelle stood before Colette, her head tilted, arms straight at her sides. It had been too long. There had been a refusal to eat and talk. She was all anger turned inward upon herself. This was a child engulfed in an inferno.

Colette had once heard, in the course of her recovery process, that "resentment kills its own container." What was at Isabelle's core? She seemed to believe she was shameful. Isabelle Sewell perhaps believed that she was defective. All the rage that should have been directed at Edward Sewell at her father, a Victorian "pillar" of society. It gnawed away at her heart.

So perhaps the very angst which Colette detected on Isabelle's face now had less to do with her physical lesions and more to do with Isabelle's apparent awareness. Because Isabelle shared Lizzie's shame-based life. Isabelle shared the wrath. Hadn't Sadie described numerous occasions when Mr. Andrew Borden and Mr. Edward Sewell were seen strolling along Second Street, apparently sharing business ideas and matters of money? So perhaps it was only every other woman who passed them on the street who sensed the insidious truth about the two men. And for those women, and girls, perhaps they tensed up, ever so slightly, when the two gents tipped their hats to them as they passed.

Unlike Isabelle however, who had crumbled within herself under the strain of fury, Lizzie Borden had come undone.

Chapter Fifteen (A)

The Historical Facts

At one point in his defense, Robinson made it sound like Lizzie was completely in agreement that Alice Russell should go ahead and tell the truth.

In the end, Robinson finally presented a somewhat feasible argument around the possibility of an intruder having come in and secreted himself in a bedroom upstairs. He pointed out the possibility that Abby Borden surprised him unexpectedly and that he was in actuality in the Borden house specifically to murder Andrew.[285]

Still, if one stopped to think through that reasoning, the theory was questionable. First of all, why would someone interested in going after Andrew Borden specifically look for the business man upstairs? On several levels, there would be questions; why would a business associate, should that have been the murderer, look for Andrew Borden, a businessman, upstairs in his home on a workday? Even if he followed Andrew Borden's everyday schedule, it was unlikely Andrew would have been upstairs. As was Andrew's habit, he actually did not go upstairs for any length of time, and in fact, actually chose most often to nap downstairs.

At last, Robinson brought up a relevant point. He asked how Lizzie could have had on one dress for the first killing, then an hour and a half later, have murdered the second victim in a different dress?[286]

Although a valid point, the same concept would have held true for that "stranger" lurking in the house. Not only would such a person not want to have been seen in the bloodied clothes, but one also wonders how he or she would have "cleaned up" so quickly, and gotten out of the house before Lizzie showed up? Secondly, and also of consideration was that surely this person would have been walking through the downtown area of Fall River on a business day, at the beginning of the lunch hour. In reality, the stranger theory presented a less likely scenario than Lizzie's possible culpability. Lizzie had full knowledge of the layout of the house. She would have known precisely where to wash up, and where to stash any blood-stained clothes.

Therefore, the following could have been Lizzie's scenario; she put on some sort of wrapper or overcoat to commit the first murder, then she stashed it. Perhaps another theory which may have followed, was that she simply took Andrew's very own black overcoat, while assisting him to lie down. Then a moment later, by placing her arms in the sleeves with the buttons at the back, and by wearing the black Prince Albert coat backwards, she lashed out suddenly and killed him.

In a perfect plan then, all the blood stains, even were they visible, would have been assumed to have been from when Andrew was murdered and blood had gotten onto the coat from his wounds. Because in actuality, it would have taken a blood splatter expert to have deciphered the causes of the stains, such as recognizing whether or not they were from splash back from the murderer wielding the hatchet, and not from Andrew's seeping wounds.

Interesting also was the fact that when it came to witnesses, Robinson discounted all of the prosecution's witnesses. There were several newspaper men. One of them, named Henry Tricky of the Boston Globe, wrote a fabricated story about Lizzie having been pregnant. Yet then he, Tricky, disappeared to Canada and mysteriously died when he "slipped and fell" trying to catch a train.[287]

However, according to witness testimony, there was a legitimate conversation overheard between a Mr. McHenry and Mr. Tricky, known as the McHenry/Tricky Affair. Basically, the original attorney for the defense, Adams, talked about a price of $1,000 for evidence from the prosecution.[288] This was simply an extension of the false Trickey story which detailed Lizzie having had a boyfriend and eventually perhaps implying she'd become pregnant by this supposed lover

Ironically, even the original defense attorney, Mr. Adams, claimed to have had proof that Lizzie was guilty. He claimed he had knowledge that McHenry and his wife had been under the bed in Lizzie's room and had overheard Adams and Lizzie discussing her guilt.

All of these tales were perhaps simply tales. However, finally, Robinson brought up the hatchet problem. He claimed no one ever found it.[289] And then there was the disagreement about which officer exactly found it in the basement? Or found just the top of it, which led to a wide search for the missing handle. So much of the case was indeed circumstantial and hearsay.

According to a newspaper article entitled "The New Sensation" from June 1893, which was nine days into the trial, specifically June 14th, a hatchet was found on the roof of the Crowe barn located directly behind the Borden house. For whatever reason, this fact was never introduced before the end of the trial.[290] So indeed; Lizzie was found innocent on July 20, 1893. That hatchet, which showed only wear from the elements, easily may have been tossed up on the garage by Lizzie herself. Perhaps the hatchet, along with the bloodied dress, may too, have been stowed away and hidden temporarily until such time as Lizzie could have disposed of them. However, eventually the hatchet turned out to have belonged to a carpenter.

This example of new evidence which may have come into play might have changed the direction of the trial entirely. Ironically, Robinson then went on to review all the doors of the Borden house and whether or not each was locked at the time of the murders, or as they would be on a typical day.

He reminded the jury and the courtroom that the front door, the one in which Bridget let in Mr. Borden when he returned from downtown, needed to be unbolted and unlocked upon Andrew's arrival.

This coincided with the sinister sound of Lizzie's supposed laughter as she came down the main staircase which led to the front door.[291]

Robinson presently pointed out that the outside cellar door, the one at the back of the house, was locked and had been locked at least on the night before, and throughout the day of the murders.[292] Robinson continued to explain that in all likelihood, the side screen door was unfastened between nine and eleven o'clock on that day. Indeed, Bridget claimed she mentioned to Lizzie that she could leave the screen door unlocked once she returned from the barn, because she would have been going in and out as she washed windows.[293]

Ironically however, Robinson made a point of mentioning that Bridget "went to the barn seven or eight times for water...it may have been more." This very statement, then, contradicted his theory that Bridget was so busy, and later off talking to the Kelly girl on the south side of the house, that she would have not have seen anyone (such as a dark mysterious stranger), going in or out of the house.[294] Because if this were true, the path running from the barn to the screen door at the back of the house, would have been precisely the same route that Bridget would have taken in order to get water to the dining room windows. In that case, she would, without a doubt, have spotted anyone going into or out of the house.

Supposedly, Bridget went upstairs for her nap around 10:45 a.m. That would have left a very short time for a stranger to have gotten in between 9:00 a.m. and 11:00 a.m. – especially if Lizzie was in the dining room at the time ironing handkerchiefs.[295]

Chapter Sixteen

S adie held a crème-colored handkerchief in her hand. She dabbed at Colette's face, her eyes intense.

"What happened to you, sweet girl?" she asked. "You fell asleep. We couldn't wake you? I was afraid you'd slipped away from us forever."

Colette sat up and rubbed her head, a bit embarrassed. She adjusted several bobbie pins in her loose bun. Isabelle had not moved. Standing by the windows with her arms crossed over her chest, she continued to gaze outside.

Within minutes, a commotion had erupted on the stairs. Dr. Warburton and his henchmen were back for Isabelle. With an air of foreboding, Isabelle studied Colette for a long moment. In fact, even as Dr. Warburton took her by the upper arm and led her down the stairs, not once did Isabelle remove her gaze from Colette.

Several hours later, the women sat around a mahogany table in the dining hall. Sadie looked around furtively, not caring if she drew attention. This was her way. Her captivity in the asylum hadn't created much concern in her of late. In fact, on this day, August 6th, she had her high-button blouse undone under her fitted taupe patient uniform. Conversely, she wore around her neck a gold crucifix. Clearly, she drew her strength from several sources.

As Colette observed Sadie, she recalled that she'd mentioned knowing Madeline, Isabelle's mother, pretty well. She leaned forward as she put a teaspoon of weak split pea and barley soup to her mouth. Much of the food was bland. Folks seemed to subsist in 1892 on mutton, puddings and stale biscuits.

"You knew Madeline pretty well, didn't you?" she asked Sadie at last, despite the fact that Sadie's attentions were elsewhere.

"So did Lizzie," she said. "Through church." Whirling around and back to Colette, somewhat reluctantly, she stared at her, sucking on a spoon. "Edward Sewell lies about her. Like so many men. They feel they can run the lives of women. You know what it was?" She leaned forward, getting as close to Colette's face as she could. "Madeline influenced women. She was persuasive. She liked to compare home-making women to squirrels who are capable of nesting and raising their young. She felt women have so much more to give. She talked a lot about the Suffrage Movement and rallying women together. Over and over she'd tell us that we, as women, needed to stand up and take an active part in government decisions and laws. Do not misunderstand me though! Children and home were of the utmost importance to her. I think her question was why women had to remain imprisoned in their large homes, and fancy parlors and sitting rooms?

Colette nodded. "Wasn't Edward dead set against her being in the church group?"

Sadie grinned, one front tooth slightly, overlapping the other. She was indeed a pretty woman who had inherited many assets naturally that, Colette thought to herself, so many women in 2011 had to pay good money for. Once Sadie spoke again, her face changed. "Edward stopped her going to the church meetings when he heard what she was telling the members. Madeline was inciting radical thoughts."

"Madeline had her way of educating all of us, wherever she was, and in whatever group she was with. The church group included. One night though, I'll never forget. It was horrible. Edward dragged her out in front of a dinner at a fancy restaurant down town. In front of everyone, he took her to the front hallway and slapped her. No one said a word. And not a single man came forward. The women too, were afraid. This was Edward's way of showing his power over all the men in town, that he made every attempt to keep his wife in line." She paused. "He slapped her with such force that her nose bled all over her white dress.

"No one stepped in?"

Sadie looked annoyed now. "I don't know where you're from, but unfortunately here in Fall River, everyone blindly minds their p's and q's. Edward Sewell is important to them, just as Andrew Borden was."

Colette sighed. She followed Sadie's gaze.

"Who are you looking for?"

Sadie said nothing. After ten or so minutes, she apparently gave up, turned to her food and started picking at her biscuits and soup. The allotted half hour for lunch passed quickly. Soon the women filed out of the large dining hall, and filtered down numerous winding staircases back to their individual rooms.

Later that evening, at around ten pm, Colette slipped out of her room with her skeleton key and started out down the two hallways to Sadie's room. At the recent insistence of Dr. Warburton, the two women had been stashed in rooms as far apart as possible.

Skirting down the first cold corridor, she felt her way with flat hands on the walls. There were only periodic kerosene lamp sconces every twenty or so feet, making it challenging to find her way. Still, in her mind's eye, she recalled watching the precise staircase where Sadie had scurried off to when they first relocated her to another room. How ironic, she thought now, that initially she had accompanied William and Edward to visit Isabelle at this very same hospital not too long before. Since that time, she'd managed to get herself committed to Perfect Pines Mental Asylum. Nellie Bly, the newspaper reporter in the 1887, who'd feigned illness to gain access to the inner workings of the Women's Lunatic Asylum in Blackwell's Island, New York, had been appalled at the conditions. Some indignities included dirty water and spoiled beef to eat. Although Perfect Pines didn't serve spoiled beef, in every other way its methods were still archaic; ice baths, chains, isolation rooms, even forcing the women to make their own straitjackets in their sewing classes. The façade of the white furniture, and the disturbing stillness about Dr. Warburton and his nurse, had convinced her that William's initial fears were valid. To think that, at the time, she was totally unaware that Isabelle was only thirteen years old.

She rapped on the door sharply, looking left and right. She didn't have much time, although it seemed like a senseless concern because the hallways in Sadie's wing of the hospital were exceedingly dim. Clearly, she had been dumped in an area for less cooperative patients, or those seen in less favor.

Finally, Colette simply turned the knob very slowly, and walked in. Sadie shared a room with three other women. They were in beds which appeared to be smaller than twin beds, if that were possible. Perhaps the size of children's beds. Colette wandered from one to the next, trying to decipher which form under the various bleached white blanket was indeed Sadie Hawthorne. Then she felt a thick rope and realized all four women were tied together. She heard a groan from a bed against the far wall.

Sadie's arm drooped over the side of the bed. "My God," Colette whispered. But she already knew. Colette felt suddenly sick. When Sadie looked up, her normally bright eyes were dull and black, devoid of any vitality. Despite the clandestine support meetings Isabelle had organized, Sadie had relapsed again. And badly.

"Who gave it to you Sadie?"

The figure on the bed didn't move.

"Who gave you the Laudanum? And what else? Pills?"

Kneeling down as she spoke to her, Colette stroked Sadie's dark hair, moving strands away from her face. Colette recalled all at once, a time in high school when she'd tried to quit drinking, and without a recovery program, at age sixteen, she'd wanted the emotional pain to stop; even if for one night. She'd not learned the tool yet of seeing her world beyond the bottom of a bottle; of seeing the night all the way through.

By the light of the moon coming through the high window, she could see a large bruise on Sadie's cheek, and there was a cut which sliced her fair skin just under her left eye. It was so odd, and heart-breaking, to see the charisma of Sadie so extinguished, her manner so reticent. This was the most disturbing aspect of this discovery. Colette had never seen Sadie defeated, not once in her short jaunt to 1892. Although they'd only been acquaintances a short time, Colette felt she knew the spirit of this young woman. That same spirit had been extinguished, snuffed out by callous fingers.

"Needed to talk to you," Sadie managed. "To anyone. He wouldn't leave me alone. Dr. Warburton let Edward Sewell spend two hours with me. He questioned me over and over. But I didn't give in. I didn't. Not for a long time. Then he brought in a tray," she stopped, tears spurted from her eyes, and she looked to be in physical pain, "a tray of bottles. Of liquor. Sweet liquors and pretty colors." Tears flowed from her eyes. "He said it would make it easier. But I resisted. Of course I knew she had not told him. That's when he hit me." She reached out her arms to Colette. "Hit me over and over."

Colette hugged her, telling her it was not the wrong thing to have done. That she did her best. "Who is he looking for?" Colette asked.

"He's hunting Isabelle. She escaped again after dinner some time. Word is, she finally boarded a train. I didn't tell him the truth…that Darren, with the help of William, arranged a new life for her, where she can go to school in Illinois. On the North Shore of Chicago in a lovely community. Valley Stream is the name. Small town. Isn't that quaint?" She looked up, one of her eyes nearly swollen closed. "He even found her a home on a lovely street, Prairie Road? No, Prairie Street. Doesn't that sound nice?"

Colette sighed. William helping was dubious news to her. It occurred to her now that William was the older brother indeed. He was sixteen or seventeen. Isabelle was thirteen. And Darren loved her more than anyone. He respected her youth. The tragedy was that Edward Sewell forced premature womanhood on Isabelle. As was the custom in 1892, and as a Victorian narcissist, his own daughter was not an individual but merely an extension of his ego; an object of which he owned like property, like a fine horse and carriage, or a distinctive pipe. Added to that, sexual abuse by the father sometimes happened in conjunction with this attitude.

"I didn't tell him," Sadie went on, her voice growing weaker. She closed her eyes. Edward tried. He violated me. He demeaned me. He said I deserved to be in this place and that women like me, and his illicit wife and daughter, were ruining American families with selfish desires. That our ideas go against what America stands for; something about a Patriarch and the pursuit of wealth, education and property. Education for men, that is. Now he's gone off in search of Isabelle. William is awaiting her at the house on Prairie. I think Darren might be there too."

Colette nodded, holding both of Sadie's hands in her own.

It troubled her greatly that she was uncertain where William's loyalties were directed?

"He said women like me, and Lizzie Borden and her sister Emma, that we're all tainted. That no proper gentleman in his right mind would ever want or desire us, much less marry us."

She sat up a bit, her eyes widened. "But I showed him," she said, "I told him I was proud of who I was. That I would travel the world. Alone if I wanted to. In whatever way I wished. That it was men that were labeling us as 'tainted.' Or that perhaps I would go to college and take on a profession. A doctor, or perhaps a professor."

Colette gave Sadie's arm a squeeze. "I need to find William," she said.

"He's in Chicago."

Sadie reclined again.

Twenty minutes later, having utilized the skeleton key again, Colette left the asylum and soon she was climbing to the first floor window of

Edward's gothic-style mansion. The air was heavy. The colors were black and green on this summer night in Fall River, Massachusetts. It was, of course, still 1892. Colette had to continually remind herself of this fact. It had only been a day since the double murders of Abby and Andrew Borden, in her time. But in 1892, more time had passed. She wasn't sure how many days, or even a week? It made sense; it occurred to Colette now that all eyes and minds were on the Borden travesty. No one, not a soul, had noticed Isabelle's deteriorated mental condition in the last year. She'd gone unnoticed. Isabelle had escaped, because of Darren's connections.

What worried Colette now was the equally untimely disappearance of Edward Sewell. He may indeed have gone after Isabelle. First, wouldn't he have had to know where she went? For certain? Colette knew where she went. Isabelle had escaped to Illinois. The odd connections between Illinois and Massachusetts continued to come together.

Once through the window, Colette unwrapped a lacy white curtain from her long dress, as she slipped inside a large bedroom. Even on this torrid night, registering well over eighty-five degrees, there was a light breeze coming through. In an instant, the blanketed silence made her forget the dismal nature of the task before her. Her cousin Glenda Morgan, an owner of an antique store, often turned to Colette for advice on the pricing of older items. Colette's specialty was the renovation of nineteenth century houses. She'd seen too many houses destroyed before they could be declared landmarks. Usually they were replaced by inferior housing. The picture she'd seen of the previous structure at 1804 Prairie Street, in Valley Stream, Illinois, had definitely been a Carpenter Gothic.

One thing was clear, Mr. Edward Sewell was well-off. Three walls of the study she'd now entered consisted of floor to ceiling bookshelves. The top three shelves were comprised of sets; row upon row of burgundy leather-bound books. The room was resplendent – so proper, and in perfect order. It was very much Edward Sewell. No, she thought, perhaps the room was what Edward Sewell wanted to appear to be. And he spared nothing to create this illusion. Everything of value was on display. In one corner there stood an ornate Victrola, one of the more expensive models judging by the large golden sound horn on top of it, and the double doors for volume control in the front. The curtains on the windows were heavy and burgundy, like the leather books. In Victorian fashion, every available space was replete with items orchestrated to trumpet the occupant's wealth. Like Andrew Borden's sitting room, the same one where he was found battered and faceless, there were several paintings on the walls hanging from long colorful ribbons.

Colette's eyes roved around the desk area. As she crept more deeply into the room, an oppressive weight fell upon her, suffocating her. Ironically, she recalled reading recently on the internet that a medium who had visited the Lizzie Borden home had detected a heaviness about it. She couldn't remember the exact words. But right now, she understood, because now she found it difficult to breathe.

Stepping behind a massive desk, she noticed two large photographs in frames. Taking out her iPhone, she lit upon the pictures to see them more clearly. Her heart jumped. On the left was what must have been a family portrait when Madeline was still in the home. Young William looked to be around ten years old, and Isabelle around seven. Her face was stern. There was an anger about her. William was not looking at the camera but instead stared at his father. The most frightening thing though was that Madeline's face had been scratched out with a letter opener or something sharp.

Looking up, Colette thought she heard something, then spotted a large wardrobe by a far wall. Scrambling, she got down on her knees. There was a large drawer at the bottom which she pulled out very slowly. Stuffed with photographs, the drawer barely opened. There were group shots of some women from the town of Fall River. Ironically, Colette recognized a few. How odd it was to be back in Fall River and know more people from Massachusetts, just from a series of days in

1892? One woman in a photo had a purposeful distance in her eyes, as if she needed to not be present, needed to be anywhere else than seated in the front row at this "damn church picnic," she seemed to say. Colette recognized a younger Lizzie Borden. The eyes were remarkably light, even in the black and white photo which had almost a purple tint to it. Her naturally curly hair was arranged delicately atop of her head, as was the custom of the day. Her cheeks were full and round. They looked just as they'd looked in the childhood photos Colette recalled studying over the years. Except now there was something about the gaze itself; at once distant, disturbed, disordered.

Right now, however, the questions in her mind revolved around Isabelle's escape. And why had young William helped Darren get his sister out of town? This was the connection to 1804 Prairie Street in Illinois. What about the hieroglyphs? Timing was key. She had to get them translated, she'd emailed her contact at DePaul University and had not heard back.   She already had an idea what the symbols may have contained. She touched her slide bracelet, even fiddled with the clasp. Still, it would not come off. Something about that bungalow had touched her simply by its strength. Once a visiting plumber to the house remarked to her, as she stood by and bounced a fussy six-month-old Olivia in her arms, that they "just don't build them like this anymore." Sure it was a humble place, especially by North Shore standards. But Colette always felt she lived in a shining example of America. A smaller house, but stronger, from a time when people actually sat on the front stoop to talk to their neighbors.

Deeply engrossed, she barely heard the front door slam. Double locks with loud clicks turned. It occurred to her that maybe Edward Sewell had the same phobia about burglary as Andrew Borden?

In a panic, she looked around to tall windows and the heavy drapes. No white eyelet here. This room screamed testosterone. Nowhere to hide. The wallpaper, a rich red floral print, matched the heavy red of the drapes. The study itself, although replete with male influences like business papers, a blotter with Edward's initials, several fountain pens and leather encased pipes had a sense of order that was obsessive. That further convinced her that Isabelle had definitely been imprisoned in this place. For a purpose. It was very similar to wallpaper she'd had clutched in her hands that day on the stairs, the day of the murder.

Isabelle tried to escape her father that day. Edward and the empty house now without her mother, left only a residual cyclone and patriarchal rage. According to Edward, women were to blame for all his troubles. Women needed to know their place. All Isabelle knew, aside from her belief in everything her mother represented, was her father's rage, intimately.

Colette slipped into a tall wardrobe with two heavy doors. Through the slats, she could make out Edward leaning over a porcelain lamp with a billowing ball for a shade. Her mind wandered to a shop in Wilmette back home, and exactly what price that gorgeous lamp would get. He lit the wick inside it just as she slipped further back in the closet. She tried to slow her heart down, even held her breath afraid that the pounding equaled the sound of kettle drums. Her disdain for this man throbbed inside her head.

Suddenly her thoughts went to the days in the asylum recently, when she and Sadie and Isabelle had talked. Isabelle had described this study in painstaking detail, and how she could tell simply by where his feet were applied, where they put pressure on the floor from up in her room, that he'd had his fill of drinks and was coming up the back stairs. He preferred the servant's stairs. Much less chance of detection, either by nosy housemaids or the wife. Of course once the wife was "gone," Edward's games became easier.

Isabelle related how she would lay there in terror, holding her breath, the strip of light under her bedroom door blocked by his shoes. If he planned to leave her alone on that particular evening, the steps would recede. But the alternative, when his steps resulted in the turning of the doorknob, the shame would wash over her from her neck up to her face and she'd pulled the covers up and fight tears. Edward

Sewell had expectations of Isabelle. And since the disappearance of her mother, Edward referred to her as the "young lady of the house."

From the restrictions of her hiding place, Colette overheard the sounds of liquid being poured. Through the slats, she distinguished the black outline of Edward's morning coat, and the sheen of his slick black shoes. He turned and posed, checking out his coat in a lavish mirror over the liquor cabinet. He drank down the first one quickly, then poured another glass.

Just like that, Colette could taste that drink. She could feel the warmth in her throat as the liquid left her mouth. That insidious trick of the mind played out a scene in her head; a vision of herself casually stopping at a liquor store for a bottle. How easy that would be? She'd have some relief from all the death and deceit in Fall River, and the feelings of shame coming up inside her. An insane urge to drink grabbed her by the neck. Despite her terror at being in this house, with this loathsome person, the insanity of her alcoholism made her want to drink. She could envision the full relapse.

Watching him intently, she concentrated on the bottom of an imaginary bottle; the drunken impulses, being foolhardy and left with immense regret. Then she grinned. How would she explain to her fellow recovering alcoholics that she'd relapsed in 1892? Would that really count? Was time travel and its environs considered a drink freely zone? No. A relapse was a relapse.

Half an hour passed. Edward still stood before the cabinet, drinking one glass after another. He swaggered over to his extravagant desk. From the back he looked like some waxen figure. The gleam from his shoes was still visible. When he turned sideways at last, his profile was severe and there were shadows under his eyes. His lips were moving.

"You really think you can run away from me?"

Her heart stopped. Then, he continued to talk.

"You? A simple woman? Just like your cheap and common mother before you."

All at once he whipped around dramatically. Colette sucked in her breath. At that, he was alert, like some rapacious beast. Strolling to the side of his desk, he slammed his hand down, toppling the ink blotter until it fell to the floor. He stalked over to the massive wardrobe closet. Colette shrunk away, pressing herself against the back of it. That's when Edward Sewell knelt down in front of the furniture where she was hidden, and she heard him pull open a drawer.

Chapter Sixteen (A)

The Historical Facts

As had been previously established, the likelihood that a stranger, who acted as murderer, was slim. He would have had to pass through the Borden house, not from front to back because the front door was locked, but rather from back to front in order to pass through the open screened door. The door was the only free and open access through which a perpetrator may have gone unnoticed by Lizzie, or any other witnesses.[296]

Yet even by that route, a stranger would have indeed been noticed. At one point in the trial, Robinson described in somewhat incoherent detail, how this murderer may have gone inside and wandered about the house, then ventured upstairs by way of the front staircase.[297] Once there, he would have murdered Abby, (even though Lizzie was upstairs at the same time, and she stated that she'd spoken with Abby), and somehow not passed Lizzie in the hallway in transit. If the murderer had indeed closed the door to the guestroom, which was the implication, that provided an excuse as to why Lizzie never noticed her stepmother laying dead on the floor. Then the critical question remained who would have opened the door ahead of time (but after the murder) which at 11:30 a.m. allowed Mrs. Churchill to see the body under the bed as evidence, from her stance on the stairs? One may recall Mrs.

Churchill had gone upstairs to check for Abby, after Andrew was discovered dead.[298]

It seemed that as the case continued to be revealed, more evidence was unraveled as it related to witness statements and it seemed that many nonsensical explanations were fabricated.

Robinson even claimed that the stranger as murderer may have been responsible for bolting the front door of the house – and then, supposedly, hidden out somewhere on the first floor? Or in the cellar? This was unlikely due to the obsessive ownership Andrew Borden had around keys to the house. The stranger would have gauged exactly when Lizzie would have gone on her time immemorial stroll to the barn and searched for sinkers, stopped to eat pears, or scrounged around for metal to repair the screen door. In other words, this stranger as murderer would have anticipated the movements of people in the house at all times. A remarkable feat.

Amazingly, throughout all this, the mysterious perpetrator would have known instinctively to stay hidden until those crucial ten or so minutes that Lizzie made her father comfortable on the sofa in the sitting room. At that time, he would have hopped from his hiding place, and successfully murdered Andrew Borden by 11:00 am. Thus, murder accomplished, he would have either then run out the front door of the house, covered in blood for all the neighbors and people walking downtown to have seen, or slipped out the screened door left open at the side of the house. Once outside, he'd managed to skirt out of the way before Lizzie had spotted him. Because Lizzie at that time, would have been en route from the barn to the house, and soon to discover Andrew's body promptly at 11:00 a.m. Subsequently, she would have called upstairs to the sleeping Bridget, and shouted "someone has killed father."[299]

Near the end of Robinson's rambling speech, where he continually called upon the men to behave in a responsible way concerning the life and death of the sweet young defendant, he finally made a point of describing how Lizzie, due to her honesty and good nature, claimed that when the guilty finger was pointed at the maid Bridget "Maggie" Sullivan, Lizzie made a point of stating clearly that "Bridget did not do it."[300] And finally, when the finger was pointed at the Portuguese worker on the farm, she said neither he, a Swede laborer, nor any of his workers would ever do such a horrible thing. Lizzie apparently continued on in this way, absolving anyone and everyone that had been accused of any guilt in the matter.[301]

Robinson attributed Lizzie's gracious demeanor to being noble. Her actions, certainly were those of an innocent person. If only the jury had looked at this logically. Perhaps as regular men, versus men who were admonished by Robinson for viewing Lizzie as anything less than a kind woman, the jury would have realized that Lizzie, had she truly been innocent, would certainly have wanted the murderer to have been caught. Why would a truly innocent Lizzie have claimed with such an amount of certainty that no one; not Bridget, not a farmer, not the Swede, not even an imaginary boyfriend, could, under any circumstances, have been responsible for the murder of her very own father? Wouldn't such a crime outrage an innocent daughter? [302] Would she not have wanted to seek out justice? Unless, of course, Lizzie herself knew for certain who the murderer was; knew for certain because she herself was the perpetrator of the crimes.

For the prosecution, Hosea M. Knowlton began his plea. Interestingly, one statement he made at the outset was significant, if carefully analyzed. Knowlton said…"the difficulty of solving this awful tragedy starts from the very impossibility of the thing itself."[303]

Examination of this statement alone on the part of the jury would have yielded a great deal of knowledge for the gentlemen who sat upon it, viewing a possible suspect as a person, rather than seeing the her as simply a woman. If they'd focused on fact, over societal and moral preconceptions, they'd have had a clearer vision of the truth.

The murders represented a Victorian tragedy in concert with the times. Putting it simply, if the defendant had been a man, for instance a son who had murdered his father and step-mother, there would have been little consideration. The jury was blinded by their beliefs and misconceptions about women.

So the "difficulty in solving the tragedy" was simply that the jury set the facts aside, due to their horror and disbelief, that a woman would have been capable of such crimes. The grievous facts against Lizzie were numerous; the suspect was at the scene in the house, Lizzie had motives – motives of rage as a victim of sexual abuse which focused internally within the family and perhaps, even unbeknownst to her, became aimed at society at large. This information covered simply the motive aspect. Because the facts in the case all clearly pointed to the suspect. This was true from the initial timing of discovery, by her location on the premises, as well as her contradictory testimonies about details. There existed purported hearsay, such as an overheard conversation described by a witness at the jail where Lizzie had been held, all these factors contributed to the aura of foggy and cryptic suspicion.[304] All eyes were on the young woman wearing her tidy hat and neat pin to the courtroom every day.

Soon it was the turn of the Prosecutor DA Knowlton to address the jury. He mentioned that certainly a person's station in life had no bearing upon his or her capacity to commit such severely heinous crimes. In fact, he stated in Porter's *The Fall River Tragedy* that "no station in life is a pledge or a security against the commission of a crime, and we all know it."[305]

Soon after, he made a statement that indeed summed up, in many ways, the totality of the human condition whereby possible abuse; sexual, physical, emotional, may well have taken place, and would have been present in the household of Lizzie Borden herself.

The statement Knowlton essentially read was, as follows: "Time and again have we been grieved to learn, pained to find, that those who are set up to teach us the way of correct life have been found, themselves, to be foul as hell inside."[306]

If Lizzie were indeed a victim of sexual abuse, the words now had been more gently put, such as, "foul with the bitterness that befits a victim of abuse, feeling like hell inside."[307]

Because the depths of despair, the self-loathing, shame and for some like Lizzie, almost narcissistic sociopathic rage, in fact, any number of these reactions may have encompassed the psyche of a victim. According to some experts, abuse victims may fall into extreme debilitating depressions. Others have even had delayed reactions whereby years after the abuse, troubles emerge later in life due to the repression of distinct memories. Others, perhaps like Lizzie, may act out in fits of violence. Because as previously stated, severe depression, aside from being a chemical imbalance, is anger turned inward upon oneself.[308] Perhaps Lizzie's depression demanded expression in the form of murder.

It may be considered a simplified hypothesis, but Lizzie may have exacted her depression turned rage on the perpetrators themselves; her father as direct abuser, and her step-mother as accomplice. Because in Lizzie's mind, Abby was equally guilty.

In Lizzie's eyes, Abby Borden was the only semblance of a mother the child had ever known. From the age of three or four years old or so, Abby was to have been her protector. Who knew that even in that all-too-proper society, that no amount of locks and keys would actually have protected her from the twisted actions within the Borden house itself.

Chapter Seventeen

B ack at the bar in his ostentatious study, there came the sounds of Edward pouring another drink. The sound of the alcohol, in combination with Colette's mounting anxiety around this sinister man, made her want a drink herself. It never failed. No matter how many years went by, there were always triggers for her. Ironically, she was grateful for what she described as "Technicolor relapse dreams." She was prone to those dreams, several times a month. In these dreams, there would be a careless relapse on her part, whereby she'd give in to a mug of beer without stopping to think. This act would lead to all sorts of human debauchery and despair. In these horrific dreams, she would do anything from committing adultery, drink and drive with her children in the car or end up with a DUI and a suspended license, cursing the police at the top of her voice from her jail cell. When she'd awaken the next morning, she'd wonder what really happened; what was reality? Some mornings were so rough; she'd meander her way through that day after a relapse dream, feeling foggy, hung over, as if she'd actually taken a drink again.

These "morning after the nightmare" days, she referred to as gifts from God; this was his remarkable and creative way of keeping her sober, and in her right mind. So now, back in 1892, she recognized that these women had no recourse. They had no support, or fellow-alcoholics nor drug addicts or victims of abuse meetings per se. Where could they go? How could they get support? Who would believe the wild talks of abuse? Perpetrated by upstanding gentlemen? Especially when even in the twenty-first century, so many repressed memories and claims of abuse, were swept aside by well-meaning family members, or simply by a society that didn't like anyone making a mess?

Peering carefully around the side of the wardrobe, it took her several minutes to realize that the room had emptied out.

Creeping out of her cramped space, she stepped around the massive piece of furniture, and checked one last time for Edward. He'd indeed left the room. She sucked in her breath suddenly when she saw his form standing in the hallway, giving instructions to some mild-mannered maid. It was the woman who had poked her head in a few minutes earlier, with a remarkably friendly "hello sir." He referenced a paper pamphlet in his hand, and every now and then she could hear him say the word "train" and "get me to Chicago."

Colette crept to the window.

The sun was setting and it cast a deceivingly serene and benign twilight to the day's end. Because it really wasn't the time to sit back and relax. Colette certainly knew this.

She looked around, half expecting Edward to come back any minute.

Colette scrambled outside and knelt down on the ledge, which was mercifully wide.

Seconds later, Edward rushed back into the room in a huff. He carried a large file in his hands. The maid had followed obediently. Colette could make out a large black and white photo of the house on Prairie Street, the one in Illinois. The Carpenter Gothic. He pointed to the houses, as if trying to explain something to her. In fact, he grew impatient as he barked out instructions on how to get him a round trip train ticket to Chicago. It was urgent! He needed to leave as soon as he could.

"I need to leave tonight," he demanded.

The maid stammered something about connections in other cities, and nodded. A rush of wind whipped up from the trees below, and the scent of hot grass was on her back. Colette leaned in; trying to hear the maid, but all she could make out was his loud condescension. This little talk had gone beyond train tickets.

"Annie," he said. "For the last time. Did you know about William and someone named Darren, and this trip to Illinois? They must have gone to the property where I found Madeline was living."

Annie trembled visibly, with her arms hugging her chest. She was simply a "Bridget" to the Victorian mentality but at least, Edward knew this Irish maid's name. Indeed, there seemed to be a racist epidemic during this time period, particularly against the Irish. This casual indifference to the names of Irish maids made Colette think of the poor beleaguered "Maggie" Bridget Sullivan, the maid at the Borden house. That Maggie would have much interrogation to endure, as well as suspicions about her loyalties, in the coming months and years, she could not even imagine. Emma and Lizzie Borden were known to have always referred to Bridget as Maggie, and the reason was not clear. Apparently their prior maid had been named Maggie, although some claimed it was a warm nickname Lizzie had for Bridget.

Soon this particular girl, this young maid Annie, had scurried out of the room and was, no doubt, racing upstairs to the master's bedroom to pack his suitcase or trunk for the journey.

Presently, Colette shimmied down the side of the brick building, gripping gargoyles and cement blocks, until she'd reached ground level. Colette fell back onto her behind, allowing her dress to hike up to her knees. She rubbed her ankles where the tie-up boots were digging into her bare skin.

There was nothing to be done now. Edward had the address in Illinois of the house on Prairie Street. He'd found Madeline there before. No good would come of it. He would follow Isabelle and William. He would hunt her down and bring her back.

All rights and freedoms would be gone for her.

Colette found a friendly wrought iron bench in a generously green park. She sat there, thinking, praying, uncertain what to do. When she looked up, she shook her head in astonishment. With one arm in a sling, and a swollen eye, Sadie had followed her.

As the two women walked, the humid night closed in, and the grey night lay upon them.

Soon, they came upon a lively little gathering of people. Colette realized it was the site of an ice cream parlor. The two women decided to rest and hide out there.

Sadie staggered a bit as they entered the shop. All at once, and quite unfortunately, it hit Colette that this may not have been a good idea. She'd forgotten it was 1892, and they were in a small town with curious and berating eyes consistently upon them. Soon there came the murmurs of "fallen women, perhaps from the local asylum" and "who allowed harlots in here?"

Still, Colette refused to leave. All along, she thought she knew the East coast, even in 1892. The judgment here seemed just as severe as it had in the Midwest. Finally, they got their two scoops of vanilla ice cream in tiny silver bowls with flatware. No Styrofoam here.

The two women settled into a small corner of the place, seated under a vast mirror with pink trim. Watching the battered, but defiant face of her companion, Colette saw herself in Sadie. Even in the twenty-first century, women who were sexually healthy and had several lovers, or more, were given labels like slut or whore.

Sadie tried to straighten her hair in the pink-trimmed mirror, but it was somewhat hopeless. Whipped by the elements, the result was a disheveled bun. She'd purposely sat with her back to the women in the place. She could still see them in the reflection of the mirror.

Indeed, a century had passed since this very time where they sat and tried to enjoy ice cream in 1892. Colette recalled too her high school years, during the late 1970s, when she'd suffered a similar sense of isolation. Due to various reasons; lack of status; money, a father who'd abandoned the family when Colette was eleven, and a depressed mother left behind with her, Colette thought a similar fate would be the inevitable end for her own life. Colette's mother reinforced the belief that some women were purposely left behind. Granted, her mother Ursula, defaulted to depression, her clinical illness, while others slid into alcoholism. The nineteen seventies may have been coined the "me" decade, but for Colette, it was anything but.

As the two women took small bites of ice cream, Colette's thoughts went back to that time in the Midwest, in Oak Park, Illinois. Ursula had started out as such a promising young woman, a direct descendent of a family who'd survived Jamestown. What an astounding feat. Still, due to cruel twists, and despite Ursula's active mind and stellar grades in school throughout her youth and university, she'd eventually settled into the married wife borne out of nineteen fifties America. There began the death knell, the insistent prognosticator of danger. If only Ursula had heard it, and heeded its warning. Because the definition of a successful woman in nineteen fifty-five had married a husband who came home from work and motored up the driveway of their three-bedroom home in a lengthy blue Buick. Awaiting him, would be the wife; sporting pearls, a wide full skirt belted, and an even wider smile. Roast beef dinner awaited on the dining room table. The children often plied dad with questions of "what did you bring me from the office?" and he would parcel out paperclips in their open palms. If all these criteria were met, there existed a happy American home. In fact, a majority of the pictures of Colette and her family from those days had the five of them crowded behind yet another massive, thickly-frosted birthday cake which Ursula had been known to bake on every festive occasion they celebrated. In those photos, the look in Ursula's eyes as she leaned over her satisfied husband, with offspring gathered around was painfully reminiscent of Sylvia Plath. Of course, Ursula had achieved the "successful life" of an American wife, but on the inside, she was suicidal. Sylvia Plath, who'd been a brilliant poet and writer in her own right, spent her short existence in the shadows of her husband, British Poet Laureate Ted Hughes. After two children and his affairs, and due to her untreated depression, Sylvia had taken her own life. Balancing bundt cakes with literary career aspirations was a life doomed to failure. Like many women, Sylvia wanted to be the best in every possible world.

So as Ursula's marriage crumbled, so did Ursula. After Colette's father left, Ursula went on to get her PhD. But in the shell which remained, and despite extreme intellectual and professional success as a research scientist, Colette felt Ursula had been stripped of her femininity by others who thought she'd not held onto her man, as a good wife should, in 1975. Ironically, no one ever told Ursula that the rules of the game had changed. The once happy house frau was supposed to have morphed into a bionic sex Sputnik in elephant-ear bell-bottoms. Ursula simply strived to be the best woman she could be.

One arm in a sling, Sadie was licking the silver spoon with her free hand, looking quite, unfortunately for her, provocative. Colette smiled, and couldn't help savoring the look of disgust on the faces of the other women, their glares of disdain shielded by their lacy hats. The women were stationed, like wilted pansies, in every corner of the parlor. Escaping into her thoughts, Colette allowed the women to blur in her mind.

The Victorian woman had it rough, after all. She was expected to make her own soap, churn butter, run a kitchen which included a massive stove, one that was impossible to light, and maneuver a complicated oven. She could easily spend an entire day devoted to an arduous laundry process, and then the next day, ironing handkerchiefs, starching blouses, dusting, vacuuming and washing windows, (if without a "Maggie" maid on hand). The Victorian woman would be responsible for all aspects of the culture and schooling for her children. Of course, she had to marry well, first and foremost. If she did not, she would end up like Lizzie Borden. A spinster. She would then suppress excessive rage, until her body would be given over to depression, and a breakdown in health. At least were she a fortunate woman of leisure, she could partake of gardening and church activities.

The American woman of 2011 could marry well, could buy soap, buy butter, and earn her own income but she must also dust, vacuum, wash windows, wash her car, tend to the garden, the lawn, and of course, the children.

Colette gazed through the silver bowl in front of her with the melting vanilla ice cream forming a milky puddle. The sounds of the ice cream parlor filled her thoughts once more and she realized Sadie too had finished. She was staring at Colette. White noise. Colette felt her mind transporting her elsewhere, somewhere less stressful where they were not being judged by eleven or twelve uptight Victorian women.

Ignoring the stares of the parlor, the two women rose and marched, Sadie, a bit unsteadily, out of the place.

The night air was fragrant, blisteringly hot, but fragrant.

"We have to leave tonight," Colette said under her breath.

Sadie gave Colette a concerted look as if to say "how?" The effects of the Laudanum were still apparent in her eyes.

"Don't you think I'm in enough trouble?" she said. "Leave to go where? We have to be back at Pines," she said, "they'll be checking for us."

"That's the last place we want to go. We need to catch a train out. I think there's one outside of Boston. We may have to take several trains, I'm not sure."

Early the next morning, the two women, wearing ill-fitting lightweight coats that Mrs. Burns the landlady dug up for them, stood surrounded by two small leather suitcases. They waited in a small station to go to Boston. There would be another connection to get to Chicago. All eyes seemed to be upon these two, apparently rogue and unaccompanied, women. Where were they traveling to alone? For once, Colette was grateful there were no computer or high-tech methods to track them.

Perhaps it was Sadie's wild expression, or maybe the way Colette kept tugging at her high-necked collar, but in the heat, amidst the steam of trains and the crowd, the proverbial costume of the day proved nearly unendurable.

Colette wore the world-weary expression of a woman from the future. It was hard for her to feign the bewildered and innocent look of the nineteenth century lady. Sadie was simply considered crazy by nineteenth century standards. In 2011, Sadie would have likely been considered lots of fun.

That's when Colette spotted him. Edward Sewell stormed through the station, cutting an angry diagonal line across the floor. He clearly knew where he was headed. He would find her. He would be damned if Isabelle would embarrass him by running away and causing more scandal, just as her mother Madeline had.

Colette grasped Sadie's arm, and held the younger woman's sleeve, pulling her aside. The two swept along silently behind the man.

The journey was long and arduous. The two women spoke very little. Amidst the constant rumble of the wooden walls of the train, which jostled them awake every half hour or so, they tried to take turns sleeping. Colette had watched Edward climb aboard a train car two or so in front of theirs.

The Chicago station was one Colette didn't recognize. Union Station would be completed a few years later. At this time however, it was a small station, and not what she'd expected. Chicago was indeed a smaller town in 1892. The two women found a corner of the station and arranged a carriage for the next part of the journey.

Colette suspected they were all three heading for Valley Stream. She worried. A carriage ride would take perhaps half the night. They might get there by early the next morning. For all she knew, Edward had a carriage and driver waiting. He would likely arrive in Valley Stream before then.

In the dim morning hours, a creeping sensation came over Colette as they approached the block of 1804 Prairie Street. It was all dirt roads. The Carpenter Gothic house would be standing somewhere near where the bungalow would one day stand. And sure enough, there was Marilyn's farmhouse, looking like it had a fresh coat of paint. The bungalow would not be there for around forty more years.

On the left there were patches of green grass and spreading lawn where in the 1920s and 1930s several craftsman style bungalows would be built. In their place, there now stood a sturdy barn, which spread across two future properties. The street lay before her, its familiarity startling. In this quick glance, it was organic and had a sacred beauty about it.

Colette felt the expanse of green, and the sound of crickets filled her up with a sense of peace. Sounds of horses hooves on the cobbled streets in nearby blocks made made clacking sounds, indicative of the muscle and dignity of the horses which pulled the heavy carriages. Prairie Street however, was muddy. Within minutes, the two women stood across the street from a haunting, brown wooden-framed house. Although morning barely had its eyes open, Colette felt confident that they couldn't be seen very well. What was this place with its sagging shutters and crumbling walkway? The trees that lined the street were small. Everything was new. The houses had just been built. There was a white farmhouse at the end of the block, and in the center, the large American foursquare she would know in later years. In 1892, this foursquare was run by a doctor who had his practice on the first floor. A century later, the house would be converted into rented rooms in the upstairs and a single family home downstairs. To the right, was the Carpenter Gothic, with one gable in the roofline directly over the front door. It was unusual. The one gable gave the cottage a quaint feel. Not a large house, but for some people right now, a sanctuary with its vertical paneling in light brown and bright red shutters on three windows. So odd to think that the house would disappear, as well as any traces of it ever having been built. In the same way, just as two bodies would go undetected under the place.

This house would disappear from all the blueprints and maps of the area. People questioned in the future, would deny it ever existed.

The pattern of striping, rather prim and proper, gave the house a uniform looking exterior like a pinstripe suit.

The air had a familiar scent to it, even one hundred and nineteen-years back in time. The Midwest was still the Midwest, apparently. Colette always noticed that certain states of the United States had particular scents; Florida, rather humid and like coconut oil and ocean, California, breezy and dry and sweet, and then the Midwest; earthy, and vital, like mud. Like buried bodies?

Looking at the Carpenter Gothic house on the site of what would be 1804 Prairie, the colors of the place struck her as unusual. The red shutters sagged a bit like tired eyes, but remained the main decorations of the only three windows on the front of the house. It was an unusual house. Definitely unlike anything Colette had seen before. It was supposed to be a haven for Isabelle, and probably for Madeline before her. Definitely not such a house in twenty-first century Valley Stream. Even Penelope at the Valley Stream Historical Society denied there ever was such a house on this very spot of land.

As Colette watched the place, her anger peaked at the thought of the men in the Sewell family. Then her pulse quickened. A dark figure caught her attention in the window on the right side of the house. The heavy curtains were opened wide.

Through the glass, Edward Sewell paced maniacally back and forth. He waved his arms about wildly. The outline of a young woman stood directly in front of him. Sadie tightened her grasp on Colette's arm, just as Colette realized who the young woman was. The scene played out before their eyes, like some sinister stage drama; a private performance just for them.

There was no one else on the street. In 1892, the town of Valley Stream was like a tiny sister to Wilmette, which at that time may still have been called "Ouimette" from the original French settlers. Valley Stream was unassuming, humble and uninhabited. Perhaps it had been a good place for Isabelle to hide? But now detection too, may have occurred too easily.

Judging from what they could glean through the windows, Edward Sewell had indeed found Isabelle. With each remonstrance, he charged after her and she seemed to cower. At one point, she turned to grab a light jacket or something by the front door, then the sound of a door slamming and screams were heard.

Colette moved quickly. Within seconds, she had raced across the street and jiggled the front door several times. There came shrieks and wailing from inside the place, followed by sounds of furniture being thrown and splintering wood.

Sadie stood in the middle of the street where a couple of chickens hurried past. She held her head in both hands and kept repeating, "no, no, no."

Colette jiggled the doorknob furiously. Finally, she slipped in behind some bushes and the front façade of the place. Looking around, she picked up a rock from the ground and threw it through the window next to the door, fumbling with the lock on the inside.

The air was still. The morning heat was unforgiving. Her efforts yielded nothing. Colette backed away from the small house a bit. Suddenly, it had the eerie presence of the house where Hansel and Gretel met their fate. This cute cottage now stood as a claustrophobic trap. Sadie stood by mutely. It took Colette a moment to realize there was someone else standing there.

Turning her head to her left, in the opaque light, Edward expanded into a dark presence that clouded the room where they battled. He had shut off the lights. Sadie reached into her linen long coat and took a swig from the laudanum. Her eyes were red-rimmed and glistened.

Then silence. Scurrying feet of small animals. Then cicadas. And nothing. The red door of the gothic cottage flew open.

"Isn't this a long way for two unaccompanied whores to be traveling?" Edward roared. His dark presence studied them. His eyes bored into Colette's. He advanced toward her, but she didn't flinch. Sadie stumbled backwards, and grabbed onto one of three trees stationed out front of the house.

"We know you followed her. Where is she?" was all Colette said, still not moving.

He sniffed, hands on his hips. "Well, you see little lady," he said."I've killed her."

Sadie let out a sharp cry. "No, no, no," she uttered under her breath. Colette's body had run cold. The night air seemed to drop temperature. In her head she still saw Isabelle standing there, in the front room, but then her mind registered his hands, having reached out for the young woman. She pushed past him and strode into the house.

It was inconceivable that her worst fears had been realized. Yet once inside the house, Colette went room by room, noticing humble furnishings and a few oriental rugs. Then she reached the sitting room at the back and side of the house.

Isabelle lay sprawled on her side, on the floor to the right of a grand fireplace. Her skin was unusually pale. Racing to her, Colette knelt down and felt for a pulse. Isabelle was lifeless. Colette saw Edward's reflection in an oval mirror over the fireplace.

"We are going to the police. Sadie and I witnessed this murder."

Edward's smile was lewd. He nodded at Sadie who by now had fallen to her knees on the front lawn, pressing her palms to her face as she sobbed. Her shoulders trembled.

"You really think the police are going to believe a couple of hysterical women? Women who have broken out of an asylum across the country no less? One," he said haughtily, nodding back toward Sadie, "a drug addict and the other, someone obsessed? Who has followed me? Stalked me? All the way to Illinois? My visit here was simply to see my daughter. She fell, and hit her head."

Colette walked past him back out into the front yard, then reached out her hand and helped Sadie up to her feet.

"Suspicion will fall upon you two!" Edward called after them. "No one will believe you! Good families fall apart because of wayward women like you."

A man and woman walked past, arm in arm. Flowing dress behind her, the woman's outfit was topped with mutton sleeves which she had rolled up above her elbows. He sported a proper bowler hat. Colette imagined how they must look to those passersby, as she was attempting to hold Sadie upright. Her eyes were glassy and there were mud stains on her skirt.

Edward's voice grew more mocking, and distant as the two women continued to walk. Soon they reached the main road, Birch Road. This same street would run through the middle of Valley Stream a century later.

Colette felt confident now, with her chin raised and her mouth set. She recalled the original Valley Stream police station had been built around 1890. She knew the way.

Colette's first thought was to awaken the doctor who she knew lived in the American Foursquare. With great urgency, she knocked on the door on the left, which would have been the residence. In a long white nightshirt, an older man answered.

Colette explained quickly that she believed someone had been murdered next door. The good doctor took one look at Sadie, dancing as she was in small circles on the lawn, repeating to herself "someone has died, someone has died."

"I know neither one of you. Get yourself off my property or I'm calling the police."

"Please do!" Colette urged him.

He shut the door on her. Sadie clutched Colette's jacket sleeve and tugged her gently as they passed a tavern. The place was fashioned in the shape of a stagecoach stop with a Dutch Colonial roof on top of it. Sadie pulled away from Colette and ran into the place, like a woman possessed. This behavior would not help matters with the police, especially if some of the men folk in town had already witnessed this behavior.

Sadie was agile and quick however. Scrambling up some side stairs, tiny hands lifting her skirt, she ended up out on a patio in front

of the place. Everywhere, men milled about in black Victorian suit
coats and matching slacks having morning coffee and cigars. There
was an equal mix of gentlemen and laborers. All at once, one laborer
grabbed Sadie as she tried to slip past him and pulled her into his lap.
At first, Colette thought Sadie was in shock. The poor young woman
had just witnessed her best friend, dead at the hands of her own father. Yet now, with a little attention, she was able to turn on the charm
and forget her troubles momentarily. Colette realized too that Sadie
was pretty drugged up at this point.

Colette noticed a spot of blood on Sadie's Jacket. It traveled down
the front of her skirt. Sadie must have gotten closer to Isabelle than
Colette realized. Why hadn't she noticed any blood on Edward? She'd
have to leave Sadie behind her now. Colette walked on swiftly to a side
yard. A string quartet was warming up for a morning rehearsal.

Colette needed to find the nearest police station. No cell phones.
No pay phones. All she knew for sure was that the station was just
across the train tracks on the other side of a tavern. Duffy's Tavern.

Still, Colette hesitated. How would she, a woman who'd escaped
an asylum, get the police to believe her? She turned back once to
check on Sadie. Several other women had joined Sadie now in her
lively conversation with the men. Colette would have to abandon her
at the place.

Racing across train tracks, Colette scooted along, then finally
lifted the front of her dress and broke into a run. For all she knew,
Edward would dispose of Isabelle's body.

An oversized frosted bulb was illuminated out front of the station,
with the stenciled word "POLICE" bending around its circumference.
It interested her all at once that the station appeared so new and clean.
There was red trim around the windows, painted to match the dark
red Racine brick.

At the station door, she clamored through, tripping and cursing
her skirt all at once. "How do women get around in these damn
things?" she blurted. Once she'd stepped inside, she realized she'd

been overheard. An older man behind a large desk looked up sharply while a slightly younger man, with a sharp-nose, leaned over the desk, smoking a pipe languidly. He paused in mid-conversation and turned.

"Help you?" the man asked, finally looking at her.

"I'd like to report a murder."

His eyes widened. He was unimpressed. The younger man set his pipe down in an ornate wooden stand situated on the other man's desk. Obviously the two spent a good deal of time in conversation around that self-same desk.

"Madam," he began, "I know everyone in Valley Stream and yet I don't know you. Do you know her, Calvin?" he asked, looking at his younger counterpart.

Colette felt the ire rising up in her, a red heat flushing up to her face. After a moment, she unbuttoned several buttons on her blouse. The thing felt so inhibiting and tight, like a straight-jacket. The younger deputy sat up straight, his eyes widening. They weren't going to believe her. She wasn't supposed to assert herself; much less claim a murder had occurred. She was one of those hysterics who'd been locked up, rightfully so, at Perfect Pines Insane Asylum.

"I need to report a murder," she repeated.

The man with the pipe stood up straight, stretched a little and pulled up a nearby wooden chair.

"Ok now, little lady. Why don't you have a seat?" he said.

Colette took a deep breath. She didn't smile. But the downward curve of her mouth would not help matters any. How could she speed this up?

"Where would this little murder be, my dear? Someone's livestock or carriage horse been slain? Is it Mrs. Olson's pig?" The Sheriff leaned over to talk to her, despite the fact that Colette stood five foot ten inches tall, and in the granny boots, probably six foot.

"My you are a tall woman." He turned to the deputy. "Why I don't think we've ever had a woman in here this tall, do you?"

"It's on Prairie Street," she said. Then an idea hit her. The only way she'd get them moving. "It's Mr. Hines from the lumber yard. Someone has attacked him and left him for dead. It's the 1800 block of Prairie. Hurry, please."

Outside, there came the frantic clanging of city fire trucks. Even for 1892, the unmistakable bell and the strong commotion signified fire.

"The fire brigade!" the young deputy cried, leaping to his feet.

Colette's pulse quickened. Somehow she knew that it was the Gothic house on Prairie. Perhaps this was it. She had wondered what Edward Sewell had done to prevent anyone from finding out about the murder? From finding out about what happened to the Carpenter Gothic house itself.

She rushed to the window. Leaning over the sill, watching as two trucks raced by, her hands clutched the ledge. The water carts were pulled by horses and accompanied by loud bells.

The Sheriff stepped onto the front stairs of the station. Two firemen who had burst from the scene of the fire, stopped to speak with him briefly. When he turned back and walked into the station, he was holding the pipe, but no longer smoking it. His gaze scrutinized Colette now, as if he'd forgotten she was there.

"Where did you say a murder happened?" the Sheriff demanded.

"Prairie Street."

"Hmmm," he said. Setting his pipe down in the stand, he turned to the deputy. He reached out a hand to stop her but Colette slipped out the front door.

Colette fought tears. No one would know about Isabelle. A fire. Had Edward set the house ablaze? As she hurried past the tavern, she saw Sadie staggering on the sidewalk, biting a clenched fist, standing too close to the street, where wagons and carriages rumbled past. Colette took her by the hand, and the two women broke into a run. Stumbling, they raced three blocks until they reached Prairie Street.

As expected, the fire wagons had screamed to a halt on the muddied street directly in front of the Carpenter Gothic house which was now ablaze. Flames roared and spat profusions of angry eruptions and roared orange with a devil's vengeance. The fire fighters, diminutive in size next to such devastation, were panicked, and held back. Hoses were raised valiantly and as high up as possible. The flow of life-saving water waned and the house appeared determined to annihilate itself in a rush of flames. As Sadie and Colette stood there, the entire front of it fell forward onto the small patch of lawn and ten or so firefighters jumped back like frenetic bugs, barely being missed. Some stood wiping their brows as they watched the house disintegrate into ashes. It was indeed, too late.

Sadie's eyes were downcast. "Isabelle was inside."

Colette closed her eyes and nodded. From simply a kernel of confusion, her rage continued to build. She bit her upper lip and shook her head. Looking across the street, she saw the present owners, the original owners in 1892, of the rental property she would someday live in. The rental house glistened in the light of the flames, bright and new. It appeared more rugged, but basically looked the same as it would one hundred years later. These were the days of lath and plaster and authentic brick, built from the drawings of architects.

Colette struggled to focus. She examined a few people who stood out front of the rental farmhouse across from them. That's when she spotted him.

Squeezing Sadie's arm, she rushed past her. Despite firemen guarding against anyone coming to the scene of the blaze, she hurried past them. It was William. She was certain. She had just spotted him. How had he gotten here?

Walking up to him, she whispered, "he was here, you know."

He turned. His eyes had a sharp glint.

"Your father was here. I saw him."

He turned suddenly and took her face in his hands, kissing her hard, brutally hard. She shoved him away and he started laughing loudly, too loudly. Everyone had gathered, in the forefront of the alarming fire. Several women stood close by, huddled together despite the heat of the night and the fires which refused to die. The night air smoldered.

"William. You need to know something. It's about Isabelle."

He stepped back, away from her, and wiped his nose with his sleeve. "I am aware that Isabelle is gone."

Colette said nothing. She studied him, then murmured, "what are you saying?" she was disoriented, shaking her head. "Listen. The police wouldn't even believe me."

"Why would they?" he asked, his eyes bright.

Ashes from the fire floated down around them like a malevolent rain of charcoal wafers, like gothic flower petals.

William looked oddly jubilant. He raised his chin and touched her cheek gently with the back of his hand. "I have put them in the coal chute. No one's going to know and father's reputation is saved.

Colette blinked. Confused and disbelieving. The smoke was frenzied. Looking past him to the billowing and tormented house, she bit her lower lip. Her long-sleeved jacket clung to her like a second skin. Whipping it off, she threw it aside. The heat was all-consuming, and suffocated the block of bystanders, with all the embers of evidence of unspeakable angst floating in the air, right in their midst. Most of the women had shrunk away, back to the safety of their homes and husbands. The fire brigade had moved their two available wagons to the next block, near a Catholic church that would also be standing one hundred years later.

"William? What are you exactly?" she breathed.

"Mother and Isabelle will no longer suffer. Nor further tarnish the Sewell name."

He stopped, then said, "you have to know in her own way, Lizzie helped us too."

"Lizzie?" Colette straightened up and rolled up her sleeves, "Lizzie?"

"Yes, it was Isabelle's World Tour three years ago. A year or so later, Lizzie embarked on her own world tour. Andrew Borden's way of keeping her quiet." William laughed again, it was a cynical laugh, uneven and forced. "Anyway, dear Lizzie also went to France and bought some lady lace and cheap geographical charts." William started to turn, blocking the fire behind him until the flames seemed to emanate from his sides. "Lizzie wanted what Isabelle had. Now Isabelle has nothing. Not even her life."

Colette said nothing.

"You see, that was all she could afford. Those little maps. But she so wanted a travel bag from France. So Isabelle had one made for herself, and one for Lizzie. Even as a very young lady, Isabelle recognized finery."

"Yes," Colette said, "I know about the bags."

"How do I know how Lizzie did it? Because I knew she'd be up to something. The murders didn't even surprise me. And I saw Lizzie drop her little bag, the one Isabelle had gotten her, from the second story window. Landed in the back yard it did." William beamed. "She thought no one saw her. And then she ran around back, right by the well and she grabbed that little bag and handed it off to the carriage driver."

He crossed his arms over his chest, his black tie a contrast with his starched white shirt. Then he went on.

So Lizzie sent the travel bag via carriage, the same carriage that had brought Miss Emma home that day. That same bag found its way to the Perfect Pines asylum. Right to Isabelle. Contents unknown. How intriguing for all of us."

"You seem to know everything," Colette said, her voice low.

"Do you believe the gall?" he went on, being very animated. "Miss Lizzie had run out and met the carriage during all the mayhem and the police crawling all over the house, right when sweet Emma had just gotten dropped off. Everyone was inside. After dropping the travel bag out the back window, as I said, she'd rushed through the house while everyone was preoccupied, and met the carriage driver with specific instructions to take the travel bag to the asylum. I had a Pinkerton stationed in the house. As soon as I heard about the murders, I got a man over there. His only job was to follow Lizzie unobserved in all the aftermath of her deeds. I'm Isabelle's brother. I know what Lizzie and Isabelle claimed went on in their private lives. Just hysterical women. All lies. So when I heard about the murders, I had someone watch Miss Lizzie. Because she wanted Mr. Borden's money. She wanted it all for herself."

As he spoke, William's voice changed. It grew deeper, more guttural.

Colette was silent. "So you would need Lizzie's travel bag with her initials to prove anything."

"I'll find it. I've alerted Dr. Warburton to be on the lookout for any luggage that doesn't belong there. Just so you are aware. I threw Isabelle's travel bag in the chute with her body. No one will find any trace of her. Foolish girl."

"I know you really believe that."

He went on, ignoring her comment. "Father is purchasing this house, this plot of land and plats of survey. He will make this house disappear, as if it was never here. No one will ever break ground here, or rebuild. Not while Edward Sewell owns the land."

"Sadie and I returned Lizzie's travel bag to Lizzie. We left it on her doorstep. I figured out you had Warburton looking for it. I'll admit, he came pretty close in the attic one day. Well guess what, we beat you to it. He won't find it now."

William's face was contorted with anger. He seemed to change right before her eyes. "Dear. Miss. Lizzie. So, she has evidence of her guilt, does she? Why, she took the law into her own hands, now didn't she?" He frowned. "They'll hang her. At least father was smart enough to handle his woman business far away from prying eyes."

Colette stared. "I don't agree with what Lizzie felt compelled to do, not at all. But what has happened to you?"

His eyes were black.

Chapter Seventeen (A)

The Historical Facts

I n 1890's America, Mr. Andrew Borden was a prominent business-man, who had lived a life free of blemish, and was entitled to all benefits freely given and allowed to men in society. Women, including prostitutes, child prostitutes, housewives and daughters, were considered property.

Next in the trial, Hosea Knowlton entered into interesting territory when he examined in detail, the differences between the sexes. Interestingly, this examination was, in its own way, reverse-sexism. This was true because, if the jury, which consisted of all men, and the society at large at the time, considered the fairer sex incapable of such violent crimes, Knowlton proceeded to steer their thoughts in an entirely new direction.[309] Even though, it perpetuated sexism, and was clearly a subjective opinion, his examples presented interesting case studies in psychology, and maybe even legitimate arguments against the defendant.

In an interesting aside, Knowlton began his lecture on the nature of women, as potential murderers. In his opinion, what they lacked in "strength and coarseness," "and vigor," they made up for it in "cunning, in dispatch, in celerity, in ferocity."[310] The only reason such suggestions held any merit was simply because such words introduced a kernel of doubt in the minds of the jurors. Specifically, Knowlton pointed out that some women were such that, "their hates" were more "undying, more unyielding, more persistent."[311] Interestingly, this argument may have garnered some attention due to a central, key characteristic of the case; the severity and horrific nature of the crimes themselves. It introduced the idea of rage-filled adrenalin rather than the brute force of a man capable of such heinous bodily injury.

Because truth be known, this fair-eyed young woman who sat serenely before them, this defendant, created quite a conundrum. She was an enigma, a devastating puzzle in the genteel minds of the late nineteenth century men on the jury.

This woman was one of their own. Whether or not they wanted to acknowledge this fact, Lizzie Borden was one of their own. She was not some indigent raised by savages. The jurors had to admit that this thirty-two year old woman, who'd committed these devastating crimes was a progeny of the self-same society. It was evident, that even in nineteenth century Massachusetts, America was male-dominated.

Certainly, Lizzie had traveled. Why she'd even experienced her grand tour of Europe at age thirty and was sufficiently cultured and refined, as was fit the proper young woman of the day. She was a product of American breeding; that faction of society that was considered acceptable, and knew what was unacceptable.

The facts stared the jurors in the face again. As Knowlton had stated at the outset, the difficulty around solving the crimes centered upon the way it had happened. The ferocity behind the motive could not be ignored. In the reality of the environment and the aftermath, no mythology could explain away what was fairly clear. Lizzie had been there and the crime was severely personal in nature. Added to that, there was no alternative explanation.

Essentially, this was Knowlton's point. There simply was no other implicit explanation. Even were someone to examine the language he used, one felt truth in each word. Cunning was one descriptor and "cunning" accurately described someone who had been able to make the murders appear coincidental, and not very well thought-out. In this way, such a haphazard method could have implicated a disgruntled renter, or even a business associate. This did not account for the ferocity of the crimes.

Someone with cunning had brooded for a very long time over the horror of his or her life. Someone like Lizzie, for instance, would have been determined in this way, to seek revenge for a lifetime of hurt; such as abuse at the hands of her father, such as the looking the other way of her step-mother, and such as the repression of a Victorian-American society.

It was noted in recent writings that Lizzie's grand tour may have exposed her to more luxuries than her life on Second Street had not revealed to her. In a sense, the trip reiterated what her father's stinginess would not provide. It may also have enlightened her to the lives of other women in the world; European women, who were granted greater freedoms to express themselves than were their American sisters. Central to Lizzie's personal trauma experienced during her European tour, was that although she accompanied wealthy young women on the trip, Lizzie lacked their social status. Therefore, on the surface she measured up, but the actual money in her purse did not.

Sadly for her, in the end it was not a sense of jealousy at the excessive wealth of the other woman, but rather her personal horror at having to wire home for more money. After several minor purchases, she wired home to her father, only to be denied by him.[312] Perhaps in her mind, of all the people in his life, he truly owed her. As previously stated, she actually received more money from her sister, Emma.

This rebuff on the part of her father, and the resulting embarrassment, reached deeply into her core, possibly to a very shameful place for Lizzie. This place of shame was perhaps a destination for which her father was responsible.

Lizzie as a young woman, and one who was taking her place in society, still had a low opinion of herself. Her odd home life further stifled her from truly learning any of the social graces.[313] So except for her being involved in church activities, she was perpetually suffocated, repressed and under scrutiny at the hands of her father. The extent of their outings may have been limited to church and visiting their farm.

The next word, "dispatch" was also well-chosen by Knowlton, because certainly, the murders having happened upon her home turf, located right in Lizzie's own world, presented a great advantage.[314] Had these been murders at the hands of thieves or business associates, wouldn't the arena have been different?   In other words, why indeed, would a business associate venture to Andrew Borden's home when he may more easily have cornered him downtown? Or even have invited him to dinner at an eating establishment in town? Would not a work associate have preferred to have him alone? There would certainly have been fewer witnesses. Because wouldn't such a person have anticipated high pedestrian traffic on Second Street on a workday in downtown Fall River? On the other hand, an inside job such Lizzie Borden herself, would have had no alternative. Thus, the location pointed suspicion further in her direction. As was mentioned before, the extent of her forays into society included nothing more than moving from point A to point B, and always escorted. As it was, even attending church with neighbor Dr. Bowen, had at one time caused a considerable stir.[315]

So spending a couple of months in Europe presented ample time for Lizzie Borden to have tasted the freedom that women in other cultures of the world were experiencing. Lizzie now aspired to loftier ideals. It well could have been the instigator, the very continent upon which she had hatched exactly how to orchestrate the murders of her father and step-mother, by navigating the Borden house on Second Street back home in Massachusetts.

Ironically, "celerity" would also have described Miss Lizzie Borden's physicality and the good shape she was in at the time. Rumor had it that she'd been witnessed by several women, as had been stated, working out at the local gymnasium. Lizzie may easily have been increasing muscle mass and strength in her arms and back. Perhaps this would enable her to wield a heavy weapon? So, although men believed and perpetuated the widely-held belief that women were weak physically and in other ways, exactly who on this all-male jury would have believed she'd have been capable of murder? A murder, much less, which involved swinging a hatchet and murdering two humans with it, around twenty-eight times in total, would indeed have been difficult to believe.

Of course "ferocity" as a descriptor of the crimes, was an extremely accurate term. No one questioned the fact that it may have required super-human strength to have done what this murderer did. Super-human or perhaps adrenaline-charged?

Knowlton next addressed the erroneous belief that no other avenues were explored.[316] Despite the fact that the usual suspect in a homicide is almost always a husband, wife or other family member; it appeared that every organization from the woman's suffrage, the WCTU and various Christian organizations rallied around Lizzie Borden in droves. At least in the beginning, this was true. In the end, many of those same groups deserted her once the trial was over.[317]

Knowlton went on to assuage any doubters in the jury, and the townsfolk as well, by explaining at length, the process of trailing other suspects. One such suspect would include a purported half-brother who lived on the outskirts of town, in the less fashionable area of town, and an individual who indeed owned a hatchet. Added to the half-brother theory, there was the question of a boyfriend. However, as was pointed out, this mythology may have been borne out of an over-zealous reporter who created the story.[318]

Chapter Eighteen

Colette pictured what the scenario must have been on the morning and early afternoon of the murders; Lizzie in a panicked state, desperate to get her bloodied L.A.B. travel bag out of the house while the police searched upstairs and down, in the frame farmhouse at 92 Second Street. Lizzie would have been wearing the wrapper so many claimed to have seen her wearing, the pink striped one, over yet another blue dress. While the rapidly cooling bodies of her parents lay in the study and the guest rooms, with steely determination, Lizzie had scurried past all the police, her sister Emma who'd just arrived home by carriage from a trip away, Mrs. Churchill and all the others who stood by. With eyes downcast, Lizzie had to hide whatever she could.

After lengthy discussion with Isabelle, Colette managed to map out the day of the murders in her mind. Apparently, Lizzie had run up to the second story with the L.A.B. travel bag, the one with her initials, and walked steadily to the back window situated asymmetrically at the back of the house. This story confirmed what William had shared. A callous and changed William. Colette recalled numerous photographs of the back yard and barn of the Borden house. There were several windows, and conveniently there was one that may have been at the top of the stairs. According to Isabelle, Lizzie had stashed the hatchet handle and bloodied dress into the L.A.B. bag, dropped it out the second story back window and it had traveled via Emma's carriage to the asylum.

So what had Lizzie thought when her crazy L.A.B. bag found its way back to her front door? Dr. Warburton was suspicious, so Colette and Sadie had returned the bag from the asylum to Lizzie's house the night they'd time traveled. That had been the very afternoon of the murders. Colette worried that Lizzie had certainly come to the front door, picked it up frantically, looked furtively left and right, on a bustling Second Street for any culprit. Lizzie perhaps cursed to herself as she scurried back into the house, travel bag under her arm until she could hide it in the wardrobe upstairs. Further, Colette thought perhaps Dr. Bowen helped her and initially took the evidence, the hatchet handle and bloody dress and shoved them into his doctor's bag.

If some woman claimed she'd seen Lizzie exercising at the gym, lifting weights and building up her body strength, then all this arduous running around may have been plausible.

A tired Sadie sat up a bit. The effects of the Laudanum had worn off.

The next morning, Sadie and Colette, with their heads leaning against the red velvet drapes of the sumptuous train car, pulled into Boston's station. Over an hour later, their carriage reached the Perfect Pines Insane Asylum. The carriage slowed and jostled a bit, accompanied by sounds of the horses' hooves which marched in place on the cobblestones. Within a minute's time, the gates opened and several orderlies in white rushed over to meet the carriage. It was not out of courtesy, as displayed by their rough treatment of the women. A rotund shorter man in white shook Sadie's head by pulling on her hair. She kicked him in the shins which made him yank her along even more brutally. As they were forced out of the carriage, no one spoke. Dr. Warburton stood on the front steps of the massive grey stone structure, his arms crossed over his chest, the white of his coat blinding.

The two women were split up and dragged to their separate rooms. They were dumped at far distant locations in the asylum from one another. Colette sat on her small cot, staring at the floor. Her mind raced. She knew now that Isabelle packed her own checkerboard I.A.S. travel bag and braved her way over to Lizzie's house in the middle of the night to say goodbye.

Seated on the cot, Colette suddenly noticed it. Did her eyes play tricks on her? It was dark. Was she just overtired from the trip? It had been an extensive trip to get back from Chicago. Clearly, she'd never realized what people endured in 1892 just to get from a train, to a carriage and home. Not entirely. She may have thought she knew from books and movies that the pace was slower. But the journey was actually grueling having to take turns sleeping and keep an eye out for asylum scouts sent to find them, or for Edward or William. Suddenly, Colette found herself unable to budge. The sight of the object filled her with dread all at once.

She'd had moments like this before in her life. It was a moment when disbelief made her unable to move, immobile with fear. Like some dissociation, she would feel herself somewhere else entirely, which didn't seem possible. Yet there it sat on the cold floor. Her mind would take her away. Terror filled her up. The idea that what she might be seeing was actually real. The curve of the sides of the small travel bag were clear enough in the shadowy room, as her eyes adjusted to the black in that magical human way. It was as if she sensed her pupils growing larger.

The object started to take shape. Finally, she pulled herself up and walked stiffly over to the bag. Kneeling, she put her hand over the top of it. It was Lizzie's travel bag with the initials L.A.B. Who had brought it back from the Borden house? Colette was certain she and Sadie had gotten it out of the attic away from Dr. Warburton, and taken it to Lizzie's house? She'd have to hide it here in her room. It was still covered in blood stains. Oddly, it had changed. It now had smears of color and ink. Like strange chemical reactions.

Colette ran her hand over the top of the case, touching the initials "L.A.B."

The bag was gritty and had raised patches on it, as if someone had tried to mix a solvent on it. Whatever it was, it made the bag look purple and black now. Or was she losing her mind? The bag had changed or been changed by someone. Why would there be raised bumps on the treated canvas exterior? She'd been hallucinating. Maybe someone, perhaps Lizzie, had tried to clean it. Of course, she thought. A bag she valued from Isabelle. Lizzie had wanted to fix it.

Pulling back on the small gold-filled button that unlocked the clasp, Colette fully expected to find it locked, as she had that time in the attic a day or so before. A day in the time travel past of 1892, passed in slow motion, like a month. The bag opened up easily. The days all tumbled into one another in this odd time travel experience. She'd once heard the definition of time travel described as seeing time pockets as existing at all times, able to be visited like time shares at foreign destinations. That time travel was less linear and moreso, concurrent, with varying stops.

Standing, Colette turned and checked the lock on the door. She still had the skeleton key for the lock. Sadie Hawthorne was forbidden to have one. Apparently, Colette rated a bit higher on the sanity scale. At the time of entering the asylum, Colette had merely feigned a depressive state. Sadie, on the other hand, was a Victorian girl's worst enemy; a free-spirited sexual woman with forward-thinking ideas. A histrionic.

Colette moved to a nearby table and lit the kerosene lamp.

Even as Colette sat there, not daring to move, her mind filled up with the realization of exactly what the bag held? Colette was aware that this had been the bag within which Lizzie had originally stashed the wooden handle of the hatchet and the bloodied clothes she'd had on.

Colette worked the interlocking clutch at the top of the bag, and it pulled apart quite easily.

The sides of the bag were soft, despite a firm structure to it. Such a soft bag to have carried such harsh realities. Opening it up, she gazed at the cream interior. Contained therein were several journals and the handle to the hatchet. Buried under the journals was a stained blue dress. Gingerly, she lifted all the items out, and examined the inside of the case next to the kerosene lamp. Sure enough, there were many stains around the bottom.

Definitely not a bag that Lizzie would ever have been allowed to buy for herself. Colette believed the rest of the contents from the L.A.B. bag were initially stashed in Dr. Bowen's bag, when the police were kept out of her room. Then after Dr. Bowen grew too nervous to keep the evidence, it had been transferred to the L.A.B. bag. For that reason, someone, likely Lizzie herself, had the L.A.B. bag brought back to the asylum, by the same carriage which brought Emma home. Although she tried to fix it originally, because she wanted to keep it, she realized it was too badly stained. These thoughts swirled in her head and she lay down on the cot. She continued to examine the bag, suddenly feeling drowsy. At the same time she could feel the slide bracelet tightening. Opening her eyes slightly, she could see the telltale lavender dust, as she called it, powdered about on her pale skin.

All at once, she heard a noise outside the door. She blew out the lamp, a bit disoriented, and shoved the travel bag under her cot. Then there came the gentle but insistent knocking. Whoever was rapping had awakened her before she could time travel.

"It's me, let me in. It's Sadie."

Colette let her in, checked the hallway left and right, and closed the door quickly.

"What are you doing here? They're watching us." As she spoke, Colette relit the lamp. Sadie's eyes were wide. "Lizzie is in the Taunton jail," she said. "She has been arrested for the murders of her parents." Colette shook her head.

"Already? How can that be? It must be August 11th?" Sadie looked bewildered, then her eyes fell upon the bag which she'd just pulled out from under the bed.

"What's this?" she remarked, her voice hushed. "Isn't that Lizzie's travel bag?"

"It is," she said. She touched the side of it. "You see, it even has her initials 'L.A.B' on the side."

"How did it get here?"

"I have no idea."

"My God," Sadie said, "that damn bag has gotten around, hasn't it?"

"I think Isabelle had two bags made in France. This one has Lizzie's initials."

Sadie rummaged through the bag all at once. Deep in thought, Colette watched her as she pulled out the journals.

"They're Isabelle's. I think Lizzie was holding on to them for her."

Sadie nodded. Colette started to formulate a scheme.

"Sadie? Would you take another field trip with me?"

She nodded. Her swollen eyes still looked a bit purple.

"I know what the blood stains are from in this case. In fact, I know where the murder weapon is. This is Lizzie's travel bag, and we're going to tell her we have it. Inside is the stained hatchet handle and bloody blue dress. "

Sadie lifted the Laudanum flask out of her pocket and took a long sip. "You really think Dr. Bowen would do that for her? That Lizzie. She has friends everywhere."

"We are going to let Lizzie know that we have her bag. And we will guard the secrets inside. I will keep the bag for her, for good."

Sadie squinted and tilted her head, looking confused.

"Just come with me. And remind me, what's the date today?"

"August 12th."

"So Lizzie will be arraigned and will go on trial," Colette murmured, thinking aloud.

Sadie looked at Colette with a solemn understanding in her eyes. Colette knew Sadie was more savvy than she let on, especially in front of the doctors and the hardened wardens at the asylum. After all, the women who assisted at the asylum were careful not to appear too intelligent, or too competent, around the men. In fact, that was a general truth of all women in 1892, as Colette had learned. One nurse Colette discovered, was secretly studying at a local university.

"Murder weapon? Lizzie's? Her parents?"

Colette nodded. Sadly, this had become the state of affairs during Colette's sojourn in the past. First the double murders of Lizzie Borden's parents. Now, Colette, and Sadie were privy to two additional murders. Except these two murders had happened without notice, without whimper or uproar or outrage. Something had happened to Madeline and Isabelle. As if the silent murder of Lizzie's soul at the hands of her abuser was not enough, the reactionary and violent murders of her parents which followed, were horrific and sensational. They were all Fall River could handle at the time. Because surely, prior to and after these murders, numerous other indignities such as alcoholism, racism, inequality, spousal and child abuse, continued to flourish in the "gay nineties."

"The murders Lizzie committed," Colette finished.

Sadie didn't flinch. They looked at one another; Colette's eyes a pale green, and Sadie's, a washday blue, had thick long lashes. Neither shed a tear. They both knew something had to be done. Fall River, 1892 started to speak out loud, about what previously went unspoken. Just like the whispers Colette thought she heard growing up, now there were the unspoken atrocities that occurred within the society of young women, and children. Sometimes at the hands of strangers, or trusted uncles, or even one's own father. The polite society, then, as now, Colette thought, would definitely not have talked about it.

So then, how many of these young girls had grown up to become angry young women? Confused young women? Women who either chose a path to God and righteousness, or completely tried to escape feelings, drowning in opiates and laudanum, or piling on layers of fat to further hide themselves? Like Sadie. Trying to squelch her sexual desires because she'd been ostracized. At the other extreme, there was Isabelle, who fought against her oppressors. Finally, Lizzie Borden, who had been sexually abused, and had her own way of dealing with the enemy.

"My father was good to me," Sadie said quietly. "I've never suffered at the hands of someone who should not have desired me. But I'm free with my feelings as you know. As everyone seems to know."

"Do you know how to get to the Taunton jail?" Colette asked her.

Sadie jumped up and grabbed her boots from the door. "Let's go. We'll figure it out." The blue eyes studied Colette. "I think it's only a half hour ride to the station."

"Yes, maybe a forty minute train ride," Colette agreed.

Sadie tilted her head, still looking at Colette. "Still don't know how you, know things? This is more of your spiritual knowledge, right?"

Colette grinned. This is what Sadie called Colette's spirit sense. She didn't understand Colette, she revealed, but she was intrigued by her. It seemed to be the only way she could understand Colette's foresight. Sadie had decided in her mind, without telling Colette, that Colette was simply an angel out of time, and that she'd come down to enlighten women in some way.

Slipping into the hallway, Colette edged ahead of Sadie, peeking around corners. Soon, they made their way to the basement, which always worked well for sneaking in and out of the place. For a bunch of militants, Colette thought they let patients get out pretty easily. Colette figured most of the patients were so drugged, Dr. Warburton and the staff, didn't worry. Maybe this was an advantage of being locked away in an asylum reserved solely for the wealthy? The security for 1892 was a bit lax.

Outside, the night enveloped them. At first the heavy clothes, the underskirt, the over skirt and the tailored jackets and blouses, cinched tightly at the waist and blouse fastened by cameo at the neck, initially felt fine. But after five minutes in the oppressive heat, freedom of movement was hampered by the heaviness of the skirts, and the leather of the boots which were clamped tightly around her ankles. A trickle of sweat rolled down her spine.

Finally they reached the cobblestone street. It was Taylor Street. Part of it was still mostly comprised of mud, with just a few cobblestones. The asylum remained on the outskirts of town. Ironically, the entire town knew when even a wealthy woman in town needed help for "hysteria," "incurable neurosis," or "uncivilized behavior." The first stop, and sometimes final resting place for these unfortunates was often Perfect Pines. Most of the luggage Colette had seen in the attic, according to Sadie, were simply relics of long dead patients.

Sadie paused next to Colette and caught her breath. Colette amused herself having turned fifty years old, and still being proud that she was outrunning a twenty-something. Granted, Sadie was twenty-four in the year 1892. Certainly life at that time was rigorous. Women made their own soap to wash their hair. Women spent an entire day catering to the God forsaken stove for heat and meals and spent several days hunched over the daunting task of family laundry.

"How does one catch a carriage?" Colette said, turning to Sadie, who was turning in circles at the edge of the road.

You mean a hack? Typically, a man finds one for you. Women don't look for their own rides."

"Of course they don't. What was I thinking?"

Colette stepped into the street and started waving at a horse and buggy a half block down. The air and grass smelled of mud and dust and was sweet. Her senses filled up with earthy greenery. The echoes of the horses' hooves clomped nearby, repetitive, then idled in place like some nineteenth century 303 Taxi.

When neither the driver nor the horse noticed her, she progressed along the cobblestones toward them. Sadie had by now stepped off the curb. She pulled her blue tailored jacket around her more tightly. Impressed by Colette's bold move, Sadie still held back in silence, allowing the older women to lead. Little did she know Colette was essentially one hundred years younger than she was.

Colette stepped up to him, hands on her hips. The driver rose from his perch and glowered there, eyes on her. He cleared his throat and lowered his hat over his eyes.

"Hello," she said. "We need a ride. We need transportation to the train station. We need to get to the Taunton Jail."

"What are you doing out alone, Miss? What's wrong with you? Who is that with you? It's getting on to dinnertime."

Colette eyed him, her eyes narrowed. "Just take us to the station."

Sadie withdrew a flask from her pocket and took a swig of the liquid. Colette knew it was laudanum. Dr. Warburton provided patients with whatever kept them quiet and submissive. Usually addictive poisons. Addictive deaths.

It intrigued Colette that the early night calm was not as quiet as she would have imagined it to be in 1892. As they cobbled along, now and then loud arguing reached them from someone's house. A simple peek out the window revealed an angry husband here, or an errant child there, getting a bottom smacked by a mother with a wooden spoon and rushed into the house. To think the Prairie door was responsible for this magical mystery tour in the nineteenth century, allowed her to see that roles hadn't changed. Women as wards of the children and home had bled into the twenty-first century as well.

Suddenly she heard a thud. Heavy. Deafening. Looking up, she spotted a man carrying out a large block of ice. He dropped it on the front stoop of a farmhouse. Children ran in circles in the front yard. One refreshing difference here was, there were no electric fences or video games or electronic devices. Families frequented the yards. This was definitely something new. People in the town were out and about, not shut up indoors. Certainly, the heat drove them to public spaces. But again, at least there was not the monotonous hum and the white glow of television screens in every house.

Once the street noises died down, there remained a lingering sound of crickets. Typical hot and lazy afternoon on the East coast. There was the occasional whisper of leaves swaying too. Massachusetts was reaching out to her in its way. Her imagination had been playing tricks on her of late.

Colette ran her hand across the plush leather seats of the carriage. The décor of the carriage had cushions that were fashioned in lattice-work quilting.

Sadie had slipped down in the seat. Her head dropped to one side. The flask had fallen to the floor. Colette picked it up. Someone's initials were inscribed on the side. Not Sadie's. They were "PH." Perhaps those of her former fiancé? Percy? That was his name. That's right. Percy had fostered a penchant for alcohol as well.

Colette called out to the driver, annoyed. Sadie straightened up all at once.

"Here! Go back! That's the train station right there," she said. She pointed out the side of the carriage, trying to loosen her sleeve when it seemed to stick to her skin. She'd already peeled off the Jacket in disgust. She swore she could see white dots floating around. The heat made her dizzy.

The carriage stopped. There came the sound of boots on gravel.

"Train to where miss?' he asked her, his head tilted as if certain she was insane.

"That's where we catch the train. I know that's where Lizzie was dropped off and taken to the Taunton Jail. Isn't that right Sadie? Isn't that what you told me?"

Sadie was silent. Finally, a slow smile crossed her face and she nodded.

"Indeed it was," she said steadily, eyeing the man intently. "The one and only station where they loaded Lizzie up with the blue hat and blue veil."

The man puffed on a pipe, frowning, "I know you two. You're from Perfect Pines. I saw where you come from when I picked you up. Don't try to fool me. No proper woman in her right mind would be wandering around. Especially when there's a maniac on the street. Why I knew Mr. Borden. He was a good man. Some crazy beast chopped up two church-going people? Into little pieces! You women need to go back to the asylum where you belong. Your husbands put you there for a reason."

Sadie studied the sky, seeming to admire a visible archway of sprinkling stars and a crescent moon. It was as if she purposely ignored the driver. Colette, less forgiving, bit her lip while the driver ranted. She pushed him aside and with one motion, jumped from the carriage. She grabbed her carpet bag from the top of the buggy and called after Sadie.

"Let's get to the train my dear," she said.

In her mind, the man's comment didn't merit an answer. She tripped on her dress, hoisted it up angrily, and then started to jog to the station.

The train ride lasted under an hour to reach the Taunton Jail from Fall River. Breathing in and out, she recognized that the chance to speak with Lizzie might actually happen. She had to keep her mind on other things; like the beauty of the train car or watching Sadie, who was reading a small prayer book. Something extremely sinister had been going on in Fall River, Massachusetts, and most likely in many communities. Colette tried to appreciate the craftsmanship of the train and that sometimes there was beauty inherent in the creations of humans themselves. Nineteenth century trains certainly were quite elaborate, with gorgeous drop lighting and wood everywhere. The nylon reclining seats and flat carpeting of the twenty-first century trains contrasted with what had been so eloquent in the previous centuries.

When at last the train pulled into town, and they approached the wide brick façade of the Taunton Jail, it looked smaller than Colette had imagined it would be. In fact, it resembled a high school. To think Miss Lizzie Borden would spend another year in this place awaiting trial.

"Let me do the talking," Colette told Sadie.

Sadie smiled. "I like how you talked to that carriage driver," she said.

Colette grasped a massive door handle of the place, and muttered, "things don't get any easier for women in my day my dear Sadie."

They reached the foyer.

"In what day?" Sadie asked, her voice hushed.

"Well, how does a woman in this day and age typically spend her days?"

Sadie wrapped a loose tendril of hair around her finger, looking thoughtful as they entered the entrance to the jail.

"What do we do?" She straightened her bun in a hallway mirror and pinched her cheeks. Colette knew the habits of Victorian women. Women wore no makeup and rarely had money of their own to cart around.

"Let's see," Sadie began. "In a typical day, it would be much like Lizzie's day a week ago Thursday, without the murders."

"Right."

Sadie didn't notice how strange that sounded. "Anyway," she went on, "I may start out by lighting the stove and even start dinner when I get up in the morning. I need to put in a roast or mutton. Laundry begins on Mondays and takes several days. Builds strong arm muscles though, I will tell you. So basically, clean the house, make soap, domestic chores and the like. If you're a married woman, which I had hoped to be," she hesitated. "Until the engagement ended. We buy fabric, and make our own dresses and wrappers, you know, the smocks that go over the skirts and blouses."

Colette stood in the dim light of the foyer. It was illumined by two simple kerosene lamp sconces. The two women had trouble seeing one another. Sadie squinted at Colette, into the face of her time traveling friend. "We have to take care of our husbands you know. They work so hard. They do so much for us."

"So as wife, you'd basically raise the children and take care of the homes you live in. Homes, most likely, owned completely, or in part by your husbands?"

"Entirely by our husbands." She gazed at Colette. "So what do your women do where you come from? Are you telling me you own the homes and the husbands do domestic chores and bring up the children? You're always a bit evasive when I ask where you're from.

"Basically, a majority of what you just listed is part of their days, but add to that working jobs themselves all day long."

"How is that possible? You would have to be two women?"

Well, not all women choose that life. But where I come from, out of financial necessity, some women need to perform both roles. Other women want careers to show their intellectual or business prowess, yet they are still expected to complete all the household tasks. And of course there are those women who do not wish to pursue outside professions. They marry men with the intention that he will earn a majority of the money and take care of the family."

Sadie stared at the floor, shaking her head. "All the major lengths some women have gone to, just to get away from a life of drudgery. I'm surprised." She stopped, then looked up. "Why would anyone choose just to do housework? So what you're saying is some women have the opportunity to pursue the arts freely, or become business owners? Like Andrew Borden?"

"Yes."

"Well, what's all the damn efforts about with the women of my time? And if you're saying women have the opportunity to go to college and even extra schooling why the Hell don't they? And they're able to vote? And have a vocation of her own? What is their reason for not going after business or medicine or the law?"

"They choose to marry the men they see as good prospects. They usually meet them in college themselves. Now there are some women who realize they are giving up their own interests by allowing the man to be the sole monetary provider – but they don't mind. Of course there are men too, who choose to stay home and the wife works."

Sadie's mouth dropped. "That's not true, is it?"

Colette laughed. "Yes, it is. However, what both fail to realize is whomever decides to not bring home any money, they kind of give up their power. My utopia has not been realized as yet, and may not ever be realized due to the influences of people used to doing things the old way."

After a moment's silence, Sadie asked, "utopia?" Sadie let go suddenly. She wiped away moisture from her forehead. The hallway grew hotter.

"Yes," Colette whispered, "my utopia would be twenty hour work weeks for both the man and the woman, equal time with both bringing home about the same amount of money. Then each would have two 10 hour days work, two days with the children and a fifth day where the whole family could be together. They would share household tasks – one could cook, the other clean and vice versa. Then weekends could be time to socialize with others and spend less time in front of the television or computers."

"Tele-who and what's a calm pewter?"

"Another time," Colette said.

"Why go to college at all?" Sadie put in. "Aren't there men at social events? Or proper introductions? I met my Percy through friends, but I can tell you, they deeply regret it now. Apparently, I have ruined their reputations as well as my own."

Colette shook her head. "We are both out of time and out of step, aren't we? Remember, let me do the talking."

Sadie nodded absently. Colette took a deep breath. This would be more than observing Lizzie Borden through a peep hole, or reading about her in a book with the now infamous photos of Abby and Andrew, post murders. This would be face to face conversation. That is, if she could convince the Sheriff and his wife. From what Colette had read about the case, they actually knew Lizzie from the time she was a little girl and played around their yard. Colette knew she needed sharp cunning to convince the authorities to let her converse with a suspected murderer. She needed to create the opportunity to have a conversation with Lizzie Borden, right here in 1892 not so much for Lizzie's well-being, but perhaps for Colette's.

Chapter Eighteen (A)

The Historical Facts

The list of alternative suspects were purported to have included a supposed "boyfriend," although one was never discovered, nor even known to exist, either as a platonic relationship or as a lover. Other possible suspects included Emma, several business associates and renters of a property belonging to Andrew Borden. There were quite a few possibilities in the business realm. The police and investigators traveled to towns nearby, following all leads, regardless of how unlikely and obscure they may have seemed. Inevitably, it was the severity of the crimes, as well as the proximity of the suspect, that led them back to Lizzie's door time and time again. Means, motive and opportunity. It was a macabre crime with concise circumstantial evidence and a textbook solution. The jury, however, brought back an acquittal.

The facts of the case contrasted with society and the time, including ignorance, or a blatant denial of child abuse, and the extreme repression of women, which played against the backdrop of the all-male jury. This jury wished desperately to believe in the male-dominated pseudo-ideology they'd created. The evidence and the outcome were destined for war. This jury of men wanted nothing more than to believe in the farce they'd created; that women were docile creatures, incapable of the "cunning" of which Knowlton spoke, nor capable of a devious nature.[319]

Ironically, it was the acquittal, or the finding of Lizzie as innocent in the face of such strong evidence, that made a social idiom quite clear. That idiom was that Lizzie Borden may have been less on trial, than the social consciousness of the men folk of Fall River themselves. Indeed, the men and their orderly society were on trial. Was Miss Borden a murderer? Likely, yes. Should the men have truly examined the society they created, they would have found themselves placed in the hot seat of judgment. The trial was sensational simply because Lizzie was a woman. The evidence contradicted their sense of logic and their pre-conceived belief systems about men and women in a civilized society. In actuality, the evidence of the case was shouting out its anger, its vengeance, and its sense of purpose and retribution. This was not a crime over money or property. To repeat, this crime reflected abject rage. Any juror in his right mind, who clearly understood and could analyze the evidence presented, would have perhaps admitted to that fact.

As Knowlton indicated, after the investigations and once the stories were connected, a clarity of conviction had to have come to the jurors. He felt there was only one explanation which could not have been denied.[320]

In the end however, the facts were flatly denied. This group of men could hardly have arrived at any other conviction or belief – and still have called themselves true Victorian men. To have found Lizzie Borden guilty, these revered men of the time would have had to have found, in fact, themselves guilty as well. Any authentic examination of the facts would have pointed, irrefutably, to one of their own. Andrew Borden, exalted and honored, and a successful businessman, was the everyman for Victorian East coast America in 1892.

Knowlton made a case for the validity of circumstantial evidence. His theory, mapped out quite lucidly, the unlikelihood that a planned-out homicide, much less two homicides, would be witnessed by anyone. As crimes of passion, it was unlikely that they would have been observed.[321]

The jury considered it much more likely that a stranger off the street would have done it. Some maniacal madman would have been a much more likely suspect. A madman, who would not have had any idea about the workings of the house, with its countless locks and keys, or the comings and goings of Bridget Sullivan, or Abby Borden, or for that matter, even how to stay out of the way of Lizzie herself.

Knowlton further stated that any traces of a crime would have been "attempted" to have been "obliterated." [322] Obviously, the house was located in the center of town, and, as was stated before, was in the business district. Therefore, any decision on the part of the perpetrator would have been a strange one if he had indeed practiced any forethought. Not only would he likely have been spotted, but how would he clean up after the crime, much less stash a weapon? Clearly, whether or not the male jury wanted to believe it, this perpetrator was indeed a devious, and deliberate individual. This was no crime of passion. This was a carefully conceived, long-imagined, well-planned and highly organized massacre. The rage was the clarity, and the driving force.

Circumstantial evidence then took on fresh meaning when Knowlton described the analogy to the footprint in the sand, discovered by Robinson Crusoe. The evidence, as the story went, and as Knowlton discussed, was how Crusoe believed that after years of living on a deserted island where he thought he'd been alone, he was shocked to discover human footprints in the sand. This surprised him because that clearly indicated that he was not alone on the island as he had thought. [323]

Knowlton drew up this small example of circumstantial evidence in order to exemplify how a collection of events, strong events, versus a "chain of events," would have easily led to a logical and accurate conclusion. "Chain" of events Knowlton referred to as a misnomer, because it implied an accidental series of events having simply happened. [324]

Knowlton's point was; given the preponderance of circumstantial evidence to analyze, such as comparing and contrasting all of Lizzie's stories and witness testimonies, would have led anyone, irrefutably, to a calculated outcome. In other words, there was nothing happenstance about the numerous occurrences, observations and facts which culminated in the end, to equate to one explanation; Lizzie Borden had to have been the murderer.

Witnesses were not always reliable. This fact Knowlton pointed out. Men were fallible, and witnesses could have been wrong. His point was that circumstantial evidence, like the observance one makes when leaves float along in a river, which indicate which way a river flows, may have provided a logical conclusion.[325]

Soon Knowlton explored the idea that, had it been any murderous man off the street, he may well have entered the premises and murdered anyone and everyone. One may have wondered why nothing had been burglarized and why, there was no sign of anything having been taken.[326]

Rightfully and accurately, Knowlton declared this to have been the work of an "assassin." And should one examine the word "assassin," one finds it literally defined as "one who" is "designated, either through financial motive or any other strong desire, to terminate the lives of certain people."[327]

Whether or not the jury or anyone recognized it, Bridget and Lizzie were miraculously left unharmed. One would have had to ask, as a juror back in 1893, why, undoubtedly, would this have been the case?

Chapter Nineteen

E ntering the front hallway of the prison, Colette thought they'd strolled into a bed and breakfast by mistake. The air was breezy. All the windows were thrown wide in every direction. Lace eyelet curtains lifted like delicate sleeves with each gentle gust. On the desk there was a vase of wildflowers.

Clearly startled by their entrance, the Deputy looked up; shoving something he was doodling on, in a drawer. Proper jailhouse decorum was instantly restored.

Next to the outer cell door, which was thrown wide, Colette spotted another small vase of flowers in the window well.

"You the maids?" he asked. "Mrs. Wright mentioned you'd be coming."

"Sorry no. We're not maids," Colette said. "We're here to see Miss Lizzie Borden."

The deputy let the fountain pen he was writing with fall to the table. He rose quickly, knocking over the wooden chair he'd been comfortably settled in.

There was a lull of silence as he scrutinized them. Finally, Colette said, "tell her it's about her travel bag." When the Deputy just looked at her, she added, "she'll know what it's about."

"Don't know that anyone can see the prisoner," he whispered. "That's Mrs. Wright with her now. She and her husband run this jail."

"Would you ask Mrs. Wright to allow me to talk to her? We're with the," she paused, "the Sacred Heart Sisters."

Someone with a feminine touch had decorated the cell specifically for a woman. "Mrs. Wright feels pity for Lizzie. Lizzie played with her daughter, Isabel, as kids. Hasn't been a female suspect in Fall River since I don't know when. Nowhere to put the suspect in Fall River. That's why she's here," he added. "Let me ask Mrs. Wright."

The deputy disappeared through the doorway. Colette could see the two properly placed feet of someone seated across from an older woman, she assumed to be likely, Mrs. Wright. Draped across the cot was a quilt and extra blankets. The prisoner's boots were black. They were perfectly still until the deputy started to talk. Suddenly they scooted inward toward the bed as if she wanted to stand. A silver spoon clanked on the terra cotta tile floor when it fell off the side of a just visible cup of tea she held in her hand.

Soon there came sounds of quick whispers. Sadie and Colette were escorted in and she saw her. She stood face to face with Lizzie Borden for the first time.

The young woman had leaned forward, straining to see who had come to see her. Indeed, the almond-shaped eyes, and the steady gaze with no perceptible smile, created a flash of feelings in Colette. Colette couldn't move, as if frozen to the spot. She fingered a cross around her neck absent-mindedly. Sadie, as well, seemed to be losing focus next to her. Finally Sadie pulled out her flask and took a long, lazy swig, her eyes looking black with torment.

Colette's eyes however, were on Lizzie. Lizzie Borden returned Colette's look with her own steady gaze and placid expression. Colette overheard the young accused mention as an afterthought, that she was not a Catholic? Colette had to think of something quickly as she shuffled into the room. The cot and the cup of tea came more clearly into focus. Now for the first time ever, Colette truly was stepping beyond the velvet ropes in a museum. Why, she had always wanted to do this! At Mount Vernon and Colonial Williamsburg and on the Freedom

Trail in Boston. Those ropes had kept her away from touching furniture or stepping on the rugs. She knew people like this; people who hid behind museum ropes in life. Withholding feelings, warmth, affection.

Colette stepped into the face of notorious history now.

"Excuse me, Miss Borden. I apologize for showing up like this," she said, pausing, standing at the end of the cot with her hands clasped in front of her, attempting piety. "We are with the Sacred Heart Sisters," she said, eying Mrs. Wright. We have just come here to pray with you and see if there's anything we can do for you in your time of incarceration.

Colette stood there waiting. Her knees trembled under her long skirt. She felt a clammy sweat under her blouse and jacket. Somehow, the room smelled sweet, like youthful perfume, or the flowers in the window. Mrs. Wright, the Sheriff's wife sat across from Lizzie.

Lizzie shook her head when Mrs. Wright started to say something.

"It's fine," she said, still studying Colette's face with a quizzical but determined brow. "I think I'd like to talk to these ladies alone if that is fine with you, Mrs. Wright?"

Mrs. Wright gave Colette a profound once over, head to toe.

"Of course," she said, then after a glance at a slightly tipsy Sadie, she added, "are you sure you don't want me to stay?"

Lizzie shook her head. Mrs. Wright rose and indicated her chair for Colette to sit. Sadie followed her in and plopped down at the other edge of the cot. Colette's mind went blank. She had not planned this out. She never thought she'd get this close to Lizzie Borden. At once she felt empathy, and curiosity. Never in her life did she imagine she would have the opportunity to ask Lizzie about her life. That she would have the chance to hear Lizzie speak. As she looked at her now, the round young face and slightly embittered eyes, she felt a pang of regret about the ruse she'd used to get into her prison cell. Lizzie seemed determined to head this conversation off with the first comment. Colette spoke up quickly.

"I have your checkerboard travel bag."

"I do not own a travel bag. Not of any sort."

"It's your French bag Isabelle bought you in Paris? She'd had it made for you by the House of Vuitton? With your initials L.A.B.?"

Lizzie took a deep breath and sat up straight. She nodded. "Well yes. I did have a bag like that."

Lizzie's expression was stoic but one eye twitched. It seemed like minutes before she blinked. Without waiting for Lizzie to answer, Colette went on.

"It is safe," she said. "No one will ever see it. I just need to keep it out of sight at the asylum. Dr. Warburton, who runs the place, he's been keeping a sharp eye out for anything amiss.

"Perfect Pines," she said, her tone even, her gaze averted. It was not a question, it was a statement. Then, after a moment, she understood. Her eyes met Colette's.

"I knew Isabelle at Perfect Pines," Colette said.

Lizzie looked down at her hands. "I understand she is still imprisoned there."

"You know she isn't."

"I know nothing of the kind, I am sure."

"As you know, she and Darren have gone to Chicago." Colette lowered her voice and leaned forward, "you tossed your L.A.B. bag out the second story window at 92 Second Street, with the hatchet handle inside, and the blue dress. The actual bloodied blue dress. Because the blue dress you burned in the kitchen fire really did just have paint on it."

Lizzie nodded. "Bad timing. I know."

"Then you retrieved the bag in the back yard and brought it to the carriage driver, a friend of Sadie's. He's the same driver who had delivered Emma to the house."

"The travel bag with my initials ended up back at my house. It confounded me," Lizzie said quickly.

"I'm afraid Sadie here," she nodded toward Sadie who now reclined on the cot, "and I, came over to your house with it. Dr. Warburton was looking for anything to get Isabelle, or any of us in trouble. He was hanging around the luggage on an afternoon when we were picking costumes for a yard party."

Lizzie's expression didn't change. Her mouth was firm. Her eyes betrayed nothing.

The sound of footsteps came from behind Colette. Mrs. Wright hovered in the doorway, as did the Deputy. He attempted to achieve a respectable stance by smoking a small pipe. Turning back to Lizzie, the young woman seemed altered. Slowly and methodically, she shifted her booted feet, straightened her posture, and then set her tea down, folding her hands neatly in her lap.

"I suppose you're wanting a donation to the convent? Or the Sacred Heart Catholic Church in town," she said, raising her voice in hopes of being overheard. "As far as I knew, I thought we only had one congregation of Catholics in town."

Colette took a deep breath and looked at the floor. "That would be wonderful. A donation to either, wouldn't it Sister Sadie," Colette said, tapping Sadie's shoe with her own shoe. Sadie sat up and nodded, gazing through the far wall. "We welcome anything," Colette went on, checking out her performance with a quick glance back at Mrs. Wright.

Mrs. Wright, in turn, receded out of the room, shooing the Deputy back to his desk.

Colette continued in a whisper, "How fortunate you are to have such a friend like Dr. Bowen."

Lizzie's eyes widened, slightly. Then the placid demeanor returned. She was good, Colette mused. She would do well in front of the jury.

Colette feared losing her audience. Lizzie's eyes revealed nothing. Sadie sat up suddenly on the cot, startling Lizzie who turned to look.

"Lizzie," Colette said. "Hear me out."

Lizzie's chin trembled noticeably. A wooden Seth Thomas clock next to the cot ticked out a rhythmic dirge. Certainly the accused's mind was reeling with what was being discussed, right out in the open, right there in her prison cell. Perhaps she envisioned Colette and Sadie as blackmailers? She couldn't be sure they were there to help. Hadn't Lizzie already endured several trials and inquisitions, and insidious gossip? Why the very town in which she grew up was, at this moment, mired in silent scrutiny of their town daughter.

Victorian America. A life for women replete with abandonment, frustration and even deprivation of the simplest rights such as the vote, a right to higher education and control over their own bodies. The treatment for "hysteria," or literally "womb disease," which was essentially a normal need for a woman to orgasm, was treated by specialists with massages of the genitalia. This special "treatment" was of course only afforded by the wealthy who were usually widows or with husbands who wanted their melancholia and hysteria to be handled efficiently. Ironically, perhaps in today's modern interpretation, such wives were often simply married to men who could not please them sexually. Left untreated, such women were prone to "irritability" and in more serious cases, committed to asylums or had surgical hysterectomies. In a male-dominated society, often such needs were simply frowned upon or ignored. Clearly, due to the fact that women did not supposedly enjoy sex, nor were they capable of sexual pleasure, that in the end there had to have been something wrong with womankind entirely.

Mrs. Wright returned to the threshold. Lizzie gave her a look, and shook her head and the older woman receded. She turned back to Colette, taking a deep breath. Lizzie's smile was plaintive and slight. Her eyes brewed with a type of fury, smoldering with some pious torment.

This Victorian woman, this woman in particular, had endured much more. In Colette's estimation, from having studied all the literature, the articles, the biographies and the blogs around the Borden case, she believed Lizzie had indeed been a victim of her father's unwanted desires. Unwanted. Uninvited.

Lizzie leaned over to her left and withdrew an embroidered handkerchief from a generous leather traveling bag. Colette's eyes lingered on the handkerchief. It was covered in blood stains. Quite a bit of missing information became clear.

Lizzie's eyes blinked several times, then quickly followed Colette's gaze.

"Please add this to the travel bag you're keeping for me."

Colette nodded and took the kerchief from Lizzie's hand. She felt certain Lizzie was behind the bag's final return to Perfect Pines Asylum.

"And then, it would be best if you go," Lizzie added quietly, starting to rise.

Sadie had by now sauntered over, appearing lost and detached, she regarded the conversation between Lizzie and Colette with adolescent bravado. Colette knew better. She knew that Sadie too was friends with Isabelle and knew Lizzie well. It was common knowledge between the three of them, that Andrew Borden and Edward Sewell were both violators of women.

Colette took a deep breath. "I know about the key on the mantle that unlocked the doors in your house on Second Street. I know the location of your bedroom and perhaps why Emma switched rooms with you. Your older sister took the smaller room." Colette hesitated, then added quietly, "why did she feel she had to do that, Lizzie?"

Lizzie inhaled sharply at the mention of the bedrooms. Sadie reclined on the cot again and turned to hear better. Lizzie's gaze didn't leave Colette's. It was as if she thought she could prevent something catastrophic from happening. Hatred around her deceased parents festered there. It was no longer self-loathing, but rather vengeance. It was vengeance. The murders had served as Lizzie's release.

Colette studied Lizzie's face. Amidst nervousness, Lizzie's eyes traveled to the side of the cot where Sadie was slumped. At the foot of the bed on the floor, there sat a large, light brown distinctive bag which was wider at the base and tapered up to a leather latched top. It had a buckle fasten in the middle and two long handles. It made Colette think of another bag just like it.

"Dr. Bowen," she started.

Lizzie looked up. "What about him?"

Sadie sat up with her eyes wide, as it something was greatly amiss.

"Colette," Sadie warned, a bit unsteadily, "I'm really tired."

"He's always been good to you. He knew about the abuse. In fact, because he's been your personal physician since birth and during your childhood, he understood unlike anyone, right?"

She nodded ever so slightly. "He is a good doctor. He's well."

"The time your parents were out of town, and you were alone at the house? He took you to church with him, didn't he?"

Lizzie reddened slightly. "We were proper people going to church. We had nothing to hide."

Colette leaned forward, her hands in her lap. "No. He asked the police to wait before searching your room on the day of the murders, didn't he? And he did that specifically so that the two of you could come up with a place to stash the blue dress and the hatchet handle, right? Then you put on that pink wrapper by the time the police and neighbors had gotten to your house. That blue dress, the one you would burn a day later in the kitchen, wasn't the bloodied dress. You hid that one away. What better place?" Colette said, eyeing the brown bag by the cot, "than the good doctor's bag?"

Lizzie's gaze was unmoved.

"I assume when people saw him on the street the afternoon of the murders, and he looked so panicked, it was because he knew, that poor wretched man knew, that you two had the bloodied evidence and that his doctor bag, one used for healing, was full of bloodied evidence. I would bet he still has the same bag. The doctor bag where you both hid the dress, and the handle to the hatchet."

Without hesitation, Lizzie replied. "He was simply concerned with his reputation."

Sadie stood up all at once pulled over a chair, knocking it over in the process. Mrs. Wright hurried to the doorway. Lizzie flashed a quick look to the woman standing there.

"Mrs. Wright. We're just finishing our conversation. My Protestant friends may not understand, because you know how they are. Nothing I can do if they assume I have turned to idol worship."

Brows knit quizzically, Mrs. Wright nodded. She eyed Sadie who was holding the chair with a tight grip. The three women sat in comparative silence for a moment. Outside could be heard the clomping of horses and the cries of children being called in by their mothers. Mrs. Wright exited the room again and she and the deputy conversed in hushed voices by his desk, indiscernible, serving only as background. Sadie took another sip of Laudanum and shoved the flask back into the small reticule she had attached to her belt.

When Colette rose to go, Lizzie too stood up. Colette was surprised at how small she seemed, but her build was solid.

"Although I empathize," Colette murmured slowly, "with your extreme pain, you are nevertheless, a murderer."

Lizzie averted her eyes. At the moment, she embodied all the stoic photographs Colette had seen of her repeatedly over the years.

"I don't know how to tell you this, but I firmly believe your dear friend has gone away for good. I don't know that you'll see Isabelle again. People in Fall River will talk, but don't listen. Don't listen to the talk. They will say she ran away out of shame or fear. That's what her father will say too."

Then she pulled out of a larger potato sack, the L.A.B. travel bag she'd secreted inside. "Lizzie," Colette whispered to the suspect, "I will take this bag to a place where it will never be found." Then she touched Lizzie's hands, which she had clasped in front of her.

Silence resounded. Lizzie gazed at nothing. Out of nowhere, a tear came to her eye. Fully aware, Lizzie knew she had ended the tyranny of her own abuse with violent force.

Lizzie had felt helpless. This tear now, was for her. And for her friend. Even though it was too late for Isabelle.

Sadie's eyes were glazed. Colette reached out her hand to her nineteenth century friend, and helped her out of the chair. Before departing, Colette turned one last time to Lizzie. She recalled reading that Lizzie had gained weight and appeared well-cared for when she finally reached the trial. Colette nodded to her with a slight smile. Lizzie was not a woman unable to sleep or eat out of a guilty conscience. This was perhaps someone who recognized she'd murdered two people, but felt she had to. This was a woman who felt she'd righted a wrong.

"Lizzie," she said. "Wear your favorite hat with the bit of flowers to court. I have a feeling you will be acquitted."

Lizzie's face didn't change. She swept away the tear from her cheek.

By the time they'd reached outside, Sadie was dragging. Colette felt certain it was a combination of Laudanum and the actual meeting with Lizzie face to face. Sadie had the sensory perception of a gentle animal. It was as if she'd absorbed Lizzie's agony.

Colette felt the same as Sadie did. Yet, she didn't cry. They crept along the uneven sidewalk, out onto the front walkway. Soon they reached the street. At Colette's request, the carriage driver waited, so that as they approached the deserted cobbled street, the singular sound of a horse adjusting his long legs, resonated throughout the hot evening air.

As Colette assisted Sadie into the carriage, she turned once to look back at the Taunton Jail. Through the first floor cell she could see the light of kerosene lamp behind the lacy curtained room which housed Lizzie Borden. In the final vestiges of the day, she could see the much maligned murderess watching them.

The carriage ride back to the train station dragged. Both women sat with slumped shoulders in the velvety slats depleted of energy. Sadie was sobering up, and the shame-filled realization that she'd been on a binge was evident in her gaze. She stared out the carriage window, careful not to make eye contact with Colette. Of course, Colette held no judgment against this woman. She'd spent ten years of her life drowned in alcoholic drinking. While trying to quit, she'd changed alcohol brands, tried new friends, new bars, new hours, new cocktails, drinking only on Mondays, or never drinking on Mondays...finally, waking up with her clothes on backwards, and having no memory of how she'd gotten home. That would have been precisely ninety years after Lizzie Borden killed her father for abusing her. Some abuse, abuse of all kinds, persist despite the passage of time.

Colette remembered the shame. Looking down, she noticed Sadie had fallen asleep on her lap. Colette grinned. She'd been about Sadie's age when she'd given up liquor for good. Over twenty years had passed since then.

As she studied the sidewalk, she barely noticed the occasional fellow carriage rambling past theirs, and fell again into deep thought. She'd read recently, supposedly the latest statistic was that women were surpassing men in problems with alcohol. The advances of women seemed to Colette, to often be illusory; unreal and inauthentic. After all, no one but Colette had put herself in harm's way by drinking alcoholically, and suffering several assaults and other horrific experiences while drunk and in blackouts. There were holes in her nights. There were nights where she seemed "normal" to everyone around her when in actuality, she'd been functioning sufficiently on the outside, without any memory or awareness of her behavior or conversations. These were alcoholic blackouts. Ways to forget her days. Ways to not feel rejection, from her mother and the men. Ways to nearly end her life. Despite all claims to the contrary, or making light of drunken acts, such experiences became more frequent and ever-more terrifying.

Finally it occurred to her one foggy-headed, disastrous morning after, that it was not normal, not normal at all, to feel compelled to check the front bumper of her Toyota Celica to see if there was blood on it or dents. This was the life of an alcoholic. In reality, it was not a life.

So had she really gotten more freedom than Lizzie Borden? Hadn't women started to define themselves as heroines of their own lives in the 1930s and the 1940s only to charge back into the banal life of a housewife in 1950? The bargain included perhaps a life shackled to domesticity in the home, but enjoying financial freedom through a "good" marriage.

Some women who pursued careers may have lost the chance for children, simply due to age. Of course, they were blamed for that too. How dare they aspire to careers, be they creative or professional?

All at once, Colette's mind cleared. In fact, far too quickly. Because walking swiftly as they approached the train station, she saw a tall angular man, half-hidden under the rim of his dark hat. The profile was menacing, determined, and clearly in search of something at the train station. He scanned left and right, searching for someone in particular. Five or so men waited with him. Pinkertons. Some roamed the platform and circled the waiting area.

Colette was so startled that Sadie awakened from the movement of her friend. They were looking for them. Colette sunk down in the leather seat of the carriage, trying to figure out how to warn the driver to continue and keep going past the train station.

Sadie was groggy. She rubbed her head and the back of her neck.

"We're here already?" she asked. "It went well with Miss Borden, then? Did it?"

Colette knew that Sadie's memory of the event was incomplete. Right now Colette's immediate concern was how to avoid letting Edward see them while also telling the driver to keep the carriage moving. The deafening sound of a train pulling into the station blew its horn several times, filling the air. Edward swept along, wearing a long duster which touched the ground. He pulled his bowler hat down low over his eyes. A black tie contrasted sharply against his white shirt. Even from inside the carriage, Colette could see his stride was provoked and driven. She saw him reach the station where he stood by, arms held stiffly at his sides. He looked left, right and finally turned around completely. He was definitely looking for someone.

Colette reached out the left side of the carriage and positioned her boots on the stairs at the side. She still held the potato sack and a roomy satchel which had somehow time-traveled with her. Rummaging around in it as quickly as she could, she found an old Totes fold-up umbrella at the bottom. Popping it open, Sadie jumped. Colette grinned and apologized, then started poking the driver up top in the front.

"Turn us away from the station right now."

Sadie was huddled in the corner of the carriage. She had withdrawn into herself. Although still an avid runner back in 2011 Illinois, Colette felt her legs beginning to shake. She could not hold onto her position with her boots planted on the exit stairs much longer, and soon she collapsed back into the carriage.

Within minutes, they were within a city block of the man in the long coat, who stood by eagle-eyed and ready. The carriage slowed, and the horses turned their heads to the left. The carriage changed direction and they trotted off, moving at a swift gait in the opposite direction of the station.

"Thank God," Colette whispered, catching her breath. She had both her hands flat against the walls inside the compartment.

"What craziness is this?" Sadie mumbled, her eyes half closed. Her lids were heavy. She was disoriented. "We've missed the train?"

What had William called him? The devil? Because Edward was capable of cold-bloodedly murdering not only his wife, but also his own daughter. He would, of course, claim he and Isabelle argued and that she'd fallen and hit her head. Perhaps more of her talk about going to university or marrying Darren. Colette knew that Edward Sewell, who possessed a typical narcissistic personality, felt that anything he believed, including the way women should behave, should be obeyed. It occurred to Colette now too, that William had likely gotten Darren out of the house before Edward arrived to confront Isabelle.

The carriage stopped suddenly. The horses were neighing wildly. Colette jumped from her seat to the outside. The scent of grass and mud filled her nostrils. The carriage driver had already jumped to the ground. His face had the sinister aspect of an attacker. His expression vacillated between pity and disbelief.

"Well what are you expecting me to do with the likes of you two ladies, now?"

His voice was gruff. Colette had acted hastily. She'd forgotten what era they were in. Still, she knew there were not real hazards on the nighttime streets of Taunton, surely?

"How about you two come over here," he said from the side of the road. "Show me just how grateful you are that I bothered to pick the likes of you up outside a jail?"

Colette leaned into the carriage and yanked out the potato sack and Sadie's carpet bag they'd thrown in when they'd skipped out on the asylum. Sadie was shaking her head, clinging to the doorframe of the carriage. Although usually willing to try just about anything with a bit of joie de vivre, Sadie held back now, at least momentarily.

In the next instant, Sadie had emerged and yanked out the L.A.B. travel bag. and swung it with a mighty backhand, hitting the driver squarely on the left side of the head. He stumbled backward and fell.

"Sadie, now!" Colette grasped the young woman's hand. Edward is looking for us. There are only trees hiding us from view."

The driver sat in a puddle by the side of the road, rubbing his head.

A maddening trickle of sweat rolled down Colette's back. She unbuttoned the top two buttons of her blouse which seemed to be a daily ritual since arriving in 1892. She could feel the heat around her ankles from the boots again. In the twilight, as follows the dinner hour, the night felt moody and distant.

Slumped at the side of the road, the carriage driver rubbed his head, then took a swig from a flask in his coat pocket.

He started to stand, a bit unsteadily. "It occurs to me," he started, "that no proper women would be out on her own, at night. I don't know either one of you. So if you want me to keep your little secret, you'll do what I ask."

He nodded toward the station. "I have a little room over there, next to the depot."

Sadie charged the man suddenly, waving her arms and wailing. It proved effective and the man and the carriage took off.

Twenty minutes later, the two women, with weighted down bags, had walked back to the Taunton Jail. In the distance, lights still emanated from the foyer and first floor cell of the place.

All at once, Colette pulled Sadie away from the beam of a streetlight which a gaslighter had just finished illuminating. Although still only around seven thirty, the late summer evening was awash in a sky of charcoal greys and pinks and temperamental clouds.

"Miss Colette?" she said, backing into the shade of a towering Oak Tree.

"He must have had the same idea," Colette said.

Sadie followed her gaze. A tall man with a bowler hat and a long overcoat filled the space of a window at the jail.

"Why is he here?" she said, her voice sounding transparent.

Colette assessed the situation, trying to get a better view. The Deputy stood perched out front of the place. He faced the opposite direction, gazing up as if the moon held him captive. His face chalky white, he looked like an apparition. Somehow, Edward Sewell had forced his way through the front entrance of the Taunton Jail.

From the street, Colette could see a dim light in Lizzie's cell which persisted. It occurred to Colette that the matron, Mrs. Wright, may have gone to bed and with the deputy outside, having a smoke or whatever he was doing, there was no one in the jailhouse watching Lizzie's cell.

"Sadie. Wait here," she said. "Stay put."

Sadie wiped her brow. "So hot," she said, throwing down her carpet bag. Wandering away, she plopped under a nearby tree in the darkness.

Colette turned back only once to catch her fishing the flask out of her carpet bag. Colette paused, thinking it through. From her own experience with addicts, including herself, she knew there was nothing to say in this situation.

Although Isabelle had pioneered a makeshift group for patients fighting drinking issues, in the asylum, Edward had made sure to shut them down. He addressed a group of suffering patients claiming Isabelle had grown bored with all of them. Isabelle's father made sure she would be of no further use to other addicts. Never mind that she had been an addict too."

A thought came to Colette. She had the L.A.B. travel bag. Aside from the hatchet and the blue calico dress, there were also the journals Isabelle had given Lizzie to hold for her. When Colette described the black velvet bag she'd found, Sadie said she knew what was inside. Colette did not tell her she found it in a green shoebox in the year 2011. Sadie knew all about the contents of the black velvet bag. It was an oval ruby ring.

"It's an engagement ring," Sadie said. "I'll bet it was for Isabelle from Darren. Where did you get this trumpet music and the ring again?"

They'd traveled from a coal chute under a bungalow not yet built, in the year 2011, she thought. Instead, she said, "Isabelle gave it all to Lizzie. She must have added them to this bag of evidence. Thing is, that worries me. It's as if Isabelle knew she was in real danger.

Her thoughts went to Edward. She was holding the trump card. Perhaps there would be a way she could get something out of him.

Twenty or so minutes passed. Colette positioned herself behind bushes outside the window. The deputy leaned back against the wall, eyes closed, enjoying an evening nap while on night duty.

Eyes intent upon the two of them, Colette strained to hear Lizzie's responses. Edward grasped the bars of her cell, spewing words at her. Thinking how unsafe and toxic he was, Colette's mind went to Olivia and the cement stairs. To think it had only been two hot summer days since she'd spent time with her daughter in the year 1994. Oddly, more than a week had passed here in 1892.

The first time travel had centered upon the hieroglyphs. The hobo writing at 1804 Prairie. That had been where this entire business with the past had started. The significance of the miraculous Prairie door, and her insistence upon keeping it after the house was razed, all coalesced now. Why had her daughter Olivia been chosen? Was it her innocence and the curiosity of a child that was required to bring the symbols to Colette's attention?

If someone were to believe in the power of inanimate objects, or in other words, the connectivity of humanity and houses, that they somehow hold energy, or the souls of their predecessors within them, then perhaps that little bit of open-mindedness on her part is what allowed her to travel via the Prairie door. In her own way, Colette too had the curiosity and the ability to transcend, at least somewhat, the constraints and the earth-bound beliefs of the general population. Maybe once the door had been severed from the house, through its untimely demolition, someone like Marilyn, or "something" made sure the Prairie door with the music box survived.

Drawing nearer to the jail, Colette alerted herself to hear Lizzie's responses to Edward's corrosive raging.

"You're the only woman who knows. I know Isabelle confided in you."

Lizzie said nothing. He grew more incensed.

"Someone sent me a note. Something about evidence having to do with my daughter. It had to be you. What could you possibly know about my relationship with my daughter?"

"Quite a bit," she said firmly.

"You're lying! You spinsters play games. Isabelle was no spinster. She was fallen like her mother. They brought me nothing but shame. And you're threatening me? You're a murderer. He was a good man. A great man! You never respected your father the way you should have. You will pay. No one will believe you."

With those words, he reached between the bars of the cell, and grabbed her by the pink lapels of her Jacket. Lizzie pulled away just in time, catching the sleeve of her pink and white striped dress. Maybe Sadie had a point. Lizzie was dressed up a bit for someone in jail awaiting trial for double-murder.

That's when someone laid a heavy hand on Colette's shoulder.

Chapter Nineteen (A)

The Historical Facts

If one added up the circumstantial evidence, identifying the corpses discovered when the massacre ended, they consisted of a husband and wife, a mother and father. So what person would have motive enough to enter into a man's domestic life? A man such as Andrew Borden and his wife? How would it not point directly to the maid Bridget, or the daughter Lizzie? If it were a random attack on 92 Second Street, by some crazed stranger who simply had murder on his mind, why not do away with everyone? After all, Bridget and Lizzie, both viable witnesses, managed to avoid being killed. Both survived.

The killing mimicked a professional hit. These murders were carefully planned and chosen. As Knowlton pointed out, the one and a half hour lag time which passed between them further solidified the assumption that the victims were carefully chosen beforehand.[328] In fact, this assassin was willing to hide out and wait for the second victim, risking discovery simply because these killings were so very, not random.

Knowlton announced to the jury that the Borden family had skeletons, and that these skeletons were tucked away, kept secret by a close-mouthed family. And in the Borden family, the secrets were literally kept under lock and key.[329] Did it not hold true, and hadn't it been proven over countless years, that dysfunctional families replete with alcoholism, physical, sexual and emotional abuse, eventually cracked in some way? That the degree to which smiles appeared on the outside, or "normalcy" reigned on the surface, implied that something was likely amiss. In Victorian America, alcohol abuse was especially common and reached horrific levels. In a sense, the alcohol crisis led to the formation of the Women's Christian Temperance Union. The disease of alcoholism indeed could have run rampant within the finest pristine homes of Fall River. In the same way, behind the closed shutters at 92 Second Street, emotional chaos bounced off the walls. There were indeed numerous cracks in the lath and plaster of the Borden family.

So too, had Lizzie and numerous other women, then and now, showed one face to the public and another in private. The actual truth told of an existence much more beleaguered, which involved a woman's spirit being under siege.

As Knowlton pointed out, the Borden family "did not parade their difficulties." Knowlton cited Lizzie's reactions to the cloakmaker, who mentioned Abby Borden.[330] Lizzie had retorted that Abby was not Lizzie's mother, but her step-mother, and that she was a mean and awful thing.[331] Soon after, while conversing with Mr. Fleet, with Abby's dead body lying nearby, Lizzie again clarified Abby as having been nothing more than her step-mother.

Interestingly, Knowlton went on to point out that Abby had acted as a mother to Lizzie since Lizzie had been three or four years old, and in all that time, there was no warmth between them.[332] Beyond that, these many years together for step-mother and daughter only further solidified that the crimes, which seemed greatly personal, were replete with extreme hurt.

So, whether their many years together were good or not, Lizzie knew Abby quite well. Clearly, there may have been lifelong resentment for Abby, one that perhaps only a close family member could have developed. There existed close proximity, but neglect as well. As several experts continued to point out during the trial, these crimes were brutal specifically, just because of how intimate they were. Even the locations were intimate; Andrew Borden while napping serenely and Abby Border replacing shams on the pillows in the guest room.

Next, Knowlton discussed a series of assumptions. In this way, he created several scenarios for examination. The first proposition explained how a three-year-old Lizzie lost her real mother at an age when, as he said, she could scarcely pronounce the word "mamma."[333] Up until this point, the picture he painted rang true. However, after the age of three, much, if not all of what he claimed to have been fact, may have been conjecture. The portrait he attempted to paint at this point did not coincide with a tragic reality which eventually revealed itself. Still, Knowlton attempted to depict a step-mother who acted as a loving replacement for Lizzie's birth mother. He claimed that, she had "come in and had done her duty by that girl and had reared her," and had stood in all "attitude which characterized the tenderest of all human relations."[334]

Knowlton went on to describe how Lizzie had certainly sought out her step-mother over the years to provide relief, sympathy, or perhaps simply a shoulder to lean on, or as he said exactly, "it was on her breast that girl had sunk as have our children the breast of their mothers."[335]

Ironically, Knowlton further described how, after all that maternal devotion how something as trivial as money and property, could have incited Lizzie to reject her step-mother, as a mother figure. This was his way of chastising Lizzie, but at the same time claiming her innocence simply because the motive was too infinitesimal.

Knowlton went on to expand upon the fact that Abby came between Lizzie and her father, both financially and personally.[336] For this very reason, Knowlton unknowingly reiterated that it was likely Lizzie murdered both of the Bordens. If Abby came between Lizzie and her father, she'd have likely killed Abby. The problem with finding a stranger, as viable suspect, was the basic fact that both individuals had been murdered.

Knowlton pointed out that the bizarre and out of control method by which the hatchet had been wielded, revealed someone driven by blind fury. He further described how misdirected and out of control the hits from the hatchet were. He mentioned that a strong man, versus an enraged woman, would, in his opinion, more likely have hit with a major strike and been done with it. These killings were perhaps even clumsy and drawn-out.

To further his point, about the unlikelihood that a stranger could possibly have been responsible, Knowlton described the barbed wire at the bottom and tops of the fencing.[337] He mentioned too that the cellar door was always locked. In fact, early on in the investigation, it was discovered that there were cobwebs in and around the doorframe of the door leading to the cellar; webs which connected the door to the frame serving as a bit of proof that the door had not been opened in a long time.[338] The barn was also locked at night.

Of particular interest was the closet up at the head of the main stairway in the house. This closet had always been kept locked. Whenever Mr. Fleet, or anyone wanted to gain access to the closet, it was necessary to see Lizzie for the keys.

In the end, there may have been any number of items stashed in this closet. For instance, a missing bloodied calico dress, a weapon or evidence of the crimes having been committed may have been easily stashed there. Perhaps only temporarily, but still a possibility.

Knowlton even went as far as questioning the entire practice of ironing the handkerchiefs. He posed a hypothesis around the question of why Lizzie would not have chosen to perform such a task in the cellar instead? If fact, he brought up the entire idea that Lizzie should not have been doing chores anyway, stating that she actually "had no duties around the household."[339] In other words, Knowlton implied that by ironing a small number of handkerchiefs in the dining room, Lizzie created a chore for herself to do, in order to give her an alibi around her location and her reason for being there.

Knowlton pointed out that the cellar would have been a more appropriate place for such work, unless Lizzie purposely wanted to be in close proximity to Mr. Borden.

Chapter Twenty

C olette whipped around, her hand raised, ready to strike.
"Mrs. Browning," it was Mrs. Wright. "Your visit with Miss Borden is over."

"We're leaving Mrs. Wright," Colette assured her. "But what about him? He's harassing Lizzie."

The jail keeper turned in the direction of Edward, in time to catch him storming out of the station.

"I left the deputy in charge," she said, shaking her head. "Unfortunately, all the men folk allow Edward Sewell too many rights and privileges."

Colette nodded. Sadie stood by, waiting.

"Be on your way," the older woman went on. "And take care in the dark."

She walked off then, and disappeared with the shadows.

"First time someone didn't tell us we needed a chaperone," Colette said.

Sadie was shaking her head. "I don't remember much of what was said just now talking with Miss Lizzie. Warburton gave me so much of the elixir. Medicinal, he says. He says, 'the female mind needs something because it's the weaker sex.' Happiness lies, he claims, in having a good home, and being a good cook and housekeeper. He says if I had a proper husband instead of being wanton, that I wouldn't crave the Laudanum."

Colette nodded. "Well, the home part might lead to happiness for some people. But, of course we know the rest isn't true."

With that, she smiled and put her hand on Sadie's shoulder. It felt angular and bony. "I don't think they're feeding you well at Perfect Pines."

Sadie turned away, and the moonlight caught her profile. Colette could see she was drinking from the flask again.

Sadie you know how addiction takes over? Laudanum is made from opium tincture, codeine and morphine. They seem to prescribe it around here like cough syrup."

"It's good for that too," Sadie said, with good intention, then, "and aches, and pains. And for the curse. You know, the ladies' time."

Colette sighed. "It's a potent narcotic, Sadie."

Up until now, they'd stayed back out of sight, under the cover of large Pine trees. They both watched as Edward charged past on the sidewalk and threw himself into a lavish carriage.

They walked along in darkness, back toward the window of the jail. No street lights in this part of town. The only sounds were the gravel under their boots and their tired conversation.

"I just miss Isabelle," Sadie mumbled through tears. "And the meetings she started."

Colette nodded. "The support meetings really helped?"

She nodded, biting her lip.

They positioned themselves outside Lizzie's window again. "What is it about Lizzie that upsets you right now?"

"Well just look at her!"

"I don't understand?"

"Isabelle knew Lizzie was driven to madness. But to do what she did? What about her soul? What will happen to her now?" Then her voice dropped, "see what she's wearing? Pastels. She's in mourning. Doesn't she know that's like admitting guilt?"

Colette turned for another look at Lizzie. The moon was radiant, a white wafer of hope, silvery, fluid and spiritual.

The receding sounds of horses' hooves were turbulent as the carriage rattled away, breaking the silence of the night. Edward Sewell had clearly had an agenda with the murder suspect. He'd wanted whatever it was that Lizzie knew. Like everything else in his life, he thought he could take hold of her heart, wring it out and get the information he needed. Instead, it had ignited the shame which had always held her captive, and turned it inside out. Her anger had protected her from him and gave her, at least temporarily, the strength to fend him off. As narcissist patriarch, he blamed her for exposing his dark deviance, which he saw simply as the private life of an "upstanding" man. The only difference between the two families was that Edward had gotten rid of the victims, whereas Lizzie had rid the world of the perpetrators, her perpetrators.

The sounds of the wooden wheels dissipated into the night. Colette felt certain that the note, likely sent by Lizzie, was aimed to rattle him a bit, and revealed possession of Isabelle's journals. Clearly, this man insisted upon subservience and did not take well to Lizzie's obstinance.

While they waited, the deputy returned and stood flush against Lizzie's cell door. He chatted her up, his stance casual. Perhaps he wanted to present the façade of a gentleman; polite but not timid, masculine but not brutish. Perhaps he knew how sinister a man could be. Certainly he was conflicted, and perhaps a little mad at himself for allowing Edward access to Lizzie at all.

The two women turned away and walked arm in arm. Sadie was still unsteady. They reached a quiet corner where they'd found the friendly ice cream parlor earlier. It was terribly late on this nineteenth century night, especially for two women unaccompanied. They may as well have been prostitutes.

They strolled the cobbled streets and came to what appeared to be a back alley. This was the sordid side of town judging from several authentic street women who suddenly surfaced, and two or three drunken men who spilled out of a tavern.

Colette pulled her friend further into the oily black of the slick alley, somewhere behind the main building. The wooden tavern sign creaked, and had gold lettering on it which read "The Sly Pig." Colette leaned back against the wall of the main bank building. She glanced up to the side of the brick structure, so sturdy, and her eyes traveled to the top where gargoyles spat their opinions from the four corners of the place. The air was a combustion of sickly sweet incense and the foul stale smells of liquor and bar food. What food was indigenous to bars in 1892, Colette mused? Mutton bites? Biscuits? Barley soup?

She squeezed her eyes closed, tears coming freely now, and took a deep breath. Sadie was more or less slumped again the wall now, also defeated. They wouldn't last much longer on this night. Colette ached everywhere, and just wanted to sleep. Opening her eyes then, Colette's gaze fell upon a small form peering at the two of them from a nearby row of wooden garbage barrels.

Sadie looked too. In the ashen corner, two small eyes glistened. Perhaps thinking it was a small animal, Sadie screamed half a scream, then covered her mouth quickly. Several men from the tavern teetered to the corner and leered into the alleyway where the women hid. Colette squeezed Sadie's arm, her forefinger to her lips.

"Don't say a word," she whispered sharply. "Whatever you do, don't scream again."

Sadie was hyperventilating. "If it's an animal, it could be a rabid dog. There are dogs on the loose everywhere in these neighborhoods."

Shadows would be no safer than papier mache when it came to dogs. Still, Colette moved forward toward the small creature. Sadie grabbed her arm, digging her slight fingers into Colette's flesh. The heat had subsided to around eighty degrees. The men at the end of the alleyway started to mill about, taking a disturbing amount of interest in the two women. Surely, they'd grown accustomed to streetwalkers in the neighborhood, and now sensed new blood in the vicinity.

Pulling free from Sadie, patting her arm reassuringly, Colette took two steps toward the blinking eyes in the raven night. She intuited this was not an animal, not of the four-legged variety anyway.

Soon she reached the creature and leaned over, adopting a non-threatening posture. Gradually, as the grey dissipated, Colette could discern the slightly protruding belly of a young girl, and as the light from the back door opening from the corner bar flashed across her face, Colette gasped. The child was no more than ten years old. She wore a cotton calico shift that fell off her shoulders and cloth shoes.

The girl's eyes, however, were not those of a child. There was a compelling dispiritedness, an innate knowing about survival implicit. Even though the grey gloom absorbed her delicate features, shadow wells of fatigue rested under each eye. A vulnerability, beyond the bare skin and a flimsy dress, drew Colette closer to the urchin. Then she saw the emotionless glare.

Sadie grabbed her arm. "Leave her be. She's an unfortunate."

"Absolutely not."

Yet, as Colette drew nearer to her, the girl hissed. Her round face contorted into an impish snarl, borne out of, no doubt, years of neglect and abuse. This was a practiced unfortunate. This was a child who had been made an adult too soon. It was doubtful she could even live inside a civilized home. Tragically, the streets had devoured her. A creature of the alleys, this girl had lost a bit of her soul. She wore bitterness like a spurned lover.

"They have diseases," Sadie warned, hand on Colette's arm.

The girl's hair puffed out on the sides, a mass of tangles, like a ravaged nest. One sleeve of her dress was off her shoulder and exposed her flattened chest.

Reaching into the potato sack, Colette withdrew several biscuits she'd grabbed from Mrs. Burns's boarding house, and wrapped in cloth. The girl lunged for them right away, at the same time revealing her entire fragile countenance in the anemic yellow of a dim streetlight. Men whistled and cat-called from behind Sadie and Colette.

Then she recalled a healthy bundle of grapes she'd stashed in the bag as well.

Several of the younger men, juiced-up by booze, wandered over to where this exchange of food took place between the women. The small girl withdrew into the shadows again. Determined not to lose her, Colette kept her eye on her.

Suddenly, she heard breathing and felt it on the back of her neck. The sick smell of too much whiskey filled her nostrils.

Sadie had slumped away, and now stood to Colette's left. Gathering courage, Colette threw out her right hand and clipped one of the men, then whipped around and disabled the other one with a swift kick to the knees.

One of the men growled from his supine position on the ground, rubbing his head. "Where the hell you think you're going with our sweet little Cherry? She belongs to us. We feed her."

Furious, as he rose to one knee, whiskey-breath started toward her, but Colette knocked him down again with an elbow and a punch to the ground.

"She's not a pet," she said.

He lay there, unmoving. The other man was soon struggling to his feet and lumbering back to the tavern.

"Since when does some woman know how to fight?" he mumbled to another man.

Colette soon pulled out a lightweight white shawl she'd stuffed in the bag and threw it over Cherry's head. Sadie's eyes were wide, stunned. She said nothing for a moment, then asked, "Where did you learn to fight like a man?"

"Self-defense class at the YWCA," she said, wiping her mouth with the back of her hand.

Sadie nodded, her eyes not comprehending, but satisfied.

After whispering to Cherry for several minutes, the girl took Colette's hand and the two of them started off in a trot, for the train station. Sadie raced behind them. Several men had started after them. One in his twenties, wearing a grubby hat, grabbed ahold of Sadie and pulled her to him. In a fury, Sadie whipped him with the L.A.B. travel bag packed to capacity with hatchet handle, dress, and the bulky journals. It caught him full upon the face and he stumbled back.

"Who the hell are you?" he demanded.

"Wenches!" Another man said, storming after them, shaking a burly fist. On the surface, donned as he was, in a well-tailored suit, with top hat and patent leather shoes, this man may well have posed for a photo recently, looking very much the gentleman of the day. Yet the words from his mouth burned with rancor. "That little piece of girl you're taking off with? We own her! We've paid for her services. Why we feed her! There will be charges brought against you whores. We will find you. No man would marry the lot of you! We will just search the streets for you."

Catching up to Colette at last, Sadie appeared amazed at the older woman's athleticism.

"Do you spend a lot of time at the gymnasium? I heard Lizzie does," she said, breathing heavily. "Where are we going?"

Colette didn't wait. She leapt in front of a carriage and it careened to a halt. She hoisted Cherry up and into the compartment, secured Sadie and kicked one of the wooden wheels.

"Move it," she said. "Take us to the train station," she ordered.

A disinterested driver gave her a desultory look.

"I am waiting here for a gent from the tavern," he said. "I'm his regular ride. Anyways, why would I want to take the likes of you anywhere?"

Colette withdrew a Swiss army knife from her pocket and wielded it in the driver's face. "Because we're escaped lunatics from Perfect Pines Asylum. I've already killed two men. You want to be next?"

Before she'd finished her sentence, the driver had raised the reins and ordered the horses, "get!"

Twenty minutes later, they neared the station. Sadie had not spoken since they'd thrown themselves, wet, dirty and exhausted, into the carriage. The driver declined payment and just kept shaking his head, no. This suited Colette very well as she had no money. Minutes passed and not once did Colette unwrap her arms from the sleeping child. Now she felt tears spurting from her eyes. This child had affected her. This woman child, this "chattel" from 1892 had awakened a rage in her.

The heat exasperated the disgust. Sweat formed on the back of Colette's neck. The air lay there, heavy with sweat and booze. Exhaustion prevailed. Cherry breathed deeply, a small rattle as she did so. Asthma, or tuberculosis. The thin dress draped on her, stuck out a bit around the young one's belly. Sadie gave Colette a knowing glance and Colette nodded. Her face was grim. Sadie's hair drooped in wet black strands over each shoulder. She'd yanked out the pins holding her bun hours before. Sadie loved to have her hair flowing freely.

"We can't do anything for her," she said. "My God. We're escapees from Pines Asylum, and we have no inheritance or ready money."

"You sound like an encyclopedia or an information line from Google." Colette said, and smiled, wiping away tears.

"What's a google?"

"Forget it."

Sadie tilted her head. Despite having no idea what Colette was all about half the time, this young woman from 1892 had opened her heart and her mind to possibilities. Possibilities no less, with some woman who'd insinuated she'd arrived from the future. over one hundred years in the future. Sadie smoothed out her skirt, one which she displayed so proudly, one which she'd been forced to sew at the asylum. It was covered in mud and grass stains.

The air through the open windows of the carriage was fragrant with the summertime of a bygone era. The inside of the carriage smelled of leather, like the scent of Colette's dad from his car seats when he'd come home very late on Christmas Eve. There was something about the look her mother had given him that night in 1969, that had embedded itself in Colette's psyche. Something in Ursula's green eyes, as they'd filled up, and become wet, spoke of betrayal, like some death by drowning.

Colette thought further about Lizzie. The reality that the acquittal would come in a year's time, in June 1893, would stun many.

Regardless, Colette knew the story would not be altered. Even with the bloodied travel bag she wasn't sure if anything would have proven Lizzie's culpability in the murders. Had they seen the bloodied handle of the hatchet, and the actual bloodied dress worn in the murders, most likely in the Fall River of 1893, Lizzie still would have been found innocent by the all male jury.

Colette could, however, with Isabelle's journals, make the L.A.B. travel bag work for her in another way.

The simple yet forceful sounds of the horse's breathing filled the night. The rhythmic clomping of the hooves was soothing. This was the same calm she'd felt as a child, the swish swish of the windshield wipers in her mother's 1968 Corvaire or laying under a tree and reveling in the whispers of the leaves. Something about their momentum, gave the feeling at least, that she and Sadie were going somewhere. They were making progress even at a gentle pace. There still existed the certainty that they'd accomplish something from this series of tragedies in Fall River, and the unfortunate razing of 1804 Prairie in Valley Stream, Illinois. Simply from her couple of days, to a week enmeshed in 1892, Colette had experienced the stifling status that was the life of being a woman. Admittedly however, a similar lack of momentum awaited her back home in the year 2011.

"Do you think Lizzie is guilty?" Colette whispered, with Cherry asleep on her lap, when Sadie turned to her again.

Twisting her dark hair on her forefinger, Sadie started in surprise, "why, of course she is," she said.

"You're convinced of that?"

Sadie eyed Colette, studying the question as if it were written in the air between them. "Although it upset Isabelle, she saw it coming. She wasn't surprised. Why do you think she planned her escape from her father's basement? She'd heard the people through the windows and she knew what had happened down the street. Even with her own blood on her hands, she fought her way out. There was no more time to wait it out. He's a madman. Edward Sewell deserves the worst punishment the law can impose upon him. You know that. He's a murderer."

Colette nodded. The street urchin started to stir.

"He will pay," Colette said. "I will make sure of it. Not enough to change the course of history, but maybe enough to ruin him in this life."

Chapter Twenty (A)

The Historical Facts

Knowlton further mentioned facts which related to clear opportunity. Apparently, Lizzie had asked that Bridget be certain to lock the doors if she went out. It was known that Lizzie had attempted to entice Bridget out of the house all together, revealing to the maid that there was a notable sale at the local fabric shop.[340]

Why would Lizzie have wanted to make certain all the doors were locked? Because it was in preparation to provide total complete opportunity for the murders to have been committed, although at this juncture, no one had realized that Abby already lay dead in a bloodied heap in the guestroom upstairs.

In this way, Lizzie attempted to make absolutely certain that should Bridget have gone out, neither she nor anyone would get back in. Otherwise, why would it have been imperative that she lock all the doors if Abby Borden had gone out? In order to make sure that Abby, (were she actually still alive and had actually been called out to see a "sick friend" by note), could not gain access to her own house? Rather senseless to have been insistent about locking up?

A more logical explanation was, should Bridget have gone out, Lizzie perhaps did not want Bridget to come back early or unexpectedly, nor anyone else to pop in while the murders were being committed.

So Lizzie had decided to iron handkerchiefs in the dining room, logistically just steps away from where her father napped in the sitting room. This gave her the ultimate opportunity. Added to that, Bridget had walked upstairs, leaving Lizzie alone with her father. Motive, means and opportunity could not have been more apparent, unless Lizzie had chosen to hit the old man over the head with the hot iron itself. Because Lizzie Borden was the last person to see Andrew Borden alive. In the nineteenth century, the shame-addled minds of this all-male jury, perhaps a jury of men fully aware of the sheltered, but subservient roles of women at the time, viewed Lizzie, a Christian woman, as simply a by-product of their male-dominated society. Good or bad, there she was. So even if she'd used the iron, Lizzie would inevitably have been acquitted.

Several versions of the tale, including Lizzie's, claimed that she had actually gotten an afghan blanket, and kissed her father and practically tucked him in on the sofa.[341]

However, two contradictions followed. At 12:30 pm, Officer Harrington, who came upon the Borden house, claimed "the fire was near extinguished,"[342] when referring to the one in the kitchen. This, then, could have meant several facts were true: either the handkerchiefs would easily have been finished in ten minutes time with that force of flame (and they were not, in the end, found to have been all ironed, two were merely sprinkled and ready to have been ironed), or that at the same time, the still burning fire may have provided the suspect ample time to have burned up the original, cheaper light blue calico dress with a diamond shape on it, the one which neighbor Adelaide Churchill recalled having seen Lizzie wearing earlier in the morning. She'd also been witnessed by close friend, Dr. Bowen, wearing it, when he stated it was a "morning calico dress."[343]

The importance around which dress was the one Lizzie presented to the officers when they'd completed their search, and which one she'd actually been wearing centered on the disparity of the explanations.

The fact remained that Lizzie was likely wearing a different dress later on, on the day of the murders. Why would she have needed to change clothes at all, were she innocent? As pointed out in: Porter's *The Fall River Tragedy* her dress, which was actually, "a silk dress and dark blue evidently, a dress with a figure which 'was not at all like a diamond,' and a dress which was not cheap and would 'not' have been 'worn in ironing.'"[344]

The precise quotes gotten from Adelaide Churchill, the neighbors and direct witnesses were as follows: the dress which Lizzie had on in the morning was: "like a light blue and white ground work,…calico or cambric, with a navy blue diamond printed on it."[345]

Mr. Moody questioned Adelaide, a friend and neighbor to Lizzie, repeatedly about the dress and her statements were, "it does not look like it," and "that is not the dress I have described." She followed this last statement with, "I did not see her with it on that morning."[346]

Dr. Bowen, as pointed out, lived across the street, and was Lizzie's close friend. He also described a type of morning dress, or calico dress. This was precisely how Bridget described it as well, referring to it as "that cheap morning dress, light blue with a dark figure."[347] There followed much talk around all the dresses, in particular, the blue corduroy dress that was supposedly covered in paint. It was suggested it had been hidden away in the closet in Lizzie's room or perhaps the one at the top of the stairs where many of the other dresses were stashed.

Finally Alice Russell, Lizzie's dear friend, admitted to seeing Lizzie in the proceedings during the aftermath on that Saturday morning after the murders, burning that corduroy dress. Alice walked into the kitchen and overheard Emma say to Lizzie, "Lizzie, what are you going to do?" and Lizzie said, "I am going to burn this old thing up. It is all covered with paint."[348]

The point was, in all their searchings, the police were never able to find the purported corduroy dress ruined by paint. That had been the dress Lizzie would claim later, that she had actually burned. In the eyes of some therefore, this appeared to have been evidence tampering.

Chapter Twenty-One

S adie and Colette, with Cherry in tow, stood out front of the Borden house. Colette looked left and right as they stood there, up and down the long sidewalk of Second Street. Just across the way; mere steps in fact, stood the house of Dr. Bowen. As they drew closer to his house, according to Colette's watch, it was nearly seven a.m. A delicate pale hand pulled back white eyelet curtains from inside the house where they now waited. Someone looked out at them several times. Although they could not hear voices, there was a great deal of movement and a serious discussion going on behind the curtains in the window. In light of Dr. Bowen's recent alliances, perhaps this argument between doctor and wife would grow more volatile soon, perhaps even as Mrs. Bowen begged him not to open the door. First, this business with Lizzie and now strange women on the doorstep?

Several passersby on the sidewalk literally stopped and gawked at the two women and the emaciated girl. They stared, unabashedly, rudely and in a typically rigid Victorian manner.

Finally, a taller man with white hair opened the door. He peered at the three over a set of gold-rimmed spectacles. He looked either annoyed, or afraid. He was perhaps, a hesitant person. His movements were jerky. Colette spoke up immediately.

"This little girl needs medical care. Urgently."

It was impossible for the good doctor to conceal his disdain at the sight of the three of them. He started to close the door, but Colette shoved one black-booted foot between the opening and stopped him.

"This is not a hospital," he said evenly, eyeing the pale child. "It appears this girl has a flu of some sort. Better to take her to the hospital at the other side of town."

Uncertain of her Fall River facts, Colette could not determine whether or not the doctor was trying to get rid of them. Was there indeed a hospital across town? It didn't matter. They were going to get free medical service right here at Dr. Bowen's. He just didn't know it yet.

"Let us in," she said, stepping fully upon the threshold and gently pushing the door open with her shoulder, careful not to bump the girl as she did so. Stopping in the foyer, she caught sight of Mrs. Bowen who stood by silently. Following Dr. Bowen's allegiance to the accused Miss Lizzie Borden, perhaps this woman had lost her patience. Her decision to stay present in the room appeared to be resolute.

Dr. Bowen turned to her. "Go," he said, nodding toward the back of the house. "You must not be here now, dear," he said.

Obediently, but with clear reluctance, the older woman turned and walked away slowly toward what was, no doubt, the kitchen area and perhaps her proper place for now in Dr. Bowen's eyes.

Colette passed through the front foyer and let herself, and her small charge into the study. The room resembled Andrew Borden's sitting room to a frightening degree, except it was much more elaborately decorated. The curtains were a bright, slightly burnt orange and the generous chairs were of solid colors, decorated with tapestries. All the furniture was comprised of solid and various types of wood. The windows were thrown wide. Certainly a doctor would want all the fresh air possible in those days. The heat since the day of the murders had not relented. It was as if the sun itself absorbed the fury, the fear and the dissent which had fallen upon the town.

"I think you ladies have been misinformed," Dr. Bowen said. "In my old age, I'm not always prepared for extemporaneous visits."

Without waiting for the good doctor's permission, Colette direct-ed Sadie to a winged-back chair. Sadie's eyes were glazed with saucy disorientation, due to the effects of the laudanum. Colette settled comfortably on a silky green sofa and propped the girl closer to her. Cherry was still asleep.

Colette stroked the girl's hair. "This child needs pre-natal care. She is going to have a baby."

"Don't be absurd Madam," Dr. Bowen said. "She can't be over ten years old."

"Don't pretend you're surprised, please. Didn't you start treating Isabelle as a young girl? Were there bruises in strange places and evi-dence of someone sexually exploiting her? What about Lizzie, doctor? It's gone on for a long time, hasn't it?"

Although he sat perfectly still, now that he'd taken a seat on a nearby hard-backed chair, his vivid blue eyes shined with a determined knowledge, a knowledge that ran deeply. Yes, there was a history there. A history with the young women of the town. Not for himself, not ex-actly. Still, he had the shame of being an ally to the devil. Perhaps he had been a sinister unwitting partner to the base desires of several of the Victorian men of Fall River? Simply because he'd covered for them; for their reputations, their incomes, their social standing, he'd been an accessory to the crimes.

"She's everyone's child," Colette said firmly. "We found her out-side a bar near Taunton."

"Why were you there?"

"You know why," she said, sitting up and resting the girl's head on a velvet sofa cushion. "See to her right now. Where is your powder room?"

Dr. Bowen paced the room in a small circle, then sat in front of her. He waved his hand toward the foyer and regarded the girl as if she were a form of small wildlife. "She shouldn't be here," he said. The girl sat up suddenly, took one look at the doctor and spat on him.

Wiping his face and cleaning his glasses with his handkerchief, he turned to say something to Colette, but she turned away and left the room.

In an upstairs hall minutes later, Colette searched for the master bedroom. If she knew Dr. Bowen, he would hide something like this somewhere, anywhere that was not his office. This item was too intimate. There was certainly a lot of unprofessional, or perhaps indefinable shame attached to what he'd been doing for Lizzie over the years. Because, although some in the town had speculated about a relationship between them, which had been based solely upon their showing up to church together, and sitting side by side in the same pew, the relationship between them was not of a sexual nature. In actuality, Dr. Bowen had been her protector; which included the day of the murders, by not allowing police entry to her room. In fact, the paternal care may have gone further back, to her infancy.

Still, even a clandestine relationship of any sort caused gossip and held secrets. Because Dr. Bowen had secrets. Implacable secrets. And Andrew Borden may very well have had his faults, serious faults.

Assured that Mrs. Bowen still moved about in the downstairs, and having heard movement from the kitchen as Colette sprinted up the stairs, she searched the room quickly, thoroughly. Pulling out drawers, she found lacy handkerchiefs and cotton underthings, then moved to a large oversized wardrobe, perhaps much like the one that was also found in Lizzie's room. This one was strictly masculine, however. Colette felt assured that Mrs. Bowen dared not peek into this, her husband's wardrobe. She figured the doctor assumed such to be true.

Still, searching the wardrobe, she questioned her belief that he'd actually hidden it in the bedroom. A distinct sound of heels hitting wooden stairs sounded right outside, near the landing to the bedroom. Time was limited. In fact, perhaps Dr. Bowen had already had his wife notify the police. The periodic sound of horses' hooves outside the open window caused her to rise to her feet quickly. She tripped over her skirt stepping to the window to look. Merely a family passing by to enjoy the exceedingly bright day.

About to abandon her search, Colette grabbed a row of black morning coats and slacks, and shoved them to the right hand side of the wardrobe. Footsteps sounded closer. Then she saw it.

A small gold handle in the back of the wardrobe popped up from the shadowy rear section. A hidden compartment. Pulling the double-doors open slowly, she reached in and grabbed a black doctor's bag from the space and rolled herself to hide, squeezing under the bed.

Someone had entered the room. She could make out the bottom of a long skirt with a scalloped hemline. It swished back and forth. Then a stroll to the door and it was thrown shut. Soon she heard tears. Mrs. Bowen's tears. There came no sound of creaking springs, but instead, she paced around the room, walking to the end of the bed, back and forth. Now and then, she'd pause by the window, no doubt, looking out onto Second Street.

Colette thought about the little girl downstairs. She checked her mother's Bulova watch. Sadie, in her inebriated state, could not act as chaperone.

Finally, the older woman swept out into the hall, and closed the door behind her. Colette rolled out from the bed, hugging the doctor bag to her chest. She recognized it as the popular Gladstone bag of the 1890s. After checking the inside quickly, and discovering exactly what she expected, she crept down the main stairs and returned to the study again.

Dr. Bowen held a stethoscope to the small girl's back. The waif was still seated on the sofa but was now joined by Sadie who stroked her hair rhythmically. Recalling how vehemently the little one had fought the two of them off, it occurred to Colette now how trusting and vulnerable children were. For whatever reason, Cherry trusted Sadie.

Dr. Bowen turned to face Colette as she stepped back into the room noiselessly. His face was somber, but then his eyes widened behind his spectacles when he saw that she carried the black doctor bag.

"She is indeed, with child," he said.

"I need the name of a good doctor, a children's doctor, in Chicago."

Dr. Bowen looked startled. "Why there? Whatever for?"

"Because," she started, taking a seat in a wingback arm chair across from him. She held out the doctor bag for him to see. "Because you are going to do everything possible for this girl. It's too late for Isabelle, and obviously for Lizzie too, who took matters into her own hands."

His face was sedate. "What do Isabelle Sewell and Lizzie Borden have to do with this lower class urchin? A product of the streets? A vagrant?"

Colette stood up and walked over to the girl, leaned over her, and spoke softly. "What's your name, honey?"

The girl's mouth was set. Under angry brows, her eyes revealed a need to speak at last. "Cherry. The men at the tavern. They named me Cherry."

Colette shot Dr. Bowen a look, shook her head. "Cherry. How about you tell me your real name? Your given name?"

"I don't remember."

At this admission, even Sadie sat up and studied the girl. She touched her hair again, but Cherry pulled away, her eyes fierce.

"Is there a name you've always liked?" Colette said to the girl once she'd settled down.

She scowled, playing with the torn hem on her calico dress. Looking at the floor, she muttered, "Elizabeth."

"Elizabeth?" Colette said brightly.

Colette turned to Dr. Bowen again. "Elizabeth is going to need special care in Chicago. She will be going to the Hull House."

Dr. Bowen frowned. I don't know of such an establishment? Who are the Hull's? Why should I help you?'

"It's called the Jane Addams Hull House. Someday it will hold much meaning to a lot of people. Benny Goodman learned to play the clarinet there."

Dr. Bowen gazed at her as if she'd lost her mind. Maybe all the rumors about the strange woman at Mrs. Burns's boarding house were true.

"Benny who?"

"Forget it. Someday there will be 'jazz' and then you'll know his name." She leaned forward and opened the doctor bag to show him something.

At the same time, he grabbed for it but she yanked it back, just out of reach. When she opened it up and showed it to him, there were large stains, blackish red stains all around the lining and the insides, visible by a nearby lamp. Sadie recoiled unexpectedly at the sight. Dr. Bowen shook his head.

"It's simply my doctor's bag. An old one. It's ruined. Why should it be strange to you that a doctor's bag would be soiled with stains?"

"They're too many stains for a medical bag. The instruments wouldn't be that filthy." Colette reached inside of the bag, beneath the lining. All at once, Dr. Bowen grabbed the bag from her.

He stood up and, pointing to the door, said, "I want all of you, out of here. I've nothing to say. I refuse to defend myself."

But it was too late. The lining, very tellingly, was stained with blood. Colette had also pulled loose a large swatch of blue calico print fabric which matched the description of the dress Lizzie had worn the day of the murders. The same dress Colette had in the L.A.B. bag. Obviously, it had been transferred several times between Lizzie's bag when she threw it out the back window, and then into the doctor's bag for a temporary hiding place. Dr. Bowen had visited the suspect several times over the course of the first and second days following the murders.

Perhaps, in their haste to secrete the dress away into the doctor bag, while the police were pounding on Lizzie's bedroom door, she and Dr. Bowen had hurriedly torn the dress stuffing it into his doctor bag. Of course, no one would think to search the upstanding Dr. Bowen's bag for evidence, much less a dress. Lizzie had perhaps shoved the dress into her own wardrobe in a panic. Maybe that's why she insisted Bridget Sullivan immediately run and get Dr. Bowen. Clearly, Andrew Borden was dead when she found him.

"Lizzie knew she could trust you."

Now his eyes showed fear.

"That's why she called for you first. Even before the police. You knew the damage done over the years. You had your suspicions about Andrew Borden all along."

He closed his eyes as she spoke.

"Madam," he said. "I insist you leave, now."

Colette continued, undeterred. "I think that's why folks said you looked very nervous the day of the murders, running around town as you were. It was because you knew she was guilty. Because you had evidence in your bag. In fact, you gave the dress back very quickly. As a professional, you couldn't be implicated in any way. You may have lost your practice and your license. But what you didn't realize was that in your haste to give it back to her, the swatch of calico blue fabric, was still in the lining of your bag. Right here, see?"

She showed the fabric to him. Elizabeth had slipped again to sleep, her head resting on Sadie's lap. Her face was pale.

"So Dr. Bowen, you will arrange for a doctor's care for Elizabeth. Because this girl is in the genesis of a future where women will be facing more victimization. You'll get her help. God help her too," she added, her voice low. She leaned over and whispered to him, "I don't know how a child's body can deliver a baby."

Colette turned and nodded to Sadie, who stood up and carried Elizabeth to the kitchen.

"She needs to eat," Colette went on. "Give us money so we can feed her at the general store. I'll be expecting a note from you, delivered to Edward Sewell's house in precisely an hour's time. Tell us the name of a doctor who will be expecting us in Chicago."

Dr. Bowen's mouth was agape.

"Do you have a wagon?" she asked.

"Out in the back yard."

Colette turned and grabbed a brightly patched quilt that was draped carefully on the sofa and threw it over her shoulder. She would drape the wagon with it.

"Thanks for the quilt too, Doctor," she said.

Stunned, Dr. Bowen shuffled to a nearby roll-top desk. He pulled open a small drawer and handed her several bills of cash. Nothing more was said as the three exited via the front door. Chin held high, Colette felt impervious now to the glares and points of onlookers along the wooden sidewalk. She turned back only once, in time to see Mrs. Bowen with a handkerchief covering her mouth, watching them with narrowed eyes.

The heat of mid-morning somehow comforted her. For once she didn't mind the feel of the sun on her long sleeves. With all the vicious heat on the day of the murders, this swelter felt placid somehow. As the three marched along, Colette took a deep breath, filling up with the oxygen of 1892, feeling free for the first time since her arrival in the era. As she pulled Elizabeth along in the small wagon, she thought to herself that this was the most free she'd felt as a woman, perhaps in years. In her way, she was taking back the streets, negating, if only slightly, some of the social injustices during the dire repression once termed the "gay" nineties. Strolling down the middle of Second Street, with a pregnant child prostitute in tow, felt appropriate. It sent a bit of a message. Saving at least one girl from the streets would impact one life, and contribute to the Jane Addams Hull House initiative.

At one point, Sadie stopped and adjusted the clean, well-made quilt under Elizabeth and adjusted a pillow she'd also taken from the winged back chair in Dr. Bowen's study. As they neared a busy intersection, perhaps the busiest in town, Colette noticed two men standing on the corner.

"Have either of you seen Edward Sewell this morning?" she said.

One of the men, smoking a large cigar said nothing, and turned away from her. Clearly insulted that she'd stopped to address him in public, he stood with his back to them, tapping one shiny leather shoe. The other man, although also taken aback, simply shook his head.

"Never mind," Colette announced. "We'll find him."

With that, the two women and the wagon rolled onward. Colette stared straight ahead, trying to recall which house it was. It was located right down the street from the Borden house. Like some horror movie, she envisioned seeing Isabelle with cuts, and wallpaper stuck to her hands and clothes, emerging from the place. Now, with the exteriors of the homes so pristine and tidy, it was hard to imagine someone had clawed her way out of captivity on this very block.

The three made their way down the sidewalk, disregarding several local boys who jeered. One threw stones at the wagon. All along the way, people ceased conversation and women, all the virtuous women of Fall River, simply glared. There was something complicit in their churlish gapes, something all together entitled. One woman whispered to another, hand shielding her chin, and positioned her young daughter behind her, out of harm's way.

Sadie blazed past them with joyful disregard. It was perhaps a posture she'd practiced for years. Her blue skirt touched the ground in certain places, and not in others, revealing a dilapidated and worn hemline. Sadie's carriage was irreverent. Shoulders pulled back, she walked with a slight sway of her hips.

Elizabeth, sat up straight in the wagon suddenly. Following her brief cat nap, she grabbed the sides of it and searched all around her, disoriented. Colette stopped and reminded her where they were, touching her shoulder. Elizabeth's eyes were wide, mesmerized by the surroundings of Fall River. Blue specks in her irises soaked in everything. Even the sky burned a mystical cobalt now.

It occurred to Colette that Elizabeth, for a ten year old child, neither squirmed nor begged for anything. She possessed a somber acquiescence, and wore a too-worldly look upon her face. Elizabeth had decided that these two women, strange as they were, perhaps wanted to help her. What a motley group they were. Colette had changed into a purple fitted suit she'd pulled out of the closet back at Mrs. Burns's boarding house on the first night she'd arrived. She did this, in spite of the fact that Mrs. Burns insisted the outfit was left behind by some showgirl who'd come through town trying to spread a love of vaudeville. Unlike the routine navy and black skirts and dresses worn by many of the Fall River ladies, this raging purple suit was not easily ignored. This was the way she wanted it. Especially now.

Her mind went back to that first day at Mrs. Burns's boarding house. Was it relevant that Mrs. Burns's place was so similar to Marilyn's farmhouse back in Illinois? It was as if her position in life in the twenty-first century was replicated as a spinster in the nineteenth century. They were sister spirits in a way, she thought. Somehow the door from the bungalow traveled the conduit between the two houses. That fabulous door, Colette thought, smiling. It had stained glass, was at least four inches thick and flew with the agility of angels. The lavender fairy dust left by the slide bracelet had become a serene indicator of travel about to happen. They worked together these two; the Prairie door and the Victorian slide bracelet she'd been wearing now for over a month.

To think the first time she'd awakened in the bed at the farmhouse in Valley Stream, the door had rested on top of her? In a sense, this was how she'd verified her purposes in time traveling; to witness some of the women of Fall River 1892, whose woes were no different than many women back in 2011. It was simply a different form of control in 2011; lower wages, a back seat in politics and acting as hostess, maid, wife, mother and executive concurrently. All this responsibility and inequality under the guise of "freedom;" as in, freedom to work, freedom to be sexual, freedom to travel and socialize, except with the caveat that such freedoms occurred within reason. Reasonable constraints, devised by society. To work, but for less pay; to be sexual... unless a woman enjoyed it too much which would result in the label of "whore" or "tramp," and to travel and socialize; certainly as long as a woman didn't go where she wasn't wanted; certain clubs or venues, and as long as she remembered her secondary place and figuratively walked a few paces behind the man.

Colette acknowledged the autocracy of the past, of the present, and the weight of that door. Perhaps that had been the initial purpose of the prosaic slides on the bracelet, and the splintery insistence of the Prairie door. Such ethereal nonsense, such odd phenomena like the unexplained, like time travel, couldn't be divinely inspired, most people would think. They'd be wrong.

The house of Edward Sewell loomed before them. Several children positioned themselves behind fences, and darted in and out of trees, bellowing insults. This was fine with her. Colette had paid a lad of around thirteen to deliver several key pages from the journal of his late daughter, Isabelle. They'd been written in her handwriting of course, and clearly spelled out Edward's drunken rages, one in which she and her brother witnessed him throwing their mother across the room. In fact, Isabelle's few journals, which had been stashed in the L.A.B. travel bag told many stories. Also evident in the bag were the blood stains from the dress and the hatchet handle which Lizzie had broken off in the basement after the murders. Colette had actually witnessed her placing the hatchet in the metal vice through the window. Although the bag only stayed in the asylum briefly, it had horrified Lizzie to find it back on her doorstep. That explained why she'd tried several solvents to clean it before giving up and delivering it back to the asylum.

Several regal and well-kept horse and buggies waited out front of the Sewell house. Some women, and a large group of children had been following the three vagabonds. Colette leaned over to the wagon and checked on Elizabeth. Still wrapped in the shawl, her face had somehow become cherubic, and had a less severe expression than when they'd first encountered her. Colette wiped away thin strands of hair from the girl's forehead. Elizabeth's pupils were pinpoints and her blue speckled irises were bright. Chaos and humiliation had somehow put the girl in a more relaxed state than before. Perhaps for the first time she was being noticed and maybe believed her life on the street would soon end. Colette had a few things to say to Edward and it appeared they'd have an audience. Madeline and Isabelle may have been silenced, but keeping opinions to herself was certainly not Colette's style.

The dark mansion, with excessive gold trim and several misplaced gargoyles pulsated with something sinister, and garish. It stood like some parody of the financial excesses of Victorian America. The three paused on the sidewalk out front of the place. Colette scanned the street, fighting the charm of the towering trees and velvety down of the sun-green lawns. Two women lounged in Adirondack chairs in the neighboring yard, holding white parasols and enjoying a pitcher of lemonade. Apparently alarmed by the three on the doorstep, one woman hid behind an ornate Japanese fan draped in her hand.

Colette shook her head and thought the expressions on these women's faces were misplaced. Colette and her savvy band of misfits were a threat to these people? They represented a threat to the status quo of life in 1892. Nothing terrified the mainstream more than dissenters knocking on the front door of all good society. The only way a woman attained property or social standing, depended upon whom they married. Isabelle's mother, Madeline realized too late that the price for financial security and home was too high a price to pay. It meant the antithesis of her spirit; no life of theater and dance or self-expression, much less political views or financial opinions. Sadie had mentioned to Colette, that there had been rumors about Madeline's bawdy nights out on the town. She too liked to drink, like Edward. True or not, any tales would have been used as incendiary devices against her vibrant spirit. Edward's excessive imbibing in alcohol contributed to his abusive control of Madeline and Isabelle. But his alcoholic drinking would be acceptable, simply because he could afford it and he was an important man. If Madeline's abuse of alcohol got the better of her, she lost all power and credibility, and her drinking simply defined her as tarnished goods, perhaps requiring the firm hand of the patriarch. Some in town may have affirmed Edward's difficult situation with a house full of fallen and unruly women. Perfect Pines Insane Asylum offered him a perfect solution to his woman problem. Lock them up. Yet Edward went a step further. He silenced them all together. Sadie had attempted to wean Madeline off hard drinks like whiskey, with alternating doses of Laudanum before her disappearance. That solution was no different than stealing from Peter to pay Paul; trading one addiction for another. Many were the tales from Sadie about sitting up with Madeline, while Isabelle looked on, trying to stop the fits and tremors resulting from her seeking solace in pills, combined with absinthe, or opiates provided by her doctor to help with the beatings from Edward.

As they approached the front stairs, the strains of violins and cellos lifted in the heated sedentary summer air. The front door was thrown wide, in expectation of exclusive guests. Sadie and Colette trudged to the bottom of the stairs, and paused. The creaking sounds of the wagon wheels ceased.

For the first time, Elizabeth made a move. She leapt from the wagon, and without inquiring, raced up the stairs. A startled valet, named Jeeves in all likelihood, reached out to stop her but she wriggled beneath his starched glove.

The two women passed through the front door right behind her, whipped past the parlor and dining room and headed toward the sounds of voices now mixed with the music. Sadie took a moment to pause in front of a hall mirror, and touched up her hair with one pale hand, which was in itself comical, when considering her torn dress and muddied hem. After traipsing through what seemed like endless rooms, they reached the back of the house where Colette had hidden in Edward's office on her last trip to the place.

Men talked. There existed a milieu of cigar smoke, witty comments and visuals of nodding heads, bobbing all around.

Colette turned and put her forefinger to her lips to quiet Sadie and Elizabeth.

"But we passed a food table," Sadie whispered.

"What?"

"At the front of the house. In the parlor. There are hors d'oeuvres and fancy cakes laid out on the table. I'll take Elizabeth and find a laundry bag in the kitchen or something."

"Load it up with food," Colette said.

Sadie nodded. Her eyes were wide. Colette had a feeling they'd need their strength on this night.

Sadie and Elizabeth turned back and crept down the hallway. Elizabeth paused, knelt down, and ran her small hand over the plush burgundy carpet runner which traveled along the wooden floor. Then, standing, she traced her hand along the ornate wallpaper, and the massive wooden frames of the paintings which lined the walls.

Colette turned and walked in the other direction, up the hallway to the sound of men talking.

Colette regarded Edward Sewell, once referred to as the devil, by William. In truth however, William merely paraded around as a sympathetic champion for women. Colette had known a few such men in her life. They hid dark motivations under the guise of being enlightened about the real issues women faced. William was simply another version of Edward. William had adopted his father's ideas in spite of himself. It may have been the society of men, or simply wanting to be as powerful as his father. Perhaps William's need for approval had usurped his instincts for what was right.

Colette managed to position herself right around the corner from the man himself. Edward puffed away on an elaborate pipe. Two other men, about Edward's age, and one who appeared to be younger even than William, looked enamored with whatever it was Edward was saying. Edward prattled on, while the other three stood still, rapt, and responding to his every word with the enthusiastic nods of neophytes.

"As I informed my wife, my second wife, who ran away with some Sousa band member, I said, – 'if you women are victims, it's because you have caused your own undoing.' Madeline made poor choices," he said, puffing his pipe between words. He pointed with the pipe as he continued. "I gave her everything. I gave her home, prosperity and prestige. Can you believe she would ask for her own sum of money? Money to use for what? For herself? What could she possibly need it for?

The other men burst into unbridled laughter that fit nicely between the leather- bound books and the burgundy velvet-finished sofas. Colette stood with her back to the office wall and closed her eyes.

An older man approached, holding his lapels with large, meat-hook hands. He joined the conversation. "Well, exactly my man. Look where it got her. Women are histrionics. Hysteria is a real condition. I've been sending my wife to the doctor for treatments. Otherwise, women attach themselves to poets and musicians and believe they can handle themselves."

Nods all around. Edward went on.

"Why it could be that new massage treatment. You know, that absurd treatment by doctors to relieve hysteria? They manipulate the woman's private areas? We should lock the women away. Otherwise they run off with some trombone player! That's the kind of women which result from too much freedom. Women don't know what to do with their own unrestricted time."

The shortest and youngest of the three, a bit of a rodent-faced little man, tapped his foot and slurped his snifter of sherry quickly, then grabbed the bottle and poured another full glass.

"It's a proven fact," he said, "that most women are neurotics. This Doctor Freud is really coming up with some incredible findings."

The older man released his lapels and roared with repellent laughter. "I often think I need to have my wife diagnosed as the schizophrenic she is." He looked left and right conspiratorially, "I tell her she's imagining occurrences and having visions. She must be hallucinating. Truth is, I need to get her committed because she's a little too smart about my lady friend I see on Hickens Street. Each of you understands, yes?"

Several lavishly dressed women strolled into the study, keeping their voices low and avoiding eye contact with the men. They were younger, unmarried and unaccompanied. Edward Sewell let out a slow whistle, then rolled his eyes when one of the women gave him a knowing look and smiled. They certainly knew one another.

"Sure," he said. "They start out like that. Then they get to believing they 'deserve' better. More of their wretched talk. I'm afraid they deserve what they get. That flirtatious one, over at Perfect Pines Asylum, she'll be passed around and shunned by all good society."

Another spoke up suddenly, "say, did you hear about the expansion of the railway in Maxsonville, Florida?"

Colette felt her heart pressing against her chest, vehemently, angrily. She felt her face burn red. She knew conversations would continue around real estate, railway expansion and big business, while concurrently reinforcing the necessity of keeping women in their homes as domestic creatures pushing feather dusters, and monitoring nannies, diapers and quieting tantrums, for as long as possible.

Edward thrust his chest out, checking a pocket watch in his palm which he'd pulled from his vest. "Well men, you both know the strains I've had in my marriage. Madeline was unfit as a mother. Isabelle never respected that mental invalid as much as she did me."

The shortest of the men agreed. "I tell my wife, if she has long lonely nights because I have chosen to punish her, and locked her in her room, it is simply due to her disobedience in the matter. She lives with it. Why one time, while I was talking with a very important, albeit attractive female headmistress of the local school, she insisted on knowing where I had been that morning? I came right out and told her, I said, "my dear. That is none of your God damn business. To hell with that," I said.

The elder of the men, chortled. "The feminine mind is much more suited to more genial and manageable pursuits, like the garden club, dressmaking classes and systematic tasks." As Edward poured himself another drink, dripping onto the sideboard where he kept the bottles, Colette shuddered. She recalled in stark relief, the night she'd hidden in the wardrobe. Just the thought of a quick bit of liquid courage for what she was about to do.

"I have an ex-wife," Edward said. "My first wife before Madeline. As I said, she was loyal. She would do anything for me. I gave her a small allowance. Unfortunately, she bore me no children. She's a spinster. It's her lot. And she welcomes it whole-heartedly. She enjoys being busy, and still assists me with tending to my business affairs like light bookkeeping and office work. She would have no life without me."

Colette covered her mouth to keep from laughing. By now, Sadie and Elizabeth had found her and ducked next to her by the wall. The youngest man gave a start when he spotted them. Several people in the next room turned. Now, the somewhat haggard threesome commanded the center of the room.

"You may or may not remember this travel bag," Colette said firmly, stepping up to Edward and displaying the purplish, stained L.A.B. travel bag from the potato sack she'd tied to her waist.

Instinctively, Edward held up his free arm, as if to block anyone from stepping nearer to the women. Colette did not relent. Taking another step toward him, she opened the travel bag and displayed it for everyone in the room to see. Contained inside the bag were several leather journals. They were covered in bloodstains. She'd hidden the hatchet handle and the blue dress in another bag. The bloodstains were simply from those items but regardless, the sight was enough to embarrass him. Several women let out nervous utterances. One woman gasped, holding kerchief to her nose. An undercurrent of conversation ensued.

Edward turned back to the room where everyone held their drinks stiffly, and said, "gentlemen and ladies, you must understand," he went on, "these women are crazy. Literally. They've escaped from Perfect Pines. I got a call this very day to be on the lookout for them."

The mahogany table shook as he slammed his drink down.

"Perhaps we should stay my good man," said the young man from the group. His hair was perfectly slicked with Brilliantine and his dark eyes were earnest.

"No," he blurted, and then stopped. "This is a private fundraising brunch. I can handle foolish women

Edward slammed the door behind him, and locked it. After a moment, he turned with a grave expression to face the three. His mouth tight, he turned and picked up a decanter, splashing dark liquor into his glass. Standing with his back to them, he took a quick swig, then poured some more. Finally, he wheeled around slowly. His eyes were menacing and black, with furrowed brows.

Colette, by now, had settled into a cushy burgundy wingback chair.

"She'd had enough," she said.

Edward narrowed his eyes at her. No woman had ever taken a seat in his study. Sadie and Elizabeth likewise, had sprawled out on a camel-back sofa.

"Who'd had enough?" he demanded, his voice low and even. "Who do you think you are? This is a very important party with very important people. And none of you were invited."

"Who? Lizzie," she said. "She'd had enough. She murdered her parents, you know."

"So what. She's crazy. An ungrateful young woman."

"You know, Isabelle knew the same pain. So I am not the only one who knows about what you exacted upon your daughter for so many years. Lizzie likely knew as well. She knew Isabelle's pain was the same as her own. Lizzie took action. Very unfortunate action. But I think she was desperate."

"I don't care about Lizzie Borden."

"But you see, Isabelle took action too. Unlike Lizzie, she decided to write it all down instead. Everything. Inside her very own, personalized with her name in gold lettering inside, journals. She wrote everything she knew about Andrew Borden, and everything you'd done to her, and to her mother Madeline. Her record is as good as science.

He laughed, a short scoff. "Who are you to talk to me of science? What would you know? I threw that bag of hers into the fire with her."

Colette placed the travel bag at her feet and sat back, clasping her hands together on her lap. "Sorry but this is Lizzie's bag. Identical to Isabelle's, but alas," she turned the bag, "the initials are L.A.B. Lizzie was a dear friend to Isabelle. She kept a good many of Isabelle's journals. I have them here in this bag. Lizzie feared something would happen to Isabelle so she insisted on keeping some for her."

Seated there, Colette had an unnerving calm about her. Sadie and Elizabeth meanwhile, nibbled on the food from a laundry bag, where they'd stashed the buffet food intended for the gilded guests. Edward eyed them with a noxious frown.

"Here's what you need to know," Colette went on. "Sexual abuse by anyone, stranger or parent, robs the victim of any sense of self, and any chance for a sexuality of their own. It also hijacks all self-esteem, and the ability to hold negative thoughts at bay. So in a way, perhaps for a lifetime, if they receive no help or counseling, the spirit of the person dies. By the way, victims include women, men and children."

"Women? Do you know how much we provide for them?"

Reaching into the bag, Colette withdrew the first journal she came to. "For instance," she said, first showing him Isabelle's name and her distinctive handwriting inside, "and remember, this is one of numerous journals Lizzie and I have in our safekeeping." She started to read, 'Last night father insisted upon seeing me up to my room after the party. These events are so difficult because they're all important people in the government and education and they control the money. Little do they know what my father does once we reach my bedroom. He turns off the lights and...." She stopped and looked up.

Leaning on the mahogany counter, he supported himself with one hand and tried to control his breathing. His barrel chest heaved under the Jacket and fussy tie. He appeared somewhat foolish considering his excessive sweating.

"I'd like to add," Colette said evenly, "that she confided also in Dr. Bowen as well as Mrs. Wright at the Taunton Jail. So there are several, credible witnesses who, upon request, will collaborate these words."

He took a quick breath and finished off his drink once again. He eyed Sadie, scrutinizing her scrawny frame and sagging dress, then looked at Elizabeth, whose eyes, ringed with exhaustion, narrowed as she stared him down.

"You're unstable," he said, turning back to Colette. "Isabelle died in a tragic fire in Illinois. It has been investigated and the case is closed. I held a private service for her. Of course, she should not have been visiting the dubious friends who lured her out there to Chicago. Show people, I'm sure. Actors and those damn brass band players. He took a swig of his fresh drink. "They were probably doing drugs like opium and morphine. As far as Lizzie?" he waved his hands wildly. "She's a filthy murderer. Of her own parents. How selfish was she to kill those who loved her most?"

"Loved her most?" Colette repeated, shaking her head.

She had him. Up until now, Edward had successfully minimized the lives of Madeline and Isabelle, simply by attaching labels to them;

"whore," "unfaithful wife," Madeline? She was a canary. A canary in a coal chute that wouldn't be discovered for over 100 years.

The door which led to the festivities in the next room flew open all at once. Several women wearing elaborate hats with feathers and carrying lacy purses spilled into the room. Perhaps pumped up with the false security of several glasses of Vermouth cocktails, they gave the two bedraggled women and unsightly child a cursory glance, then went on with uproarious laughter over some private joke. In fact, the addition of the lower class dimension simply added to their merriment, like entertainment.

Pipe smoke from Edward's Meerschaum traveled up to the ceiling. With each puff he likened himself more and more to the proverbial caricature of a Victorian fool. Were the circumstances less dire, Colette would have found herself somewhat amused at the sight. The eyes that peered at her over the top of the pipe were nothing less than evil.

Colette had seen this malevolence before. Back in her century, while a practicing drunk, she'd fallen prey to the worst of them. And in her sober years since, until she'd smartened up, she'd spent years untangling herself from a web of one narcissist after another; a man as controller, a man as fixer and even a man as victim. Why had she always attracted narcissists? It hit her how it was not only through genetics that attitudes and biases could be passed on from generation to generation, but it was also learned behavior. The misogyny of certain men. The shame of victims. In the Victorian era, beliefs were giftwrapped in pretty words like "women are delicate and need protecting," they're vulnerable and incapable of thinking in certain ways. Women as costly possessions. No doubt, in the image of what man wanted women to be. Made in the image of man? Hardly. These women were built to work like horses in the 1890s, to tackle days of laundry, deal with temperamental giant stoves, make their own soaps and shampoos, and cook and appear refreshed and cool in layers of binding clothing.

"Isabelle ran away from you," she said to Edward, her voice low.

The door to the adjoining room had opened on its own now. Scents of brandy, perfume and rolls of languid laughter carried through. There was the suggestion of cruel judgment, as if it was carried upon the scents themselves. Edward now held a bottle of whiskey up in his hand, no longer steady on his feet. It was as if he didn't notice that the door had been thrown wide as he continued to mumble.

"She was a whore, just like her mother."

"What's wrong with that?"

It came from a tiny place, but the voice was fierce. All eyes turned. Elizabeth leaned against the wall with her arms crossed over her undeveloped chest. Her high button boots and well-worn ruffled dress made her look like a miniature adult somehow, like a woman shrunk to doll-size.

"You talking to me you little wretch?" Edward demanded. He exhaled his pipe, and tried to squint as if mentally willing her out of sight, anywhere from here, away from his home. Perhaps in efforts to inflate his ego, he leaned back on a shelf full of tropies and a wall devoted to mounted animal heads of foxes and bobcats.

Elizabeth smiled, her face angelic, but with the knowing grin of a swindler.

"I think," she said, tapping the toe of her small boot, and studying it casually, "we could add to the journal pages of your daughter, the fact that you tried to pay me for my services not too long ago on a trip to Taunton."

With that, Edward lunged across the room and reached out to throttle the girl until a chorus of voices rose from behind him. The door was still open and he could clearly be seen by not only the bawdy drinkers, but by the local minister and several of the upstanding women on the library board. White gloves were flying and waving in a blur until the valet closed the door briskly, shutting everyone out.

Still, the scent of perfume lingered in Edward's study, where the two women and child prostitute waited.

Colette sauntered to Edward's desk and picked up a small pad of tan paper, as well as a fountain pen. She handed both to Edward, and twisted the cap off the pen.

"Write this address down." She also withdrew a pile of papers. "It is where most of your money will be going from now on. The name is Jane Addams, Hull House, Chicago, Illinois. Sign this document. It states that you leave everything, including this house, as a halfway house for women and runaway children. And you," she said, turning to the valet, "will attest and witness to it."

Edward didn't move.

"Sign it," she said.

For the first time, his eyes narrowed. He glared at each of them, one at a time, his eyes red-ringed with disgust.

"I will not."

Sadie and Colette stood inches from him.

"Sign it," Colette repeated. Then Elizabeth stepped forward.

He signed it with alcohol-fueled vigor; bent over, and sloppy. Straightening up, his eyes blazed as he raised his hand and slapped Sadie with enough force to send her across the room. Her angular thin body knocked against a far wall brimming with shelves of leather-bound books. Colette raced to her, lifting one of her limp arms and feeling for her pulse. She'd hit her head hard. Her arm was bent at an unnatural angle. Somehow she smiled, then she just laid still, all long limbs and odd angles, looking like a destroyed marionette.

"I'm okay," she said. "Let's get out of here."

Grabbing the paperwork off the massive desk, Edward started to rip the documents apart until a sharp shot rang out and a bright red stain flowered from Edward's chest, his white tuxedo shirt instantly saturated.

Catching her breath, Colette searched frantically for Elizabeth, turning around several times, her eyes panicked. There she saw the child wielding a small silver pistol. Without hesitation, Elizabeth strode over to Edward, who had sunk down the wall to the hardwood floor and expensive Oriental rug, and was clutching his chest. With blissful rancor, she picked up the documents he'd dropped, blood-stains and all.

"Still good," she said, in her fierce small voice, "and we got the bastard's signature."

Colette checked her slides. A heavy bit of lavender dusting particles could be seen on her wrist under the slide bracelet.

"I need to get back to Mrs. Burns's boarding house right away," she said.

The three females, in a bit of trouble, abandoned a porch full of eloquently dressed women, and the telltale whistles of the forthcoming policeman filled the air. They descended the sturdy front stairs, the same stairs where Colette had first seen Isabelle trying to escape her fate. The last 1892 saw of Colette was her scurrying along, with Sadie trotting beside her and Elizabeth pulling the wagon, now brimming with buffet food.

Epilogue

E dward Sewell did not die when Elizabeth shot him. Although there were witnesses, he would not name his shooter. Sadie was recognized and returned to Perfect Pines Insane Asylum when she was discovered in what had been the room of Colette Browning at Mrs. Burns's Boarding house. Afraid Sadie Hawthorne would reveal what she knew about Edward Sewell and his involvement with Elizabeth, when she was going by the name "Cherry" and a prostitute, Edward flew in a German doctor and arranged for an experimental lobotomy to help ease Sadie's upset with her confused memories. Her spirit extinguished, Sadie died of pneumonia in her room at the asylum in 1895, but was not discovered until a week later.

Through the generous donations of an unnamed patron, train transportation was provided, with a chaperone, for Elizabeth. En route to Chicago's Hull House, she miscarried her baby. However, once arrived at Hull House, she acquired the last name of Hanrahan when a kindly couple adopted her after a visit with Jane Addams. Elizabeth grew up to study painting privately, received a university degree and became one of the first female instructors at the Art Institute of Chicago in 1910.

Perhaps the most significant event for Colette, aside from time travel to the year 1892, came when a tall, tanned and grey-haired gentleman of about age sixty-five years entered a Starbucks in 2012 Valley Stream. His name was Jake Grainger. Finding Colette there, he said a former colleague , one Steven Harmon at DePaul University, had mentioned she'd helped identify the meager remains of two women found in a coal chute in 2011. This particular coal chute, and the extension to the coal chute, had been buried to the side of a 1920s bungalow about twenty feet from the property line, buried deeply within the recesses of a much older and unknown house. Jake shared with her the story of his grandfather, a traveling John Sousa band musician, who had supposedly left a message of hobo hieroglyphs on the stairs of the bungalow. Shocked and elated, Colette displayed the symbols contained in a picture on her iphone. The tic tac toe indicated, Jake said, to "hold your tongue." The ball shape, Jake described as probably indicating there had been police involvement. Jake explained how his grandfather, Darren Haben, had loved a young woman named Isabelle who had been identified with Colette's help. Darren had a friend, a hobo who had lost everything in the crash of 1929, and the two of them had written the message on the stairs. Darren purposely built the bungalow there in 1928, knowing Isabelle had died nearby. He'd seen the fire. Yet over the years, no records existed of a Carpenter Gothic House. Jake said his grandfather had lost some trumpet music and a black drawstring bag. They were never found. Colette smiled. The bag contained an engagement ring. Of course, she could not tell him she had them. In the closet of her rented room she'd grown to love. She'd stashed the L.A.B. travel bag and the definitive evidence of Lizzie's guilt which included a blood-stained hatchet handle, and the actual blue calico dress, also covered in blood stains. Lizzie's dress.

As they parted, Jake mentioned that his grandfather Darren had supposedly placed a leather copy of an obscure book by a police reporter for the *Fall River Globe* in a shoebox of sorts. He'd said it was hidden by the same stairs with the hieroglyphs, behind a loose brick. It was rare too, he said, because the mythology existed that Lizzie had tried to buy out all the copies when it was first published in 1893.

Lizzie Borden was acquitted. She would commit no further murders. Despite being treated as a pariah, she remained in Fall River until her death at the age of sixty-six in 1927. She did shoplift again, as she'd done years before. Ironically Colette had read that shoplifting was also sometimes a way for victims of abuse to act out. She and Emma had a falling out, Emma moved away and they went for over twenty years without speaking. Lizzie spent a majority of her time with Nance O'Neil, a famous actress of the day, and other theater friends.

A photo of Lizzie in her fifties showed a plump and serene Lizzie with a favorite dog on her lap. In this photo she was seated on the porch of her graceful home, Maplecroft, she'd purchased after the trial, located on the Hill, the nice side of Fall River she had always aspired to live.

Although Lizzie had attempted to buy and destroy most copies of Porter's *The Fall River Tragedy,* Darren Haben, Sousa band musician, wanted to make sure that the reality of Lizzie's determination to free herself from the shackles of her life, would somehow connect the East coast with Valley Stream, and perhaps hope that the bodies of Isabelle and her mother would one day be discovered. After all, she and Isabelle and been friends. So Darren had slipped the book into the green shoebox, and it had survived.

Lizzie's choice to remain in Fall River may have portrayed a woman who wanted nothing more than to be a respected and valued woman in her hometown. This woman had less interest in international wealth or lavish vacations abroad, and more desire and determination to prove her own worth. Murder had not been the answer to her demise. However, in 1892, what other resources were available to her? To seek help may have brought shame upon the family, and unwarranted shame upon herself. The closest ally she may have had was Dr. Seabury Bowen. Because beneath the clear-skinned façade, there were hidden the parasites of abuse which affected how everything in her life appeared, a life without clarity, which may have been for Lizzie, like looking through muddied gauze.

One week following her meeting with Jake, Colette had another significant encounter. At a homecoming weekend at the small university where Colette's daughter, Olivia, and Louise's son, both attended, the two women somehow ended up seated side by side at the school football game. After a win for the home team, the two women continued their conversation over a couple of drinks at the local hamburger joint. It was then, for whatever reason, that Louise shared with Colette how her childhood had been marred by sexual abuse at the hands of an uncle.

Later, in the parking lot, when Louise's husband pulled up in a silver Lexus, with Talia in the back seat, Colette was taken aback when Louise turned and gave her a hug. In a way, she felt empowered, simply because Louise had smiled.

ENDNOTES

1   Axelrod-Contrada, Joan, *The Lizzie Borden "Axe-Murder" Trial,* (Berkeley Heights, NJ: Enslow Publishers, Inc) 14.

2   Porter, Edwin H. Porter, *The Fall River Tragedy: A History of the Borden Murders,* (Fall River, MA: King Philip Publishing Company, (originally published Fall River, MA 1893). 214.

3   Porter 25.

4   Porter 15.

5   Porter 110.

6   Porter 111.

7   Porter 26.

8   Porter 28.

9   Porter 29.

10   Porter 31.

11   Porter 35.

12   Porter 103.

13   Porter 38.

14   Porter 44.

15   Porter 104.

16 Porter 104.

17 Porter 28.

18 Porter 34.

19 Porter 77.

20 Porter 80.

21 Porter 81.

22 Porter 89.

23 Porter 132.

24 Porter 37.

25 Porter 90.

26 Porter 92.

27 Marcia R. Carlisle, "What Made Lizzie Borden Kill?" *American Heritage* July/August 1992, vol. 43, Issue 4. P. 130.

28 Carlisle 131.

29 Edwin H. Porter, *The Fall River Tragedy: A History of the Borden Murders,* (Fall River, MA: King Philip Publishing Company, (originally published Fall River, MA 1893) 101.

30 Porter 104.

31   Porter 105.

32   Porter 108.

33   Porter 105.

34   Porter 108.

35   Porter 110.

36   Porter 111.

37   Porter 114.

38   Porter 118.

39   Porter 119.

40   Porter 119.

41   Porter 120.

42   Porter 126.

43   Porter 126.

44   Porter 127.

45   Porter 24.

46   Marcia R. Carlisle, "What Made Lizzie Borden Kill?" *American Heritage* July/August 1992, vol. 43, Issue 4. P. 131.

47   Carlisle 131.

48   Edwin H. Porter, *The Fall River Tragedy: A History of the Borden Murders,* (Fall River, MA: King Philip Publishing Company, (originally published Fall River, MA 1893). .

49   Porter 129.

50   Porter 129.

51   Porter129.

52   Porter 171.

53   Porter 110.

54   Porter 113.

55   Porter 130.

56   Marcia R. Carlisle, "What Made Lizzie Borden Kill?" *American Heritage* July/August 1992, vol. 43, Issue 4. P. 132.

57   Edwin H. Porter, *The Fall River Tragedy: A History of the Borden Murders,* (Fall River, MA: King Philip Publishing Company, (originally published Fall River, MA 1893). 130.

58   Porter 130.

59   Porter 110.

60   Porter 136.

61   Porter 137.

62   Porter 138.

63   Porter 142.

64   Porter 175.

65   Porter 144.

66   Porter 151.

67   Stefani Koorey, *The Witness Statements for the Lizzie Borden Murder Case*, 4 August – 6 October, 1892, <http://created in 2001//for LizzieAndrewBorden.com>.

68   Koorey

69   Edwin H. Porter, *The Fall River Tragedy: A History of the Borden Murders,* (Fall River, MA: King Philip Publishing Company, (originally published Fall River, MA 1893). 161.

70   Porter 162.

71   Porter 166.

72   Marcia R. Carlisle, "What Made Lizzie Borden Kill?" *American Heritage* July/August 1992, vol. 43, Issue 4. P. 132.

73   Michael Martins and Dennis A. Binette, *Parallel Lives, A Social History of Lizzie A. Borden & Her Fall River,*(Fall River Historical Society/Fall River, MA, 2010) p. 200.

74   Marcia R. Carlisle, "What Made Lizzie Borden Kill?" *American Heritage* July/August 1992, vol. 43, Issue 4. P. 133.

75   Edwin H. Porter, *The Fall River Tragedy: A History of the Borden Murders,* (Fall River, MA: King Philip Publishing Company, (originally published Fall River, MA 1893). 184.

76   Porter 103.

77   Porter 104.

78   Porter 170.

79   Porter 171.

80   Porter 172.

81   Porter 104.

82   Porter 230.

83   Porter 255.

84   Porter 192.

85   Porter 191.

86   Porter 105.

87   Porter 108.

88   Porter 121.

89   Porter 122.

90   Porter 211.

91   Porter 44.

92   Porter 185.

93   Porter 185.

94   Porter 181.

95   Porter 175.

96   Porter 175.

97   Porter 187.

98   Porter 177.

99   Porter 178.

100   Porter 169, 224.

101   Porter 259.

102   Porter 49.

103   Porter 122.

104   Porter 244.

105   Porter 103.

106   Porter 104.

107   Porter 184.

108   Porter 184.

109   Porter 184.

110   Michael Martins and Dennis A. Binette, *Parallel Lives, A Social History of Lizzie A. Borden & Her Fall River,*(Fall River Historical Society/Fall River, MA, 2010) 473.

111   Marcia R. Carlisle, "What Made Lizzie Borden Kill?" *American Heritage* July/August 1992, vol. 43, Issue 4. P. 132.

112   Carlisle 6.

113   Edwin H. Porter, *The Fall River Tragedy: A History of the Borden Murders,* (Fall River, MA: King Philip Publishing Company, (originally published Fall River, MA 1893) 11.

114   Porter 9.

115   Porter 10.

116   Porter 10.

117   Porter Preface

118   Porter 142.

119   Porter 162.

120 Porter 238.

121 Porter 186.

122 Porter 187.

123 Porter 187.

124 Porter 193.

125 Porter 187.

126 Porter 24.

127 Porter 187.

128 Porter 190.

129 Porter 190.

130 Porter 190.

131 Porter 190.

132 Porter 190.

133 Michael Martins and Dennis A. Binette, *Parallel Lives, A Social History of Lizzie A. Borden & Her Fall River*,(Fall River Historical Society/Fall River, MA, 2010) 413.

134 Edwin H. Porter, *The Fall River Tragedy: A History of the Borden Murders*, (Fall River, MA: King Philip Publishing Company, (originally published Fall River, MA 1893) 191.

135   Porter 191.

136   Porter 191.

137   Porter 193.

138   Porter 193.

139   Porter 193.

140   Porter 193.

141   Porter 193.

142   Porter 193.

143   Porter 194.

144   Porter 194.

145   Porter 38.

146   Porter 36.

147   "Hatchet Found on Roof of Crowe Barn" *Fall River Evening News*, Thursday, June 15, 1893.

148   "Hatchet Found on Roof of Crowe Barn" *Fall River Evening News*, Thursday, June 15, 1893.

149   Edwin H. Porter, *The Fall River Tragedy: A History of the Borden Murders*, (Fall River, MA: King Philip Publishing Company, (originally published Fall River, MA 1893). 122.

150   Porter 197.

151   Porter 199.

152   Porter 203.

153   Porter 200.

154   Porter 200.

155   Porter 200.

156   Shelley Dziedzic, "Making the Grand Tour" 2008, <http://www.
      LizzieBorden: Warps & Wefts.com>.

157   Edwin H. Porter, *The Fall River Tragedy: A History of the Borden
      Murders,* (Fall River, MA: King Philip Publishing Company,
      (originally published Fall River, MA 1893). 227.

158   Porter 227.

159   Porter 203.

160   Porter 203.

161   Porter 227.

162   Porter 37.

163   Porter 105.

164   Porter 203.

165 Shelley Dziedzic, "Making the Grand Tour" 2008, <http://www. LizzieBorden: Warps & Wefts.com>.

166 <http://www.Evanston Public Library, ewhp.database.epl.org>.

167 Leonard Rebello, *Lizzie Borden: Past & Present,* "Lizzie Borden's Shameful Treatment"(Fall River, MA:Al-Zach Press, May 1, 1999) 292-296.

168 Edwin H. Porter, *The Fall River Tragedy: A History of the Borden Murders,* (Fall River, MA: King Philip Publishing Company, (originally published Fall River, MA 1893). 184.

169 Michael Martins and Dennis A. Binette, *Parallel Lives, A Social History of Lizzie A. Borden & Her Fall River,*(Fall River Historical Society/Fall River, MA, 2010) 185.

170 Edwin H. Porter, *The Fall River Tragedy: A History of the Borden Murders,* (Fall River, MA: King Philip Publishing Company, (originally published Fall River, MA 1893). 104.

171 Porter 187.

172 Porter, 49.

173 Porter 122.

174 Porter 260.

175 Porter 207.

176 Porter 207.

177   Porter 207.

178   Porter 208.

179   Porter 210.

180   Porter 210.

181   Porter 210.

182   Porter 210.

183   Porter 210.

184   Porter 210.

185   Porter 256.

186   Porter 210.

187   Porter 210.

188   Michael Martins and Dennis Binette, eds., "The Commonwealth of Massachusetts versus Lizzie A. Borden: *The Knowlton Papers, 1892-1893,*(Fall River, MA: Fall River Historical Society, 1994) letter #HK113, pg. 117, unsigned, dated December 2, 1892.

189   Edwin H. Porter, *The Fall River Tragedy: A History of the Borden Murders,* (Fall River, MA: King Philip Publishing Company, (originally published Fall River, MA 1893). 210.

190   Porter 210.

191 Charles F. Cooper, "A Most Merry & Illustrated History of the Life and Trials of Lizzie Borden," 2006 http://www.coopertoons.com/merryhistory/lizzieborden.

192 Edwin H. Porter, *The Fall River Tragedy: A History of the Borden Murders,* (Fall River, MA: King Philip Publishing Company, (originally published Fall River, MA 1893). 215.

193 Porter 210.

194 Porter 213.

195 Stefani Koorey, "The Witness Statements for the Lizzie Borden Case, August 4 – October 6, 1892," (created in 2001) <http://www.Lizzieandrewborden.com>. (proofread by Harry Widdows and Stefani Koorey, July 28, 2003).

196 Edwin H. Porter, *The Fall River Tragedy: A History of the Borden Murders,* (Fall River, MA: King Philip Publishing Company, (originally published Fall River, MA 1893). 215.

197 Porter 213.

198 Porter 214.

199 Porter 214.

200 Porter 214.

201 Porter 214.

202 Porter 215.

203 Porter 214.

204 Charles F. Cooper, "A Most Merry & Illustrated History of the Life and Trials of Lizzie Borden," 2006 http://www.coopertoons. com/merryhistory/lizzieborden.

205 Stefani Koorey, "The Witness Statements for the Lizzie Borden Case, August 4 – October 6, 1892," (created in 2001) <http:// www.Lizzieandrewborden.com>. (proofread by Harry Widdows and Stefani Koorey, July 28, 2003). 45, 46.

206 Edwin H. Porter, *The Fall River Tragedy: A History of the Borden Murders,* (Fall River, MA: King Philip Publishing Company, (originally published Fall River, MA 1893). 37, 38.

207 Porter 103.

208 Shelley Dziedzic, "Making the Grand Tour" 2008, <http://www. LizzieBorden: Warps & Wefts.com>.

209 Edwin H. Porter, *The Fall River Tragedy: A History of the Borden Murders,* (Fall River, MA: King Philip Publishing Company, (originally published Fall River, MA 1893). 300.

210 Porter 211, 122.

211 Porter 245.

212 Michael Martins and Dennis Binette, eds., "The Commonwealth of Massachusetts versus Lizzie A. Borden; The Knowlton Papers, 1892-1893," (Fall River, MA: Fall River Historical Society, 1994, letter #HK113, pf. 117, unsigned, dated December 2, 1892) and April, 2008 http://www.lizziebordens warpsandwefts.com>. Forum moderator: AdminLizzieBorden.

213 Edwin H. Porter, *The Fall River Tragedy: A History of the Borden Murders,* (Fall River, MA: King Philip Publishing Company, (originally published Fall River, MA 1893). 99.

214 Porter 216.

215 Porter 218.

216 Porter 220.

217 Porter 223.

218 Porter 224.

219 Porter 224.

220 Porter 262.

221 Stefani Koorey, "The Witness Statements for the Lizzie Borden Case, August 4 – October 6, 1892," (created in 2001) <http://www.Lizzieandrewborden.com>. (proofread by Harry Widdows and Stefani Koorey, July 28, 2003). 45, 46.

222 Edwin H. Porter, *The Fall River Tragedy: A History of the Borden Murders,* (Fall River, MA: King Philip Publishing Company, (originally published Fall River, MA 1893). 224.

223 Porter 24.

224 Porter 226.

225 Porter 226.

226 Porter 227.

227 Porter 227.

228 Porter 228.

229 Porter 228.

230 Porter 228.

231 Porter 228.

232 Porter 228.

233 Porter 229.

234 Porter 230.

235 Porter 231.

236 Porter 231.

237 Shelley Dziedzic, "Making the Grand Tour" 2008, <http://www. LizzieBorden: Warps & Wefts.com>.

238 Dziedzic.

239 Edwin H. Porter, *The Fall River Tragedy: A History of the Borden Murders,* (Fall River, MA: King Philip Publishing Company, (originally published Fall River, MA 1893). 113.

240 Porter 224.

241 Porter 224.

242 Porter 235.

243 Porter 235.

244 Porter 237.

245 Porter 259.

246 Porter 238.

247 Porter 238.

248 Porter 239.

249 Porter 24, 173, 103, 104.

250 Porter 173, 103, 104.

251 Porter 89, 90.

252 Porter 241.

253 Porter 170, 243.

254 Porter 243.

255 Porter 243.

256 Porter 243.

257 Porter 243.

258   Porter 245.

259   Porter 231.

260   Porter 248.

261   Porter 248.

262   Porter 250.

263   Porter 252.

264   Porter 252.

265   Porter 132.

266   Porter 252.

267   Porter 252.

268   Porter 184.

269   Shelley Dziedzic, "Making the Grand Tour" 2008, <http://www. LizzieBorden: Warps & Wefts.com>.

270   photo, Lizzie at Maplecroft, http://www.Providencejournal. com>.

271   Charles F. Cooper, "A Most Merry & Illustrated History of the Life and Trials of Lizzie Borden," 2006 http://www.coopertoons. com/merryhistory/lizzieborden.

272   Edwin H. Porter, *The Fall River Tragedy: A History of the Borden Murders,* (Fall River, MA: King Philip Publishing Company, (originally published Fall River, MA 1893). 254.

273   Porter 254.

274   Porter 255.

275   Michael Martins and Dennis A. Binette, *Parallel Lives, A Social History of Lizzie A. Borden & Her Fall River,*(Fall River Historical Society/Fall River, MA, 2010) 110-115.

276   Porter 227.

277   Porter 113.

278   Porter 128.

279   Charles F. Cooper, "A Most Merry & Illustrated History of the Life and Trials of Lizzie Borden," 2006 http://www.coopertoons.com/merryhistory/lizzieborden.

280   Cooper.

281   Edwin H. Porter, *The Fall River Tragedy: A History of the Borden Murders,* (Fall River, MA: King Philip Publishing Company, (originally published Fall River, MA 1893). 256.

282   Porter 256.

283   Porter 257.

284   Porter 142.

285   Porter 262.

286   Porter 265.

287   Porter 144.

288   Porter 156.

289   Porter 265.

290   "Hatchet Found on Roof of Crowe Barn" *Fall River Evening News,* Thursday, June 15, 1893.

291   Edwin H. Porter, *The Fall River Tragedy: A History of the Borden Murders,* (Fall River, MA: King Philip Publishing Company, (originally published Fall River, MA 1893). 245.

292   Porter 261.

293   Porter 261.

294   Porter 261.

295   Porter 103.

296   Porter 262.

297   Porter 101.

298   Porter 104.

299   Porter 104.

300   Porter 267.

301   Porter 267.

302   Porter 267.

303   Porter 271.

304   Porter 210.

305   Porter 271.

306   Porter 272.

307   Porter 272.

308   Carol Kurtz Walsh, "Dissolving Shame," *Pathways Magazine*, December 1, 2014.

309   Edwin H. Porter, *The Fall River Tragedy: A History of the Borden Murders*, (Fall River, MA: King Philip Publishing Company, (originally published Fall River, MA 1893). 274.

310   Porter 274.

311   Porter 274.

312   Shelley Dziedzic, "Making the Grand Tour" 2008, <http://www.LizzieBorden: Warps & Wefts.com>..

313   Marcia R. Carlisle, "What Made Lizzie Borden Kill?" *American Heritage* July/August 1992, vol. 43, Issue 4. P. 132.

314   Edwin H. Porter, *The Fall River Tragedy: A History of the Borden Murders*, (Fall River, MA: King Philip Publishing Company, (originally published Fall River, MA 1893). 275.

315   Charles F. Cooper, "A Most Merry & Illustrated History of the Life and Trials of Lizzie Borden," 2006 http://www.coopertoons.com/merryhistory/lizzieborden.

316   Edwin H. Porter, *The Fall River Tragedy: A History of the Borden Murders*, (Fall River, MA: King Philip Publishing Company, (originally published Fall River, MA 1893). 276.

317   Leonard Rebello, *Lizzie Borden: Past & Present*, "Lizzie Borden's Shameful Treatment"(Fall River, MA:Al-Zach Press, May 1, 1999) 292-296.

318   Edwin H. Porter, *The Fall River Tragedy: A History of the Borden Murders*, (Fall River, MA: King Philip Publishing Company, (originally published Fall River, MA 1893). 148.

319   Porter 274.

320   Porter 296.

321   Porter 277.

322   Porter 277.

323   Porter 277.

324   Porter 277.

325   Porter 277.

326 Porter 280.

327 Porter 280.

328 Porter 280.

329 Porter 281.

330 Porter 281.

331 Porter 282.

332 Porter 281.

333 Porter 113.

334 Porter 281.

335 Porter 281.

336 Porter 113.

337 Porter 283.

338 Porter 187, 260, 98.

339 Porter 292.

340 Porter 103.

341 Porter 24.

342 Porter 190, 228.

343 Porter 299.

344 Porter 297.

345 Porter 298.

346 Porter 298.

347 Porter 299.

348 Porter 210.

WORKS CITED

Primary Text

Porter, Edwin H. *The Fall River Tragedy*. Portland, ME: King Philip, 1985. (originally Fall River, MA: Buffington, 1893). Print.

Axelrod-Contrada, Joan. *The Lizzie Borden "Axe Murder" Trial*. Berkeley Heights, NJ: Enslow, 2000. Print.

Carlisle, Marcia R. "What Made Lizzie Borden Kill?" *American Heritage*. July/August, 1992. Print.

Clark, Denise M. "How Lizzie Borden got Away with Murder," Fall River, MA: Pear Tree, 2001-2008. http://www.LizzieAndrewBorden.com.

Cooper, Charles F. "A Most Merry and Illustrated History of the Life and Trial(s) of Lizzie Borden," 2006. http://www.coopertoons. com/merryhistory/lizzborden/lizzborden.html>.

Dziedzic, Shelley. "Making the Grand Tour," http://www.lizziebord-enwarpsandweft.com>.

"Fourteen Reasons to Believe Lizzie Murdered her Parents," University of Missouri- Kansas City, http://www.law2.unkc.edu.com>.

"Hatchet Found on Roof of Crowe Barn," *Fall River Evening News*, 15 June, 1893. Print.

"Hoboglyphs (hobo hieroglyphs)," http://www.en.wikipedia.org/wiki/List_of_hieroglyphs>.

Koorey, Stefani, "The Witness Statements for the Lizzie Borden Murder Case, August 4-October 6, 1892,"

2001, for <http://www.LizzieAndrewBorden.com>. proofread by Harry Widdows and Stefani Koorey, 28 July, 2003.

Martins, Michael/Binette, Dennis A., *Parallel Lives; A Social History of Lizzie A. Borden and Her Fall River*, Fall River: Fall River Historical Society, 2010. Print.

Martins, Michael/Binette, Dennis A., eds., "The Commonwealth of Massachusetts Versus Lizzie Borden: The Knowlton Papers, 1892-1893," Fall River: Fall River Historical Society, 1994. (letter #HK113, 117, unsigned, dated 2 December, 1892).

Mouric, Bas C. "Crime Passionel: Emotional Rage or Cold-Blooded Murder? A Review of Emotion-Induced Dissociation in Healthy Individuals." *Erasmus Journal of Medicine*, January, 2011. Print.

Rebello, Leonard. "Lizzie Borden's Shameful Treatment." *Lizzie Borden: Past and Present.* Fall River, Al-Zach, 1999. Print.

Springside gatehouse (photo). http://en.wikipedia.org/wiki/file: Springside_gatehouse.jpg>.

"Victorian History: Sexual Abuse and Sexual Exploitation of Victorian Children," 13 October, 2010. http://www.vichist.blogspot.com>.

Made in the USA
Middletown, DE
07 March 2016